Stalking the Wild Hare

Stories from the Gen Con Writer's Symposium

Edited by John Helfers, Chris Pierson,
Marc Tassin, and Jean Rabe

Walkabout Publishing • 2010

Walkabout Publishing • S.D.Studios
P.O. Box 151
Kansasville, WI 53139
www.walkaboutpublishing.com

All stories and info are copyright their respective authors. (Info follows.)
All other content is © 2010 Stephen D. Sullivan.

Edited by John Helfers, Chris Pierson, Marc Tassin, and Jean Rabe.
Cover design & art by Stephen D. Sullivan, © 2010 SDS.

Permission granted from Gen Con LLC, for the use of the Gen Con name.

Thanks to Stephen D. Sullivan and Walkabout Publishing for helping us stalk the wild hare and producing this in time for Gen Con.

All rights reserved, including the right of reproduction in whole or in part in any form. No part of this publication may be reproduced or transmitted in any form or by any means, electronic or mechanical, including photocopy, recording, scanning, or any information storage and retrieval system, without written permission of the author(s).

ISBN: 978-0-9821799-0-1

"Covenant" © 2010 by Mike Stackpole.

"Off the Rack" © 2007 by Elizabeth A. Vaughan. First published in *Pandora's Closet*. Reprinted by permission of the author.

"Stronger than Fate" © 2007 by John Helfers. First published in *If I Were an Evil Overlord*. Reprinted by permission of the author.

"The Opposite of Solid" © 2007 by Linda P. Baker. First published in *Pandora's Closet*. Reprinted by permission of the author.

"As Good as a Rest" © 2010 by Tim Waggoner.

"And a Ship to Sail," copyright © 2010 by Christopher T. Pierson.

"The Pool" © 2010 by Wes Nicholson.

"Ink and Newsprint" © 2008 by Marc Tassin. First published in *Catopolis*. Reprinted by permission of the author.

"Last Dance" © 2008 by Steven Saus. First published in *Dayton Daily News*. Reprinted by permission of the author.

"Judgment" Copyright © 2004 by Kerrie Hughes. First published in *Haunted Holidays*. Reprinted by permission of the author.

"Critical Violation" © 2010 by Daniel Myers.

"Time War" © 2010 by Stephen D. Sullivan.

"The Fourteenth Virtue" © 2008 by Anton Strout. First published in *The Dimension Next Door*. Reprinted by permission of the author.

"Blood and Limestone" copyright © 1995 by Richard Lee Byers. First published in *Blood Muse*. Reprinted by permission of the author.

"Almost Brothers" © 2008 by Paul Genesse. First published in *Fellowship Fantastic*. Reprinted by permission of the author.

"The Prince of Artemis V" © 2010 by Jennifer Brozek. First published in Issue 15 of *Crossed Genres* magazine. Reprinted by permission of the author.

"Stew" © 2000 by Donald J. Bingle. First published in *Civil War Fantastic*. Reprinted by permission of the author.

"In the Eyes of the Empress's Cat" © 2006 by Bradley P. Beaulieu. First published in *Orson Scott Card's InterGalactic Medicine Show*. Reprinted by permission of the author.

"An Animal's Nature" © 2010 by Dylan Birtolo.

"The Shattering" © 2010 by Sabrina Klein.

"Staging a Coup" © 2010 by Kelly Swails.

"Roadshow" © 2006 by Jean Rabe. First published in *The Magic Toybox*. Reprinted by permission of the author.

*For Colonel Louis Zocchi,
who inadvertently started all of this,
and for Jeannette LeGault who, perhaps
not-so-inadvertently, continued it.*

CONTENTS

Introduction, *Jean Rabe* 8
Covenant, *Michael A. Stackpole* 11
Off the Rack, *Elizabeth A. Vaughan* 26
Stronger Than Fate, *John Helfers* 36
The Opposite of Solid, *Linda P. Baker* 48
As Good as a Rest, *Tim Waggoner* 65
And a Ship to Sail, *Chris Pierson* 78
The Pool, *Wes Nicholson* 107
Ink and Newsprint, *Marc Tassin* 114
Last Dance, *Steven Saus* 133
Judgment, *Kerrie Hughes* 138
Critical Violation, *Daniel Myers* 164
Time War, *Stephen D. Sullivan* 174
Fourteenth Virtue, *Anton Strout* 189
Blood and Limestone, *Richard Lee Byers* 204
Almost Brothers, *Paul Genesse* 214
The Prince of Artemis V, *Jennifer Brozek* 235
Stew, *Donald J. Bingle* 247
In the Eyes of the Empress's Cat, *Bradley P. Beaulieu* 259
An Animal's Nature, *Dylan Birtolo* 285
The Shattering, *Sabrina Klein* 294
Staging a Coup, *Kelly Swails* 302
Roadshow, *Jean Rabe* 316

Stalking a Wild Hare - Introduction

They're almost impossible to catch . . . those crafty wild hares. But they are fun to chase. Symposium member Steven Saus sent us in pursuit of this particular one.

Steven suggested that Writer's Symposium members put together a collection of stories for release at Gen Con 2010. It was a "wild hare" of an idea, and all the writers in this book were quick to embrace it. They had to be quick, as the notion was birthed in late March, and you hold the finished product in your hands in early August. If this anthology is received well enough, we'll try to stalk another wild hare next year.

The Writer's Symposium traces its literary roots back to Gen Con 1995, when the convention was held in Milwaukee, WI. Colonel Louis Zocchi ran what was dubbed The Speaker's Symposium, predominately a collection of military men who presented fascinating seminars on various aspects of war. Lou wanted to expand his program and asked me to host a couple of writing panels as part of it. I had to say yes. You see, a few years before, on one of his trips to Lake Geneva, WI, Lou stopped by my office to say "hi." He had one of his ventriloquism dummies with him. I'd never seen one of Lou's shows, and so he gave me a one-man performance . . . ventriloquism and magic and comedy. It was wonderful. He was wonderful. The magician had caught me in his spell, and so I couldn't refuse his request to be a part of his Speaker's Symposium.

The following year, 1996, I repeated the seminars—again at Lou's request—and added a few more sessions. If I recall correctly, Chris Pierson—a displaced Canadian who was at Gen Con anyway and had some free time—joined me that year or the one after. Richard Lee Byers from Florida was reeled in, too. Later, I coaxed John Helfers from Green Bay and Tim Waggoner from Ohio.

I met Elizabeth Vaughan in one of those early years. She attended a few seminars and wanted to go to lunch to talk about writing. I was busy (I'm always busy at Gen Con). Now she's busy at Gen Con, and we still find it hard to finesse our schedules so we can go to lunch. In fact, this year Elizabeth is deservedly the convention's author guest of honor.

As the years passed more authors took part—Donald J. Bingle, Paul Genesse, Marc Tassin, to name a few—and still more seminars were added to the program. It became standing room only . . . and so the Gen Con staff had to put us in a bigger room. We broke away from the military guys (who still give fantastic seminars at Gen Con).

Somewhere in there we changed our banner to the Writer's Symposium.

The program evolved further when we got the notion to offer a full track of seminars all convention long.

Gen Con moved to Indianapolis, we went along for the ride ... and added even more stalwart authors to our panels. Too, we began providing sessions into the evening hours. Then came a second track of programming, and New York Times bestselling author Michael A. Stackpole joined our ranks.

Now participants have at least two writing seminars at any given time to pick from. At the 2010 Gen Con we showcased 82 different seminars . . . and this collection of tales.

Whew!

So Gen Con 2010 marks the sixteenth year for our writing seminars and workshops. Amazing. Time runs as fast as a . . . wild hare. In all those years we've seen attendees practice what we preached and get published. Some of those one-time attendees are now on our panels. Like USA Today bestselling fantasy-romance author Elizabeth Vaughan. And like Steven, who came up with this wild hare of an idea for a book.

Read through the assortment of stories in our fine collection, and don't be shy about picking up other works by the panelists in the Writer's Symposium.

Enjoy!

—*Jean Rabe*

COVENANT
Michael A. Stackpole

Covenant is one of those stories that squirts out when you're not thinking about it. Mike was running errands when he just started running lines of dialogue for no discernible reason. After garnering some strange looks from old ladies at the grocery, he went home and turned out the story.

Mike has attended Gen Con continuously since 1980. In the mid-1990s he started running writing seminars at Gen Con, as something of a precursor to the Writer's Symposium. Best known for his Star Wars™ novels, he's also an award-winning game designer and was inducted into the Academy of Gaming Arts & Design Hall of Fame in 1993.

They sent a representative to me on the first night of the full moon. It used to be they picked the person they viewed most expendable. They realized, after a short while, that sending the one who annoyed me the *least* was the most efficacious strategy.

Vincent came at dusk, when his missive said he would come. He had called upon me before. It had been a long time, and he had changed. His hair thinner, laced with gray, his flesh sallow and sagging, his brown eyes tinged with red; not from tears, but from life-fatigue.

He barely glanced up—not wanting to meet my gaze.

None of them ever did.

Vincent, however, came closer than most. He believed he had something of an understanding of me but knew better than to allow himself full comprehension. It was enough for him to know that he didn't know and that he didn't *want* to know.

In knowing would be madness.

"Mr. Simon," he began, the tremble in his voice matched by a quiver in his body.

"Just Simon, Vincent." I knew he preferred the diminutive, Vince. I'd heard it shouted often enough, in the distance. In jest, in "good mornings," at their occasional weekend cookouts. I'm sure they felt their voices did not carry as far as my house atop the hill. If they imagined the contrary, silence would have swallowed their parties.

They always invited me, of course. They scheduled the festivities far too early in the day for me to make an appearance, but convention had been observed in the invitation.

The covenant remained intact.

I stepped aside in the doorway and beckoned him into my domicile. "Enter, please, Vincent."

He took one last clean breath of cool evening air and slipped into my domain. The house was stuffy and musty and cluttered—lit all in sepia tones. Thick layers of ancient scent had settled. So it always is with the homes of the unforgivingly old. It's something that can't be scrubbed away. Those who come in, those who are younger, wonder if this is the stench of the grave. Their noses wrinkle at the thought of having this odor sleeping in their nostrils forever.

Vincent crossed to the old couch. Doilies had been added to the arms since his last visit. He noticed and sat a bit away, afraid that he might somehow damage something so delicate. In fact, as he set himself on the couch, he seemed to lose 50 years—once again a small child waiting to be punished for a prank.

I would take the wingback chair, but not yet.

I did not know why Vincent had come. His note had not been specific. That would have violated the covenant. He'd simply requested a visit on a small cream-colored square of stationary folded in half and secured beneath a rock on my porch. He placed it next to the burn mark where, years before, a brave child had left a burning bag of dog shit before rapping on my door and turning to run, full force, for his life and, ironically, into my arms.

It would not do to let him think I did not know why he had

come. He thought certain I did. After all, *He* knows when every sparrow falls: not because it comforts the sparrows to note that their deaths register, but it makes those who fashioned God in their image feel they have a purpose—that they are important.

Knowing was part of the covenant.

So I said to him, keeping my voice soft and dry like autumnal leaves, "I will let you explain things in your own words, Vincent, but first I shall make tea. There is no unpleasantness which cannot be made better over tea."

He believed his sigh of relief inaudible, and it pleased me to allow him that belief. I retreated to my kitchen to make tea. I do that when they come to visit. It humanizes me. It makes them think we have something in common. They can say to others, "Well, I had tea with HIM. He really didn't seem so bad."

That delusion being another bulwark against insanity.

I like making tea. The ritual challenges me. So many things to get right and so difficult to replicate the results. Definitely an art—most emphatically not a science. Science has spoiled too many things by reducing them to mathematics. Reduce any experience to numbers, and it becomes commonplace. Everyone can access it—and somewhere in the wasteland of video and data transfers, thousands of observers trick themselves into believing they have actually *had* the experience.

I returned with the tea and the cups on a tray. I poured. I knew he took it without sugar and no milk, so I had brought none along. I seated myself in the wing backed chair, crossing my legs indolently but deliberately. With saucer in one hand, and rose petal cup in the other, I nodded to him. "You may begin."

Vincent sipped his tea, then placed the china cup down. "There is a problem with the Gillespie girl."

I closed my eyes. The Gillespie girl, Jennifer was her name. Early adolescence, fourteen years old, no more than fifteen. Unremarkable child in terms of physical attractiveness. Still awkward, and I had seen no real evidence that she would grow out of it. She had taken up the violin, attacking the instrument with a passion that someday might wear down her lack of talent. To their ears, I'm sure, the music sounded bitter and sour, but I listened for the passion.

And it occurred to me then, that recently, slowly, I had heard it wither.

"She has some difficulty at school. Her only friend moved away over the summer. It's a gang of kids at school—*popular* kids, mostly jocks. They pick on her. She won't file a complaint because that will make her a complete outcast." Vincent looked down at his hands, wringing them impotently. "I have no influence there anymore. I tried to speak to some parents, but the biggest bully is Kenny—Kenneth Carson. He is our Quarterback and on track for a free ride to State. He's even been scouted for the pros."

"And her parents?"

"Mother lives out of state. Stepmother is a trophy wife. Oblivious. The father, overworked." Vincent's head came up quickly, and he nearly met my gaze. "I knew something was wrong, but I know the rules. I wouldn't have come. It was her grandmother who talked to me, who made the request."

I do not understand parents. I do not understand how they care less for their own offspring than a rancher cares for cattle, or a shepherd cares for sheep. Do they somehow imagine that there are no predators looking for their children?

How is it that they ask their children, "How was school today, dear?" and then fail to listen? Is that the extent to which they understand the parental duty: enquire, perhaps listen, but do no analysis? Are they afraid of invading a child's privacy? What privacy? Until maturity a child is as much a part of a parent as a hand or foot. How is respect for illusory privacy an acceptable excuse against exercising parental responsibility?

Children require two things from parents. The first is security. The second is to be educated in coping strategies which work. The greatest of these, of course, is critical thinking. Teach a child to think, and he will forever be safe and secure. Critical thinking will get one past most everything.

Except something like me.

I set my cup on the tray. Vincent glanced at it. I think he was less concerned with what I was drinking than if I had drunk it all. For his sake, I had.

And for his sake, I paused before speaking. I let him see me deliberate. This was important. Deep inside, Vincent knew, even before he set foot on my walk, even before he swung open the creaking wrought-iron gate, even before he left his house to come see me, exactly how things would resolve themselves.

He just didn't want to see that it was an easy decision for me.

"You will send the girl here tomorrow at dusk."

"We had hoped..."

I gently shook my head. He had already brought something of hers with him. It was in a plastic bag in his pocket. Probably underwear—undoubtedly unlaundered. The grandmother would have insisted. Dimly I recalled her and the vile witch her sister had been. How curious she sought my help now.

"You had hoped to save her some discomfort. It will be no worse than anything she feels already. You know that, Vincent, but I respect your effort to address the concerns of others."

I stood and he followed, threading his way quickly toward the door. I glided after him, purposefully silent. I opened the door onto the night. The full moon's light splashed silver over the spear points on my fence and down over the road into the valley beneath my hill.

Vincent paused in the doorway. "Will there be enough time, you know, to deal with this? I don't know if she can take another month."

"There will be plenty of time. She will come tomorrow. We will have tea. She will have a nightmare tomorrow evening, and then it will all be over."

He wanted to ask if I was certain, but that would've violated protocol. Vincent had come to me on the first night of the full moon. That was how it had always been. Beneath the full moon was when I did things. Those things they needed me to do.

I require no lunar influence to act, but I gave them this impression on purpose. Men are exceptionally good at forming patterns. They recognized them, they react to them, and they all too often see them where they do not exist. Those false patterns are the bases for superstition. I find it useful to play to them. It sets up expectations and patterns which I can break as I will.

Break as I must.

The myth of unusual things happening beneath the full moon provides comfort for those who live beneath my hill. It is nonsense, of course. Rather exhaustive and boring statistical studies have demonstrated repeatedly that nothing unusual happens on the nights of full moons. Police reports of criminal activity remain flat on those nights as compared to others. Emergency room admissions do not spike when the moon is full. Crazies are crazy at all times, and the unusual happens at all times, but it's only remembered, and remarked upon, when it happens beneath the ivory orb.

Of course, my utilization of the full moon was actually pragmatic. It limited their petitions to me. Absent it, I should have been bothered with the trivial and banal.

*

Vincent departed and I set to work. I retreated to the upper reaches of my house and lit candles. The dwellers below would be watching me, of course. The gauzy curtains over my windows provided silhouette—theatre which they could interpret into any number of things. Visions of boiling alembics, potions dripping from distillation coils, foul creatures being summoned from some nether realm to do my bidding. They would feature me in nightmares of their own making, then wonder why they had trouble sleeping.

After lighting the candles I sat at my desk and opened a laptop computer. Just knowing I possessed a computer would've destroyed the image I had spent so much time crafting. Those below me assumed that the most intricate device I owned was an abacus and that I kept time with an hour-glass.

What distinguishes man from other beasts is his ability to use tools. If one wishes to understand man, one must understand tools and their uses. The computer—aside from being able to do complex math very quickly—is primarily a means of communication. Active communication, as in e-mail and chatting, or passive.

And it is the passive mode which I find most intriguing.

With less effort than required to make tea, I had Jennifer Gillespie's life unfolding on the computer screen.

Do parents actually pay any attention to what their children write? Her torment had been writ large on social networking sites. Not so much what she said, which was very little, but in the cold and cruel remarks of those who responded to her. Here she was, a lonely child, a lost sheep, bleating in the wilderness for anyone to hear. And it was those she had chosen to friend, or had extended friend invitations to her, who tormented her. She could watch them planning their parties. She could read between the lines as they sniped at each other and largely ignored her. She did her best to remain positive, though her strength was ebbing.

She had written joyously of an upcoming violin recital. She even made it an event to which she invited her friends, but none of them had said they would attend. Worse yet, those who refused outright, tortured her. They explained they were having a party that same evening.

They even did their scheming in the comments section of her event.

And perhaps the last twist of the knife was that her stepmother—though she said she would attend the recital—offered party-planning advice to Jennifer's enemies.

*

The child came to me, not quite scared out of her wits, but close enough that she was unable to speak when greeted at the door. She had no real idea who I was. I was old enough to be the crabby neighbor who yelled for children to stay out of his yard. Alternately, I could've been the old man who skulked in the shadows and mumbled to himself. Most children her age assumed that's what I did in my house, behind my curtains, behind the silhouettes arguing in some Hitchcockian drama. A few referred to me as Norman Bates. I heard them, of course, but since fear filled their tiny voices, no action was required on my part.

But, for some children, I was that lonely old man who could sympathize with their feelings of alienation. Friendless. An outcast. Someone who didn't need contempt or pity, but understanding. A kindred soul.

This is who I would be for Jennifer Gillespie. Though this was her first trip into my home, it would not be her last. In her hand would be the invitation to join her family at Thanksgiving this year. I would, of course, decline. She would then bring me a small basket of leftovers and leave it on my front porch. Though she knew nothing of baking, she would ask her grandmother to teach her so she could bring me cookies.

And later I would ask her to bring her violin and would ask her to play for me.

And someday, some distant day, when a child of her own was feeling fretful, Jennifer would pull that child into her lap, wrap her in a warm embrace, and tell her the story of a lonely old man who smiled when she played her violin. For her, I would be a pleasant memory.

Not so the jackals who beset her.

I offered her tea, and she accepted with a silent nod. She sat where Vincent had sat, all prim and proper, holding herself tightly. She fought to be polite and realized her silence made her seem unmannerly. She struggled, and I admired that.

I asked her simple things. I asked what made her happy. I asked her to describe what she felt when a puppy licked her face or the sense of revelation when the answer to a complex math problem blossomed in her head. I mentioned that I had heard her play the violin one night as I strolled in the twilight. She shivered at that thought, that I might be out there in the shadows, but only for a heartbeat.

I assured her I had enjoyed her music.

She blushed and looked into her cup.

And that was all I needed.

But I gave her something more. "Humor me, child." I pointed toward her cup and made a swirling motion with my finger. "Very good. Now quickly, overturn your cup into your saucer."

She did as bidden and looked at me expectantly.

I made a show of pulling on glasses—little half lenses, older than her grandmother. I shot her a glance that told her my needing them was our secret. Sharing confidences creates trust. She accepted the covenant with an all-but-imperceptible nod. It bound us together forever.

I plucked her cup slowly from the saucer and turned it over. The tea leaves stuck to the cup's walls, and I pointed them out. "Oh, very good. You see this one here, near the rim, the one which looks like a violin? Something will be happening with you and your violin in the very near future."

"I have a recital. It's in two weeks." She picked nervously at a fingernail. "You could come if you want to." She wasn't certain why she had extended the invitation, but she had, and immediately took responsibility for that act. "I will bring you an invitation."

"And it shall be my pleasure to attend." I pointed to another tea leaf, one which folded itself over into an oval. "And this, it looks like one of those sports things."

Her face darkened. "A football. That's a big deal at my

school."

I shook my head. "I see misfortune there. Pity. Is there a game soon?"

Jennifer nodded. "This evening."

"And I have kept you from it."

"No, I didn't feel like going." She looked up, meeting my eyes in a way that only true innocence can. "Sometimes it's hard to be around the kids at school. I don't fit in."

I lowered my voice. "It has been my experience, Jennifer Gillespie, that those who feel they do not fit in are just not pieces meant for *that* puzzle. The quest is not to change yourself into what others want you to be, but to make others see you as you truly are."

She stared blankly for a handful of heartbeats, then blinked. Already the words were fading from her conscious memory, sinking in deeper. She, like so many others, was trapped in the adolescent dilemma. How can one stand out and become an individual while so desperately wanting to be part of the pack?

Some people never escape that dilemma. Their entire existence bounces from one trauma to another. The measure of their worth is a standard set by others. They chase after elusive and arbitrary goals created by well-paid pitchmen and sour, bitter, little people who make themselves feel better by tearing others down. The words I had given Jennifer would free her from this tyranny. It would take years, but once she chose to ignore the judgment of others, she would know the greatest freedom possible.

I smiled and stood. "I am so sorry that you have to leave to practice your violin. This has been a very pleasant visit. I do hope you will come again."

She rose a bit unsteady, but her head cleared as she came to the door. "Thank you, Mr. Simon. I will bring you the invitation."

My smile broadened, genuinely. "Sleep well child."

*

I needed her essence. I drank the lees of the tea from her saucer. I sat where she sat, taking in her fading warmth. I touched which she had touched. I looked around at the things that she had looked at, noting what attracted her and what scared her. And mostly I absorbed her sense of compassion.

It was the compassion, of course, which attracted the bullies to her. Without empathy there is no compassion, and empathy was what they saw as weakness. Not only would Jennifer flinch when they inflicted pain on her, but she would do so when they picked on *others*. And those others, though they should have been her allies, were happy to have the bullies choose her instead of themselves.

Bullies pick on the weak to cover their own weaknesses. In the dark of the night they wake from terrible dreams in which something greater than themselves holds them powerless. Only by dominating the weak can they convince themselves they have true power. They know they are deluded, but their fear will never let them acknowledge the truth.

And their fear would one day consume them.

And sooner for a few, much sooner.

From the Internet, of course, I had known there was a game. I had also seen that a postgame celebration had been arranged. Cloaking myself in Jennifer's essence, I moved into the night. The party site was not too far, but was far enough to suit my purposes. The children would drive there. I chose to walk.

I do not own a car by choice. I eschew them, much like guns. Both are marvels, mechanical marvels, engineered with all the precision mathematics and science can bring to bear. But I find them to be far noisier than necessary.

And a walk in the night air is always good for your health. Or mine, at least.

I took my time getting to the party. And I watched for a while before making my final approach. Primate behavior was in full display. Picking out the Alpha—the Carson progeny—was not difficult. The Betas made themselves apparent, too. No Omegas—no one to form the bottom of the hierarchy. A structure without a foundation is bound to collapse. So I made my appearance. Those who noticed me assumed I was Jennifer. I became instantly invisible to most. A few felt panic. They were smart enough to assume that the only way that Jennifer would show up was if she was intent on acting out the climax of a King novel.

Several of them moved away. A couple more texted nearby friends to alert them of the danger. But being adolescents, and thinking of themselves as both adult and invulnerable, none of them called authorities to avert what might be a bloody disaster.

And more than one started shooting video.

I made my way directly toward the knot of Betas around Carson. They wore letter jackets, and a couple had scraped knuckles from the game. A gang of five emerged from the center to confront me. Kenneth Carson tauntingly offered a beer. Others laughed nervously, mumbling that I had to be insane.

It was then that I chose to release her essence.

The smartest of them—not Carson—urinated on himself.

Squinting, the Quarterback rescinded his offer of hospitality. "Who the fuck are you?"

As I might ignore the whimper of a dog, I let his question pass unanswered. "You are being offered a choice. Grow up *now,* or forever remain a child."

Carson threw the beer at me.

He missed. Not because his throw was off target. Not because I made any attempt to evade. He just did not hit me.

If he drew any significance from that fact, he gave no sign. "You're a crazy old man!"

"Hardly a passing grade."

"What?"

I smiled blasphemously. "You only got one of three right."

He didn't understand. Perhaps understanding was beyond

him. For so many years he had denied his fear that he thought himself fearless. He remained blind to anything that might frighten him. He actively disbelieved that which *did* frighten him. And afterward, he actively forgot anything that had ever frightened him.

But he did understand one thing, one primal thing. His authority had been challenged. Someone—a crazy old man or *whatever*—came into his domain and mocked him. He was Kenneth Carson. He was the Quarterback. In the high school pantheon he was as Zeus himself. And though he had not the intellect to understand that mythic allusion, like Zeus he could tolerate no defiance.

Alcohol inhibits the ability of the human brain to reason accurately. Kenneth Carson had little need for reason. Big and tall, full of hormones and beer, still soaring from the victory that evening, and convinced of his immortality, Carson came for me. Fists raised above his head, he rushed forward, snarling, much as a juvenile ape does when charging a silverback.

And, as all bullies eventually learn, eons of tormenting the weak do nothing to make you stronger.

To those who watched I raised a hand to stop him, almost as if pleading for him to stop. My palm hit his sternum, and he collapsed around it. His feet came up, rising higher than his head, his fists flew past me. He crashed down on his shoulders, moaning, hugging arms to his chest.

I sank to a knee beside him, speaking for the smart one alone. That boy had dropped into a sitting position and stared at me wide-eyed while his companions crawled away from pools of fresh vomit. I took Carson's right wrist in my grasp, and though he struggled, he found himself powerless to resist.

My voice remained even and low, in much the same tones I had used earlier with Jennifer. "Carson will tell the authorities that you were horsing around, and there was an accident. In addition to having broken his sternum," I said as I squeezed fingers together and bones cracked, "he suffered other injuries. You will have to remind him that these injuries are not career ending. If I am required to visit him again, the new ones will be."

The smart boy held his hands up, as if to fend me off. "Don't hurt me."

I smiled in a way that liquefied the contents of his bowels. "This is not about you. If you don't want to be hurt, don't hurt. If you want forgiveness, show yourself to be worthy of forgiveness."

My smile shifted to include teeth. "And do not beg forgiveness of me, because I do not forgive. To forgive is divine, and I am something else entirely."

*

I slipped away into the shadows, wondering why I had not slain Carson. I allowed myself to imagine it was because of Jennifer. She would've felt guilty, and I wished to save her that. And part of me wished to see how Carson would react, how the story of the night would unfold. I wanted to read what the children would tell other children in their comments and their status messages. I wanted to watch them condense the impossible into 140 characters.

There were the pictures, of course, grainy, gray, indistinct. They appeared on websites devoted to the paranormal and were decried as being poor Photoshop jobs. I was explained away as everything from an escaped sanitarium inmate or the New Jersey Devil to an alien invader. Believers sought to define me by their superstitions. Skeptics tried to dismiss me with their mathematics.

It would be a grand thing to suggest that many lessons had been learned that night. That Carson, after only two weeks in a cast, tore the plaster apart and inserted himself into a critical game, playing through pain, to lead his team to victory. And that the mean girls had a change of heart and took all of their party planning and brought it to the Gillespie house as a surprise for Jennifer to celebrate her recital.

And that Jennifer, emboldened and embraced, rose to the top

of her class, got a scholarship to an Ivy League school, and learned that, for her, there were no limitations in life.

A grand thing, yes.

Life is seldom that grand.

A college booster compensated Carson for his injuries with the loan of an expensive sports car. It had twelve cylinders under the hood, and six empties behind the driver's seat, when Carson wrapped it around a tree.

The crash must have been very noisy.

And the mean girls had their party. Someone spiked the punch. Police were relatively certain whoever it was thought they were mixing in ecstasy. They weren't. Most of the people just had headaches. A few slipped into comas. Most who came out again, it is expected, will someday learn to be able to care for themselves.

Jennifer was not embraced by her class. But she still rose to the top, emboldened by the smile of the smart, young man who managed to regain his composure shortly after being introduced to me at her recital. Her stepmother—who was holding up well despite the abrupt departure of a very superstitious pool boy who had been working closely with her—threw Jennifer a party after the recital.

I heard a great time was had by all.

I was invited.

I did not make an appearance. I did not need to.

I think Jennifer understood I would not appear. That was part of the covenant. Which is why, late that evening, she played quietly—all-but-inaudibly—uncertain if anyone but she could hear.

But certain someone would.

Off The Rack
Elizabeth A. Vaughan

I started attending the Gen Con Writer's Symposium long before I ever dreamed that I could write a book and get it published. It wasn't until I met Jean Rabe and a host of other writers at the panels that I realized that I might be able to make my dream a reality.

My first book, Warprize, was published in 2005. I now have six books on the shelves, the most recent being Destiny's Star, released by Berkley. I also have quite a few short stories that have been published in various anthologies. You can find out more about my writing, including the story of how I got published, at www.eavwrites.com.

In fact, it was Jean who invited me to submit this story for Pandora's Closet, a themed anthology about magical clothing published by DAW in 2007. "You write romance," she said. "Make it romantic."

What Ms. Rabe wants, Ms. Rabe gets.

Sarah yanked the offending strip of paper from the calculator, crumpled it, and threw it at the basket. It bounced off the rim, hit the wall, and fell to the floor.

With a curse, she jerked out of her chair to retrieve it. The chair obeyed the law of physics and thumped back against the wall. Sarah cursed again, this at the black mark it left on the wall.

Pam stuck her head into the tiny closet Sarah called her office. "Problem?"

"No." Sarah kept her face down as she picked up the crumpled wad and dropped it in the trash. She wasn't going to tell her only employee about the red ink on that slip of paper. "Just got up too fast."

Pam accepted that, as she accepted the meager paycheck each week, with a shrug. "Listen, can I leave early? There's no customers, and I gotta—"

"Sure." Sarah didn't really want to hear it. "Go. I'll lock up."

The door was swinging shut before the words were out of Sarah's mouth. She heard the door chimes marking Pam's exit even as she turned off the calculator. She paused long enough to watch the negative number fade as the display went dim.

Sarah sighed and stepped out into her store to watch as the last few moments before closing ticked off. She stepped to the counter and started to clear away the clutter.

Outside, through the glass windows of the storefront, soft white flakes started to fill Pam's tire treads. Painted on the window, backward from this angle, was "Sarah's Closet," the gold and cream lettering still as bright and promising as they'd been a year ago on opening day.

Sarah looked away from the bright promise and cleared the counter, straightening pens, dusting the unused credit card machine and the register.

Opening day of her consignment shop had been just as bright and promising as the window. She'd spent a year researching, planning, taking out the loan, making the business plan. She'd collected the clothes for a year, searching garage sales and auctions, talking to friends of friends to build her inventory.

But consignment needs more consignments to survive, and as the months wore on there'd been few visitors who had brought in things. She'd found it hard to replace the stock and watch the store at the same time, forcing her to hire help—a cost she'd left out of her detailed and perfect business plan.

Sarah sighed again. There'd been traffic, sure, but somehow people didn't find what they were looking for, or it was not the right size, or it was the wrong color. Why go to her store, when they could go the big discounters?

She glanced at the clock. Another three minutes and she could go home and lose herself in a bubble bath, a favorite romance novel, and ramen noodles. Time enough tomorrow to think about negative numbers and looming bills.

Movement drew her gaze back to the window. Someone was trying to wrestle an old shopping cart up on the sidewalk in front of the shop. A shopping cart piled high with bags and cans, and with more plastic bags tied to the sides, all filled with questionable items.

Sarah frowned. She'd picked this location because of its higher-end clientele, and she'd never seen a street person here before. Dressed in a thin, stained sweat shirt, with old jeans almost falling off his hips. She caught a glimpse of a ratty beard when his head turned. One of the legs of the jeans was pulled up over his knee, displaying a naked leg dotted with scabs and sores. A thin ankle, covered in an old cotton sock, pushed into even older tennis shoes. No hat. No gloves. Sarah shivered at the thought.

The man was pulling at the cart, trying to get the wheels over the curb. She could hear it rattling and squeaking as he tugged. He got the back wheels over the curb, and pulled until the front wheels clanged into the obstacle. He kept pulling, as if it never occurred to him to go to the front and lift it up.

Or maybe he couldn't.

The snow that had fallen in his hair was melting, and water drops glistened in the scraggy depths. There were damp patches on his shoulders where his muscles moved underneath. Sarah looked at him with an expert eye, sizing him up without really thinking about it. A medium, easily.

There was a coat on the men's rack, a high-end winter coat that would fit him. And a warm woolen hat in the bin. Gloves, too.

She hesitated, surprised by her impulse. Generosity wouldn't put food on the table. But the loss wouldn't make any real difference. And it was closing time. And he was in front of the door.

Without another thought, she gathered up the coat, stuffed the hat and gloves in the pockets, and stepped outside.

The snow was a swirl now, the wind making patterns in the light of the parking lot lamps. Sarah took in a breath of cold air, faintly scented by the Chinese restaurant next door. The man was still tugging on the cart, and in frustration, Sarah stepped around him and lifted up the end to clang on the sidewalk.

He looked at her, startled, with pale grey eyes.

Sarah didn't bother to say anything, just held out the coat.

His eyes flicked to it, and then back to her face. His beard and mustache covered his face, leaving no hints to his reaction.

Sarah shivered in the cold. "Take it." She held it out again. "Put it on."

He reached for the coat with a filthy hand. Sarah watched as he eased it over his shoulders, moving carefully as if it would break. She swallowed hard, afraid to look too close at his leg, or take too deep a breath.

The man pulled out the knit hat from one pocket, and pulled it over his matted hair. He looked at her with those washed out eyes, and said nothing.

Sarah hadn't really expected much else. Her impulse of generosity had left, leaving her only a desire to close up and get home. But as she turned to go, the man mumbled something and started digging in the cart.

Uh-oh. Sarah winced at the idea that the man was going to reciprocate, and prayed that whatever emerged was—

He held out a hanger.

She reached out and accepted it. It was one of those old wooden hangers, with the metal rod that reinforced the wood. It felt warm and smooth under her fingertips, and she caught a faint hint of cedar.

She looked back at the man, intending to say, "Thank you." But he was already shoving the cart past her shop, mumbling something, intent on his own business.

Sarah went back in and put the hanger on one of the empty racks, right by the counter. She gathered her own coat and purse and shut off the lights. The man and his cart were into the next block when she stepped out into the snow and headed for her car.

Intent on bubble bath and book, she drove off into the night.

*

Sarah overslept the next morning; thankfully Pam had opened the store on time. Pam was chewing gum and bent over the counter, looking over one of those gossip rags when Sarah rushed in with coffee and the paper. Sarah nodded and said, "Morning," as she headed toward the office door, trying not to look as embarrassed as she felt for being late.

There was a ball gown hanging from the rack. On *the* hanger. It was a lovely low cut blue silk, with a full gathered skirt.

Sarah stopped dead in her tracks. "Where did that come from?"

Pam opened her mouth, but the chime on the door made them both turn and look. Two women, stylish and made up to perfection entered. Sarah's brain was processing the cost of their labels when the first one spoke.

"Good morning! I'm looking for a vintage—"

The other woman squealed. "Look!"

Stunned, Sarah watched as they descended on the dress.

"It's my size!"

"It's perfect for you!" One reached for the paper price tag that hung from a small ribbon off the dress. She nudged the other to look at the tag.

"I want it." The first woman announced.

Pam reached for one of the longer garment bags. The woman dug out a credit card and placed it on the counter.

Sarah still stood there, coffee in one hand, paper and purse in the other. One of the women gave her a pat on the shoulder. "I'll be back, if you get in more treasures like this!"

"That will be $1,590.00. With tax." Pam murmured. The credit card zipped through the machine.

Money worries temporarily forgotten, Sarah still stood there, stunned.

*

Pam denied all knowledge of the dress, claiming that it had been hanging there when she'd walked in. Sarah had her doubts, of course, but Pam wasn't the type to do something on her own initiative, that was for sure. Sarah decided that someone was trying to help her, except that no one had a key, or access to that kind of dress, that she knew of.

But then it happened again.

And again.

Each morning, Sarah would open the store, to find a garment hanging from *the* hanger. Each time someone would come in that day, looking for that particular garment, cheerfully paying the price on the tag.

A business suit.

A sun dress.

A leather jacket.

A wet suit.

The prices varied, the clothing varied, but without fail the hanger had something suspended from it every morning, a small paper price tag dangling in front.

Sarah couldn't figure it out. She had the locks changed, she set up a security camera. But the camera didn't work and the clothing kept appearing. As did customers, new ones who became repeat ones, who brought clothes to consign, who came back and bought other clothes.

Within a month Sarah was in the black.

Within six months, she had back inventory and Pam was full-time. She could be pickier now, setting aside the older and worn items to donate to The Salvation Army.

During this time Sarah became a bit superstitious. She forbade Pam to touch *the* hanger, and left it on the rack in all its glory. Pam, of course, just shrugged. She didn't seem to notice or care about anything other than her paycheck.

And the clothes kept coming.

A christening gown of linen and lace.

A slinky little black dress.

A 5x wedding dress, with veil and slippers. Sarah waited all day to see who would up for that one.

And sure enough, close to the end of the day, in walked a large woman with her groom-to-be. She fit the dress perfectly. And never blinked at the price. Once the sale was made, and Pam had left for the day, Sarah stood in front of the rack and stared at the hanger.

"I don't suppose you could find me a man? I'm not fussy, although I prefer brown eyes to blue."

The hanger just hung there in silence.

Sarah laughed, and shook her head. "That's okay. I'm grateful for the clothes and the help." She eyed the hanger seriously. "But it won't last forever, will it?"

The hanger remained silent.

*

And so it went.

Sarah's Closet became the in place to shop, with both the society crowd and the young people looking for bargains. Sarah had enough stock that she was starting to think about the Internet, getting a website, and putting pictures of the clothing on-line. But something deep within made her hesitate. "Nothing good lasts forever" echoed in the depths of her brain. "Wait and see" was another thought. After all, magic never lasted, now did it?

In all those stories. She took the prudent and cautious route.

So she wasn't really surprised the morning she opened the shop, a year and a day later, to find that there was nothing on the hanger.

The cold air and snow blew in as she stood there in the doorway, staring at the rack. It was indeed empty, swaying slightly in the draft.

She stomped the snow off her boots, stepped in, and let the door close behind her.

A year and a day.

It had been a year and a day ago that she'd seen that odd man, and given him a coat. He'd handed her the hanger in exchange, a more than fair exchange for the magic that it had brought with it.

Magic that had saved her dreams.

Sarah sighed, mild disappointment flowing through her like a wave. She'd expected it, but it still hurt. It had been a wonderful year, and she was in good shape financially. The store would still need hard work, but she knew that she could make it, after this year.

The magic was over and done.

But to see the hanger just...hanging there...

It hurt.

She sighed, and went about the day.

Business was brisk in the morning, but the snow kept falling all day, large wet flakes. Customers slowed to a trickle, and the radio spoke of businesses closing early. Sarah let Pam go home, and settled behind the counter and watched the snow. She tried to ignore the hanger, which was still on the rack.

Once or twice it occurred to Sarah to pack it in and treat herself to a bubble bath, but she had the oddest sense of waiting, as if something was going to happen.

There were no more customers, and the only call she got was from the Salvation Army, asking if she had anything to be picked up. She said she did, and they'd be by shortly.

Sarah had wait for the truck, and then close the store and go home. Yes, a bubble bath, that new hardbound romance she'd just bought, some General Tso's from the Chinese place next door. Good plan for a snowy night.

The Salvation Army truck pulled up; it was the regular guy, so he went in back and carried out the box crammed full of clothing. He set it down on the floor and handed Sarah the clipboard with the paperwork. She signed off, and he put it under his arm and reached back down.

When he lifted the box up, *the* hanger was tucked in among the clothes.

Sarah darted a look at the rack, and sure enough, her hanger wasn't there. She looked back as the man headed for the door.

She could just see the wooden corner of the hanger, as if it was waving goodbye over his shoulder. It seemed right somehow. Fitting, even.

At the same time, the door opened, and a customer walked in, dancing around the man with the box with a laugh and an apology. Sarah was still focused on the box, and she watched as it was loaded on the truck, the big metal door coming down with a muffled clang.

"Excuse me." The customer placed a coat on the counter.

Sarah looked down. It was a well-made coat, from a high-end designer. Warm and thick, with deep pockets. She reached out to touch it.

"You want to sell this?" She was still oddly distracted. There was something familiar about the coat.

"No," came a warm, deep voice that carried a hint of laughter. "Actually I found it, and your business card was in the pocket, so I brought—"

It was the coat that she'd given away, a year and a day ago! It had to be.

"Where did you get this?" She looked up into a smiling face and the warmest pair of brown eyes she'd ever seen.

The man laughed again. "Well, that's kind of a strange story, truth be told." He smiled even wider, and Sarah caught her breath. "I'll tell you," he continued, then hesitated for a moment as he seemed to study her. "I'll tell you, but only over some dinner. Do you like Chinese?"

STRONGER THAN FATE
John Helfers

I picked this one because it received the best audience reaction (at a Gen Con a few years back) out of my many readings at various signing and conventions through the years. Plus, it's a rare foray into humorous (more or less) fantasy.

A writer and editor for the past fifteen years, I've alternated working with authors such as Charlaine Harris, Stephen Coonts, and Mercedes Lackey at my day job as Senior Editor at Tekno Books, and writing original and tie-in fiction in the Dragonlance, BattleTech, *and* Shadowrun *universes, among others. Future novels include more tie-in works set in the* Deathlands *and Executioner franchises from Worldwide/ Gold Eagle, as well as more original fiction at some point. I've been with the Writer's Symposium for more years than I care to count.*

Deep within his Ebon Citadel, ensconced firmly, if not altogether comfortably, on the Throne of Black Blades, Khazerai the Undying drummed his thin, ring-bedecked fingers on the cold arm of his chair, and wondered where it had all gone wrong.

How could it have come to this, when everything else has happened according to plan? he thought. Granted, his rise to total dominion over the entire continent of Cauldera had not been without its setbacks, but overall, things had worked out exactly as he had expected.

First, he had deposed the weak and ineffective ruler of the small kingdom of Yulen after quickly working his way up the royal chain of command to become the king's personal advisor. A nip of poison in each of his twin sons' drinking goblets to emotionally cripple the old man, and a series of successively larger glasses of

Stronger Than Fate

wine before bedtime had ensured the old fool's complete ignorance as Khazerai had slowly replaced the guards and stuff with men loyal to him. When the coup happened in one swift stroke, the people were actually hailing him as their savior, which he was, he supposed, of a sort.

Next came the annexation of the surrounding lands, during which his agents sowed unrest among the peasants by promising them their own property in return for harsh but not totally crushing taxes to fund the monarchy, leading to an uprising when he invaded each country with his small but well-trained force. Soon Yulen was four times its original size, and its army was anything but small.

Khazerai then had his men trained and equipped with the best weapons and equipment that could be made or bought, and declared brutal war against the rest of the kingdoms. Often his announcement was initially met with derision, as several of the other lands had been unwilling to believe that Yulen, previously known only for producing exceptionally fine chicken eggs, was now on the warpath. Several swift victories ensued, with Khazerai's trained men overwhelming the ill-prepared, unwieldy enemy armies in a series of swift tactical strikes.

Others thought themselves safe behind the ramparts of the Duchy of Tolera, which was twice the size of Yulen in both holdings and its military. But Khazerai's spies had also brought that kingdom down from within, each one whispering to each of the three sons that he should be in charge when their father passed on. When he suddenly expired from an overdose of a sleeping draught in his nightly wine; each of the sons, thinking that both of the others had moved to kill their father and claim the throne, declared war on his siblings, dividing up the armies and navies and battling each other. All of which left the kingdom's borders wide open. With such an invitation, how could Khazerai refuse?

Once again, the ruler of the Yulen Empire was hailed as a savior both behind and in front of the scenes. His men had brokered treaties with each of the three armies in turn, then destroyed each prince when the time was right; one vanquished on the battlefield, one assassination, and the third one's by mob reprisal after it was learned about his (completely false, mind you) unnatural attraction to farm animals. Each prince's death had been blamed on one of the other two, and Khazerai had gladly stepped in to stop the princes' reigns of battle and bloodshed, and replace it with his much more moderate reign of fear and secrecy. With Tolara's rich farmland, ore-laden mountains, and healthy population under his control, the rest of the continent only needed to be mopped up. Khazerai did this using his own form of diplomacy—usually by parking half of his army at a soon-to-be-subjugated land's border while sending the other half around to flank. While his army was out consolidating his rule, Khazerai did not fear reprisal at home either. As soon as he had taken power in Yulen all those years ago, every able-bodied man and woman had been required to serve a two-year term in the military, and spend one weekend a month and three weeks a year fulfilling their duties, making them more than able to fend off an invading army until he could return. But who would even dare try such a thing? *No one, that's who.*

The Churches? Hardly. As soon as Khazerai took over a kingdom he banned all religion, stating a policy of "Humans first, everyone else after." Once he exposed the prelates, bishops, and priests of the local churches as, "the hypocritical, greedy swine that they are, the fat, bloated ticks on the backside of the populace, sucking the hard working men and women—you people—dry, and what do they give you in return? Nothing in this world, that's for certain." The commoners had eaten it up. And since the all deities in the pantheon of Cauldera were dependent on the unwavering faith of the masses to grant them their powers—well, in his infamous speech to ten thousand Tolerans, Khazerai had said, "Those who giveth can also taketh away." The gods' influence had disappeared almost overnight.

Regardless, with Khazerai standing in front of his seemingly endless Yulen Legions and requesting to "parley," swift acquiescence soon followed. And so, a mere quarter-century after he had taken over the small country of Yulen, Khazerai now ruled the entire continent.

And it had all been so easy, he thought. *Too easy?* No, there had been a fair share of difficulty along the way. The attempted coup in the early days of his reign by a trusted lieutenant, leading a small contingent of soldiers still loyal to the old Yulen king. They had been dispatched immediately, and announced as traitors to the new regime, which they were. He could count a half-dozen assassination attempts by other rulers, which had always insured that their land moved up to the number one position on his "next to be conquered" list. There had been spies in his own camp to root out, laughably under-planned and under-equipped treason plots to uncover, tributes to collect, the usual business of running an all-powerful empire.

And yet it could all come tumbling down around my head if I do not stop what is happening, he thought. Now Khazerai heard the clash of swords on steel outside the Citadel, as his troops engaged the invading enemy. The two immediate options were fight or flight, and yet he sat on his throne for a few more seconds, pondering the inexorable chain of events that had led to this exact moment.

It had all started about a year ago, when his lieutenant had come to him with a report on what the dictator had thought was a minor matter. "My Eminence, there has been a disturbance on the outskirts of the Western Marches. A family was in arrears for taxes, and the local magistrate had them executed and their pig farm confiscated as an example of your far-reaching will to the rest. However, the youngest son of the assistant pig-tender survived, and has vowed revenge on both you and the Empire."

"The orphaned son of an assistant pig-tender is coming after me?" Khazerai was hard-pressed to contain his mirth. "Post a ten

Khaz reward for his head, and send the local patrols out with orders to kill him on sight."

"It will be done, My Exaltedness."

And that, Khazerai had thought, *is the end of that trifling matter*. However, a few weeks later, as he had been deciding whether to expand his empire to the east, where the Torlingan horsemen roamed the grassy plains, or to the west over the mountains, long-rumored to be a land of untold wealth and strange, foreign races, his lieutenant strode up and bowed low before the Throne of Black Blades.

"Most-Powerful One, I have news from the Western Marches."

"Whatever about? Is the mud harvest especially good this year?" Khazerai asked, having long forgotten about the son of the assistant pig-tender.

"Remember that orphaned boy who swore revenge against you?"

Khazerai looked up from his maps. "Orphan, orphan—something about swine, wasn't it? What about him?"

"He has eluded or ambushed several patrols, claiming that they are a tool of the Evil Empire—"

Which they are, but calling my realm evil is a bit much, Khazerai thought.

"—And people in the area are already talking about him as a leader of the small group of rebels in the mountains there."

Well, that won't do at all, Khazerai mused. "Increase the bounty to fifty Khaz, and send a troop of my Night Guards down there to eliminate this local pestilence. Also, if he really wants to come after me, I expect he'll need some weapons training. Instruct your men to find all of the weapons masters and either hire them or remove them."

Khazerai was about to turn back to his maps when a thought struck him. "You know, not that I don't trust our men's abilities, but I do believe in being thorough. Hire a squad of Ladian assassins and send them there as well. Do not let either group know of the other's mission. We'll see who gets him first."

"Immediately, Exalted One."

With that Khazerai turned his mind back to more pressing matters. Two of his overbarons had been squabbling for weeks over a border dispute, and he decided to tour both holdings, and see for himself what the best way would be to handle the matter. During his month-long tour, he discovered malfeasance on both sides, and had promptly arrested both men and had them put to death, installing easily controlled puppet rulers in each one's place.

But that had taken up an inordinate amount of his time, and he had scarcely returned to the gates of the Ebon Citadel when his lieutenant ran up, sweaty and disheveled.

"Forgive me, My Master, but this assistant pig-tender's son—"

"Who?"

"The one who swore revenge on you a few months back when the local guards killed his family for nonpayment of taxes."

"Ah yes, been killed, has he?"

"No, I'm afraid not. In fact, there are several fiefdoms that are fomenting open revolt against the Empire. They are led by this youth, who claims to have brought back the power of the gods to Cauldera."

"What? What about the Night Guards that were sent over to kill him?"

"Lured into a trap in the mountains and crushed under an avalanche."

"And the Ladians?"

"Um, well, that's partially how he's claiming to have brought the gods back, My Majesty. Apparently, while they were able to poison him, friends of his managed to find the leaves of the rare *deusex* plant, make the even rarer antidote, and save his life. He claims that during the time he was suffering from the poison's effects, he spoke to the gods, and was charged with bringing their might back to your lands, and also eradicating the quote 'blight of evil' unquote that hangs over Cauldera."

"How melodramatic. Well, if it's a fight he wants, then let's give it to him. Assemble the Third, Fourth, and Fifth Dark Brigades and send them to the Western Marches. Scour the land and destroy this boy and anyone that stands with him. Do not take any prisoners, do not bring him back alive. Just kill him. Handle this yourself." For a moment, Khazerai was seized by the mad impulse to add, "and you know the penalty for failure," but with an effort, he restrained himself. However, in the back of his mind, he wondered *where did that come from?* Of course his soldiers knew the penalty for failure; demotion and, if they really screwed up, corporal punishment. He wouldn't just kill them on a whim because they couldn't complete one assignment. Good lieutenants were always hard to find, and killing the ones he had out of pique wouldn't help morale at all. *Perhaps this assistant pig-tender's boy is bothering me more than I'd like to think. However, I'm sure that this will be the end of the matter.*

Unfortunately, that was not the case. Although Khazerai's lieutenant did return with the charred remains of what he swore was the body of the rebel leader, along with a fairly stirring account of how the Dark Brigades had flushed the rebels out, encircled them, and burned almost all of them alive, reports over the next few months kept popping up about sightings of the leader of the rebels, the populace's new messiah. Khazerai speculated that either the peasants were trying to keep his memory alive as a martyr, or the tenacious little bastard had somehow escaped the trap, and was running around sowing discontent throughout his empire. Neither option was acceptable to him, and so the chase was on.

"Dispatch a Shade Legion to every location where this assistant pig-tender's son has been sighted, and track him down. I want his head—nothing else—delivered to me within the next month."

But even that hadn't worked. Oh, his legions had done their

job well, sowing fear and terror throughout the populace wherever they marched, but the assistant pig-tender's son, through some arcane legerdemain, managed to escape several dire predicaments, such as:

—When his Legions had trapped the youth in a network of caves and then flooded the entire complex, drowning several dozen miners and their families.

—When his Twilight Riders had harried him to the cliffs overlooking the Teglan Sea, and one of them had even wounded him with a lucky shot from a crossbow (earning him an increase in rank; Khazerai always believed in promoting from within) and sent him plunging two hundred feet into the churning waters.

—When one of his most trusted vassals had actually captured the youth alive and thrown him in jail. Apparently this lord had not gotten the "kill on sight" memo, for by the time a messenger had been sent informing Khazerai of the capture (he hadn't even finished reading the message before sending a three-word message back—*Kill him immediately*), the boy had escaped, getting the vassal killed in the confusion.

And on it went, with the assistant pig-keeper's son escaping mortal situation after situation, sometimes sacrificing a trusted companion, but always popping up after Khazerai was sure he had been killed. And always along the way, he gathered followers to his cause like bees to honey.

Like vultures to a dead carcass, if I have my way, Khazerai thought. He couldn't believe the boy's luck, and a small part of him wondered if indeed this one was protected by the gods. Shaking his head, he dismissed the thought—the gods were no more, Khazerai himself had seen to that.

So then, what to do with this boy? Whatever he was going to do, it had better be quick, as Khazerai now heard the clang of sword on shield and the shouts of the victorious—overshadowed just a bit by the screams of the dying—right outside his main chamber. *And I'm sure he's there, leading the way, just like in the legends . . .*

The thought gave Khazerai pause, just as he was also resisting an insane urge to go out there and to see if he could lend a hand. Direct confrontation had never been his style, he always preferred using the more subtle arts to achieve his goals, and failing that, following up with the army. *But it would appear that my army is in the process of being routed, which doesn't leave many options left.* Flight wasn't an option, for even if he could make it out of the Ebon Citadel, his face was known throughout the Empire, for in a moment of supreme egotism several years ago he had ordered his own face placed on all the coins—well, that, and to stop the rampant counterfeiting that had been devaluing his currency. Regardless, he wouldn't be able to go as far as the next county without being caught. Surrender? Not likely, as they no doubt would tear him limb from limb before he could even reach trial, assuming that they would even bother with such a formality, and not just try to burn him alive.

Khazerai tried to concentrate, as something about the legends of the people was niggling at his mind—something about the stories of the heroes who, no matter what the odds were against them, always managed to defeat evil at the end. Impossible odds, odds like—

—Exactly like what has been stacked against this boy from the very beginning, he thought. *And he has come through all of it, not without difficulty, but he has vanquished everything in his path to destroy me.*

The thought rocked Khazerai. Could it be true, could they somehow be caught up in a cycle that was larger than the both of them, the endless struggle of good versus evil? Could there be a force beyond men, beyond the gods, beyond even his incredible comprehension, that somehow ensured that evil was defeated in every confrontation, no matter how long it took?

If this is true, that would certainly explain my odd impulses lately, he thought. But if that was the case, how would he manage

Stronger Than Fate

to salvage victory from what looked like certain defeat?

Before he could even begin to contemplate the answer to that question, the huge double doors burst open, and his trusted lieutenant backed into the room, valiantly fending off what could only be the assistant pig keeper's son, now clad in gleaming chain mail, and swinging a shining sword like a man possessed. The fighting pair was followed by several other men from both sides, all cursing and hacking at each other with crimson-streaked blades. Khazerai stood up as the approaching battle spilled toward him.

Although Khazerai's lieutenant was a most capable warrior, he had also suffered several other wounds during the fighting, and was now hard pressed to defend against the crusader's relentless assault. As Khazerai watched, the young man slashed his henchman across the wrist, disarming him, then beat upon his shield with hammering blows, driving him to the ground. The lieutenant's shield arm buckled, and his battered armor fell to the side, exposing his chest and head. The young warrior raised his sword to finish him off, and when his sword was just about to come down, Khazerai spoke.

"Don't kill him, if you please. After all, it's me you really want."

At the sound of his voice, the young man started and looked up. When that happened, Khazerai's lieutenant managed to draw a small blade from the back of his shield and glanced up at his liege's face, waiting for the command to strike.

Khazerai shook his head just enough to negate his man's intended action. He felt it more strongly now; the sense that theirs was a battle that had raged for centuries, millennia even, since before the dawn of time itself. He knew how this would play out, indeed, how it must play out for the cycle to continue. And strangely, he was content with this. *After all, I had a good run*, he thought. *Perhaps it is time to pass the torch on.*

What? Absolutely not! another part of his mind said. *This is not how it will all end, accepting this fate like a mewling lamb to the slaughter.*

But how am I to defeat him then? Khazerai thought. *Everything is on his side, the army, the gods, momentum—*

And in a trice Khazerai had the answer. He nodded to the young man, who was breathing hard with his exertions as he stood there in his armor the likes of which this world had not seen for hundreds of years. Seeing the glint of wildness in his enemy's eye, he chose his next words carefully. "You have defeated my army, and destroyed all that have come against you. Now you have me at your mercy." He spread his arms, palms up, out in a show of submission. "Congratulations, you have won."

"Not yet I haven't," the young man snarled, raising his sword again. "Not until your foul stain is erased from this world!"

Before anyone could move, the young man bounded up the steps to the dais of the Throne of Black Blades and stabbed Khazerai in the chest, right through the heart. "With the Sword of Laighmon, granted to me by the gods themselves, I strike you down. And before you die, know that Ardon, son of Laot the assistant pig-tender, was the one that destroyed you."

Even through his pain, Khazerai couldn't help smiling at the boy's theatrics. "So...be...it."

The youth pulled his sword out, and with dazzling speed, whirled and beheaded Khazerai in one smooth, powerful stroke. The despot's head bounced down the steps to land facing the young warrior, his eyes open in sightless accusation. The headless body fell back into the chair, the jet of blood from the neck already subsiding.

The young warrior turned to the assembled soldiers before him. "People of the Yulen Empire, your suffering is at an end. Your cruel overlord is no more, and today heralds a new dawn of peace and tranquility—"

He might have gone on like that for hours if Khazerai's body hadn't risen from the chair behind him, grabbed the young man's sword out of his hand, and lopped off his golden-haired head in one stroke. As the young man's cranium bounced to the ground,

Khazerai's body kicked the shaking torso off the dais and strode to where his head lay. Everyone watched, aghast, as the body dropped the sword of the gods, picked up its head and set it on top of his neck again. As the men in the room stared, the flesh of Khazerai's neck knitted together, drawing the wound closed until there was just a thin red line marking the injury, and in a few seconds, that was gone as well. The hideous gash on his chest had already closed as well, leaving no trace that he had ever been cut at all. The men all knelt down on the floor, first his own, then the soldiers of the former enemy army, each one prostrating themselves before him.

He walked over to his lieutenant and motioned him up with one hand, then addressed the rest of the men in the room. "Go forth and let the rest of your people know that your leader is dead, and if they lay down their arms right now, I will be merciful. However, this is not negotiable, and they have, oh—about five minutes to decide. Now get out of here."

The vanquished men wasted no time in scrambling out of the throne room, Khazerai's intense gaze following them the entire way. Swiveling his head back and forth, he tested the muscles in his neck, feeling them stretch and pop as he moved. He rubbed his jaw, which throbbed when he touched it. *That's going to bruise nicely*, he thought. Picking up the once shining sword, he wasn't surprised to see that it was just an ordinary weapon, with no magic about it at all. Dropping it, he glanced over at the quivering body of the young warrior, blood now staining his once-gleaming armor a blackish-red, and shook his head.

"What part of 'Khazerai the Undying' didn't you understand?"

THE OPPOSITE OF SOLID
Linda P. Baker

I was thrilled when Jean Rabe accepted "The Opposite of Solid" for her anthology, Pandora's Closet. *Of all my stories, it's the one that's the most me. Like Charles, my main character, I really did want to run away and be a hippie. I guess I just had too much common sense to do it. But still, sometimes when I hear a period song or see a picture of a woman dancing with flowers in her hair during the Summer of Love, I wish I'd been a little less sensible and a bit more adventurous. However, that choice might not have led me to where I am now—a writer living in Mobile, AL, with my pack—husband, Larry, and Airedale Terrier/Dragon, Grady. I've been with the Writer's Symposium as far back as when we were in Milwaukee, WI. www.gradysheart.com*

"The more you live, the less you die."
—Janis Joplin

Solid. That's the word that sums up my life.

Rock-solid, my momma called me. Rock-solid and steady. "You're gonna make some woman a good, steady, dependable husband," she would say, all proud and approving, as we sat in the kitchen, peeling potatoes for Sunday dinner. "Rock-solid."

She thought it was a compliment. Wouldn't my momma have been shocked to hear her compliment turn into "stolid and plodding?" That's what my last girlfriend called me, as she slammed the door on her way out.

I think that's why I noticed the woman wearing a faded red hippie jacket, sitting on a park bench in the afternoon sun. It was her transparency that drew me. She was ethereal.

Ethereal and luminous, with coppery, Irish red hair and light like sun sparkling on snow around her head. It almost seemed I could see the wood slats of the bench through her shoulders. That's why she drew me...she looked so much the opposite of solid.

I wouldn't have normally had the nerve to ask a strange, beautiful woman if I could sit with her, but today, enjoying the early spring sunshine of Golden Gate Park, watching the flitting of butterflies and hearing the buzzing of bees, I felt particularly daring. I mumbled my request and remained standing, just on the off chance that she would refuse.

She looked up at me with eyes that for a moment seemed clear as water, then darkened to a good, hard blue. "You see me?!" Her voice was like orchids, throaty and fragile, like she didn't talk much.

"Yeah, sure I do." I answered immediately before I could think what an odd question it was. I sat beside her as close as I dared and put my newspaper and my lunch salad and my bottle of fancy spring water between us.

Up close, she was less fragile, more visible, and the fairy light that danced around her head settled down and proved to be the noon sun reflecting off the bay. She smelled like gardenias with a touch of carnation, almost a taste rather than a scent. Almost funereal, but...pleasant.

Flower power. This woman had it, from her long red hair to her deliberately scuffed bell-bottom jeans to the tips of her sandaled feet.

"Don't people normally see you?"

"Not normally," she confessed. "They just sort of . . . look past."

I thought of how her shoulders had seemed to disappear into the back of the bench. But she was plainly solid up close. Thin as a model and pale, but substantial. She was wearing a jacket a bit too big for her that must have once been a deep, ruby red, but now was faded to a streaked pink. It had gold embroidery around the cuffs and running up the front, a kind of flowery *fleur de lis* design that had frayed and cracked with age. It looked weirdly familiar, like it was something I'd seen before.

I picked up my salad and fought with the supposed easy open corner. "I don't see how anyone could look past you. Not with that hair."

She fingered a long copper curl as if she'd forgotten she was wearing a halo of fire around her head.

"It's beautiful," I offered, "especially with the sun shining on it."

She looked at me as if she was as startled at being paid a compliment as I was at giving one. She blushed, a pale pink that touched only her high cheekbones and just above her eyebrows. "Thank you. No one's said something like that to me in a long time."

I was smitten. In addition to a funky retro jacket and hair like new pennies, she had the smile of a siren, bright as sunflowers.

"I'm Charles." I held out my hand.

She touched her small hand to mine. Her skin felt strange, cool and there, yet . . . so not there. Like the brush of dandelion fluff. "Arizona."

I can't help but laugh. "Arizona? That's your name?"

The smile faltered. Her hand slipped away, leaving a ghostly impression of coolness where her fingertips brushed.

I rushed to patch my faux pas. "With hair like that, I thought you'd be Caitlan or Maureen or . . . "I searched my mind for another obviously Irish American name and couldn't think of a single one.

She relaxed, her smile returning. "It's from a song."

And immediately, the lyrics popped into my head. "Arizona, rainbow shades and hobo shoes. Paul Revere and the Raiders."

She smiled even wider, surprised and delighted that I would get the reference. "My mom and dad were sort of hippies."

"I wanted to be a hippie. More than I ever wanted anything in

The Opposite of Solid

my life. I even bought a map of San Francisco and a moth-eaten old duffel bag and kept it packed and hidden in the back of my closet." I couldn't believe I'd just told her that. I'd never told anyone about the stuff I'd dreamed when I was a teenager. It all just seemed so silly and flighty. The exact opposite of the rock-solid person my parents expected me to become. And I guess, there was a bit of disappointment in there, too, that I'd never shinnied down the pear tree that grew right outside my window and lit out for California.

I'd missed the Summer of Love and Woodstock and Monterey Pops. The closest we'd come to anything hippie in East Texas was Jimmy Johnston, who wore his kinky blonde hair in a 'fro and went around saying "Groovy, dude," to everyone, until he slipped and said it to our English teacher in class one day and got sent to the principal's office. The Haight-Ashbury district that had seemed so exotic and exciting was now just The Haight, home to Gap and Starbucks. I hadn't moved to San Francisco until I was forty-something, and only then because I was promoted into it.

Arizona and her shining hair and the strangely familiar, flowery, faded embroidery on her sleeves brought back the bittersweet smells and sounds of those summer nights. Lying in my bed, listening to Hendrix and Janis Joplin and Joe Cocker and Jefferson Airplane, with the radio turned low so my parents wouldn't hear. Smelling the warm, growing earth and the green pears. Dreaming of hopping a freighter headed west.

"What was in your duffel bag?"

I still remembered that, too. "A pair of bell bottomed jeans that I bought off a guy named Jimmy Johnston. And a poster for a Janis Joplin concert. And clean socks."

She laughed, a rougher sound than I'd have expected from such a delicate woman.

I looked down at my sensible leather dress shoes and smiled. I would have been the only flower child in Haight-Ashbury wearing clean, white cotton socks. I guess solid and rebellious are strange bedfellows.

"Why did you want to be a hippie?"

I opened my mouth to be glib, and again, wound up telling the truth. "I didn't want to be sensible and steady. I thought being a hippie sounded like a magical way to live. Free and alive, the way Janis Joplin was. Unfettered, spontaneous. Music, drugs, free love."

She frowned, as if I'd said something goofy again.

"I know it probably wasn't like that. I mean, living moment to moment may sound glamorous, but not knowing where your next meal is coming from isn't all that . . . groovy."

We both grinned at my use of the word.

"I guess the fact that I thought I'd need clean socks tells you I wasn't cut out for it."

"I think you can be glamorous and free and still have clean socks," she said, and for a moment, I saw that sparkling light again and caught a glimpse of a Monterey Pine, needles shifting gently in the breeze through her forehead, as if her brain was clear.

I rubbed my eyes. Seeing things like that sounded like all the stories I'd read about LSD trips. When I looked up, her forehead was just a forehead again, solid and wrinkled by fine concentration lines.

"Why didn't you do it?" she asked. "Why didn't you run away and become a hippie?"

"I don't—I'm not sure exactly." I didn't like the sound of the words coming out. "I guess . . . I guess the right time just never came. And then it was too late."

"I was there once," she said. "For a while. It was cool, just like the books say."

"There . . . where?" A bean sprout fell off my fork onto my thigh. I brushed it away. Why did I feel like our conversation lulled her into saying something she didn't mean to? Why did I, for just minute, think she meant she'd been to Haight-Ashbury, in the Summer of Love?

Then she looked at me, straight into me. Like she could see

through me. "San Francisco, back then. I was there for a while."

"Huh?"

"I don't know about taking you there, but . . . I think I can take you somewhere you've never been before. If you want to go with me on my next trip."

Because I was still in that whole Woodstock, Summer of Love frame of mind, I immediately thought she meant a *trip*. A drug trip. But . . . would I do it? I sat there, staring at her. Kind of stupidly, I imagined. Like a big, dumb rock with a heart beating triple time. Would I do it? Wasn't that the kind of recklessness I'd always wanted? Hadn't I always intended to try tripping, just once? But I wasn't that fourteen-year-old dreamer anymore.

What if she was a cop? What if this was a set-up? My appetite shriveled, and I put the salad down on the ground. "Is this a joke?" I looked around, trying to do it casually. I couldn't see anybody who appeared to be watching us, but that was the point of surveillance, wasn't it?

"No, it's not a joke." She held out her hand.

I glanced over my shoulder, then at a guy who was sitting nearby on the ground, leaning back against a tree.

I looked back at her. She hadn't moved. She was just sitting there, her small hand extended, palm up. But she was doing that shimmering thing. One minute so transparent that she almost wasn't visible, the next as solid as . . . well, not as solid as me. Few people were as *solid* as me.

It must be something about the area, about the way the bench was positioned to the sun and the water. There was something about her. Something about the way she was barely there, but so much more there than anyone else I'd ever met, that drew me like a magnet. I took her hand. And the world shifted.

It felt like—it felt like sparkling. Like sparkling should feel, if you could feel it. It felt like I'd become one of those sparklers that all the kids played with on holidays. Like I was giving off sparks, showers of them, but they didn't burn. I didn't burn. I gave off sparks of multi-colored light, but I didn't diminish. I was still solid and stable.

Then slowly the fiery pricks of light began to die down, and I could see. The world around me was hazy and thin, but I could see. The world was becoming more and more solid, more and more color leaching into the walls and the floor beneath my feet.

Floor? I was sitting in Golden Gate Park, watching the noon sun sparkle on the bay, holding hands with a girl named Arizona. There shouldn't be floor beneath my feet. Especially not floor with shag carpet. Or walls with flocked gold and green wallpaper becoming more solid around me. There shouldn't be—I looked around in a panic. Where was Arizona? But there she was, right beside me, her thin fingers still gripping my thick ones.

"Arizona? What's going on?"

"I don't know yet," she said, her voice calm and even. There was none of the panic in her tone that I'd heard in my own. "It'll come clear. It always does."

"What does?" I turned slowly, not going so far that I had to let go of her hand. At the moment, she was my only connection to solidity.

We were in a hotel room. It looked and smelled like there'd been a raucous party there. The air was thick, almost unbreathable with the sour scent of aged cigarette smoke and the sweet scent of whiskey. There was an unopened bottle of booze on the nightstand and one overturned on the floor just under the foot of the bed. Cigarette butts and potato chips overflowed from several ashtrays and from what looked like a large, shell shaped soapdish on one bedside table. On the floor, beside the almost empty bottle of whiskey, was a newspaper. I leaned over and picked it up. A Los Angeles newspaper, dated October 4, 1970.

"I don't understand. Where are we? Is this some kind of joke? Did you have this made up at that shop over on Page?" But of course, a fake newspaper wouldn't account for how I'd gotten here.

Arizona's lack of confusion and fear only made me more frantic. Up until that point, she'd seemed fluttery and ethereal, like a butterfly or a wispy cloud or some fey fairy creature. Here, in this place that I couldn't account for, she seemed solid as stone and as dangerous as rattlesnake backed into a corner.

"How did we get here?"

"I don't know exactly. It just happens." Arizona said. "It'll have something to do with this." She caught the edges of her jacket and held it out from her hips.

The red jacket with its gold embroidery had seemed strangely familiar from the moment I saw it. But that was some jacket, if it could take me on a LSD trip without the LSD. "I don't understand."

"It'll come clear."

"Stop saying that! This doesn't make sense. Did you drug me? Have I passed out? Is this a dream?" Would I wake up in a few minutes, annoyed that the alarm clock had gone off and that yet another boring, plodding day was beginning?

"We've traveled in time."

"What?" That made even less sense, and now I was starting to get angry. I kept trying to remember if she'd touched my food. Or if I'd put my water down on the bench between us.

"I don't know how it works. I just know it happens. And we'll know what needs to be done. Once it comes clear."

For some reason, I wanted the panic of my first few minutes back. It seemed like a solid, logical response. At the same time, it didn't seem right, that a guy as big and broad as me should turn into a gibbering mess while a tiny woman stood by so coolly.

Arizona seemed to understand. She took my hands in hers, and it was only because her hands seemed so hot that I realized how cold my own were. "It'll be all right," she said. "I promise. It scared me, too, the first few times, but I got used to it."

"How many times has this happened to you?"

"I don't know. I quit counting after a while."

"How long is 'a while'?"

"I don't know. Ever since I bought this jacket at a junk auction. A long time, I think."

I circled the room. I stopped in front of the door and put my hand on the knob. The dull, tarnished gold of it was cold and solid in my palm. It gave me an idea.

I rushed over to the window and shoved the heavy curtains aside. The sliding glass door opened onto a dinky balcony that overlooked the street below. In the hotel parking lot right below was a mint Volkswagon van that I would have killed for in my youth. It had the finest psychedelic paint job I'd ever seen, even down to the giant peace sign on the front. And down the street, a yellow Corvair and a red Ford Mustang mixed in with a dozen huge, heavy period cars. So much for the theory that it was all just an elaborate joke. A newspaper could be faked, but an entire street of 1960s vehicles?

As I stepped back into the room, there was rattling and coughing behind a door that I assumed was a bathroom. A woman cursed softly under her breath. There was the sound of water running. More cursing, then the bathroom door opened.

I gasped, so loudly that the woman who strolled into the room should have heard me.

She looked exactly like Janis Joplin. The Janis Joplin I'd listened to long after my parents thought I was asleep. The Janis Joplin who epitomized everything I'd wanted in the depths of my unsolid soul when I was thirteen.

The woman walked past like I wasn't even there. I put out my hand to touch her, and it was like touching a cloud. It was like on the television when someone touched a ghost. My hand went right through her shoulder.

The Janis lookalike didn't even flinch. She just walked past and threw herself down on her stomach on the bed. The springs squeaked under her weight, then settled.

"What the hell!" There's only so much even a rock-steady guy like me can take. I crossed the room in what seemed like only two giant strides and grabbed Arizona. Her shoulders were thin, but solid. "What the hell's going on here? What kind of game is this?"

"No game."

But my mind wouldn't stop gibbering. It carried my tongue right along with it. "What's going on? I want to know right now. What is this, some kind of set-up? And where did you find that woman? She looks just like Janis Joplin." I knew about look-alikes, those people who do impersonations of celebrities. I'd seen a couple that could make you stop in your tracks, but this one . . . This one could have been Janis Joplin's twin.

"She *is* Janis Joplin," Arizona said, as matter of fact as if she'd been discussing next week's menu. "I told you. We've moved through time. You're connected to her somehow. That's why we came here, to this time. This place."

"I'm not connected to her. She died thirty years ago! Today." I picked up the paper from the floor and shook it at Arizona. "She died on this day. When I was just a kid."

Arizona nodded, but she wasn't paying me any attention. She was watching the woman on the bed.

She had rolled over on her back and pulled a large cloth purse up off the floor. Propping the bag on her stomach, she dug into it, scratching around like whatever she was looking for was eluding her. Things began to fall out of it, an ink pen, a wad of papers, keys.

The next thing she found was a cigarette pack. She ran her finger down in it, then shook it, as if there had to be just one more cigarette in it. When it stayed empty, she gave a sound of disgust and threw it into the overflowing ashtray on the nightstand. Then she sat up and pulled open the nightstand drawer and stuck her hand in. She found another empty cigarette pack. She cursed, eloquently and musically.

That's when I knew, really knew, that this really was Janis Joplin. Because a lookalike might fake her pockmarked face, or her eyes, or the frizzy hair. But no one, *no one*, could sound like Janis. No one could sound like that, rough and sweet, gravel on satin.

Then she pulled something else out of the nightstand. A paper bag, brown and so new it sounded crisp. She slowly opened the bag and upended it. What toppled out made my breath freeze in my throat.

Janis stared at what had spilled out of the bag . . . a syringe, a small folded packet that looked like wax paper, a spoon, a short piece of rubber hose. Even a stolid and plodding guy like me recognized a drug kit when he saw one.

Janis picked up each item one by one and turned them over in her hands. She picked up the wax paper packet last, opened it slowly. It had fine white powder in it. I knew what it was.

Janis looked like she might cry. Or laugh. Or scream.

I looked back at Arizona. She was watching us, her gaze flitting back and forth between my back and the packet in Janis' hands.

"Has it 'come clear' yet?" she asked. "Why we came here?"

In a flash, I remembered why I'd never taken my duffel bag with its carefully folded clean socks and my guitar and hopped a train for Haight-Ashbury. It was because of Janis Joplin.

Janis Joplin was a Texas girl whose hometown was just like mine, uptight and boring and predictable. But unlike me, she'd escaped. She'd lived her dream. I'd dreamed of hopping a freighter for California and standing right in front of the stage for one of her concerts. I'd dreamed of being carefree and unpredictable, of living for the moment.

Then Janis Joplin had died.

First Hendrix, then Janis just a couple of weeks later of a heroin overdose.

And suddenly, I'd seen the dark underside of the carefree, hippie lifestyle. Several months later, Jim Morrison also died. But Janis' death had been the end of my dreams of Haight-Ashbury and life as a barefoot, dancing flower child.

The Opposite of Solid

I wheeled to Arizona. "I just remembered. This is why I didn't run away from home. Janis died and all the light seemed to leak out of my dreams." I wasn't sure the light had ever come back.

Arizona nodded and smiled.

"Does that mean. . . ?" I stopped and squeezed my temples between my palms. It was all so weird, so very far out, that I couldn't quite wrap my mind around it. But I'd read science fiction, like every other kid with dreams of something different, something better. Some of the stories about time travel had stayed with me. "Does that mean, that if I save her . . . my life will change? Does that mean that I'll be the person I always wanted to be?"

Arizona sort of shrugged and smiled and nodded, all at the same time.

I started to question that weird, ambiguous response, but I was too taken with the idea that I might not have to be stolid and plodding. That the woman behind me on the bed didn't have to die. But how would that work, if I couldn't even touch her?

As I thought it, Janis jumped backward, sending the drug paraphernalia scattering across the bed. "God damn, man! Where'd you come from? How the hell did you get in here?"

She could see me! She was talking to me! For a minute, I just stood there, a big, dumb rock. Janis Joplin could see me. *Janis Joplin* was talking to me!

"I asked you what you're doing in here?" She was regaining her equilibrium, coming up on her knees on the bed, reaching for her purse.

My voice came back in a rush. My muscles decided they wanted to work. "I'm sorry, Miss Joplin, for scaring you. I just came for . . . I just came for this." I leaned over the bed and gathered up the drug stuff, dropping the syringe, dropping the hose, but making sure I tucked the little wax packet of white powder into my pocket. Then I gathered up the rest of it a second time and stuffed it back into the sack.

At any moment, I expected Janis to whack me over the head

with her bag, or reach into it and pull out a gun, or start screaming her head off. But she just gaped at me, opening and closing her mouth like a guppie. When I got back to normal, if I got back to normal, maybe I would have a good laugh over making Janis Joplin tongue-tied.

"What—? How—? Who the hell are you, man? How the fuck did you get in here?"

"It's kinda hard to explain." I grinned with what I hoped was a reassuring expression. "I'm just a fan. A fan from Texas. I've been listening to your music . . . Well, all of my life, and I just—well, It's really great." I knew I was starting to babble, but, hell, who wouldn't babble, standing near enough a childhood hero to smell her toothpaste?

Arizona touched my elbow. Actually, she sort of pinched my elbow. Her fingers dug into the soft flesh right above it. I could see the sparkles starting around her head. She was losing her solid edge. Did that mean that we'd done what we were supposed to do?

But there was still one more thing I needed to say, even if it didn't help in the long run. "You've been clean for months now. You need to stay clean, to make more music for all your Texas fans."

Janis nodded, staring at my face. She was slowly losing her solidity, just as I suspected I was losing mine. The sparkles grew larger, stronger, and the burning arcs clouded my vision. The room around me faded, the flowered comforter and the wadded pillows at the head of the bed, and the petite, rumpled woman in front of them, losing their sharp edges. Janis had become even more transparent than Arizona had ever been.

Weirdly, as the room faded, it seemed to double. Like I was seeing two cloudy, see-through Janises, two fuzzy hotel rooms, slowly splitting apart, slowly, slowly becoming separate, y-ing out in two different directions. But there was only one Arizona, only one me, in only one of the rooms. The last thing I new of the time and space we'd been in was Janis Joplin's husky, trademark voice,

The Opposite of Solid

saying softly, "Godd-d-d damn!"

Going back, or traveling through time, or coming down from the trip, whatever it was, wasn't easy. Going had been like expanding, like turning into a sparkling cloud. Coming back was like being stuffed into a container that was much too small. Like being split in two, then twisted back together. The sparkly, transparent Charles was twisted and shoved and collapsed back down into solid Charles, and it hurt.

I hit the ground hard. Like falling out of the sky without a parachute. The scent of crushed and bruised grass slammed into my lungs. My eyes filled with tears. The weight and pressure of now was almost more than I could stand. The brown paper bag fell out of my numb fingers.

It was a rude way to ride back into San Francisco. I lay on the ground, gasping for breath, and watched Arizona rematerialize above me. Obviously, she had a better handle on time travel tripping than I did. It looked almost like she floated into being, slowly becoming solid enough that I couldn't see the clouds above me.

Arizona leaned down and held out a hand, as if a flyweight like her could pull someone as solid as me up. "Are you okay?"

I was. But I wasn't. I felt weird and different. But . . . the problem was, I didn't feel different enough. I didn't feel like jumping up and running around Hippie Hill in my bare feet. I didn't take her offer of help. I just lay there, staring up at her and her faded red jacket, outlined in blue sky.

"I don't feel any different," I said. "If we just changed my past, why don't I feel different? Shouldn't I have different memories? Shouldn't I remember running away? Shouldn't I be—" I stopped myself before I could say it. 'A better person.' A *better* person. It was a revelation to realize that deep down, I'd always seen myself as a coward and a cop-out because I hadn't had the courage to make my dreams come true.

I sat up and picked at the knees of my wool blend trousers,

wiped a piece of grass off the toe of my shiny dress shoes. What if I'd changed my whole life, and it didn't make any difference? What if I was destined to be stolid and plodding and solid, no matter what? "Shouldn't I be a different person with a different job, and maybe, different clothes?"

"You are," Arizona said gently. "In that other universe."

"Other universe?"

"Didn't you see it, as we were returning? Didn't you see it branch off?"

"What the hell are you talking about?"

Arizona pulled her red jacket tight and sat down beside me on the grass. "I don't know really know how it works. I just know that each time I go back, each time I change something, I see the result splinter off into another future. I've done a lot of research on it, and I think it's got to do with parallel universes. Did you know there's a theory that there are infinite universes, all running parallel to ours?"

"I don't give a crap about parallel universes! I care about this one. I thought I'd be different."

"Aren't you?" Arizona asked. "Aren't you different just a little bit? Doesn't it make a difference that somewhere, sometime, the boy that you were took that step off the edge? Don't you feel . . . thinner?"

I stared at her. A cloud skittered across the sky, across one cheek, up and over her nose, out the side of her forehead. Thinner. Not transparent. She was thinner, so thin I could see through her!

"Oh, my god." I looked down at myself, felt my arms, my chest. I felt solid. I couldn't see the grass through my thighs. I couldn't see anything through anything. It was the first time in my life I've ever been glad to apply the word 'solid' to myself.

"Every time it happens," she said softly, "a little bit of me splinters off, too. A part of me lives on in those other universes, goes on, in another life. I've been doing it so long, there's not much of me left in this one." She slipped the faded jacket off one

The Opposite of Solid

arm. "I knew when you saw me that it was a sign. Then when you told me about what you wanted to be when you were a kid, and about Janis Joplin, I knew you were meant to take the jacket."

I could see individual blades of grass, swaying in the breeze, through her thin shoulder. I could smell the salt scent of the bay, blowing through her. I dug my fingers into the grass, into the ground. The earth was solid beneath me. The sky above had never seemed so hard and blue. It was my mind, my thoughts, that seemed wispy and skittering, like clouds. How crazy was she, to think a faded, old jacket could take her back in time? To think that she could pass her craziness on to me? To think that because I liked Janis Joplin's music, it was a sign.

She was shifting, trying to slide the jacket off the other shoulder.

I stood up before she could get any farther. "I—Look—I've got to get back to work." I looked at my watch, as if just the act of reminding myself of the time of day could tame the skittering thoughts. As if doing something normal and monotonous as checking the time could settle the panic that was battering around in my stomach.

She stopped tugging at the jacket and looked up at me with eyes that seemed to swim and waft and shift, clear, then solid blue, then clear again, like a fish's eyes. "I thought you wanted to be different."

For a moment, I smelled her again, a quick waft of funereal gardenias. I smelled ripe, ready-to-pick pears. Felt the lure of night stars and Janis Joplin's singular voice. "I'm sorry. I—" I looked at my watch again, but I couldn't see the hands. "I have to go. It was nice to meet you."

Before I could smell that scent again, that scent of Texas night, I rushed away. I hurried across the park, taking shortcuts over the grass. I didn't stop until I'd joined a clump of people who were waiting at the edge of the park for the light to change. After several seconds, I forced myself to look back.

63

Arizona had followed me and was standing several yards away on the grass. She was looking at me, but her expression was remote and sad, and disappointed, as if she could no longer see me. She had put the faded red jacket back on. As I watched, she reached inside it and pulled out a pair of sunglasses. They were huge and round, pure 60s sunglasses, nothing like the tiny, expensive aviator-shaped glasses that were so costly and popular today. She put them on. They dwarfed her small, luminous face.

Recognition hit me like a blow. I *knew* the red jacket. That's why it was so familiar. It was Janis'. There was a picture of her wearing it, on one of her albums. Janis sitting on a motorcycle, wearing a red jacket trimmed with gold embroidery and enormous sunglasses, her frizzy hair lit by the sun. Her expression was luminous and faraway, like she could see something the rest of us couldn't.

The light changed. All around me, people started across the street. A couple of people shoved past me. Another one growled at me to get out of the way if I wasn't going to cross.

I stared at Arizona. Smelled pears mixed with salt air. I stepped off the curb and plodded after the surge of people heading back to work, Janis Joplin singing in my head.

As Good as a Rest
Tim Waggoner

Tim Waggoner has participated in the Gen Con Writers' Symposium for the past ten years and has loved every minute of it. His most current novels are the Nekropolis series of urban fantasies and the Lady Ruin series for Wizards of the Coast. In total, he's published more than twenty novels and two short story collections, and his articles on writing have appeared in Writer's Digest *and* Writers' Journal, *among others. He teaches creative writing at Sinclair Community College and in Seton Hill University's Master of Fine Arts in Writing Popular Fiction program. Visit him on the web at www.timwaggoner.com and www.nekropoliscity.com.*

The door to the office of Archetype Management burst open, and into the sterile reception area stalked a tall, broad-shouldered, well-muscled woman dressed in skimpy leather and bronze armor covered completely in gore.

The receptionist shouted as gobbets of bloody flesh slid off the warrior woman and landed on the plush ginger-colored carpet with meaty-wet plaps.

"Look at the mess you're making!" the thin, bird-boned woman said. She stood, eyes blazing over the tops of her granny glasses, hair bun so tight it looked as if her head might explode any moment. She stabbed a slender finger at the door. "Get out of here before you make it any worse!"

The blonde swordswoman—the very picture of a Norse valkyrie with a touch of stone-age savage thrown in for good measure—dropped a callused hand to the hilt of the sword hanging at her side. "I would consider it a personal favor if you wouldn't speak to me in that tone," she said evenly.

The receptionist's face reddened in anger and her jaw muscles tightened. The already severe lines of her suit seemed to become sharper, sharp enough to draw blood.

"Don't think you can intimidate me, Ms. Tugenda. As Mr. Abernathy's executive assistant, I deal on a daily basis with all manner of archetypes, from thunder gods to demons. I don't threaten easily."

Tugenda didn't usually encounter this sort of resistance and wasn't quite sure what to do next. She decided to try to bull her way through. "I've come to ask for a reassignment. Is Mr. Abernathy in?"

The receptionist glanced toward a closed door behind her immaculately ordered desk. "Yesssss . . . but he's booked solid. Perhaps you could return tomorrow? After you've bathed a dozen times or so," she finished cattily.

Tugenda gritted her teeth but otherwise ignored the taunt. "I can't stand another day of mindlessly hacking my way through barbarian hordes. I must insist on speaking with Mr. Abernathy." She scowled darkly. "Now."

The receptionist's expression hardened. "That's not possible, Ms. Tugenda. You'll have to make an appointment." She took a seat at her desk once more and flipped open her appointment book. "How about next Thursday at 11:15?"

In answer, Tugenda drew her sword in a single swift motion, raised it above her head, and brought it down on the appointment book. Pages scattered into the air as the book, as well as the desk beneath it, split in two.

The receptionist didn't so much as blink. "I take it Thursday isn't good for you. How about Friday?"

Tugenda didn't bother to reply. She sheathed her sword and stomped toward Mr. Abernathy's door, leaving bloody bootprints on the carpet behind her.

The receptionist dashed forward to block her way. "I simply cannot allow you to see Mr. Abernathy without an appointment! It isn't—"

"That's quite all right, Clarisse," came a pleasant voice from within the now open door. "I always have time for a client as important as Ms. Tugenda."

The receptionist frowned, clearly not approving, but she stepped aside and Tugenda walked into the office. Mr. Abernathy, a small, rather rotund man in a charcoal gray business suit, gave Tugenda an overly practiced smile and stuck out his hand.

"Good to see you."

Tugenda displayed her gore-slicked fingers. "I think you'd prefer I didn't shake just now."

Mr. Abernathy's smile faltered. "I see what you mean."

Tugenda realized then that Abernathy wasn't alone in his office. Before his desk sat a massive man in an ill-fitting but expensive navy blue suit. His long dark hair was pulled back and bound in a pony tail, and a leather briefcase sat on the floor next to his chair.

Tugenda was about to ask who he was, when she recognized him. She was shocked. The Cimmerian looked quite a bit different than the last time she'd seen him.

"I'm sorry," she said. "I didn't realize you were here. If I'd known—"

He held up a huge, powerful hand to forestall Tugenda's apology. "That's all right. I was just about to leave anyway." He stood, bent to pick up his briefcase and stuck it awkwardly beneath one arm. "I have to get going to my new assignment." He sounded like a beaten man, with none of the fire and passion she was familiar with.

He turned to Mr. Abernathy. "One last thing: can you tell me exactly what in Crom's name a *tort* is?"

Mr. Abernathy chuckled and patted his client on one of his log-sized arms. "You'll figure it all out, don't worry. After battling monsters and wizards for so long, I think you'll find your new assignment with Hyperborean Law to be a breeze."

The man snorted doubtfully, turned to Tugenda, nodded

once, and then left the office. Mr. Abernathy followed and closed the door on the sound of Clarisse spraying a can of industrial-strength air freshener into the reception area and muttering to herself about how in the Omniverse she was ever going to get these bloody footprints out of the carpet.

Mr. Abernathy smiled at Tugenda once more and gestured to the now empty chair. "Please, sit down."

Tugenda did so, ignoring the wet smack of her blood-smeared body at it came in contact with naugahyde.

Mr. Abernathy looked as if he suddenly regretted inviting her to sit, but he said nothing. He sat behind his desk and clasped his hands together before him. "So, what can I do for you today?"

Tugenda got straight to the point. "You can reassign me. I'm sick to death of slicing and dicing hordes of enemies. And I've really had it with this outfit." She wriggled uncomfortable. "Not only doesn't it provide much protection during battle—not to mention against breezes! —but it chaffs like a bear!"

Abernathy shrugged. "I always thought that what it lacked in practicality it made up for in style."

"I doubt you'd give much of a damn for style after you've picked as much troll flesh out of your cleavage as I have. But it's more than my outfit. It's the saddlesores from riding all day on a flatulent excuse for a horse. It's not being able to get a decent date because I'm too busy toppling an evil monarch or questing after some fabulous magical artifact. And when I finally do meet a man, he's either afraid of me or, if he's a warrior, he's only interested in the sort of empty-headed submissive females that evil priests are always serving up as sacrifices to their gods.

"And just try to have a decent conversation! All sorcerers ever want to talk about is how they're going to conquer the world and how much better everything will be once they're running the show. And all male fighters want to discuss are fighting techniques and sexual positions—and not in that order." She brushed a clumpy, matted lock from her forehead. "And do you have any idea what blood does to a girl's hair and skin?"

"I can see why you're so unhappy with your current assignment," Abernathy said with just the right amount of understanding. "Actually, it's rather fortuitous that you came to see me today. I was just about to send for you."

Tugenda was surprised—and more than a little suspicious. "Oh?"

"Recently we've been updating some of our assignments, trying to bring them more into line with today's needs."

She jerked her head toward the door. "Is that what you did with him? Bring him 'into line'?"

"Sometimes an archetype needs a bit of modernizing in order to stay relevant." Abernathy smiled. "He'll still be a warrior, just a different sort."

Tugenda thought of the way the barbarian fighter had almost slunk out of the office. He hadn't looked much like a warrior to her. "And you intend to do the same with me?"

"Yes, we do. It's true that your particular archetype—that of the battle maiden—has grown in popularity over the last few decades, but we feel it's time to move on, to explore new and more exciting possibilities. After all, that's why you came to see me today, isn't it?"

True, but Tugenda didn't relish the prospect of ending up like her male counterpart. She'd do her best to make sure that didn't happen.

"Very well. But there's one thing, Abernathy."

"Yes?"

"If you ever refer to me as a 'maiden' again, I'll have your balls for earrings."

Abernathy's ever-present smile faltered. "I'll, uh, try to keep that in mind. Now let's see what we've got for you." He turned to the computer on his desk and worked the mouse for a few moments. "Ah!" He turned back to face Tugenda, smile once more in place. "Tell me, have you ever heard of something called a sitcom?"

INTERIOR, EVENING—THE IVERSON HOUSEHOLD.

TUGENDA IVERSON, home from a busy day at the office, rushes into the kitchen, carrying an armload of groceries that are about to spill. Running in behind her are the three adorable but smart-aleck Iverson children, five-year-old BILLIE, eight-year-old JOEY, and sixteen-year-old DIANE.

HOLD FOR AUDIENCE APPLAUSE.

TUGENDA lays the groceries on the counter just as the bags rip, spilling boxes and cans everywhere.

LAUGHTER.

TUGENDA
By Caolan's cast-iron girdle! (TUGENDA looks up at the audience. In a demanding voice.) What's so damn funny?

MORE LAUGHTER.

TUGENDA's hand reaches toward her side, as if for something that should be there, but isn't. She scowls.

DIANE
Mu-therr! I swear, you are such a klutz sometimes!

BILLIE
I think she's getting old.

JOEY

Maybe we should start looking at nursing home brochures.

LAUGHTER.

TUGENDA

Why you little mud-sucking plague worms! (She grabs for her terrified children as the audience roars with laughter.)

Enter FRANK IVERSON.

FRANK

(Pausing for applause.) Hey, everybody, I'm home! (Noticing that his wife has all three of his children in headlocks.) Ah, there's nothing like family togetherness!

LAUGHTER.

TUGENDA

(Looking out at the audience and bellowing.) SHUT UP!

FRANK

Honey, I hate to spring this on you at the last moment, but my boss and his wife are going to be coming over to dinner tonight. (Checks watch.) In about forty-five minutes, to be precise. Do you think you can whip up one of your famous gourmet meals by then?

TUGENDA roars her fury, grabs a knife from the butcher block and slaughters her entire family.

RIOTOUS LAUGHTER.

TUGENDA

(Looking out at the audience and grinning maniacally.) Now it's your turn! (Brandishing her blade, she leaps into the crowd.)

ASSORTED SCREAMING.

*

Tugenda sat before Mr. Abernathy's desk again, this time wearing a business suit and skirt, but still covered in blood.

Abernathy sighed. "That assignment wasn't to your liking, I take it."

"I fail to see how it related to my archetype," she said stiffly.

"The strong modern woman trying to have it all, juggling husband, kids, career, all the while maintaining her sense of humor . . . Don't you see how it applies to the role of a warrior maid—er, I mean, a warrior? I admit, it's a bit on the abstract side—"

"I'm a swordswoman," Tugenda said. "I kill things. I don't do abstract."

Abernathy furrowed his brow in thought. "You know, you might consider going the route of your male counterpart who was in here the other day. Despite his initial hesitancy, he's thrown himself into his new role with gusto. He's already won a class action suit against Eldritch Pharmaceuticals, and he plans to take on Stygian Tobacco next."

Tugenda wasn't sure. Still, it if was good enough for *him*. . . .

*

"So you unequivocally deny that you killed your wife for the insurance money, Mr. Carcosa?"

The defendant—a wormy little man with pale, pock-marked skin—answered calmly. "Yes, I do. I couldn't have. I . . . just don't have the heart to murder anyone, let alone my own wife." A slight quiver of his bottom lip, a hint of tears welling in the corners of his eyes.

The defense attorney, a wolfishly handsome thirtysomething male, flashed Tugenda a quick, self-satisfied grin as if to say, *Some performance, huh? We've got the jury right where we want them*, before turning to the judge. "No further questions, your honor." He strode back to the defense table, strutting like a particularly vain peacock dressed in a four hundred dollar suit.

The judge, a white-bearded man with stern hawk-eyes, looked at Tugenda. "Do you wish to cross-examine, Prosecutor?"

"Uh . . ." The former warrior rifled through the papers scattered on the table before her, unable to make head nor tails out of the chicken-scratchings which covered them. Reading wasn't exactly a prime job requirement for a barbarian.

"Prosecutor?" The judge was beginning to sound annoyed.

Tugenda looked up from the bewildering papers and took a deep breath. "Yes, your honor, I would." She stood and approached the witness stand, her high-heel shoes clack-clack-clacking as she crossed the highly polished wooden floor.

She could feel the jury leaning forward in anticipation as she carefully framed the first question in her mind. "You claim to be innocent?"

A small smile, as if he were thinking, *That's the best you've got?* "I don't claim. I *am* innocent."

Tugenda nodded. "Very well, then you will have no qualms about facing me in ritual combat."

The defendant blinked. "Excuse me?"

"If you are truly innocent, then the gods shall lend strength to your sword-arm and you will defeat me. If not, I shall defeat you."

The man turned to the judge. "Your honor?"

The judge scowled. "Ms. Tugenda, if this is your idea of a joke—"

Tugenda ignored the old man. "Defend yourself, Carcosa!" She lunged for the defendant.

*

"The man was dead before he hit the floor," Abernathy said, a trifle queasily.

Tugenda grinned. "At least I learned one thing: he *did* have the heart of a murderer."

She reached into a blood-soaked pocket of suit jacket. "I have it right here if you'd like to take a look..."

"NO! I mean, thank you, that won't be necessary." Abernathy fell silent as he thought for a moment. "It's clear that you need a career that will allow you to be more... physical. Something with opportunity for a bit of adventure." Abernathy consulted his computer. "It appears we have an opening in romance novels."

Tugenda had to admit that the law did have its rewards—she patted her wet pocket—but overall it was a little too mundane for her tastes. She wasn't sure exactly what a romance novel was, but the adventure part sounded appealing.

"I'll take it."

*

Tugenda stood on the swaying deck of a sailing vessel, the strong breeze carrying the scent of saltwater, gulls crying above her, the sound almost lost in the creak of the ship's rigging and the singing and shouting of sailors at work. The summer sun blazed down upon her, its heat at once unbearable and somehow stimulating.

She wore a blue and white dress which had been beautiful at one time, but was now little more than tattered rags barely covering her lush and ample form.

Standing before her was the captain of the vessel, shirtless, with long, flowing blonde hair. He was well-built, his chest hairless and coated with a sheen of sweat. His black pants hugged his legs and trunk, leaving nothing to the imagination. A thin rapier (nearly useless as a weapon, Tugenda thought) hung at his side.

Not bad. Nothing to compare with a certain barbarian turned lawyer, but she wouldn't kick him out of bed. Not until she was finished with him, anyway.

"My love," said Captain Ignazio as he struck a pose and flexed his pecs, "these last few days have been a gift from God, a blessed respite in the wearying struggle that is a pirate's life."

Tugenda had trouble understanding him, the man's accent was so thick.

"Uh, yes, for me too. I guess."

He gestured dramatically toward the port side of the vessel. "Even now my twin brother's ship, *The Revenge*, draws alongside, and we shall finally settle our long-standing feud once and for all!"

Tugenda glanced at the oncoming ship. "Twins, huh?" This assignment was looking better all the time! She began contemplating the geometric possibilities when another thought intruded.

She turned back to Ignazio. "What are you doing going around in this sun without a shirt? You'll burn like crazy! And your hair looks awfully bouncy and full-bodied for someone who spends a lot of time in this salty air."

"Never mind that, my treasure." He put his arm around her waist and drew her manfully to him. "We have only moments before my brother attacks. We must make the most of them."

Tugenda grinned. "Now you're talking!" She undid Ignazio's sword belt, dropped his rapier to the deck, grabbed the waistband of his pants and yanked downward.

The pirate captain pulled back, horrified. "What are you doing?"

"You said we only have moments, so let's get to it, sailor-boy!"

Ignazio stumbled back, feet caught in his pants, and fell onto his posterior.

"But you can't do this! Y-you're a lady!"

Tugenda sighed. It was the same old story. Men were all hands and sweet talk—as long as they held the reins. But let a woman show the least bit of aggression in romance, and they acted like confused little boys.

"Nevermind, Ignazio. I'm not really in the mood anymore." She reached down and picked up his ridiculous excuse for a sword. It wasn't much, but it would have to serve.

"What do you intend to do with my rapier, my sweet?"

Tugenda faced the oncoming ship. "Find out if your twin is a better man than you are, Ignazio." She swished the blade through the air a couple times to test it. Then she glanced back at the still prone—and pants-less—captain. "And whether or not his sword's bigger than yours."

*

"One hundred and twenty-three dead, including the captains of both ships," Abernathy said.

Tugenda shrugged. "I was bored." She stood in front of Abernathy's desk. She was so covered with blood and other less-identifiable substances that he'd refused to allow her to sit this time. "That was hardly a suitable scenario for my archetype."

"What do you mean? A woman in a rough-and-tumble man's world, trying to survive—and perhaps win a little love—with only her wits and femininity to—" He broke off and sighed. "Yes, I suppose it was something of a stretch." He turned to his computer once more. "I'll check to see what else we have, Tugenda, but I have to be honest with you, the prospects don't look good. I don't know if we have anything that falls within the parameters you've outlined."

"Actually, I've been thinking about that." Tugenda wiped a clotted dark-red mass off her forearm and flicked it onto the floor. "Even though fighting day-in and day-out gets a little tiring at times, I *am* awfully good at it."

Abernathy eyed her crimson-soaked frame. "I'd say."

"And it does satisfy me in a way nothing else seems to. So

maybe I should go back to doing what I do best."

Abernathy hesitated. "There's a slight problem with that."

Tugenda frowned. "Oh?"

"We've reassigned the particular milieu where you used to work. It's being used for computer role-playing games now."

Tugenda stepped forward and put her hands on Abernathy's desk. She leaned toward him until her nose was just touching his. A drop of pirate blood ran onto him and rolled down his cheek.

"Then find me another *milieu*, whatever in Caolan's name that is, and be quick about it!"

Abernathy swallowed and got to work.

*

Tugenda stood amidst a decayed cityscape, photon sword held high above her head, its hungry thrum announcing its bloodlust to the world. Surrounding her was a horde of misshapen creatures that supposedly had once been men, though there was little sign of humanity in them now. As one, the mutants charged, bellowing as they came.

Tugenda thumbed the switch on her forearm control panel to activate her battlesuit's defenses. The hi-tech armor was still skin-tight—and its molding quite unnecessarily exaggerated her feminine attributes—but at least she wouldn't have to worry about any nasty bits and pieces of mutant sliding down her front.

She lay about her with the energy weapon to the accompaniment of sizzling flesh and shrieking, dying monsters, quickly falling into a familiar, comfortable rhythm: hack-slice, hack-slice, hack-slice.

What the hell, she thought as she decapitated yet another mutant. *It's a living.*

AND A SHIP TO SAIL
Chris Pierson

Chris Pierson has eight published novels, and has appeared in numerous DAW anthologies, including Boondocks Fantasy, Timeshares, Gamer Fantastic, *and* Terribly Twisted Tales. *He has been involved in the Writers' Symposium almost since the beginning (depending on how you count it), after being offered his first novel while lurking around the back of a seminar in 1997. "And a Ship to Sail" was one of his first published stories, appearing in* Dragon Magazine #239. *He lives in Jamaica Plain, Massachusetts, with his wife Rebekah and daughter Chloe, who is one year old and already telling stories.*

When I was a lad and the world was bright, my da asked me what I wanted from life. I told him I only needed three things: a lady fair, a purse full of gold, and adventure.

That wasn't the answer he'd hoped for, but I reckon it was the one he expected. "Oh, Radesin," he said. "There's more to this life than all that. You mustn't listen to old Harmag's stories."

My da, bless his soul, was never a man for imagination. He was a sail-dyer down at the harbor in Medella-town, and that was all he'd ever be. Tell it true, it was all he ever *wanted* to be. A simple man, but happy.

Not I. I wanted to hunt pirates for the king like old Harmag: cutting through the surf at the prow of my own ship, sails full, chasing down the scourge of the Twin Seas. Most of all, I wanted out of Medella. I dreamed of getting away from all my father's yards of sailcloth and boiling vats and smelly dyes. My mistake, I reckon, was in telling him so—but the view behind is seldom blind, as they used to say.

"But I want to make something of my life," I said—well, be fair: *whined*. "I don't want to waste away the years like—"

Though I shut my mouth before I could say another word, my da knew what I meant anyway. Ask any father, he'll tell you: the sharpest thing in the world is his own child's tongue. I'd cut him to the quick, and I still feel ill remembering the look on his face. I've only seen the like once since, and that was on a dead man they found under Eight Dogs Quay, with a knife stuck in his heart.

Some lads' fathers have no temper for lip—make a slip like that, your hide gets tanned. But my da was never much for beatings. He just shook his head.

"Go on, then," he said. He always had watery eyes—the curse of working with dyes all your life—but I could tell that he was trying not to cry. It was the look he got when he saw a woman who reminded him of my ma. "Get you gone. Go with Harmag, find your fortune on the brine. And when some sea-dog spits you on his cutlass, remember your old da, wasting away the years."

I never went with Harmag, of course, and though things between my da and me were never quite the same, he left me his shop when he died. And though I'm not as good as he was, I've become a fair sail-dyer in my own time.

*

It was late summer and there'd just been a beast of a storm through, the first of what would be a bad season for them. For most men who make their living by the sea, such times are like a curse, but for those of us who truck in sails, it's the other end of the oar entirely. Besides ripping off roofs all over Medella-town and collapsing a fair bit of the fish-market, the storm-winds had split half the sails in the harbor.

"Bleeding dogs should know better, should come back to port when the seas get high and gray," growled Harmag. By that time he was older than Ustach the Black and had long since sold off his boat and retired. "Fools."

"Aye," I told him, "but if they *did* know better, I'd have no work. And then I'd have nothing better to do than sit around another man's shop, bitching all the day."

Harmag gave me one of those squinty looks where you weren't quite sure whether he was grinning or snarling at you. "Show some respect for your elders."

"I'd like to, but if I showed you as much respect as you want me to, I'd not have time for aught else," I said, and he laughed. "Anyway, it's a busy day. I just got Lagerl's new jib off, and already there's three new orders in this morning."

"Ten gold falcons say one's for Earbern," Harmag said, with a nod at my hands.

It's hard for a dyer to hide his work: up to my elbows in the vats half the time, I rarely see the real color of my hands. On this day they were Hadeshi crimson, a shade favored by Earbern Redlocks, a grizzled privateer who'd long been one of Harmag's fiercest rivals. I spread my fingers and shrugged.

"He gave me a bigger bag of silver than *you* ever did, old man," I said.

"That's because the man's dense."

I did a passable imitation of his squint, and he laughed again.

You'd think that, since I'd followed my da and not him, Harmag would have little time for me, but then, you didn't know Harmag. We'd always be friends, we two, whether my hands were red with dye or pirate's blood. Still, even a friend can outstay his welcome, and Harmag was spending more and more time in my shop. He'd been there since I opened, and tell it true, I was wondering if he'd ever leave. Midday had long passed, though gloaming-hour was still hours off.

"Sun's riding west," I said. "The Shark's probably opened her doors by now."

The Shark and Anchor was the other place Harmag spent his time, now that he didn't go asea any more. It was a dark, smelly taproom a few docks north of my shop, and a favorite haunt of old sea-dogs like him. He spent most nights swilling grog and singing chanteys with men he'd known—and, in most cases, hated—since long before I was born. Sometimes I joined him.

Now he grunted and creaked to his feet from the stool where he'd been perching. "Well, since you're so keen on getting rid of me, I'll get me gone. I've got something of a throat on me anyway."

"Grousing the day long is thirsty work," I said.

He squinted and hobbled out.

Chuckling, I went in the back of the shop and checked Earbern's mainsail. It was stewing in the biggest vat, but it wasn't yet done. You've got to take care with Hadeshi crimson. It needs to set well, understand, or the first time it rains it'll fade right to pink. And then, like as not, the dog you did the dyeing for will come back and thrash you stupid for making him look a fool. Pirate-hunters are a rough lot. Flying a pink sail's just asking for trouble.

I grabbed a paddle and stirred the vat, then went to check on the other sails I'd started that day—one worm-green, one black. They both still needed time, too.

The black vat was in the far back of the shop, which is why I didn't hear her come in.

"Excuse me?" called a voice from the door, and I jumped. I wasn't expecting anyone just then. I looked up in surprise.

It was easy to see she had no business being down at the docks. Her clothes were fine, and she held a perfumed handkerchief to her nose. Now, my dyes don't smell like a lilac bush, but anyone from the docks gets used to much worse stinks from a young age—rotting fish, sewage, sailors who've been at sea for weeks, that sort of thing. My dyes were mild beside these, but she looked fit to faint. I hurried to her with a steadying hand, but she drew back quick.

That was another thing that marked her as someone other than a dockswoman: she carried herself with a noble's arrogance. I swear to Hameth, up on the hill they must teach their daughters to look at people like that from birth. But then, if someone stinking of dye and with blood-red hands came lurching at me in a steamy room, I'd probably step back myself.

I got a good look at her, and she was beautiful, tell it true. Long, coppery curls, tawny eyes with flecks of green, full lips painted the color of summer plums, cheeks flushed the faintest shade of rose...

Well, I *am* a dyer by trade. I tend to notice colors first.

Anyway, she was lovely in a way most noblewomen aren't—many are too cold by half, but she had a warmth in her face that made me look at my hands and try to wipe the crimson off on my smock. Of course, it didn't come off—for that, you need a hunk of pumice and a lot of time—but I reckon I'd have rubbed them raw if she hadn't spoken first.

"Are—are you—" She stopped, looking troubled. "Do you dye cloth?"

"Aye, that I do," I said. Well, tell it true, I stammered a bit at first. "But, milady, my main work's in sailcloth. You might prefer going to the Merchant's Quarter—"

"No!" she yelped. It wasn't loud or anything, but it was a yelp, all right. I wondered what that meant. She took a deep breath. "That is, good sir, I was hoping you would do me a service nonetheless. I have silver."

She reached for the purse at her belt, but I raised a hand to stop her.

"Stay yourself, milady," I said, trying my damnedest to sound as well-bred as she did. "I've no doubt you have the means. I merely meant—"

"Please," she said, and grimaced just a bit. She was fighting back tears, like my da used to do.

I swallowed. "Maybe you'd prefer to speak in the front room, away from these." I waved at the vats of dye.

She nodded, and I led her back to the shopfront, got her sat

And a Ship to Sail

down, and pulled the front door shut. From the look she gave me, she appreciated the privacy.

"Now, milady," I said, "what do you require?"

"I need a garment dyed," she said. "A sash."

I nodded. Sashes were very much in fashion in the Upper City in those days. The queen wore them, so all the ladies had to, too. "Do you have the cloth?" I asked.

She nodded and reached into her hand-pouch. It was all I could do not to whistle at what she pulled out—it was a sash all right, but it was made of Lyrian silk, from across the sea. I'd only ever seen the stuff a couple times before. It was worth more than a dozen full sails, easy.

I took it from her with care—silk's slippery stuff, and I wasn't about to risk dropping it on my grimy floor. I looked it over and decided I'd take the job. Well, be fair, I'd decided that when she first mentioned it, but now I told her so.

She was so relieved, for a moment I thought she might throw her arms around me. "Thank you, sir," she said. "I am greatly in your debt."

She went for her purse again. This time, I *did* reach out and touch her arm. She stiffened a little, but didn't draw back.

"Please, milady," I said. "That won't be necessary. The sight of you in this place is payment enough."

Aye, I can have quite the silver tongue when I set to it. But I meant it, too. She must have understood that, because she looked right at me with her tawny-green eyes, and there was something in them that I couldn't read: sorrow, fear, pride. Probably all of them. It was like falling into two green-flecked pools.

"The—the color, milady?" I babbled.

She looked away, and I leaned against the counter, suddenly come over all wobble-kneed. She stared at the sash, and twisted her long, green skirts in her hands.

"Purple," she murmured. "I want you to dye it purple."

*

Of course, I told Harmag all about it.

As it happened, I was able to close up early that day. The lady—it wasn't until later that I realized I hadn't even asked her name—was my last customer. I hung the crimson, green, and black sails up among the rafters to dry, set the silken sash in a pan to soak, then locked up and went to the Shark and Anchor to lift my elbow.

Harmag was sitting with Blind Gefnath in their usual corner. He saw me come in, and by the time I pushed my way past all the drunken sailors and docksmen, he'd poured me some Plecath red. In a reasonably clean cup, even.

"Little Radesin," said Gefnath as I squeezed into my chair. It always surprised me how he could pick me out, blind as he was, in such a noisy, smelly place as the Shark. But then, he'd been a sea-wizard before the pirates took his eyes, and wizards have their own ways of seeing.

"You'll not guess who came into the shop today," I said.

Harmag squinted. "The Prophet Urul and all his holy retinue?"

Blind Gefnath cackled and gave a toothless smile. Harmag took a big gulp of some foul stuff or other. I once caught a good whiff of what he liked to drink, and my nose burned for a whole day. I think they use the same stuff to clean barnacles off the dock-pilings.

"No," I said. "A lady from the Upper City."

"Oh, aye," he said, and laughed, "and the Bishop of Jaresh stopped by our table earlier for a quick game of hobbledy-wink."

"It's no joke. Noble blood, she had."

"He's right," said Blind Gefnath. "I thought I smelled jasmine when you sat down. The lady's perfume, aye?"

How he could pick out such a delicate scent, when the Shark reeked of sweat and stale wine and worse, and I had four different kinds of dye on me—well, again, Gefnath was a sorcerer. He could summon up wind on a calm day, charm a man with just the sound of his voice, and even farspeak, sending messages from shore to ship and back again without uttering a word. He was whip-smart besides, and I never knew him to speak aught but truth.

I reckon Harmag could have said the same, because Gefnath seemed to convince him I wasn't fibbing.

"Was she pretty?" Harmag asked, flashing an old sea-dog's leer. "Take a fancy to her, did you?"

I must have blushed, because he roared and clapped me on the back.

"Mark me, Radesin," he said, and poured himself another cup. "You don't want any lady fair who'd come all the way down to the docks. Up to no good, I bet. What was she after?"

"She wanted a sash dyed."

Blind Gefnath straightened in his seat, staring right at me like he could see me. He did that now and then, and it always gave me the shivers. "What color?"

"Uh," I said, trying to look anywhere but at the empty holes where his eyes had been.

"What color sash?" he asked again. Now Harmag was looking hard at me, too.

"Purple," I said. "Cholene purple."

"Urul's beard," Gefnath swore. He clenched his hands and made a face like he'd just bitten into a raw mackerel. Harmag looked a bit odd, too.

"What's wrong?" I asked.

"Unlettered pup," Harmag said. "You don't know. Where'd you get your schooling, anyway?"

I bristled at this. I may not be as sharp as some, but I like to think I know something of the world.

"Listening to your lies, mostly," I said. "Anyway, you always say you taught me everything you know."

"Reckon I was wrong," he said. "You truly don't know what a

purple sash is for?"

"No, for Hameth's sake!" I shouted. "What are you two on about?"

"She means to end her life," said Blind Gefnath.

Well, it was like someone had clouted me over the head with a belaying pin. I may have said something, but it couldn't have made much sense, because my mind went to about twelve different places at once.

"The purple sash has been a token of death in the Upper City for nigh on eighty years," Harmag said. "Remember what I told you about the Duchess Fielle?"

It took me a moment. Harmag had spun me more yarns than I can count. But I can still remember every one, and for obvious reasons the tragedy of Fielle and Nytenbreg is strong in my memory to this day. It's too long for telling now, but the important part is that Fielle, out of unrequited love for the selfish Prince Nytenbreg of Creos, cast herself into the sea to drown. I recited that part to Harmag, as best as I could recall.

"Well," he said, "what do you reckon she was wearing about her waist at the time?"

The belaying pin smacked me again.

"That happened a few years afore I was born," he told me. "Since then, lovesick lasses with more gold than brains who decide to throw themselves off Fielle's Cliff have worn the purple sash."

I didn't say a thing. I was too busy gaping like a landed fish.

"Your lady friend must not want anyone on the hill to know what she means to do," said Blind Gefnath. "That's why she came down here to the docks."

"That's—that's *horrible*," I said.

"Aye," Harmag agreed.

"I have to do something!"

Harmag scowled, and squinted, and shook his head. "Don't try it, Radesin. She'll just find another fellow who'll do it for her."

I wasn't listening to him, though, or to Gefnath, who

counseled me about the folly of getting involved in Upper City affairs. For the rest of the night, all I could think of were those tawny-green eyes, staring glassily at some poor fisherman as he hauled her body out of the sea. Of that copper hair tangled with seaweed, that rose-flushed skin turned bloated and blue. I felt sick.

I decided then, even as Harmag and Gefnath told me otherwise, that I was going to save her.

I went to bed late that night. First I went back into the workroom of my shop.

*

She was due to come for the sash at midday. Of course, it was my luck that Wanscit the Wearisome stopped by that morning.

Wanscit the Wearisome was something of a legend on the wharf. You see, he was beyond a doubt the most boring, long-winded rattlemouth this side of Khun. Once he started talking, you practically had to stab him in the eye to shut him up. Unlike Harmag, who could talk the claws off a lobster but keep you amused the whole time, Wanscit rambled on forever about nothing at all—getting to the point was a concept he'd only ever seen from a distance. Some said he could move his ship through calmed seas simply by talking while pointing at the sails, and there were more than a few tales of sailors jumping overboard rather than enduring a conversation with him.

And in he came, right before *she* was due. He didn't even have work for me. He just wanted to talk.

"Good day, Radesin," he said. "Although, maybe it's not so good after all. It looks like it might rain, and when it rains that bone I broke in my wrist starts hurting, and one of my men has the gray fever, and I'm worried it might spread about the boat, which reminds me, I ought to see about getting some more pitch put on her hull, and—"

And on and on and on. You'll notice I hadn't said anything

yet. He didn't give me the chance. I handled it the way everyone handled Wanscit: I nodded, smiled, and prayed for the strength not to strangle him.

"—and I noticed during the storm that the main spar's a bit loose, so maybe I should get someone to tighten the bolts because if another wind like that one comes up—"

Most times, I'd have thought up an excuse to close the shop, bustle him out, and huddle in the dark waiting for him to go away. But *she* might arrive any moment. I shuddered to think of what might happen if Wanscit started prattling to her.

"—and, of course, I had to let my second mate go last week, because he wasn't fitting in, didn't seem to have much spirit whenever I was around, so I—"

"Wanscit? Can I talk to you for a moment?"

Now *there* was a sentence I never thought I'd hear anyone say in my whole long life. It didn't come out of my mouth, of course; rather, it was Harmag. He'd poked his head in the door while I wasn't looking. I stared at him in wonder.

"Well," said Wanscit, "I was just telling Radesin about how my second mate wasn't fitting in—"

"Yes, yes," Harmag said. He stepped over, put a friendly arm around Wanscit's stooped shoulders, and steered him, still nattering, out the door.

I've heard many tales of men facing gruesome death in the name of friendship. I reckon this was just about as brave. Before they disappeared out into the street, Harmag squinted at me to make it clear that I owed him.

I could still hear Wanscit, blithering off into the distance, when *she* came in.

Tell it true, I'd been worried she wouldn't be as lovely as the day before—that some witchery of the light had made me fall in love with the sight of her, and it would have faded overnight. Worried—or maybe a bit hopeful. After all, the woman was both far above my station and set to leap to her doom off Fielle's Cliff.

Not good courting material.

The sight of her crushed both my worries and my hopes. If there was a witchery to the light, it followed her around, because she was just beautiful as the day before. I froze as she approached the counter. All of a sudden my tongue was stuck to the roof of my mouth, and my belly felt like it was full of eels.

Reckon I must have stood there gaping a while, because she finally cleared her throat. "I—I brought in a sash yesterday."

And then I saw it, in the depths of those remarkable eyes: doubt. Some part of her wasn't set on her fate. My heart about danced a hornpipe.

"I'll get it," I said. "But first, I must tell you I lied about not wanting payment."

She reached for her purse, but I held up my hand.

"I don't want your silver," I told her. "I want to know something."

She swallowed, clutching her skirts like she had the day before. She was wearing pale blue this time. She must have known what was coming, because it was a while before she answered.

"Very well," she said.

I drew myself up, trying to look stern but compassionate, instead of frightened and smitten, which was how I felt. "Why?"

She lowered her head, letting her copper curls fall over those eyes. "What do you mean?" she asked.

"The purple sash." I wasn't about to let her demur her way out of this—not while that doubt was there. "Not exactly the sort of thing a lady wears to the Highsummer Fair."

She flinched, and I was sorry I'd been so glib. She looked up at me, her eyes shining. "I hardly think it should trouble you," she said, trying in vain to sound haughty.

"I disagree. You want me to craft your death-token. I believe I ought to know why."

She could have walked out. All it would have cost her was a bit of Lyrian silk—something her family could afford, no doubt. But instead she leaned against the counter, sighed, and told me everything.

Her name was Armena, and she was the second daughter of His Grace the Count Gyldith, one of those minor lords who spend their whole lives finding ways to increase their status on the hill. One way he'd set on was to arrange for Armena to wed Lyscerl, the son of . . . well, some duke or other. I can't remember his name.

"But I don't love him," she told me. "Lyscerl's a fool who cares only for his own pleasure. He drinks too much, he bets on dice, he beds too many women."

I nodded, my mouth as dry as a dead man's bones. I swallowed a few times, and managed to coax some spit to wet my lips.

"He doesn't deserve your love, then," I said—and winced as soon as it was out of my mouth. It was so *blatant* . . .

"No," she said. "He doesn't. But my father won't have it any other way."

"What—" I began, then coughed and fell silent. She leaned closer—just a bit, but it made every part of me go warm. "What would it take for your father to—to change his mind?"

She gave me an odd look: surprise, maybe a bit of hope. But it vanished right away, her brow furrowing. "You presume too much, sir."

Her words may as well have been a slap. I drew back, stung. "I am sorry, milady," I said, and turned to go back into the shop, to fetch her sash.

I had my hand on the door when I heard her rise from her seat. "Wait," she said. I stopped, hoping she couldn't see me tremble. "Bide a moment, if you will."

I was back at the counter before I even knew I'd moved.

"I am the one who should apologize," she said. "I have been rude when you tried to help. You only offered your ear for my troubles."

If only she'd known how much more I was offering. Then

And a Ship to Sail

again, if she *had* known, it might have frightened her off.

"Nonetheless," I replied, "my bluntness has offended you."

"Nonsense. I've had my fill of delicate talk, words whose meaning gets lost in nicety and decorum. There are times, sir, when I would give up all my riches and station just to be able to speak as plainly as you."

I'm not ashamed to tell you I blushed. "I reckon you just did, milady," I said.

She smiled, laughed a little. It wasn't a polite, mannered laugh, either—the sort of sound she might have made in her father's company, or Lyscerl's. It was real mirth, and gods, if I'd thought she was beautiful before. I felt my mouth starting to go dry again.

"I suppose you're right," she said. She looked at me again in that odd, surprised-hopeful way, and I don't know how it got there but her hand was in mine. "You're the first man to make me laugh in . . . longer than I care to think."

It took some effort, but I forced myself not to gibber at her. I just smiled, and held her green-flecked eyes with mine.

Then, all at once, she realized what she was doing. We were close to each other—far closer than a lady and a commoner should get. We were *touching*, for Hameth's sake. She drew back, her face red, putting a hand to her breast.

"No," she said, not daring to look at me. "This is my lot, and I cannot marry Lyscerl, so I have no choice. I have vowed before Amassi and her daughters that I will follow Fielle into the sea instead."

I opened my mouth to speak, to tell her what I felt. Then I closed it again. I hadn't the ghost of a clue what to say. She was right: a countess-to-be and a low-born sail-dyer were no match. So I kept my tongue and stared at the scuffed toes of my shoes.

"Please, sir," she said, her voice small and tight. "I implore you. Bring me the sash."

I did. What else could I do?

And then she was gone, in a billow of blue skirts, the scent of jasmine hanging in the air behind her until the docks' stink smothered it. I leaned back against the wall, feeling ill, and prayed that Wanscit the Wearisome was right, and there would be rain.

*

They were all singing in the Shark, as they often did. There was a bounce to my step, I'll admit, because my prayers had come true: it was raining knives out, and had been most of the afternoon. The chantey the old dogs in the tavern sang lifted my spirits even more. It was one of my favorites, "A Sword and a Ship to Sail." That's the one where the chorus goes:

Give me a sword and a ship to sail
and I'll never come home again.
I'll travel the waves and kiss the maids
and fight a hundred men.
I don't know why I'm leaving, lass,
I don't know where or when,
But give me a sword and a ship to sail
and I'll never come home again.

Harmag had sung me that song when I was a lad, more times than I can remember. I still know all five traditional verses, as well as some particularly salty licks he and his mates had made up as well. I heard them hollering in something like harmony as soon as I entered the Shark, and I was bellowing the tenor part in full throat by the time I shoved my way to them.

For that, I got a sound thumping on the back and a foaming mug of Blackfalcon ale. The singing went on as I drank. Harmag pounded his fist on the table with glee as he boomed the baritone. Blind Gefnath and a huge ox of a captain named Holm were with him, crowing in the higher registers. Holm, in particular, was

And a Ship to Sail

wildly off key—but no one would ever tell him so. People who annoyed Holm didn't get to keep their teeth.

Harmag made up the last verse, something about a mermaid and a swordfish that would surely have caused mass faintings in the Upper City, and the song fell apart into laughter. I started on my second beer. When I could make myself heard above the noise, I thanked Harmag for rescuing me from Wanscit.

"'Twere nothing," he said, though I knew there'd be four moons in the sky before he let me forget about it. "I saw him go into your shop, and I knew you were expecting your lady friend. I didn't want him spoiling your chances at *true love*."

I went red to the tips of my ears, which is what Harmag intended. He and Holm howled. Blind Gefnath turned toward me and sniffed the air.

"Jasmine," he said. "So she came back. Did you ask for her story?"

Someone put a third flagon in my hand, and I told them about Armena and her betrothal to Lyscerl.

"I've heard of him," Harmag said, and spat. "He's a right bugger, that one—but a *rich* bugger. Which is what really matters. Reckon that ends it, then. Too bad."

I shook my head. "No. It's raining tonight. She'll come back."

Holm chuckled. "If she's jumping into the sea, I doubt she'll care about the weather."

I explained what I meant, what I'd done. Their reaction was predictable.

"Are you daft?" Gefnath asked.

Harmag squinted. "Where's your head at, lad?"

Fair enough. But they hadn't seen the doubt in Armena's eyes, nor that other thing that had been there when I held her hand. Harmag shrugged when I told him this, as if it were neither here nor there. I told him and the others that I was going to win her away from both Lyscerl and the sea.

"And how, exactly, to do that?" asked Gefnath. "If you

challenge him for her hand, he'll demand satisfaction. And while I'm sure you know which end of a sword is pointed, he's surely a trained duelist. He'll gut you like a cod."

"We don't have to fight fair," Holm said. "I know some lads'll jump to go at a noble with gaffs and pins. Give the word, Radesin."

He'd have done it, too. I just had to say so, and they'd have been fishing bits of Lyscerl out of the water for weeks. That wasn't what I had in mind, though, so I turned him down. He looked disappointed.

"What, then?" asked Harmag. "If you're set on this—"

"I am."

"Then," he went on, "you must play to win at a single stroke, or you'll wake up to find your head mounted on a pike on the hill. And if you want to win, you have to go after *her*. Not Lyscerl."

I spread my hands, asking for ideas. They had none.

For a while, I sat and mulled over my fourth—or maybe my fifth—flagon, thinking about what Harmag had said. Even if I won Armena over, it would be scandalous for someone as low-born as me to take the hand of Count Gyldith's daughter. He and Lyscerl would probably have no qualms about getting *their* friends to cut *me* into little bits.

So I had to give him a reason not to. But what?

Well, if there's one thing a nobleman understands, it's the clatter of a coffer of coins, as my da would say. But that didn't help much. True, I had some silver—a fair bit for a docksman, tell it true—but nothing that would set His Grace's eyes atwinkle. How, then, could a mere sail-dyer slake a noble's thirst for riches? I'd need more gold than I could count—maybe even a whole sea of the stuff.

And there it was. I had the answer—or the beginning of one, at least—and it about near knocked me off my chair. I reckon it showed, because even Blind Gefnath glanced my way.

"Methinks the lad's got a plan," he said.

I held up a hand to stave off their questions. My idea was just forming, and I didn't want it to slip away. After a while, I had most of it worked out in my head, and I nodded.

"I know," I said. "I know what to do."

*

"Good gods," Harmag said when I was done telling them. "You'll need every sailor in Medella-town to agree to that."

I shrugged. "Not all. Nine out of ten should be enough."

"I like it," Holm said. "I don't know if it'll work, but I like it."

Blind Gefnath made a sour face, but I could tell by the way he was leaning forward over the table that he was intrigued. "How are you going to do it?"

"Well," I said, "that's where I'll need your help. The three of you—Harmag's tongue, Holm's muscle, and your charms and farspeech."

It was one of the few times Harmag genuinely smiled—no hint of a squint there. He laid a gnarled hand on my arm. "You've got it," he said.

Holm put his beefy fist over Harmag's, and after a moment Gefnath nodded and let me place his hand atop the rest.

Harmag was still grinning. "How long will you need, lad?"

I considered. "Three days."

"It's settled, then," Blind Gefnath said. "Three days. You know, I truly wish I could have my eyes back, so I could see this when it happens."

*

The rain tapered off an hour before dawn. I know this, because I was still awake, in my shop, my arms deep in sailcloth and dye. It was a busy week, indeed—all my vats were full, the ceiling hung with drying canvas. And there was much work left to do. Harmag didn't come in that day: he, like Blind Gefnath and

Holm, was too busy to chat.

Armena returned that morning, as I knew she would. She was angry, as I knew she'd be. Myself, I felt fit to jump up on the counter and dance at the sight of her.

"Sir!" she shouted as she stormed in.

I came out to the front of the shop before she could stomp her way into the back. She was wearing green again, more a hunter's hue, deeper than before.

"My name is Radesin, milady," I said.

I could hear the smile in my own voice, but I didn't let it show on my face, so in her anger she didn't notice. I bowed, keeping my hands behind my back.

"Very well, *Radesin*," she snapped. "Explain this."

She slammed the sash onto the counter, her hand trembling with rage. I had to fight back another smile as I looked upon it. Where it had been the rich violet of the sea-snails of Choleth, it was now pale, mottled lavender.

"The dye ran in the rain," she said. "It ruined my blue gown."

I thought that rather odd, considering what she'd meant to do while she wore that frock, but I didn't mention that. I tried my best to look penitent, hoping she wouldn't guess I'd deliberately not let the dye set—that the sash had faded because I'd *wanted* it to fade.

"Milady, I am sorry," I lied. "I will, of course, pay for your gown."

Her reaction was what I'd hoped for. The doubt was back, stronger than before, a candle-flame where it had been a spark. Some more fanning, I hoped, and it would blaze like Hameth's own hearth.

"That isn't necessary," she said. "Just dye it again. Properly this time."

I bowed again, kept my hands out of view, didn't reach for the sash. "As you wish, milady. But I fear I can't have it ready for three days now." I nodded—didn't point!—back into the depths of my workroom. "My work's piled up to the rafters. You may seek another man's services, if you so wish."

She didn't so wish, as I bloody well knew. She wrung her skirts, the doubt gleaming in her eyes.

"No, sir—Radesin. That will do. Three days it is."

For a moment, she looked ready to say more. It seemed all I had to do was ask her, and she would have forsaken and forgotten Lyscerl and Count Gyldith altogether. Unfortunately, they wouldn't have been so absent-minded, so I held my tongue, bowed a third time, and bade her good day.

With a small sigh of what might have been disappointment, she left the shop. I looked down at the faded sash on the counter and finally allowed myself a smile.

*

The days passed in a blur of canvas and dye-fumes and captains coming to collect their sails, one by one. Sleep and I became strangers. Tell it true, though, I wouldn't have been able to fall asleep even if I'd had the time. I'd have lain abed the night through, without so much as a wink for thinking of how much work I had yet to do, and *why* I was doing it. And, most of all, whether it would all work.

I slaved like a wizard's golem, going from task to task without thought, my mind roiling like a storm. It's one of the world's great wonders that, in my distraction, I didn't fall into a vat of dye and drown myself.

Of Harmag and the others I saw nothing at all. They were busy at their own tasks, and since I left the shop only twice to buy new supplies at the sea-market, I never had the chance to look for them. I had to trust that they would succeed.

Sometimes I look back on those three days and they seem like an eye-blink; others, they seem like years. I spent so much time hunched over the dyeing-vats, I lost a fair bit of my sense of smell—which, as I've said, isn't such a bad fate on the docks. My eyes ran like gutters after a storm. And, even now, my head sometimes feels like a blacksmith's been using it for an anvil, and I have to stop what I'm doing and lie down with a wet cloth over my eyes until the pain goes away.

Was it worth it? I'm getting there.

Came the third day, and I ran out of money. I had nary a copper bit left to my good name—even what little I'd inherited from my poor da was gone. If he'd known what I'd done with it, he probably would have cried. Or, then again, maybe he wouldn't have. It's at such times when I wish I'd known him better.

Not long after I'd spent my last silver, I ran out of sailcloth too. I had to turn a few dogs away, and they were fit to spit for it, but what choice did I have? Once the last of my stock was gone, I realized the full spread of what I'd done: I'd put so much into my fancy over Armena, I had nothing left. If I failed, I'd have to close up my shop, or borrow silver from some moneylender or other. And, then as now, it was best not to be having debts on the docks.

Done be done, though, as they say: the view behind, and all that. When I'd rid myself of my last scrap of canvas, I saw to the sash and closed up the shop. I was just reaching to lock the door, in fact, when Harmag came a-barging in.

He squinted me up and down and barked a laugh, hobbling over to a stool to sit. "You're a sight," he said.

I ran a hand through my hair, which had gotten to looking like an ill-tended haystack. "You look halfway dead yourself."

Harmag didn't laugh. I reckon if I'd known he was ailing and would be gone before Year-end, I'd never had said such a thing. But there you go—like the song says, the only things you can never lose are your regrets.

"*You* try walking up and down this bloody wharf, chasing down every dog with anything bigger than a rowboat to his name," he said. He nodded to my hands, which were stained even more brightly than when I first met Armena. "You'd best keep those covered tomorrow."

I reached behind the counter and pulled out a pair of gloves. "I gave a thought to that."

"I won't take more of your time," he said, rising from his seat. "Just needed to find my wind, that's all. And to make sure you were well."

"Well enough," I said, trying to sound confident even though my guts had been tightening all day. By that point, they felt about the size of a walnut. "Tomorrow, around midday. Wait for the signal."

"Tomorrow, midday," he answered, and turned to go. He paused with the door half-open on the darkening street and squinted back at me. "Good luck to you, Radesin."

I nodded and smiled. It's good to have such friends.

*

Exhaustion, it seems, is stronger than impatience. I slept sound as a dragon that night. I seldom remember my dreams, but I still recall seeing coppery hair, flowing around green-flecked, doubtful eyes.

Mercifully, I forgot to close my shutters before taking to bed, or I might have slept the day away while all my plans fell to pieces. Instead, sunrise streaming through my window dragged me out of slumber. I washed and dressed in a panic, and nearly forgot my gloves. I caught myself at the last moment, though, and was pulling them on as I came down the steps from the upper floor of the shop, where I slept at night.

Armena, as with many nobles, was a late riser. It was almost midday before I heard the heels of her shoes on the cobbles outside my shop. I gripped the edge of the counter to keep my hands from shaking as the door opened and she entered in a swirl of satin. Her gown that day was the red-orange of dying embers. I found I was having trouble breathing all of a sudden.

"A fine d—" I started to stay, but my voice shook and finally broke.

I looked at the floor, but not before I saw the roses bloom in her cheeks. I made myself take three slow, deep breaths, then looked up at those tawny eyes. The doubt in them shone as bright as a lantern.

I must have stared too long, because she blinked and cleared her throat. "Good morning, Radesin," she whispered. She, too, was trying to keep her voice steady. "The sash, please."

I stepped into the workroom, fetched the sash, and brought it to her. But I didn't hand it over. "Milady," I said, my heart battering against my ribs, "I'll give you this, but first I must ask one last favor."

She sighed and squared her shoulders. The doubt blazed hotter and brighter.

"What is it, then?" she asked.

"Allow me to accompany you," I said. "Let me go with you to Fielle's Cliff, so I may be the last man to see you alive."

From the way her shoulders slumped, that wasn't what she'd expected. I reckon she'd thought I'd beg her to reconsider, not to jump, to abandon Lyscerl and her family. I knew, though, that that wouldn't work. And so, without another word, I handed over her death-token.

She stared at it, wringing it in her hands. Then she nodded. "Very well," she breathed, so soft I barely heard her.

*

The Duchess Fielle, as well as being shamelessly romantic, had also had a bent for melodrama. Fielle's Cliff, north along the shore from Medella-town, afforded the best vantage on the entire city, both Upper and Lower. Most of all, it gave a breathtaking view of the harbor, which was dotted with ships going about their day's business.

Or seeming to, at least.

Hundreds of eyes had watched Fielle plummet to her death eighty years before. Hundreds of eyes would see Armena do the same—and for a while, as we climbed the narrow path in silence, it seemed she might balk at the notion. At the last, though, she found the strength that had brought her that far, stepped to the bluff's edge, and began folding the purple sash about her waist.

I said nothing. I checked the sun: midday was close. I looked at Armena, whose eyes were shut and whose lips were moving in silent prayer. Then I glanced over my shoulder at a large clump of redmottle bushes near the path. They rustled, and I took a deep breath and turned back to Armena.

She tensed to jump.

I grabbed her arm.

With a yell, she stumbled back. Then the shock wore off, and she struck me—not a dainty slap, but as hard a punch as any sailor might deliver. Tell it true, she was really quite strong. I reeled, but I didn't let her go.

"How dare you interfere!" she shouted. "If I had known this was your intent, I never would have let you accompany me. Now let me go, Radesin!"

"No," I said.

Blood pounded so hard in my head. I could barely hear my own voice. But she heard, and her face turned ashen. The fires of doubt glowed like a furnace.

"There are other choices to make besides death," I told her.

"Choices like what?" she asked, trying to put on an air of arrogance. Instead, she just sounded frightened. "You?"

"Yes, milady." Suddenly I was as calm as the sea on a windless day. "Choices like me. Look down upon the harbor."

Reluctantly, haughtily, she did.

"There's something odd about the ships today," I said. "Can you tell me what it is?"

She scowled, annoyed to be playing a game. Then she blinked.

"They—they fly no sails."

I nodded. "Unlike your betrothed, I have little gold to give you," I said, raising my voice so it carried across the cliff's breadth. "But I would give you all I have."

The sun crested the sky. The redmottle bushes rustled again. And out on the water, the ships unfurled their sails as one.

*

Harmag and the others had been busy indeed. Persuading the captains of well nigh every ship in town to fly a sail that's not his own is every bit as hard as it sounds.

Over the past three days, while I toiled over my vats, Harmag had gone from pier to taproom to brothel, cornering all the sailors he could find. Most agreed to the plan straight away, or near enough—it helped, of course, that I was giving them new sails without asking for a copper bit in exchange.

Some dogs, however, are stubborn or dumb or just plain mean. They took convincing. Between Holm's muscle and Blind Gefnath's magic, though, almost all of them fell into line. While I'd be lying if I said *every* captain flew one of the sails I'd prepared for that day—no one had wanted to talk to Wanscit the Wearisome, for one—those who didn't were few.

The rest was simple. That morning, Harmag went out aboard his old ship, which now belonged to his former first mate. About the same time, Holm led Gefnath up to the bluffs, where they hid together in a particular clump of redmottles and waited for me to arrive. When I did, and spoke the words we'd settled on, Gefnath farspoke a word to Harmag ... who, in turn, raised the first of the sails I'd spent the past three days dyeing a warm, orangey yellow in the depths of my shop.

Following his lead, the rest of the dogs on the water did the same. So, blossoming like some bright yellow flower, the harbor became a sea of gold.

Armena gasped, and even *my* eyes widened. It was quite a sight, nearly every ship flying the same hue. We were far from the only ones to see it, too: as we looked on, a wondering crowd began to gather on the wharf. Smaller groups formed at vantage points throughout the city. Among them, I learned later, were Lyscerl and His Grace the Count Gyldith.

But I cared for none of that. All that mattered, all my toil came down to, was the look in Armena's eyes. Feeling both triumphant and nauseated, I removed my gloves, revealing the deep, golden stains upon my hands, and looked in her eyes.

They were different now. The doubt that had burned so brightly in them was gone. In its place, certainty shone as bright as the sun above.

She said nothing—words wouldn't have described what was between us then. Instead, she reached down to her waist, removed the purple sash, and let it slide through her hands, out over the cliff's edge.

It fell for a moment, then the wind caught it and bore it high into the sky as Armena let me take her in my arms.

*

When I was a lad and the world was bright, my da asked me what I wanted from life. I told him I only needed three things: a lady fair, a purse full of gold, and adventure.

Well, I won the first of those that day, high on Fielle's Cliff. His Grace, while far from overjoyed that a commoner had wooed his daughter, could ill afford to scorn the man who'd filled the harbor with gold. Reluctantly, he gave his blessing to our wedding that autumn. Lyscerl the ducal heir didn't take it so kindly, and got himself killed in a drunken duel. No one beyond his family really missed him.

The second thing, the gold, came soon enough as well. Armena's dowry aside, I became famous in Medella-town.

Chris Pierson

Demand for the work of Radesin Goldensea spread all over the city, even up on the hill. I moved from dyeing only sailcloth to all manner of things, from royal fabrics to wizard's robes. My fortune was made, and while I would never be truly rich, I was happy enough. And each year, on a day in late summer, every ship captain in Medella raises a golden sail in place of his usual. They even made a festival of it, with me at its midst. So, though I've never been truly wealthy, since that day my heart and purse have never been empty.

And adventure?

I'll tell you about that someday.

*

Give Me a Sword and a Ship to Sail (And I'll Never Come Home Again)

Well I was born with my feet on the deck
of a ship upon the brine,
My father was a fighting man,
his cutlass keen and fine.
He set me up upon his knee
when I was nine or ten,
And said "get you a sword and a ship to sail,
and you'll never come home again."

CHORUS
Give me a sword and a ship to sail
and I'll never come home again.
I'll travel the waves and kiss the maids
and fight a hundred men.
I don't know why I'm leaving, lass,
I don't know where or when,

*But give me a sword and a ship to sail
and I'll never come home again."*

I left my home soon afterward
and bought myself a sword.
I fought for silver and for gold:
I built up quite a hoard,
And so I went down to the wharf
and bought a boat and then,
I had me a sword and a ship to sail,
and I never went home again.

CHORUS

For many years I've plied the seas,
I've seen nigh every sight.
I've cut the throats of men by day,
loved lasses in the night.
I've fought and drunk and learned far more
than many a wise man's ken,
And with my sword and ship to sail,
I'll never go home again.

CHORUS

The sea has always been my love,
the blade has been my life,
But one morn after too much wine,
I woke up with a wife.
She kept me home and scolded me
and clucked at me like a hen,
So I gave her a sword and a ship to sail,
and she never came home again.

Chris Pierson

CHORUS

And now I'm old and stooped and gray,
my eyesight's growing dim,
But when I die, I'll happily go,
I won't be glum or grim,
For I have seen the great wide world,
I didn't stay in my den,
'Cause I got me a sword and a ship to sail,
and I never went home again.

CHORUS AND END

THE POOL
Wes Nicholson

"The Pool" was my first foray into the horror genre. It was written in a hurry when Jean Rabe told me of a horror anthology that was looking for writers. I wasn't successful in getting it into that anthology, but the rejection letter taught me a lot about what a horror story needs. What you're reading in this book is the first printing—third rewrite—of "The Pool." In the past two decades I've had numerous role-playing products published, as well as a handful of short fiction pieces. I've written a YA book, and I'm working on a novel, in between my "real" job and keeping my kids entertained. This is my second year in the Gen Con Writer's Symposium. Since I had such a great time with it in 2009, I'm back for more.

The sign on the pool fence read "No Midnight Swimming!"

Gene and Jean had never felt like midnight dips, skinny or otherwise, even when they were dating as teenagers. But the sign had been on the fence when they bought the house, and Gene had thought it was cool, so it stayed.

As the kids grew older, Gene Jr., or GJ as most folks called him, wanted to have friends over for a pool party. As happens with younger siblings, when GJ got the okay to host his first pool party, Becky started whining that she should be allowed to have her friends over too. Their parents explained that they weren't really able to look after a gaggle of eight-year-olds in a pool, on top of GJ's friends . . . especially since they didn't know who could swim and who couldn't.

So Becky had to wait until she was ten, just like GJ.

The pool was the focus of the family's leisure time. In summer, they spent at least an hour most evenings relaxing in the cool water, or lounging on the deck with a cold drink. GJ usually had at least one friend over, and Becky was allowed a friend . . . sometimes . . . after it was worked out who could swim and who couldn't.

In autumn, the children took a swim every afternoon until it got too cold to go in. In winter, GJ and Becky took turns marking off the days until spring arrived. And when it finally rolled around, they were into the pool faster than the blink of that proverbial eye.

Becky was allowed a pool party for her tenth birthday, and she couldn't wait for the chance to have her friends visit all at once . . . even the two boys she wanted to invite. She'd even managed to convince her parents to let all the girls stay for a sleepover. Becky hadn't asked to have the boys included in that part. Boys could be fun, but they didn't understand dress-ups, and they hated getting their hair braided, so there wasn't any point in them staying.

To be accommodating (actually, to escape) GJ was going to Jake's house for a sleepover, so there would be no annoying big brother to bug her friends.

The day of the party came, and all of Becky's friends arrived in their finest clothes—the girls in gorgeous, lacy dresses and the boys in bow ties and dress shorts. Each child carried a present for Becky under one arm and a shoulder bag with their swimmers and towel over the other. Mums and dads toted overnight bags for the girls—the looks on the parents' faces telling Gene and Jean they were insane for having a gaggle of ten-year-old girls on a sleepover.

The looks on Gene and Jean's faces saying "yes, we know."

Gene tried to cover his ears, he even tried ear plugs, to block out the squealing and giggles as ten kids, swam, dived, paddled, and tossed a beach ball around the pool. The pitch of their young voices was just right to get by anything he tried.

Jean grinned and shrugged her shoulders. "What did you expect?" she mouthed, not bothering to try and be heard over the racket. Gene shrugged back and went to roasting the corn dogs on the barbecue.

The sign on the pool fence read "No Midnight Swimming!"

but nobody really noticed.

By midnight they intended to all be sleeping, or applying make-up to each other's faces and smearing it all over the pillowcases when they lay down.

Joanna was the loudest squealer, and the best swimmer after Becky. The two girls kept sneaking up on the other children from under the water, ducking them or bursting up from behind and splashing everyone within reach.

After a couple of hours in the pool, it was no surprise the kids ate all the corn dogs, and the chips, and the cocktail frankfurts. And they drank all the soda—even the soda water. Gene had to call out for pizza, the kind that came with a bottle of soda and large garlic bread with every two ordered. Kids being what they are, none of them would touch the garlic bread when it came.

Around nine, the boys' parents picked them up, and Gene and Jean made an attempt at getting the girls to bed. They knew it wouldn't be that easy, but an early start gave them some hope of getting everyone asleep by the early hours.

Jennifer had brought a music DVD with her—a band called Water or something like that. The girls set it up on the TV and started dancing to a song that went on about a fantastic life in a plastic world. Gene and Jean let it go—at least the girls were all in the lounge room and one step closer to bed.

An hour later, the girls were struggling to stay awake, but there was so much they hadn't done yet. One girl had given Becky a deluxe junior cosmetics set, and there was no way it wasn't going to get a serious workout. They plastered each other with lipstick and clogged their eyelashes with mascara. They smeared blusher on their cheeks and got eyeshadow just about everywhere except where it was supposed to go. And they told each other how beautiful and grown up they all looked.

By 11, the adrenalin had run out, and the girls climbed into their pajamas and snuggled into their sleeping bags. Within a few minutes they were all asleep. Gene and Jean heaved a collective sigh of relief and took themselves off to bed.

Time enough in the morning to clean everything up—after the girls had gone home.

The sign on the pool fence read "No Midnight Swimming!" but there was nobody outside to see it.

Shortly before 1 a.m. Joanna woke up. She was hot. The party had been fun, but it was crowded on the lounge room floor so she quietly tiptoed outside to get some air. From the patio the pool looked very inviting. Since there was nobody else awake to see her, she took off her pajamas and slid silently into the cool water.

Jean went into the lounge room just after 8 to wake the girls. She and Gene had already had breakfast and had done a bit of cleaning around the barbecue area, but not the pool. The parents were all expected around 9, and the girls had slept as long as Jean thought was doable if they were all going to be dressed, fed, and ready to go home.

She didn't notice right away that one girl was missing.

In the tangled mess of sleeping bags, blankets, and pillows there could have been five or fifteen kids buried and nobody would have known.

It didn't take more than a few minutes of scrambling for clothes and falling over each other in the race to get dressed and out to the kitchen for pancakes. It was then the girls realized Joanna wasn't there. And she wasn't in the bathroom either—Becky checked. A quick search of the house turned up nothing, and Gene was getting annoyed. Joanna had been the life of the party yesterday, but today wasn't the time for her to be playing tricks on everyone. Gene called her parents, in case she'd taken herself off home. No luck there, but her worried mother came straight over. By the time she arrived, Joanna's pajamas had been found beside the pool, but there was still no sign of Joanna.

Of course, the police had to be called in. They arrived within minutes, missing children being high on their response list. They talked to all the girls, but had to wait for their parents to arrive

The Pool

and OK it all. They talked to Gene and Jean. They looked all over the house, and under it. They looked around the pool, and took Joanna's pajamas away to the lab for testing. They didn't say what kind of testing. They saw the sign by the pool that said "No Midnight Swimming!" but it was just a sign, so they didn't think anything of it.

The rest of the girls went home as soon as the police were done with them. Their parents gave Jean, and especially Gene, very odd looks. GJ came home from his sleepover and wanted to know what all the fuss was about. The police talked to him, too—to make sure he really had been away all night.

Being an election year, the mayor was on the phone to the local police chief insisting this be sorted out quickly. He wasn't interested in being told there were few clues, and the lab tests on the pajamas would take at least a day. That wouldn't get him re-elected, and it wouldn't keep the chief in his job—if the chief understood the mayor's meaning. He did.

By the afternoon the police reached only one conclusion: Gene, either alone or with help, had kidnapped Joanna, taken her somewhere, probably molested her, and almost certainly murdered her. The evidence was all circumstantial, but they figured the tests on the pajamas would give them something more concrete, and for now they were seen to be doing something. That night they arrested Gene and charged him with Joanna's abduction and murder. They took him away in handcuffs as the neighbors watched with all those "I told you so" expressions that neighbors get when there's something strange in the neighborhood.

Jean sent GJ and Becky off to bed and wandered around the house in a daze. She tidied up where she'd tidied already, and some places she even tidied a third time. Eventually, around 11, she took herself to bed and tried to get some sleep. But it wouldn't come. She couldn't believe her husband had done any of the things he was accused of, but she had been so exhausted during the sleepover, she couldn't swear that he was in the bed with her all night.

The night was hot, and Jean tossed in the bed, still unable to get to sleep. She got up and took a nip of brandy from the liquor cupboard, but it didn't help. She went outside to look around the pool, the light of the moon showing her the cool, inviting water. It was just after midnight and Jean needed to unwind, so she slipped off her housecoat and nightdress and slid into the water. It felt soft and welcoming.

In the morning, the children found Jean's coat and nightdress by the pool, but mum was nowhere to be seen.

On the pool fence, the sign read "No Midnight Swimming!"

Naturally, "everyone" knew that Jean had staged her own disappearance to take the heat off Gene, and the police weren't greatly concerned about finding her. The figured she would come back once she realized the children were going to be left alone in the house. However, when she hadn't turned up by the next morning, the police didn't oppose Gene's bail application, and he went home to be a dad.

The forensic tests on the pajamas came back two days later—all negative, of course. With no hard evidence against Gene, the charges were dropped. But that didn't stop the suspicious looks from neighbors, or from GJ and Becky being taunted at school about their dad being a child killer. Threats of a lawsuit from Joanna's parents surfaced, the police continued to investigate Gene, and the afternoon visits from friends of the family stopped.

Jean hadn't reappeared.

Gene and the kids were devastated.

After a month of emotional agony, Gene decided enough was enough. He put the house on the market—for considerably less than it was worth. As soon as it sold, he packed up the kids and moved to a new town. Jean still hadn't reappeared. On the pool fence, the sign read "No Midnight Swimming!"

The new owners had two young children and didn't think it was safe to have a pool, so they filled it in. They threw the sign out in the trash.

The Pool

*

Jimmy McCarthy was captain of the high school basketball team.

He hadn't known Gene or Jean or their kids . . . or the people who bought the house and filled in the pool.

But Jimmy was tied to them all nonetheless.

Jimmy was suspended from school.

He'd been caught skinny dipping in the school pool with Angela Somers, and Principal Somers had wanted to expel him. The basketball coach managed to convince Principal Somers that a two-week suspension would suffice. After all, Angela wasn't being expelled, and both teenagers were at fault. And, besides, often teenagers slipped into the school very late at night to go swimming—especially on the weekends. None of them had been expelled.

Jimmy had two weeks of "nothing to do."

So, with nothing better to do, Jimmy went scavenging at the dump. His eye was caught by the glint of sunlight on a metal sheet. He picked it up and started laughing—it said "No Midnight Swimming!"

Jimmy knew exactly what to do with that sign.

After dark, when everyone had gone home, Jimmy snuck into the high school pool and wired the sign to the safety fence. Then he went home.

The next morning, the swim coach thought Principal Somers had arranged the sign, and Principal Somers thought the swim coach had done it. So, neither of them said anything.

On the high school pool fence, the sign read "No Midnight Swimming!"

INK AND NEWSPRINT
Marc Tassin

Marc Tassin was enthralled by books from an early age, and he often considered trying his hand at writing. Then Marc attended the Gen Con Writer's Symposium. Inspired by the advice and support offered by the panelists, Marc stopped thinking about writing and started actually writing. Since then, Marc has published numerous short stories, articles, and game materials, and this is his third year as a panelist for the Symposium. His story, "Ink and Newsprint," is a tale about technology's impact on the written word – from the point of view of a cat.

Sophocles paced in front of the rack of newspapers, his fluffy grey tail swishing back and forth with the precision of a drum major's baton. Ears back, he padded across the shop's asphalt-tile floor, turned at the comic book circular, and headed back the other way. Passing the counter, he glared at the big, round clock on the newsstand's wall, its Plexiglas casing coated with dust.

Ten after nine.

Ten after nine and still no sign of Coffee Man. For three years, Coffee Man had arrived at 8:50 a.m. every day. Coffee Man always carried a fresh cup of coffee from the diner next door, always the exact same variety – some sort of cheap Colombian blend, Sophocles deduced from the aroma – and always black. He purchased a *New York Times* and always paid for it in coins. But for the past two months, no sign of him. Sophocles found this pointedly disturbing.

It wasn't the man's absence alone that bothered the old, gray British Shorthair. Customers came and went at the little newsstand. It was all part of life. In his fifteen years, he'd learned that much at least. Rather, it was Coffee Man's absence *combined with* the absences of Too-Much-Perfume Woman, Guy-Who-Doesn't-Bathe, Muddy-Boot-Man, and countless others. (Although to be honest, Sophocles didn't miss Muddy-Boot-Man, who made a terrible mess every time he came in to the store.)

The disappearances were part of a growing trend, one had that slowly appeared over the past five years. Where once the shop had been a bustle of activity in the morning, now the little bell over the door had fallen almost silent, ringing just a few times each hour.

Sophocles twitched his nose and narrowed his eyes. With the exception of Herbert, the old man who worked the store's counter, Sophocles didn't trust humans. They were notorious for their inability to maintain regular schedules. Things always "came up," as they liked to put it, and interrupted proper and respectable routines.

He stopped his pacing to survey the newspaper rack. Publications from around the country and the far corners of the world shared space. *The Times*, the *Detroit Free Press*, the *San Francisco Chronicle*: Ehgleman's Newsstand had it all. At Ehgleman's, customers weren't limited to the one-sided, local point of view. The expatriate wasn't reduced to getting irregular, and certainly inaccurate, information by phone or letter from friends across the sea. Certainly not.

No, at Ehgleman's customers could find the facts, plain and simple, printed in a sharp 7.5-point Nimrod Cyrillic font, on sensible yellow-white newsprint. That was, after all, what the news was all about. The facts, clearly stated, in a form you can sink your claws into.

And yet, the people no longer came.

Checking the clock, Sophocles saw that it was a quarter past nine. He sighed and plodded over to the big, plate-glass windows at the front of the store. With a bit of effort, he hopped onto the wide sill. The east-facing windows made for excellent morning sunning, something Sophocles did daily at 9:15 a.m. sharp. He stepped onto the little cushion Herbert had placed there for him, turned a few circles to loosen the stuffing, and settled in.

Sophocles watched the crowds passing by: rushing off to their jobs, towing children to daycare, balancing steaming cups of coffee while negotiating the sea of people moving along the sidewalk. No one even glanced at the wooden bench in front of the shop, the paint on its slats faded and chipping. Herbert had placed it there years ago, back when people actually sat and read their papers right after buying them. On most days, the bench remained empty. People just pushed past, at most using the bench as a place to set a briefcase while negotiating the removal of a phone from a pocket.

As Sophocles sat gazing out the window, mulling over his troubles, a strange thing happened. Someone *did* sit on the bench: a young man, wearing jeans and a T-shirt. No more than thirty, Sophocles estimated, although he was never very good at guessing their ages. Like the others he had a coffee – a rather large one at that – but he didn't carry a briefcase.

Sitting there on the bench, the man reached into his pants pocket and pulled out a hand-sized device. A phone, Sophocles thought at first. He'd seen the little devices proliferate like fleas on an alley cat over the past few years. He could appreciate the desire to remain in contact with others, but voice communication was seldom as efficient as the printed word. It all seemed rather silly.

But as Sophocles watched, it became clear that this was no ordinary phone. The man tapped a button on the front, and the shiny black face of the thing sprang to life. Colorful icons appeared on the screen, some animated, all of them begging to be touched. The man made a few deft motions, tapping here and there on the screen, the screen flickering as it switched from one view to the next.

And when the man stopped, what Sophocles saw sent shivers through his body. The world spun, and Sophocles struggled to his feet, stepping over to press his face closer to the window.

There, on the screen of the strange and terrible device, was a newspaper. *The Times*.

*

That night, the moment Herbert stepped out the door, Sophocles raced to the phone. He batted the receiver from the cradle so hard that it went flying off the desktop and clattered to the floor. Sophocles had to fish it back up by the cord before he could make his call.

He pawed the numbers, let the phone ring a single time, and then smacked the contact back down to hang up. It was a signal he and a friend of his had developed for calling one another during human waking hours. They'd picked it up from other cats they'd talked to at the vet. He'd heard humans talking about the strange calls they got that ring once and no one is there, but fortunately the humans attributed them to telemarketers or trouble with the lines.

A moment later the phone rang and Sophocles answered.

"Hello," he mewed.

"Hey, Sophocles. I had to sneak the cordless under the bed to call you back. What's the big emergency?"

"Mr. Snuggles! We have a serious problem over here. I need advice from someone who knows about those *crazy* phone things the humans are all carrying."

Sophocles hissed the word "crazy." He despised the trappings of modern society, seeing its many technological marvels as little more than showy glitz designed to sap the time and money of the working cat. Probably true for humans as well, but he hadn't given it that much thought. Of course, after today's incident he realized he might need to reconsider.

"Why don't we get together tomorrow and—" Mr. Snuggles began.

"No. Tonight. We need to talk right away," said Sophocles.

"Okay, okay, don't choke on a hairball. Look, the boy is going out with his friends in a few minutes. When he leaves, I'll slip out and come right over. Will that work?"

"Yes, fine. Don't delay. This is of the utmost importance."

"No problem. Just try to calm down, and stay away from the catnip. I'll be over as soon as I can."

*

Mr. Snuggles lived in an apartment a block from the newsstand. He and Sophocles had met at the vet's a couple of years back. Although their personalities differed dramatically, for some reason they'd hit it off. Where Sophocles was old, almost fifteen by his own count, and fond of all things traditional, Mr. Snuggles was young, a mere kitten in Sophocles' eyes at three years. He loved everything new and exciting.

Sophocles propped open the bathroom window for Mr. Snuggles, then busied himself counting copies on the magazine rack. If anything was low, he'd make sure to sit near the copy and mew tomorrow, so Herbert would remember to restock. The man was frustratingly unobservant at times.

An hour later, Mr. Snuggles arrived.

"Hey, Sophocles," he said, his coppery eyes glinting in the half-light.

"Oh, thank goodness you're here," Sophocles said.

Mr. Snuggles made his way around the room, sniffing the corners and taking the place in.

"Man, you're lucky. I love this place, Sopho. The ambience is fantastic. It's like stepping back in time. I mean, look at this," he said, hopping onto the counter and sniffing at a clear plastic jar of candies. "You guys even have Squirrel Nuts. Seriously, Sopho, where do you even *order* Squirrel Nuts? I didn't even know they still made them. Places like this are an endangered species."

Sophocles jumped onto the counter and swished his tail under Mr. Snuggles' nose. "If you'd stop rambling on, you'd find out that this is *exactly* why I called you."

Ink and Newsprint

"What do you mean?"

Sophocles sprang from the counter to the desk behind it, and dragged a heavy binder out from between two bookends shaped like the front and rear of a Spanish galleon. With a bit of effort, he flipped open the cover and pawed through the pages until he reached a section near the end.

"Look," he said.

Mr. Snuggles hopped over and glanced at the page. Columns of numbers filled it from top to bottom. A startling number of them were written in red ink.

"Wow, this is amazing," said Mr. Snuggles.

"Isn't it?" sighed Sophocles. "Shocking, I know."

"Yeah. I didn't think anyone had done their books by hand in the past twenty years. I mean, sheesh, Sophocles. Haven't you guys ever heard of QuickBooks?"

Sophocles swatted a paw down on the page.

"Not that, you imbecile. These balances. We're hemorrhaging money. In the past five years alone we've lost almost sixty percent of our regular customer base. For a while, I thought perhaps another newsstand had opened nearby, but now I *know* what's happened."

Mr. Snuggles quirked his head, half-smiling.

"Oh, really? And what did you discover?"

Sophocles jumped to the floor and marched over to the magazines. With a flick of his paw, he knocked a copy of *Smartphone & Pocket PC Magazine* from the rack.

"This," he said, pointing at the cover. "*This* is the problem."

Mr. Snuggles jumped off the desk and sauntered over. He checked out the magazine cover, which displayed an array of high-end cell phones.

"What?" he asked in mock surprise. "Phones?"

"I know! It sounds unbelievable. I hardly believed it myself at first, but did you know –" Sophocles lowered his voice in a conspiratorial fashion "– that you can read *newspapers* on these?"

At first, Mr. Snuggles looked shocked, but then his eye twitched and he fell on the floor laughing. Sophocles stared at him, aghast.

"Wha... what's so funny?"

"Sophocles," Mr. Snuggles said, "people have been able to do that for years. *And* take pictures, *and* read books, *and* listen to music, *and* send letters..."

"Letters?" gasped Sophocles.

This only sent Mr. Snuggles into further fits of laughter.

"Stop that! Stop that at once! This is my *life* you're laughing at. My store is going to close!"

Mr. Snuggles stifled his laughter, took a long breath, and wiped tears from his eyes with the back of one paw. Rolling back onto his feet, he gave Sophocles a look of compassion.

"I'm sorry, Sopho. I keep telling you to *read* the technology sections of those papers you love so much."

"Fah," Sophocles scoffed. "That's not news. It's corporate gossip. It has no business in a proper paper."

"You can't hide from it forever, Sophocles. This is the future. This is why all your customers are drifting away. They don't *need* newspapers anymore."

"What? Of course people need newspapers. Without the news we wander in shadow, ignorant of the world around us. Without the news we wallow, confused, with no understanding of our place in the world. Without the news..."

"I didn't say people don't need news. I said they don't need news*papers*."

Sophocles stared, bewildered. Mr. Snuggles sighed.

"Look, Sopho. Remember when I told you about the internet?"

Sophocles nodded. "The thing humans use to watch each other mate."

"Well, yeah, partly. Okay, mostly, but it's more than that. It's become an interconnected version of our own world. People meet. They talk. They post their own news. Even the newspapers see this. They all offer their news online. With a few clicks, anyone, anywhere, can read news from everywhere else in the world."

"But . . . but what about the papers we have here? I mean, we offer papers from the far corners of the earth. We already keep people connected to the events of the world!"

"So does the internet, only you don't have to wait until the afternoon print run is complete, or days for those out-of-country editions you carry. You can find out right away, the moment the news happens."

Sophocles walked over to the rack of newspapers and ran a paw over a copy of the *Detroit Free Press*. "And they can get this on their computers, as well as their phones."

"Yes, Sopho. Almost everyone can."

Sophocles' head drooped. He sat down, his tail swishing slowly across the floor. When at last he raised his head and gazed at Mr. Snuggles again, his eyes were damp.

"That's it, then," he said. "We're no longer necessary."

Mr. Snuggles padded over and sat next to Sophocles. For a long time they just sat there together, in silence. Finally, Sophocles stood and headed back to the counter.

"Where are you going?" Mr. Snuggles asked.

Sophocles stopped, head low, and gave a long sigh.

"I'm going to run the numbers, see how much time we have."

Mr. Snuggles narrowed his eyes and raised his tail.

"Hold on," he said. "Don't close those books out just yet, Sopho. I have an idea ... but we're going to need a computer."

*

The two cats scurried down the alley behind the shop. It had taken a bit of coaxing to get Sophocles outside. From the day Herbert brought him home, Sophocles had lived within the confines of the newsstand. His only forays into the greater world consisted of trips to the vet and a couple of accidental lockouts during his more adventurous youth. A close encounter with a taxi, however, had convinced him of the folly of such explorations, and he'd settled into a safe and comfortable pattern of life within the shop.

Now, he found himself in the unpleasant position of making the block-long trek to Mr. Snuggles' apartment. It was all he could do to keep up with the younger, livelier cat, and he had to remind Mr. Snuggles repeatedly to slow down. Each time they passed an opening onto the alley, Sophocles instinctively stopped. Engine noise, distant sirens, pungent unfamiliar odors, and the strange, pink-orange light of the street lamps left him cowering.

"Relax," Mr. Snuggles said. "I do this all the time. It's perfectly safe."

In the end, a single thought pushed him onward. His shop. His talk with Mr. Snuggles had finally driven the reality home. The shop wouldn't survive much longer: six months, a year at most. He'd managed to hide this truth from himself for a long time, but saying it out loud made it seem real. This reality burned hot within Sophocles' mind, like no other idea had burned in a very long time.

If there were a way to save his shop, by his tail he would do it. And if it required him to travel a block – hell, *two* blocks – then he would make that sacrifice. Taking a long, deep breath and holding it, he dashed across the alley mouth.

Soon they stood behind Mr. Snuggles' apartment building. Sophocles marveled at how simple the trip had been. Not nearly the horror he'd imagined. A breeze blew through the space between buildings, ruffling his fur. He lifted his head and sniffed, taking in the crisp, outdoor air. His muscles twitched with an urge to run and dance among the trash in the alley. Maybe even hunt.

"You coming, old man?" Mr. Snuggles called.

Sophocles looked up and saw Mr. Snuggles standing on the

fire escape above. An overflowing dumpster offered a simple path to him – simple, at least, for a younger cat. His newfound vigor faded as he struggled up the pile. A few jumps in the shop were one thing, but this was something else. His muscles burned and he breathed heavily as he clambered, with effort, to the top.

Finally, he arrived. Mr. Snuggles grinned at him.

"What's so funny?" Sophocles demanded.

"*You*, old man. I'll be honest. I wasn't sure you had it in you. You're pretty tough for an old cat."

Sophocles raised his nose and tail, then sniffed.

"You will find, little kitten, that age hasn't diminished my spirit. My muscles may not have the same strength as yours, but I assure you, I more than make up for it in determination."

Mr. Snuggles smiled again, then dashed up the stairs. Sophocles followed, appreciating the relative ease of climbing the fire escape. In moments they sat outside a window, looking in on a darkened dining room.

"How do we get in?" Sophocles asked.

Mr. Snuggles responded by tapping on the window, claws extended. From around the corner, a shapely, young Blue Point Lynx appeared. Her body swayed as she walked, ringed tail teasing the air behind her, blue eyes shining. Sophocles started to feel light-headed, and realized he was holding his breath.

"My word," he gasped. "She's beautiful."

"Isn't she, though? Her name's Evette," Mr. Snuggles said, beaming.

"You never told me you lived with another cat."

"They only got her about six months ago. I'll admit things didn't go well at first. They almost sent her away. Heck, they almost sent *me* away when I started marking rooms to keep her out of my space. But one evening, after a really big blowout, all that tension melted into something a bit more, um, enjoyable. We've gotten along great ever since."

Effortlessly, Evette hopped onto the dining room table, and

then virtually floated to the windowsill. Standing on her hind legs, her smooth, white underbelly pressed against the glass, she undid the window latch with her front paws.

"Gracious. She's a vixen, isn't she?" whispered Sophocles.

"Hey. Watch it, old man. That's my girlfriend you're talking about."

"Right, sorry. No offense meant."

"Ah, none taken. And you're right anyhow." Mr. Snuggles chuckled.

The latch undone, Mr. Snuggles and Evette worked together to open the window. It resisted at first, but once they broke the seal, the weighted lines in the frame took over and the sash slid open. They closed it behind them, then the three cats hopped over onto the table. Evette padded over to Mr. Snuggles and rubbed her body down his length.

"Hey, lover," she purred. "You didn't tell me you were bringing company."

She gave Sophocles a sly, appraising look, which made him feel nervous and excited all at once.

"He's an *old* friend," Mr. Snuggles said. He smiled over his shoulder at Sophocles. "But he's got a problem, and I've got an idea on how we can help. We're going to need the computer, though. Is everyone asleep?"

"Dead to the world," Evette replied. "The place is ours."

"Excellent. Okay, Sopho. Come with me."

"You boys have fun," Evette said, bounding off the table and heading for the far doorway. "I told Boots I'd call her tonight."

Mr. Snuggles hopped down and headed out the other exit. Sophocles followed. The house held so many new and unusual scents that Sophocles had to resist stopping to sniff at them. After so many years in the store, he'd forgotten how rich and exciting the rest of the world could be.

In the living room, Mr. Snuggles hopped onto the coffee table. Sophocles did the same, and found Mr. Snuggles opening a laptop computer. Sophocles had never seen one this close. Once the computer was open, Mr. Snuggles tapped the power button. The screen glowed, illuminating the room.

"Okay. We need to get online."

Mr. Snuggles sat in front of the computer and tapped away at the keys with one paw. At one point he placed his paw on a flat bit of plastic near the edge of the computer, swished it back and forth, then clicked a button with a claw.

A few moments later, the screen filled with an electronic version of a newspaper. Again, Sophocles felt light-headed. He was having trouble breathing, and instinctively popped his claws, trying to sink them into the smooth, glass table for stability.

"I want to show you something," Mr. Snuggles said, unaware of Sophocles' trouble.

A few more paw motions and the screen changed to show an old diner. In front of it was a mob of people holding signs painted with slogans, like "Save Our History!" and "Keep Our City Alive!"

"I read this article," Sophocles said. "October 23, 2007. 'Activists Save Local Diner.'"

"Exactly. A bunch of those Save Our City people, the same ones who made the stink last year about the 'homogenization of our cities.' They went crazy when they found out that place was set to close and a fast-food joint was going to take its spot. That diner has crappy food and is about as clean as a sewer grate, but people saved it because it represents a part of the world that's fading away."

Sophocles began to nod, then shook his head. "This isn't the same. No one is taking over the newsstand. We're just running out of money. Protests won't help."

"We don't need protests. We just need to convince people that they're about to lose something important to the city. How long has Ehgleman's been open?"

"It was established in 1946. Mr. Ehgleman had just returned from the war and..."

"Right, right. I remember the story. And in that time, how often have you remodeled?"

"Well, Herbert purchased a new cash register when he took over the shop in '65. Oh, and we replaced that light fixture, the one that fell when the people living upstairs had that party in '95."

"That's what I'm saying, Sopho. That newsstand is like a freaking museum. It's like someone froze it in time. These folks," Mr. Snuggles said, tapping the picture of the protesters, "eat this stuff up. And if they find out that you might close, they'll swarm the place."

Sophocles thought about this. Something about the plan nagged at him. It didn't feel quite right, but all the pieces were there. It *could* work.

"It's a decent idea," he said. "But how will we let them know? Do you have their phone numbers?"

Mr. Snuggles laughed.

"We don't need to call them. Remember how I said the internet can connect people together?"

He tapped the keyboard a few more times. The screen changed, revealing a page with a series of dated entries titled "Snugg's Place." Sophocles narrowed his eyes and stared at the screen.

"What is it?"

"It's my blog. We're going to take Ehgleman's Newsstand into the blogosphere!"

Sophocles stared at Mr. Snuggles. "You do realize that I haven't the slightest idea what you are talking about."

Mr. Snuggles sighed. "A blog is sort of like an online diary. You post entries and can talk about anything that interests you."

"I'm not seeing the point."

"Other people read the blog and post their own comments, and if they like what you wrote, and have blogs of their own, they can connect *their* blogs to your story."

"A sort of ... web?"

Mr. Snuggles laughed. "You could say that."

"But why would anyone want to read the ramblings of a rank amateur? No offense, of course."

"Well, first, they aren't all amateurs. Authors, politicians, all sorts of people have blogs. What's more, and I think you'll be especially interested in this, bloggers have started breaking news stories the major outlets didn't even know about. With a blog, anyone can be a reporter."

Sophocles mulled it over. It was like the small-press papers they carried on the big circular rack at Ehgleman's, the ones published in garages and old warehouses by fringe groups or fans of esoteric topics. Still, he had his doubts.

"This is all well and good, but how will anyone find what you've written? I mean, just because you *publish* an article doesn't mean anyone will *read* it."

"Fortunately, I've got that covered," Mr. Snuggles said.

He tapped away furiously, alternating between the keys and the smooth plastic square. A moment later, a list appeared on the screen.

"These are the blogs of other cats, all friends of mine."

"What?" Sophocles asked. "You mean there are more cats writing blogs?"

"Oh yeah, hundreds. Thousands, maybe. Who knows? On the internet everyone's anonymous. Almost anything you find there could have been created by a cat."

Sophocles gaped at the computer, dumbfounded. He felt as if someone had taken his entire world, turned it inside out, and handed it back to him.

"So all I have to do," Mr. Snuggles said, "is email the other cats and let them know what I'm trying to accomplish. They'll link to the story and we'll start building momentum. We help each other out like this all the time."

He turned to Sophocles.

"Now what I need from you is help. If anyone who knows how

to write news, Sophocles, it's you. We'll save your newsstand yet!"

Sophocles stared at the screen, taking in the dozens of names in the list.

"I need to get a computer," he said.

*

Over the next few weeks, Mr. Snuggles kept Sophocles posted about the progress of their campaign. It wasn't necessary. Within a few days of the story hitting the web, strange new people started drifting into the newsstand.

Some were young people with little handheld computers, like the device the man outside the window had used.

"Oh my god," they would gasp. "Can you believe this place? This is awesome. It's like something out of a movie!"

Others were older, their hair steely-colored, and wore sensible shoes and worn sweaters.

"My father and I used to come to a newsstand just like this when I was a boy," they'd say. "He'd buy a *Times*, some pipe tobacco, and if I was good, a comic book for me."

More than one of them came in with cats of their own, held in their arms or in special travel totes they opened once they were inside the door. As their owners explored the store, the cats came over to talk to Sophocles.

"We think it's really great what you're doing here," they told him. "The humans don't always appreciate their history, so it's up to us to preserve it."

Sophocles nodded, unsure what to say, unused to so much company after years of living alone in the newsstand with Herbert.

The most important change, however, was that people bought things again: newspapers, cigarettes, maps of the city, penny candy, comic books, magazines. The little bell of the cash register rang over and over, a wonderful music to accompany the new, swirling dance of life in the newsstand.

After visiting Ehgleman's, many people drifted next door to the diner, an old greasy spoon in as much financial trouble as the newsstand had been. The boost in customers helped it too. At one point, the diner's owner, an older woman with a long nose who always smelled of bacon grease, came in to talk to Herbert. The two of them marveled at their unexpected new success, wondering at what had changed.

Beaming at their good fortune, they laughed and chatted, becoming good friends and spending many of their evenings together. All the while, Sophocles sat on his cushion in the window, filled with warm feelings. He and Mr. Snuggles had saved the newsstand and the diner, in the process bringing some extra happiness into Herbert's and Bacon Grease Lady's lives.

At one point, Herbert decided he should use some of his profits to remodel. Mr. Snuggles panicked, and made it very clear to Sophocles that remodeling was *out of the question*. People didn't want a shiny, new newsstand. They wanted classic urban grime. It took some effort, but Sophocles erased messages from the contractor, "lost" paperwork, and otherwise interfered with the process until Herbert gave up on the idea as more trouble than it was worth.

The high point for Sophocles came when the city's major paper ran a story about Ehgleman's in the Lifestyles section, outlining its history and proclaiming it one of the city's "pulp gems of a disappearing classic urban landscape." Sophocles even appeared in one of the photos. The most satisfying part, however, was that he got to read it the way he liked: in strong, black ink on yellow-white newsprint.

Sophocles did get a computer. A few carefully placed technology articles caught Herbert's attention and put the idea into his head to buy one. Herbert used it twice and promptly gave up on it. At night, while Herbert went home, Sophocles learned its arcane secrets. After a month of effort, he proudly opened "Sopho's Stories," a blog about the news and newspapers where he wrote short essays about the state of journalism and the modern news media.

And yet, despite the now-solid financial position of the newsstand, something still bothered Sophocles. For a long time it nagged at him, often in the depths of the night, just out of reach and tickling the back of his mind. Then one evening, while Mr. Snuggles was visiting, it came to him.

They were sitting together on the desk behind the counter, going over Sophocles' latest story on the computer.

"I think I finally figured it out," he said.

"What's that?"

"That thing. The thing that's bothered me from the beginning."

Mr. Snuggles maneuvered the mouse to click the Back button on the browser. The home page for "Sopho's Stories" came up on the screen. "I'll bite. What is it?"

"We saved the store, and that's important, but we saved it by turning it into a novelty."

"So? Wasn't that what you wanted?"

"No," Sophocles said, lowering his head. "What I wanted, what I *truly* wanted, was for things to be the same as they were. I wanted people to care about those little black words on the page. I wanted them to pick up that newspaper, to feel the newsprint, smell the ink, and know they held the world in their hands – the combined knowledge of sharp, creative minds, working together to bring the truth to the people.

"But I know the truth, now. We saved the newsstand, but we can't save the magic those little black printed words represent. We can't save *newspapers*."

Mr. Snuggles sat back on his haunches and gave a little chuckle.

Sophocles whipped his head around and glared at him. "Why do you do that? Why do you always laugh at me when I'm feeling the worst?"

Mr. Snuggles shook his head. "Sopho, my friend, you're one of the smartest, wisest creatures I know, but sometimes you're blind to the most obvious things."

"What are you talking about?"

Mr. Snuggles scrolled to the bottom of "Sopho's Stories" clicked on a blue link labeled "web stats." A series of bar graphs appeared on the screen.

"According to this," Mr. Snuggles said, "around ten thousand people – or cats maybe, you can't tell – have read your most recent article over the past two days. That's ten thousand people whose lives you've touched, people you've opened doors for. People with whom you've shared wisdom and understanding they might never have discovered on their own."

Sophocles glared. "I'm aware of the stats, and I'm pleased people are interested. Still, I don't see your point."

"Sophocles, it isn't the *paper* that holds the magic. It's the *words*. It's words that give the paper the magic you love, words that saved your store, and words that will preserve that magic for those who come after us."

Mr. Snuggles rose and walked over to a newspaper setting next to the computer. He swiped at it with his paw, rustling the pages.

"Without words, this paper is nothing but a piece of flattened tree. It doesn't matter whether they're printed on paper, appear on a computer screen, or, I don't know, get zapped straight into your head. It is, and always will be, the *words* that hold the magic.

"What you love isn't dying, Sophocles. Just the trees the words get printed on."

*

Sophocles never forgot their conversation. Through joyous occasions, like the birth of Mr. Snuggles' and Evette's kittens the next year, and sad, as when Herbert passed on two years later, that simple conversation stayed with him, and gave him hope.

Herbert's son took over the shop, and Sophocles kept on posting to "Sopho's Stores" for three more years. Then, one day, the posts stopped.

Mr. Snuggles realized something was wrong almost right away. Others noticed as well, and soon emails and comments bloomed throughout the internet, as admirers of the blog wondered what had happened.

When a second night came with no new posts, Mr. Snuggles knew. He raced over to the newsstand, hurrying down the alley, fearing the worst. When he arrived, the bathroom window was closed, so he crept around to the front of the store.

A little light sat in the front window. It hadn't been there before, and it shone on Sophocles' cushion. Where the old cat should have been sleeping, there was a framed picture of him in his youth, serious and sitting atop a stack of newspapers. *The Times*, Mr. Snuggles noticed. Beside the picture lay a handwritten note.

"Goodbye, old friend. Take good care of Dad."

Mr. Snuggles posted the news on "Snugg's Place" as soon as he returned home. The word travelled quickly, and within hours, a memorial appeared on a popular social networking site. A few humans tried to puzzle out who Sophocles, the respected news commentator, had been, but every lead came up short.

Cats, of course, knew.

It wasn't until three days later that Mr. Snuggles found it. He'd missed the message at first: his voracious spam filter had eaten it. It was a single email from sopho@sophostories.com, with the subject "To My Friend". The date and time stamp showed it had reached his mailbox at 3 a.m. on the day Sophocles' posts stopped.

For a while, Mr. Snuggles just stared at it, unsure he even wanted to read it. Finally, he worked up the courage to open it. Inside he found two simple, magic words.

"Thank You."

LAST DANCE
Steven Saus

The second year I went to the Catholic Youth Conference, I overheard a guy mention Cthulhu. We spent the rest of the conference talking about Lovecraft and gaming; luckily I now live close enough to him that we still game on a regular basis. "Last Dance" is largely drawn from my memories of those conferences. An earlier version of this story won an honorable mention in a local writing contest. I stumbled onto the Writing Symposium three years ago, and it's become my main reason for going to Gen Con. You can find more of my work at www.stevensaus.com.

    The mixed crowd of the state youth conference danced and wound through itself while I fought my way to the exit. After I uttered my last unheard "excuse me" and slipped past the final dancing body, I stepped out of the makeshift dance hall. I let the smell of nearby pine trees clear out the funk of sweaty teenagers and the spaghetti they'd served us from dinner. A summer evening breeze slid through the weave of my polo shirt, cooling my skin. The steady, bright blue streetlight in the counselors' parking lot was a calm change from the improvised strobes and disco ball inside. The chow-hall door closed behind me.
    I'd made it out. I'd escaped the noise, the chaos, the bodies.
    I'd escaped the polite and final "no, thank you."
    The world came back into focus as I slipped my glasses on. My cabin was across the quad, but nobody was over there. Nobody I wanted to talk to, anyway. I shrugged and started walking toward the end of the cafeteria's porch. The woods hunkered around the conference grounds. I imagined myself in them. A cloak over my head, and I would move from tree to tree, watching the others as they went from one cabin to the next. Then, when the time was –

I whirled at the blast of music, sudden and loud. I nearly fell off the edge of the porch, just catching a glimpse of someone entering the building, the logo of a high school football team on his jacket. The door's springs slammed it shut again.

Kristen was still in there, somewhere, lost in the noise and crowd. She was not over-stimulated. Her heart wasn't pounding in double-time syncopation with the music. I'd watched her navigate the crowd, sailing smoothly among people and music. I was just a nervous wave that had splashed against her hull and swirled in her wake.

The sob came from the parking lot across the road. Only counselors' cars were parked there. Our parents wouldn't come to get us until Sunday morning, and even the oldest "youth" at the conference was still a year away from a learner's permit.

I walked over and found the girl sitting on the curb, hidden between an Escort and a rusted pickup truck. Her hair was plain and straight, meeting her knees tucked under her chin.

"Hi," I said.

She didn't look up, face hidden behind a shield of knees and bangs. Still, I recognized her. She was in Kristen's cabin. I'd seen her with Kristen earlier – they might have even come from the same town. I sat down beside her, feeling the cool hardness of the concrete through my shorts. This far from the noise, I could hear the soft chirping of crickets in the grass.

I tried again. "Not having much fun tonight, huh?"

Her smile was bitter, but she looked up and wiped a tear from her face.

"No. I . . . well, no." Her hand swept her hair back behind an ear. "I've decided I don't like dances."

I smiled back at her. "I don't like them either. Completely stupid." I got another smile for that, a little more honest this time. "So why aren't you hanging out with Kristen? I'm sure she's having fun."

The girl's smile dropped away. "Because *she's* hanging out with

Michael. Who made it very, *very* clear that he didn't want to hang out with *me*."

I knew him, too. Michael was on the first floor of my cabin. He lived only a few miles from me, but we never talked. He was interested in football, lifting weights, and expensive shirts – all good signs he wasn't interested in talking to someone like me. I'd seen him talking to Kristen inside. I hadn't put it together – hadn't wanted to put it together.

The girl leaned back, resting her hands on the grass. "So why aren't *you* inside? Do you know Kristen?"

I made a sound then – a sound I'd never made before. Maybe it was a laugh, but it came up short and caught in my throat and became more of a choke. It was new to me, but the sound fit perfectly.

"Just a little bit. I wanted to, you know, talk to her more. Tonight." I leaned back too, shoving my fingers between the blades of grass. "But she didn't want to."

The girl made a small, sympathetic sound in her throat, but didn't say anything else.

"Yeah," I said. "I guess it was Michael."

Our eyes met, and a laugh, a real laugh, billowed up between us and silenced the crickets.

"Cigarette?" she asked.

"Oh, God, yes," I said. She rummaged through her purse as I continued. "My mother went through all my stuff before I left. I haven't had one all weekend."

She handed me a cigarette, and I was glad it wasn't a menthol. She lit it for me, the lighter so new that the warning sticker was still attached. A gust blew out the flame, so we tried again. My hand, cupped against the wind, brushed against hers.

Once we'd gotten my cigarette going, she took care of her own. "I got these from my cousin Therese," she said. "She's a counselor here. This is her car." She smacked the Escort's bumper. "She didn't lock it, the idiot."

We smoked next to Therese's car. Stings of music blared every time the doors opened to let kids in and out of the dance. Nobody even glanced our way.

"You should know," I said, "that Michael drools in his sleep."

She smacked my shoulder.

"No, really! He skipped third session this afternoon. I saw him taking a nap, and he was totally drooling. There was a puddle and everything. *Loooooooooser.*"

She grinned, the bitterness gone. "Okay, how about this. Kristen was plucking her eyebrows for tonight and overdid it. She pulled out all the hairs – her eyebrows are totally drawn on now." She laughed. "Are you trying to catch mosquitoes in your mouth? C'mon, close it!"

"Are you serious?" I asked. "All of them? Completely? On purpose?"

Her right hand made a small cross over her breast, and then she kissed her fingertips.

"But what was wrong with her *eyebrows*?"

She shrugged. "Just trying to be beautiful, I guess."

I pushed my glasses back up to the bridge of my nose. I took a last drag and tossed the butt onto the ground. We still completely failed to attract attention from the direction of the dance.

"I mean, that's just stupid, right?" I asked. "Why can't she – why can't *women* just be accepted for who they are? Why have some dumbass standard of who and what is attractive?"

She scooted a little closer. "I don't know. I mean, it's like, who decides how many buttons to leave undone?"

She leaned over and unbuttoned the top button of my shirt. She didn't lean back again when she was done.

"There," she said. "Isn't that better?"

I felt her breath on my cheek when she spoke again. "Do you want to go back in there?" she asked. "With me?"

I heard a blast of music, and looked up to see if it was Kristen leaving. The girl had pulled away when I looked back.

"Not right now," I said. "If you want, go on in. I'm going to see if I can catch Kristen on the way out."

She stood up, brushing off the back of her skirt.

"Thanks for talking," she said.

"No problem," I said. "Thanks for the cigarette."

She nodded and walked across the street. I didn't recognize the song when she opened the door and went in.

The girl came out later with another boy's arm around her shoulders. They were laughing, looking like every other couple that had come out of the dance. They joined some others at the end of the porch, then headed off behind the buildings.

I sat on the cold curb, my legs slowly cramping under me. I wished I'd asked that girl for another cigarette.

I watched the doors until the last cleanup lights were off.

I never saw Kristen leave.

JUDGMENT
Kerrie Hughes

Judgment was Kerrie's first short story sell in the DAW anthology Haunted Holidays *in 2003. Since then she has become an editor of nine DAW anthologies, the latest of which is* The Girls' Guide to Guns and Monsters, *which was released in February, and* Love & Rockets *which will be out late in 2010.* Chicks Kick Ass *is her first Anthology with TOR and will be out in May, 2011. She also has several anthology and research projects in development and is working on two paranormal novels. She has been with the Writer's Symposium for several years.*

Far beneath the earth, or rather, existing within the earth, the Feast of Samhain reached its peak. The inhabitants of the kingdom of the dead ate and drank to excess, toasting those they had left behind, Jesters and dancers wove around the crowded tables, partaking of a bite of food and a sip of wine whenever offered. The merriment was at its highest on this evening, but not everyone was at the festivities; many had secreted themselves in their rooms and peered into scrying bowls to watch the living. The scrying was a nightly activity but tonight was more of a temptation, for the veil between the two worlds was at its thinnest on Samhain. Some tried to reach across the boundaries to communicate with departed loved ones, or to exact vengeance on their enemies. Most were mournful souls and longed to fill the void between life and death. The feast was to distract those who might violate the boundaries on this sacred night, but it was also a farewell dinner for those who were preparing to return to the living, if they were allowed.

At the head of the feast table sat the Dagda and the Morrigan, the King and Queen of the Otherworld, toasting the people at the long table in front of them. These were the dead who had successfully petitioned for their right to leave. To the royal couples right sat the Cerridwen, the Servant of the Cauldron of Life. She was the one who would be approached when those who had won the right to leave decided to exercise their privilege. On any other day their duties consisted of allowing the petitioners of the next life to plead their cases. One by one they came before the Royalty of the Otherworld and asked for passage beyond. The script was always the same; Cerridwen asked the petitioner their name and why they wished to go back. The petitioner would answer respectfully and wait while the Morrigan and the Dagda conferred with their advisors to each side of them...and then the answer came.

*

Erin Smith stood in front of her latest painting, *Judgment*, and answered questions from her classmates on its execution and meaning. She wore paint-spattered jeans and her usual long sleeve black tee shirt with the name of some band that was popular only with the local Goth kids. She wore a clean one today for her semester review at the London School of Art. Her hair was dyed cherry red with black streaks and was a shoulder length blunt cut that she usually pulled back into pigtails. Her brown eyes were heavily lined with kohl, and her lips were resplendent with dark purple lipstick. Around her throat she wore a wide black ribbon with a cat-head dangle charm. As far as she was concerned this would do for a Halloween costume, let everyone tell her that she dressed for Halloween every day. Small and pale, she looked like dozens of other Goth children in the clubs of London, except Erin was eighteen, an American, and struggling with her studies.

"Erin, why do you leave all of your paintings unfinished?" asked her painting professor, Mrs. Rollins. It seemed an absurd question coming from someone dressed in rabbit ears for the so-called holiday.

The students in the class murmured at the answer they expected to hear. Erin was known for her adamant views on everything and anything and the class expected to hear a firm answer. One they could either mock or admire based on their own narrow views of art and the world. They also wore a haphazard jumble of tacky costumes for the holiday, but no one seemed to notice that they were too old to go trick-or-treating.

Erin looked at the painting and brushed her fingers along the bare canvas at the bottom right corner. The rest of the painting was an abstract creation of angry faces and clenched hands done in dark, muddy reds and black. The only bright color was a spot of brilliant blue ethereal wings attached to an eye. Behind the faces and hands was a large grey tree with branches that contained green doors. This had become a theme in Erin's art and she could talk about the meaning for hours.

She sighed and pondered the question. Why couldn't she finish any painting she started? Erin felt it would be better to ask why she couldn't finish anything. She never finished food, finished a book, or completed a painting. She couldn't even plot her own suicide to its final end. The long sleeves she wore hid the cut marks of practice slices that she made when she felt particularly empty. Erin refused to drink or do drugs, she hated not being in control of all her actions, but she could not explain why she would cut her arms with a razor when she was alone and unoccupied with art. The night before last, she had toyed with the razor along her scars and thought about slicing deeper this time, but something stopped her. Something that felt like a hand on her shoulder and a whisper in her ear," *No, this is not the way. Go the other way.*"

But this was today and she stood there and scratched at her latest wounds, they were itchier than usual, and answered Mrs. Rollins's query.

"I don't know," was all she could say.

Judgment

*

Later that evening, Erin watched an old man settle himself on the cold sidewalk outside the McDonalds at Piccadilly Square. He leaned against a light pole and busied himself with items he pulled out of his coat pockets. She sat uncomfortably on her stool inside the greasy-smelling restaurant and ate her hamburger, too far away to identify what held his attention. Her meal distracted her for the moment; it tasted like any other assembly line burger from any other McDonalds in any place she lived. *It never ceases to amaze me.* She thought as she half enjoyed the salty ketchup and the chopped, reconstituted onions. *Everywhere I go, no matter how remote, there's a Mickey D's.*

She resumed her study of the elderly gentleman in his tattered overcoat, non-descript brown slacks and a navy blue sweater that had seen better days. He was becoming as familiar as the pickles on her burger. One semester in London and she had counted ten sightings in as many places, and always he seemed to be searching for something. Erin felt no threat from him, she had lived in Chicago for ten years and was used to homeless people to the point of being able to assess someone's potential for danger within seconds.

This is England after all, she mused to herself, *no one here packs a gun and the fights all seem to be contained to sporting matches and pubs.*

The homeless were plentiful in this city known colorfully as 'bloody, poxy London.' The only difference between these people and the street people of Chicago, other than an occasional weapon, was the eye contact. The panhandlers in London kept their heads down when they held out their begging cups to request change and did not heckle the colder hearts that had none to spare. Ironically the receptacle of choice in both places was usually an empty McDonalds coffee cup.

Once again proving that fast food has become the religion of choice to subjugate and control the masses. Erin thought as she guiltily ate the last bite of her burger. Normally she shunned the doors of what she considered to be a slave-wage market that ruined the environment and caused poor health, but she was sick of English food. *If I eat one more piece of fruit that tastes slightly of fish-meal or eat one more dinner that comes with minty peas I'm going to become anorexic,* she resolved.

Erin listened to the sounds of the restaurant and eavesdropped on the couple in the booth to the left of her. They were arguing in a manner that was uniquely American, loud and with drama, oblivious to others around them. She suspected him of hitting on her girlfriend while he accused the same of being a liar and a slut. *How boring,* she thought as she dunked, nay bathed, her fries in ketchup. *Who decides how much salt to put on fries, and why ketchup?* She mused. *The English like malt vinegar on their "chips" and the Dutch use mayo.* She smiled as she changed the subject in her head. *Such deep thoughts, perhaps I need to bring a book for times like this.*

Hoping to occupy her mind with something more interesting, she looked back out the window and wondered what kind of life did the old man have, and how did he come to his current fate? He looked up from his task, whatever that was, and stared at her as if in answer. Erin did not avert her gaze, his eyes had a familiar warmth, and for a moment she felt a strange kinship with him.

Do I know him? She thought to herself. Relatives of infrequent visit filed through her head but none matched those wizened eyes.

A touch on her shoulder asked for her attention, and she turned to see the man from the street at her elbow.

"I have been looking for you. It's nearly time to attend the judgment." He said with quiet concern.

Erin sat up quickly and almost fell off her stool. She looked back out the window to where the man had been moments before to see him shuffle past the crowded street, his profile toward her, munching on French fries. Erin's eyes went wide as she turned full toward where the same man was standing beside her...and he wasn't there.

What the... Her head felt light and she braced herself against the table with both hands. *Am I hallucinating, is the salt and boredom getting to me?*

She glanced back at the remnants of her meal and found that her fries were missing. She looked on the floor but they were not there either.

Did that old man... Maybe he?... I... think it's time for bed... and perhaps I won't eat junk anymore... my body... no... my brain can't handle it anymore. Erin puzzled over what had just happened as she gathered up her things and tossed her remaining food in the trash.

*

After a long shower and a cup of tea, Erin picked up a newspaper and began to read. The headlines were not as shocking as the ones in America, but every so often a horrendous story made the front page. *Woman Kills Husband of 25 Years- Feeds Flesh to Children. I hope she hangs,* Erin thought before continuing on to the less gory articles. She was suddenly too tired to care about the upcoming exhibits and openings around London and decided to lie down on her dorm-sized bed and read a book about Pre-Raphaelite Femme Fatales. *These chicks knew the score,* she thought as she leafed through the stories about women who lured men to their doom.

Her concentration kept drifting to the sounds of traffic outside and the noises of the building. Erin heard a few dorm mates coming down the hall and chattering to each other.

"I'm going to get soooo drunk," said one voice.

"How's my costume? Is there enough cleavage?" said another.

Morons, she thought with just a hint of jealousy.

Her stomach gurgled, not settling well after the junk she had eaten. *My next answer to "Would you like fries with that?" will be a definite no and keep the burger too.* Fortunately sleep overrode the nausea in her belly and the book soon lay unread on her chest.

*

Erin felt herself drift through a green field toward a cottage. It had a thatched roof and stone walls, but no window glass. The wooden shutters were thrown wide to welcome the summer sun, and she drifted inside. Below, Erin saw a girl about twelve years old, dressed in a clean peasant's frock and long sleeve shift. She was sitting on one side of a large wooden table peeling potatoes. Her long brown hair was pulled back in a single braid and a healthy glow was on her skin from laughing. Her brown eyes sparkled with glee while an older man with a face Erin couldn't see clearly whittled a piece of wood while telling the young girl a story that must have been funny. Erin strained to see the old man's face, but her attention kept going to the figure of a cat that he was making. It was sleeping, curled up with its tail tucked under its chin. He added the eyes and the whiskers with a few deft strokes, then inspected it one last time and gave it to the girl. Erin watched the old man reach across the table and she extended her hand to take it as though she were now in the young girl's body. Her eyes met his eyes, green with brown rings and gold flecks . . . just like the man at the restaurant.

*

Erin sat up in bed, her book falling off her chest and tumbling to the floor. Her reading light was still on and the bedside clock revealed that she had been asleep for only twenty minutes. Embarrassed by how easily this short REM journey had startled her, she leaned over the side of the bed to retrieve the fallen book. On the floor where the novel should have been was the whittled cat from her dream. Erin's chest clenched and her heart beat faster with surprise.

I have lost it! I have really, truly lost it! she thought with alarm. Erin spent the rest of the night with every light in the room on.

*

Saturday morning found Erin overtired and restless. Everywhere she looked she saw reminders of something familiar, but somehow unremembered. She found it unnerving to sit still, but the more she moved about the more restless she became. Finally she decided to go to the National Gallery for inspiration and meditation.

In the tube station Erin thought she glimpsed the old man, and was both disappointed and relieved when it turned out to be a different but definitely homeless man. She placed a quid in his cup and proceeded to her stop. *That could be me one of these days if I don't get my act together,* she thought.

On the train she saw two young men pretending not to look at her. The pair wasn't English and when they saw she had noticed their attentions they smiled. Erin felt a moment of panic, her mind told her they were harmless tourists from America who recognized a fellow American, but her eyes saw something else.

*

Two young scruffy faces smiled at her from the yard. She was inside the cottage again, but only saw the old man and not the young girl. He was outside speaking to the two men. They had approached the cottage on horseback, and led a line of three other horses behind them. Erin recognized two of the animals as belonging to neighbors. She wondered what these men were doing with the property of the Erskines and the Halorans. Both were young and dressed in slightly tattered clothes. One wore the jacket of a soldier and the other a thin coat that was once fashionable but worn through at the elbows. Erin got the impression that the men were neither farmers nor employed . . . and probably trouble.

She did not hear them speaking but could guess what they were saying. The one in the soldier's coat was demanding her Grandfather's horse for a paltry sum. The argument went back and forth, with the rude young man quoting the recently passed penal laws that forced Catholics to turn over any horse worth more than five pounds for the sum of five pounds. Her Grandfather argued that he had heard of no such thing, and ordered the young men away before he lost his temper. Erin picked up the short carving knife and concealed it in her apron pocket before going to the door. When she appeared, the men first looked concerned and then amused. The one in the thin coat approached her with a leer on his face.

*

Erin snapped back to reality when one of the men spoke.

"Is something wrong?" he asked with genuine concern, "You look like your blood pressure just went through the roof."

The man next to him nodded, and Erin realized she was clutching her chest with one hand and was flushed with heat.

She took a deep breath and with great effort mumbled, "No, no . . . sorry . . . I'm . . . okay."

Before the two men could say anything else, the next stop was called and she exited the train, leaving the concerned pair behind.

Erin climbed the steps of the underground to emerge at Trafalgar Square. The tourists were doing their usual bit with the bold pigeons there, and she quickened her pace to get to the National Gallery. Her thoughts muddled over these recent events, and she worried that she might need Prozac or some other form of mind candy for the masses. *Screw that, I'm not letting the empire of pharmaceutical overlords take my brain!*

By the time she reached the museum and headed for one of her favorite paintings, Erin had decided that the old man and the grandfather in her dreams/visions were one and the same, and perhaps she was subconsciously trying to tell herself something.

But what could the message be? she wondered.

As she gazed at a pastoral scene, Erin thought the cottage looked familiar. Even the old man driving the cart looked like . . . well, the old man.

Just as this thought passed through her head she felt someone sit down beside her. She turned, knowing it would be the old man, and raised an eyebrow of silent inquiry. He smiled, and the space around them vibrated softly while a low buzz made her head feel thick and heavy. She closed her eyes but opened them again when he laid a gentle hand on her arm. The noise and sensation evaporated and she found herself still sitting on the museum bench but now surrounded by a green meadow. In front of her was a water fountain of a simple design, round with a spiral design carved along the rim. It was made of obsidian and water bubbled down from the sky to fill it.

"I need . . . some . . . answers." Erin managed to stammer in a near whisper.

The old man patted her arm reassuringly before beginning, "These things are never easy to do in the short time we need to do them," he said, more to himself than to Erin. "I was your grandfather in your first life on earth, and I have been asked to be your Guide to a judgment before I myself walk through the passage of rebirth."

Erin blinked twice and asked, "I am being judged?"

"No," he quickly answered. "You are to be the judge."

"The judge of who?" she asked.

The old man looked back at the well, but did not take his hand off her arm. He seemed not to be looking at the water but beyond it, and after a minute of reflection finally spoke. "You will judge the man that killed you."

His words hit Erin in her forehead, where her spirit, or nethereye, would be. Her mind flooded back to the memory of her last minutes on earth when she was a young girl in Ireland in 1705. She saw the two young men grab her grandfather, one punching him across the temple hard enough that he crumbled to the grass. She took the knife out of her pocket and ran at the man who was about to kick her grandfather in the chest. His companion moved to catch her and took a cut across his face for his trouble. Screaming, he clapped his hand to his cheek and let her go. The assailant of the old man looked up just as Erin stabbed him in the stomach with all her strength. It had all happened within seconds, and before she could scream or run, the man she had cut first put a knife to her throat and slashed her through.

In real time Erin sobbed into her hands until her grandfather placed his arm around her. "There now girl, it's been a long time ago, and you have much time ahead of you."

Erin gained control of herself and pulled a wad of tissues out of her coat pocket to blow her nose. Wiping her tears, she composed herself before speaking. "Did you survive?"

"Ah lass, you were always concerned with my health before yours." He said with a smile. "I lived only long enough to see you die and to see the one who slew me die as well. The one who killed you placed our bodies and his companion's inside our cottage and burned it down after ransacking it. He would not hang for stealing the horse of a Catholic, but he might for killing an old man and his granddaughter."

"So he got away with it?" Erin asked.

"In this world, the physical world, he went unpunished for your death, but in the Otherworld, where we all must pass before moving on to a new life, he is punished," he replied, and then added, "Come with me."

They walked toward the well while he talked. "When you died, you passed to the Otherworld where you existed for several years." He took a cup from the edge of the well and filled it half full before handing it to Erin.

"This isn't going to trap me here forever, is it?" she asked.

The old man laughed, "No you will not become Persephone in Hades. This is the Well of Memory. It is necessary for you to recall your life here and the ones you lived on earth. We want to do the Judgment quickly and without distressing you unduly. The longer you are here in your current form, the more danger there is of remembering this place when you go back. I'm sure you realize that would not be right."

Erin thought it would be fine with her, but she accepted the cup and took a sip. Her grandfather added, "Do not worry if the memories do not come right away, sometimes it is difficult."

But Erin did not feel distressed as thoughts flooded her head and embraced her mind. She knew the stone walls that were now forming around them. Trees of the Otherworld filled her peripheral vision, and she smiled with the joy of knowing she had climbed every one of them. This world was like the inside of a castle and the outside in a park tumbled into a maze. The sky was nighttime dark, but the light felt like dawn to the east and sunset toward the west, and the effect was intoxicating.

"I remember now, I loved it here. I didn't want to leave," Erin said as she looked around. Ten yards in front of her was a spiral staircase carved from an impossibly large tree. The steps were two feet deep and five feet wide at their narrowest. Branches and roots seemed to reach out in all directions. Lights adorned every appendage, dimly lit but in a large enough quantity to create a marvelous beacon against the endless sky and landscape. This was the tree she had sketched, doodled, and painted over and over again. Erin had spent nearly fifty years in the Otherworld climbing up and down the Tree of Knowledge, exploring the branches and the rooms they led to. Her own sleeping room had been located in a lower branch looking over an ethereal forest of Othertrees. These were the spirits of trees on earth, for only trees could exist in both the Upper and Other world at the same time. They were immune to the process of death and rebirth of the soul. The ancient druids understood this fact and used the natural portal of a tree to try to commune and gain favor from Otherworlders. Sometimes they had succeeded. Erin shivered at the memory of watching an Otherworlder attempt to achieve power over the living Druids by asking for sacrifice and sex-magic. But the ephemeral fairies were everywhere in the Otherworld and reported all activities to the council. They meant no harm but they were tattle-tales, she recalled. The Otherworlder had met a harsh fate, with penitence extracted for his victims before he was judged and declared unforgiven.

Grandfather spoke, "We must be hurrying to court, lass, your case will be coming up soon." He gestured toward a tall clock to their left. It was a large and grand construction embedded in a stone wall. The timepiece made no noise as it marked off the minutes and hours from the Upperworld. It also displayed the day and year. A larger clock dial marked off Otherworld time, which was measured in larger increments. Essentially the time on each clock face was equal minute by minute, but the Otherworld clock was in literal alignment with the Sun and Moon. No months or leap year were displayed on this dial, only seasons and major events like Samhain and Solstice. Below the two great dials were scrolls in gilded frames lined up on the wall. They announced the events of the day in beautifully written calligraphy. Erin clearly saw her own announcement, **Liam Healey: to be judged by Mary McLean of 1705**. Below the title were details of the event and a ticker counting the minutes down till the appearance.

Judgment

The two walked past the Tree of Knowledge and entered a clearing where a large stone wall held a closed pair of ornate giant doors closed. Metalwork in the shape of a large spiral covered the wooden doors. Two guards were posted, one at each door, each holding a long spear and wearing a dagger at their waists. They were dressed in violet leather pants that were fitted but well made for fighting. Their shirts were white and their vests had the emblem of the spiral the same as the door. Erin followed her Grandfather as he approached the guards.

"Good day, do you have business with the council?" The taller guard asked.

Grandfather answered, "My once granddaughter, Mary McLean, now Erin Smith of the Upperworld, is to judge Liam Healey."

The second guard consulted a scroll on the wall behind him and turned back before stating, "Yes we have been expecting you."

The taller guard bowed slightly to Erin, and spoke, "Welcome back. If you have any questions while inside the court, address them to your guide first and he will direct you."

"Thank you," answered Erin. As she walked in behind her grandfather, she lost herself in memories. "Mary McLean, that was my name for 12 years above and 55 below. She recalled that amid her wanderings of the endless and beautiful Otherworld, she also longed to see the Judgment of the one who slew her. She harbored a hatred for Liam Healey that worried the fairies and the council until they asked her to appear before them during a Beltane meeting. In the Otherworld, Samhain was a feast before judgment and Solistice the time of rebirth, but Beltane was a time of reflection and planning. At this time the council concerned themselves with citizens of the Otherworld who were unhappy and festering in pain or regret of their past lives. A common theme in the Otherworld was "Renew and move forward." It was a farewell saying that was the equivalent of "Have a nice day" in the Upperworld.

Erin had chosen not to go through the rebirth during her fifty-five years in the Otherworld. Instead, she had delighted in exploring the realm and had marveled at the endless feasting, games, and conversations that, when alive, she had not been able to afford. But she had also dwelled on the past. She had dwelled on the murder and the tragedy of her first life and that of her grandfather. She had even taken to haunting the area where she was murdered, hoping to hear news of when Liam would die and be forced before her for Judgment. Sometimes she would sit over a scrying bowl for days and try to communicate her hatred to him. This was a violation of Otherworld rules, but she no longer cared. She knew she would deny him the luxury of a day's rest in this peaceful realm and call for his Judgment the moment he died. It was her right to call Judgment if she existed in the Otherworld when Healey died, but it was his right to call for his own judgment once his penance was served. When Erin had existed here as Mary she had seen at least two hundred and fifty Judgments, but she had been perplexed when the council had summoned her during the Beltane time, when Judgments were not done. They had questioned her about her activities in this realm and when she intended to proceed to the rebirth ceremony. Erin pronounced that she would not go until she had condemned Healey to the Afterdeath.

The Dagda himself had reminded her that a verdict before a trial was not the way things were done.

Erin had recklessly answered, "Even if I have to go to hell with him I will condemn him no matter what, no matter when."

It was these words that brought red to her cheeks now as she realized she was only moments away from going before the court, and the Dagda. *Please let him not remember me*, she thought.

As they entered the courtroom, Erin and her grandfather were greeted by a female clerk who quietly asked their names before checking her roster. Once she was sure they were participants and not observers she led them away from the visitor area to a line of

Judgment

oversized chairs built into the wall. The architecture in the Otherworld was reminiscent of Celtic design and natural bloom. Trees grew at regular intervals, pruned to look identical, yet each one was still unique. Fireplaces were positioned to cast a warm glow throughout the courtroom and to prevent dark corners where conspirators might gossip. Even the vines that grew around the rafters of the tall ceilings and the posts that supported the walls tangled in an orderly and balanced fashion. It was as if disorder were in bad taste once anything entered the court. The clerks also wore uniforms that featured a symmetrical leaf design, appearing as a natural extension of the nature around them.

Erin sat down next to her grandfather and noticed there was room for a third person on each bench. She had never sat in this area before, and had only observed from the raised gallery at the back of the court. The seats were cushioned in green velvet and they relaxed in comfort for the moment. Her grandfather leaned over and whispered, "Do you have any questions, my dear? Do you remember how the proceedings go?"

Erin whispered back with just a hint of her old malice, "I remember enough and I already know what my decision will be."

"Granddaughter, please do not pre-judge the accused. The Morrigan does not look kindly on those who do not listen before they speak."

"I am sure I will be attentive and she will not look upon me as disrespectful, Grandfather, but I do not now nor have I ever understood why you forgave the man who killed you and allowed him to go through the rebirth without penalty?" she nearly hissed in her effort to be quiet.

Her grandfather looked a little hurt and somewhat disheartened. He turned away for the moment, and missed the instant regret that crossed her face. He turned back and before he could speak she said softly, "I'm sorry. I don't mean to hurt you." Then she took his near hand in hers and squeezed it lightly.

He squeezed her hand back and spoke, "You have a right to

your anger, and some of it is the pain of having lived only four times, and short lives each time."

Erin felt immense shame. She could recall all of her past lives, and was well aware of her suicides in the last two. The torment she felt in her current life was the same torment she felt in the lives she had lived since the first one when she was murdered. Each time she had come back to the Otherworld she had tormented Liam Healey as he carried out his tasks as a servant. The penance for most murderers was a life as a servant for the ones who did not take life. Liam had been sentenced to clean the floors of the court and to repair the endless walls on the landscapes of the Otherworld. Those who were to be judged took turns cleaning the court floors as a reminder of their own coming Judgment. Erin knew it was bad manners for a victim to torment her accused while they was serving penance, but each time she saw him she called his name and sneered at him. She sought him out just to make sure he knew she was still waiting for him, but he had born it with good humor and continued his chores in silence. It infuriated her, but she could not judge him till he served his full term of penance.

Her grandfather's voice interrupted her train of thought. "I have done seven lives now, and my happiest was with you as my beloved grandchild." He paused, then continued before she could answer his declaration of affection. "My dear, I have the advantage of six lives that were well lived, but I also hold the memory of my second life, when I was not a kind or innocent man."

Erin was stunned for a moment. It had never occurred to her that her Grandfather had lived a life that was not . . . her grandfather. Thoughts swam in her head. *Why did I never ask? Am I so young that I cannot see beyond myself?* . . . and finally, *What did he do?*

The old man sensed her last question and spoke in a low, quietly guilty voice. "I killed many people, and burned many villages as a Viking long before they knew the shores of Ireland. I was a raider and a..." He stopped and looked aggrieved but did not continue this line of thought. Instead he continued in a different direction. "... if it had not been for the mercy of the Morrigan and the Dagda, who are the only ones who can judge a man who has killed in times of war and famine, I would have been condemned by my victims to go to the unknown, the Afterdeath." Tears ran down his face now and he reached for a kerchief in his pocket.

Erin rubbed his back and felt both guilty and foolish. "I'm sorry." She said again.

"No, no lass . . . I am the one who is sorry, I should have told you this when we were together here in this world. But I was afraid. You were so angry and upset over your own loss of life and mine that I could not face you." He sat up a bit and wiped his face before continuing, "I went through the rebirth ceremony to avoid telling you and spent my last life regretful and depressed." He turned and looked at Erin with full attention. "My dear, dear granddaughter, do not allow yourself to carry bitterness from one life to the next. I know that the life you live now is sad, but it is sad because you feel unfinished. It drives your...suicidal ...well, it controls you."

Erin was stunned. She knew every word he said was true and while it felt difficult, she became aware of a deep calm pushing away the rise of panic that came at his word . . . unfinished.

At that moment another court clerk, this one male, walked up to the pair and said quietly, "It is time...please come with me."

Before the Court, Erin stood in her dirty jeans and t-shirt. Her Grandfather was a few feet behind her in case she needed support. Erin did not feel she needed any help at this point. She was well acquainted with the process, but understood why someone might want a guide to stand with them. She could not imagine the bewilderment a newcomer might feel to these proceedings. Her lack of balanced and Otherworldly attire made her feel very shabby in front of the spectacularly dressed court and attendants, but her lack of fine clothing was secondary to the embarrassment that grew as the Dagda and the Morrigan looked her over.

The Cerridwen approached, wearing robes of light green with the pattern of the trees stitched throughout them. She held a large scroll and unrolled it gracefully, then announced, "Mary McLean versus Liam Healey," to the Royal Court in a voice that sounded like life itself. The Cerridwen spanned the world between life and death more closely than any other soul dwelling in the Otherworld. It was the Cauldron of Renewal that lent her this advantage over death. Hers was a position, like all Royal positions in the Otherworld, which was bestowed by the reigning monarchy to the next holder of title. To be the Cerridwen was to be declared the holder of life itself. Her Cauldron was under constant protection by her own personal guards, two of which watched over it now. One male and one female, they would send those who would drink from it without permission to the Afterdeath before they had a chance to let its elixir allow them to cross back to the Upperworld.

After announcing the case to the Royal Court, the Cerridwen handed the scroll to the male clerk who now read the charges, "Mary McLean, now Erin Smith, stands before us. She has been summoned by her assailant Liam Healey to judge him."

At this cue, Liam was led into the room to stand off to one side, but in full view of both court and Erin. He wore gray robes with a swirl of patterns resembling birds and dogs, symbols of his violence on earth. Erin felt a quick shiver run through her shoulders as sweat beaded her brow. She worried she might faint. Sensing her discomfort, her grandfather stepped forward to touch her shoulder. She turned and patted his hand before speaking. "I'm okay. I'll be all right."

When Erin turned back the Morrigan was smiling at her. Erin was overwhelmed by the woman's beauty. Even as a child she had stared at her, afraid to meet those emerald eyes that danced with knowledge and concentrating instead on her heavy curls of dark brown and robes that were stitched with thread that sparkled like diamonds. Her pattern was that of the Triskelion, representing the three phases of women, Maiden, Matron and Crone.

The Morrigan addressed her, "As you are in the middle of your fourth life, I shall address you by your current name . . . if you don't mind?"

This was less a question than a command, and Erin bowed in agreement while murmuring, "Thank you."

The Morrigan grinned slightly. Erin loved that smile as did all, or most, of the inhabitants of the Otherworld. It was the knitted brows and frown that everyone dreaded. The Morrigan was loved but feared. She suffered no fools and looked upon everyone as her children, as was her right. It was rumored that she had lived a hundred lives before earning her term as the Morrigan from the previous one.

"Erin," she began, "It is unusual for someone to be summoned from their current life to judge someone from their past, but not unheard of. Liam has been a servant here for two centuries in penitence and has spent this time atoning for what he feels was a horrendous mistake. He now has the right to wait for your death in relaxation and if you deem it, to be Judged."

The Dagda gestured that he wished to speak, and the Morrigan nodded her relinquishment. He had silver gray hair pulled back in a long braid and a tightly cropped beard. His eyes were blue and mirrored in them was a great deal of pain and woe. Crows' feet creased the edges and revealed his constant worry. He had confessed to one hundred thirty-five lives lived and had patience, but could be very distant. His robes were dark blue and patterned with the symbol of the Stag, as his was a position as consort and protector of the Morrigan, though his position was equal to hers.

"Young lady," he started, "I remember your determination to convict this man, and as I wish to get you back to your current life as quickly as possible, I will be blunt."

Erin felt her heart beat hard in her chest, she was uncertain at a time she thought she would be brave and determined.

The Dagda leaned forward and continued, "Liam has violated a basic law ... the requirement that the dead not interfere with the living."

Erin knew this law, and had violated it herself when she had tried to torment Liam long ago. She looked over at Liam, but he did not return the glance, instead he was looking twice as nervous as she felt. *Good, you should be shaking.* The thought gave her courage.

The Dagda continued, "He sought to influence your life so you would not cut it short by your own hand a third time."

Erin felt intensely aware of her heart in the back of her throat now as the Dagda continued. "He has prevented you from cutting your own wrists on several occasions, and while his intentions were good, he has still broken the law—"

The Morrigan interrupted at this point, sounded like a scolding mother, "My dear child, you have thrown away the precious gift of life twice and without thought of those you left behind. The grief you have caused is selfish and unforgivable."

Erin suddenly felt as though she were the one on trial now, and her eyes watered at the thought of her past failures.

The Dagda placed his hand on the Morrigan's arm. She quieted noticeably, and he continued for her, "Erin ... Liam has decided that if he cannot 'stay your hand,' he will give up his right to wait for your natural death and allow you to judge him now. He knows the consequence could be your condemnation, but he hopes it will allow you to take this weight off your soul and move forward ... to live this life to a natural end."

Erin felt her head spin, it was all too much to take in. *Liam* had been the presence that kept her from making that final cut. She looked at him directly. Yes, it was him she had felt each time she was alone and distressed, loathing everything she could not finish and herself. He met her gaze and smiled weakly.

"May I address my accuser?" he asked the court timidly.

Judgment

Both the Morrigan and the Dagda nodded their consent, with the Dagda commanding, "Just be brief and mind your words, we cannot keep her here much longer."

Liam bowed while murmuring his thanks, then turned to Erin. "I have no excuse for what I did beyond greed and fear. I knew this for all sixty years of my life. Then, for the next two centuries I watched you on Earth as a child and sometimes here when you returned as well. I felt horrible shame when you took your life the first time. I knew it was your subconscious hatred of me and your fear of life that kept you from living fully.

"The next time you returned to the living I secretly delighted in your every word and action. It was as if you were my own child and . . . and my shame . . . my guilt was immense. I had no right . . . to harm you the first time . . . I'm sorry, I sound like a dottering fool. All these years I've practiced what to say to you, and it isn't enough. But I need you to know that when took your life again . . ." he stammered and tears filled his eyes. ". . . I knew I needed to make sure . . . I mean, I've watched you as I've watched my own children . . . when you died . . . I'm . . . I'm horribly sorry . . . I know it's not enough, but I am deeply and truly sorry. Please, judge me, for better or worse, please judge me and live." He was sobbing now and no one comforted him. Both the Dagda and the Morrigan looked at Erin, avoiding his shame.

Erin looked at him, feeling conflicted over what her grandfather had told her about his own past but also feeling the knot of hatred that she had fostered for this man. This hatred burned in her now and she did not see the pathetic plea before her. She saw a vicious youth with a knife. *He's like half the people in prison, more sorry they got caught than sorry for what they did. Why should I believe him?*

Erin spoke her thoughts out loud, "Why should I forgive you? You didn't kill in self-defense or by order of your King in time of war. You preyed on an old man and his granddaughter!" Erin paused as she realized she yelled her last question. *I need to be calm,* she thought before continuing. "How do I know you aren't lying to me, to the court? How do I know you won't go back and commit worse crimes? How do I know it was you who stopped me from killing myself?"

Liam looked stunned and was about to say something but the Dagda spoke first. "Young lady, I can assure you that the Watchers..." he gestured to the myriad of glimmering blue lights that were actually small fairies who reported the activities in the Otherworld to the council, "... observed this man stop you from suicide on two occasions in the last six months. That fact is not open to question." He stated firmly.

Erin felt humbled and continued in a less defiant voice, "I'm sorry... I have to believe the Watchers of course, but how do I know he is sorry? How do I accept the apology of a man I have hated for so long?" Her eyes began to water much to her own dismay and she turned to look at her Grandfather. He stepped forward with a nod to the court and spoke quietly to Erin.

"My dear, you are becoming hysterical." He embraced her and whispered in her ear. " Remember, this is for you. You can forgive him and move on with your life, or you can condemn him and still move on with your life." He then released her and spoke normally. "Do what you feel is right."

Erin felt better and her thoughts became more coherent, *I was wrong to take my own life. I know that. I know I need help, and I know it was Liam who stopped me from suicide. But I also know he had no right to take my life in the first place... my god, I sound like a whiny child. People die every single day from hundreds of diseases and wars. Famine takes the life of thousands every year, but who gets judged on that? Government? I can't keep letting my own tragedy run my life.*

As her Grandfather moved back to his position, she looked back to where the prisoner was standing and knew what to do. Liam seemed scared but resigned to whatever would happen next.

He was avoiding her gaze.

How dare you not look me in the eye, she thought.

Erin walked over to where Liam stood. At her small height she looked into his face and he could not avoid her. The guards did not move forward, as they did not perceive Erin as a threat. The court, however, took great interest in her movement and everyone became quiet.

"Liam Healey," Erin started calmly, "You look me in the eye and tell me you were wrong."

Liam seemed stunned by what she asked, but quickly met her gaze and answered, "I was wrong and I am sorry." The answer sounded sincere, and he did not drop the gaze until he was done.

"Fine, then I know my verdict," she said out loud without taking her eyes off of his face. Then she slapped him, hard.

Liam reeled from the slap, he had not expected one and was not braced for it. He fell to the floor as the spectators of the proceedings gasped.

"What do you think of that?" she asked him.

"I think I deserved it." He answered as he rubbed his offended cheek without moving to get up.

"Good," she answered as she held out her hand to help him get up. "I forgive you."

Liam rose with her aid and looked surprised, "Thank you."

The Dagda smiled, suppressed a chuckle, and spoke, "I believe we have a verdict."

The clerks announced the verdict, and Liam was led away to prepare for his renewal ceremony with the Cerridwen. He looked back at Erin before leaving, and smiled, then bowed to her. She did not respond.

Her attention was then commanded by the words of The Morrigan, "Erin Smith, thank you for your time, but Samhain is about to end, and you need to return while it is still easy for you to pass through. Please hasten, as we don't want you to be stuck here until next year's Samhain. Farewell, renew and move forward my dear."

Erin followed her grandfather, back outside but by a side door so they did not have to walk back through the gallery of spectators. *I have to go back to my life now.*

As they approached the Well of Memory, her grandfather spoke, "I wish we had more time, but we have only a minute to get you through the veil safely."

Erin hugged her grandfather and told him, "Thank you, I'm not sure what to say other than I loved you very much." Tears again welled in her eyes.

Her Grandfather smiled and agreed, "I know lass, I know. I loved you more than anyone I knew in the past."

Erin was about to say more but was stopped by him, "No, no there is no more time for words now. Walk past the well and through the shimmer you see behind it and hurry. There are only seconds left," he said urgently.

Erin didn't waste any time, she remembered the stories of those who became stuck in the veil. They rarely survived with their sanity intact. She did not hesitate at the veil, but stepped quickly through, then found herself walking down a city street in London.

She could remember what had just happened, but it was fading fast. *I want to remember! Maybe if I try to hang on to the images in my head.* Erin struggled, but her body felt as light as her head and she wasn't sure if her feet were really on the ground. She stopped walking and thought she might faint till she saw the old man from McDonald's next to her.

He placed a comforting hand on her arm and said, "Are you alright my dear?"

"Yes, yes . . . I think I'm just hungry." She answered and looked at her wristwatch to see that it was quite late, a minute past midnight to be exact.

Erin heard him mutter, "Well goodnight then, you best be off home."

She looked up to see him walk away, but he was gone, and by the time she realized it was dark and she was definitely hungry, she had forgotten all of it.

Across the street was a fish-n-chip shop with a small sign stating it was the best in town and open late for pub hours. Erin walked across the street and decided to judge for herself. She ordered a large helping and sat herself at one of the small tables inside. The shop was noisy and people were talking to one another about nothing in general. She looked at the malt vinegar when she saw no ketchup on her table and much to her own surprise tried it on her chips.

Pretty good, I would say this is the best meal I've eaten in a long time. Then while she munched on the last of her fish and chips she thought of her next painting and it was complete in her mind. Erin sketched it quickly on a napkin and headed toward her studio to start it.

CRITICAL VIOLATION
Daniel Myers

Back in 2003 I stumbled upon the Writer's Symposium panels at Gen Con. This was a bit of a revelation, because it showed me there was a place where all of my interests could come together. Two years later I was participating in the panels and giving seminars about medieval European cooking and how it relates to both gaming and writing. Since then I have been slowly (and painfully) developing my skills as a writer. I seem to be drawn to stories of a rather grim nature (a compulsion which sometimes worries me). Add that to my other interests, and I guess it's not too surprising that I'd write a horror story from a cook's viewpoint. If you're interested in my historical cooking research, I keep it all online at MedievalCookery.com.

Juan slammed the door and slumped against it, the chef's knife held loosely at his side all but forgotten. Moments later he heard a soft thump as something pressed against the other side. An image leaped to mind, one of something small and furry and . . . no! It just wasn't right. He glanced around, hoping for something else to think about, anything. He stopped when he saw the empty basket that had held granola bars. It had all started with the granola.

*

He'd been head cook at the lab for a little more than two years, charged with the task of providing breakfast, lunch, and the occasional dinner for a hundred and fifty or so scientists, and in all that time he'd never had any problem with pests until the past week. The kitchen was top-notch, which was quite a relief in comparison to his previous assignment. There he'd been working by himself in a converted closet, making lunches for a couple dozen computer geeks who only wanted pizza. Here he had all new equipment, an assistant, and free reign over the menu. The customers appeared to be happy with anything he made. He didn't even have to worry about the budget—the government paid for whatever he ordered, no questions asked. Then early last week, Tony came out of the back room while they were cleaning up.

"Boss, you need to see something. I think we've got mice."

"Mice?" Juan was sure he'd misheard, and he started going over everything they'd received in the latest delivery that sounded like "mice."

"Yeah, it looks like something has chewed into the case of granola."

Chewed. He was talking about mice, the animals, real mice. Crap. That could be a big problem.

"Ok," Juan said, "I'll be there in a second. Oh, remind me to order some more oyster crackers. I think the guys in the bio section are stealing them to feed to the animals."

Tony laughed and went to collect the trays.

Juan finished wiping down the steam table to buy some time to think. It could be worse. The factory where he once worked had vermin. Every morning he had to wipe the droppings off the cutting boards, and the plant foreman kept telling him to shut up and do his job. After landing this new job, it took months before he no longer felt tainted somehow. Sill, mice were a critical violation of the health codes. They carried diseases and got into everything, and one mouse seen usually meant dozens unseen. He had to do something or it would just get worse. Juan tossed the washcloth into the bucket of sanitizer, took a deep breath, and headed to the storeroom.

A glance around didn't reveal anything out of place. He checked the shelf by the box of packets of gourmet granola, but everything looked intact.

"Not that stuff," Tony had followed him. "The big box in the back corner, next to the cleansers."

Juan bent down to look at the bottom shelf. The granola bars had been a miss-order. Last month he'd meant to get a single box to give the scientists an option for a healthy snack. What was delivered was a full case. If he'd thought about it he would have returned them, but no, he'd opened them up and put some out. Almost none of them sold. No one liked the healthy granola bars. They all wanted the soft, chewy, chocolate-covered ones.

He'd stopped wasting counter space on them, and instead tried crushing some of them up as a topping for yoghurt. No one liked yoghurt parfaits, they wanted pudding with banana slices, vanilla wafers, and whipped cream. Juan gave up on the granola altogether and the rest of the case had sat mostly ignored.

The front of the box looked okay, but there was a scattering of crumbs on the floor. A little way under the shelf he saw more crumbs and some droppings. Juan pulled the box forward to check, and sure enough there was a hole the size of his fist chewed in the back. He started to pull out the bars that had been torn open and noticed that they were months past their expiration date. The whole case was. That made things easier, as the whole thing could go in the trash.

The rest of his evening was spent checking boxes and bags. Every shelf was emptied and wiped down with bleach. Then he swept and mopped the floor. Hopefully it was just a field mouse that had managed to get inside. He wanted to tell the facility manager and have her bring in someone professional, but that could mean closing down the cafeteria, possibly for weeks. He couldn't do without the pay, and Tony probably couldn't either. He'd try to take care of it on his own, and if it turned out to be more than an isolated thing then he'd go to her.

On his way home that evening, Juan stopped at the hardware store and bought a package of mousetraps.

*

If only it had been so simple, Juan thought as he sat with his back against the door. On the other side there was a soft brushing sound, as something moved back and forth against it. Juan scrambled to the other side of the room, his back pressing against the cold steel of the walk-in refrigerator's door.

His throat tightened and breathing became difficult. Were they chewing their way in? They didn't move fast, but they didn't stop for anything. A small pink paw poked under the door, scratched weakly at the floor a couple of times, before it withdrew. He looked at the knife in his hand and then quickly back to the door.

Someone would come to help him, but would they get here in time?

Several days ago, when he came in before dawn to prep for breakfast service, he'd found a rat caught in one of the traps. It was still alive, but wouldn't last much longer. The spring arm had snapped down on its neck. Juan put on a pair of disposable gloves, and used a broom to sweep the rat, trap and all, into a dustpan. He took it out to the Dumpster by the loading dock—there was no way he was going to just throw it into one of the kitchen trash cans. He set the dustpan down by the Dumpster, peeled off the gloves, and went back inside to wash his hands.

An hour later he went back out to see if it was dead yet. The rat was still alive, and had somehow managed to drag itself and the trap off behind the Dumpster. It moved, seeming no weaker than before. He put on new gloves and used the broom handle, first to drag the rat and trap out into the open, and then to bash the rat over and over until at long last it stopped moving. The rat, trap, dustpan, and broom all went into the Dumpster, followed by the gloves. Back inside, Juan washed his hands three times while feeling like a sissy for overreacting.

On the way home he picked up some bigger traps, this time made specifically for rats. Two days later when he came in for the morning, all the traps were full.

Again the rats were all still moving, but given their state they shouldn't have been. These all looked like something had been chewing on them, with cuts here and there and the odd missing piece of tail. To make matters worse, the rats all reeked of spoiled meat. They had to be diseased. This time he put a plastic bag over the end of the broom and used it to push the traps into a cardboard box. With gloved hands and at arms' length, he carried the box out to the Dumpster. The smell that came from the box was horrid, and it was all Juan could do to keep from throwing up. As soon as he was back inside, he called the facility manager and left an incoherent message on her voice mail that basically said he'd seen a rat. She called back and told him that an exterminator would be in later in the week. She suggested he set some traps in the meanwhile.

Juan went numb.

The next time he took out the trash he found the cardboard box on its side, empty. On the other side of the driveway, a feral cat sat motionless, watching him. Juan picked up the box and gagged as the smell of it washed over him. He tossed it into the Dumpster and went back inside to wash his hands.

*

That smell was hard to forget. Juan looked down at the knife in his hand. His favorite knife, its broad ten-inch blade had a dark smear on one edge. Not blood, not exactly. There wasn't anything nearby that he could use to clean it off. It really didn't matter though. He didn't think he ever wanted to use it again, at least not on food. He looked around the room and wondered how long the emergency lighting would last.

How long had it been since the lab went on lock-down? The messages over the PA had stopped what had to be hours ago.

How much longer would it be until someone came to get him?

There had been some loud bangs, possibly gunshots, and he'd

expected that someone would knock on the door at any moment. Then there was silence and he waited, and as the silence grew so did his doubt.

In the days after finding those first rats it almost turned into a routine. He'd get in before Tony, as usual, take the full traps with their struggling victims to the Dumpster, mop and sanitize the floor, place new traps, and then check through the stores to throw out anything that had been chewed on. On his most recent trip to the Dumpster he'd noticed another cat across the driveway, unmoving. It stared at him, waiting. That would have been okay, after all, cats are weird. But this one looked a bit mangy, almost like it had been chewed on. It didn't wander around, or hide, just sat and looked at him without even the slightest twitch of a tail.

Juan hurried back inside and pulled the door shut behind him to make sure it was tight. At least he hadn't seen any rats other than the horrible ones caught in the traps. Of course, until the banquet he hadn't had to be in the kitchens at night.

*

The dinner was an annual thing for welcoming new interns. The scientists always wanted the same food every year—roast beef, garlic potatoes, green beans, and chocolate cake. It went off without a hitch, and the scientists appeared to love it, but Juan probably could have cooked it in his sleep. Tony helped with serving and keeping the coffee urns full, and then stayed for the cleanup, happy to pick up the overtime.

After they had run the last load of dishes through the Hobart and sanitized the counters, Tony said goodnight and left Juan to lock up the office. That was when the alarm went off and the lights went out, leaving Juan standing in the dim glow of the emergency lights.

Juan thought it was a fire alarm at first, and was almost out of the cafeteria when the words over the PA system finally sunk in.

"SOME ANIMALS HAVE ESCAPED FROM THE BIO-TESTING SECTION. THERE IS NO IMMEDIATE DANGER. PLEASE REMAIN IN YOUR WORK AREA WITH ALL DOORS CLOSED UNTIL FURTHER NOTICE."

Juan thought about leaving anyway, but figured it would be pushing his luck. They always fixed these things pretty quick. He could kill the time with a game or two of solitaire on the computer in the office. As he turned back, he saw a dark shape at the bottom of the cafeteria doors. A large rat was squeezing through the gap under the doors. Once through, it stood still for a moment, and then moved slowly toward him, pausing every few feet to sniff the air.

Juan wanted to run, but his feet froze in place.

The rat shuffled into a clear space between tables about ten feet away, and now Juan could see that this one looked just as bad as the ones in the traps. Its fur and skin had come away in patches, and its tail was mostly gone, but the worst part was that much of the skin on its head was missing, letting the skull show through. It sniffed the air again, and then crept closer.

Juan backed through the cafeteria, through the line, and to the back room, watching as the rat continued its slow approach. There was a rack of knives at the prep area on his right, so he grabbed one without taking his eyes off the rat.

He could kill it, it wasn't moving that fast, but still he didn't want to get that close. Maybe one of the traps? He backed into the storeroom, carefully picked up one of the large rat traps, and stepped back to the door.

The rat had passed the last of the tables and reached the cashier stand. Much farther and it would be in the kitchen, where there were a lot of cabinets and shelves and places to hide. Juan knelt and slid the trap across the floor toward the rat.

Perfect!

The trap skidded to a stop inches from the rat's bony jaws.

The rat didn't flinch, but continued forward, not interested in the bait. It looked like it would climb over the trap and miss the trigger completely when it managed to bump the bait. Juan thought he heard the crunch of bone as the trap snapped shut. He stepped closer to get a better look.

The trap had struck the rat on the back, near the tail. It had snapped hard enough to sever the rat's spine and hind legs. It was lying belly up and twitching. Juan waited for the involuntary movement to stop, but instead it seemed to move more as the seconds passed. Then the rat managed to roll over. It lifted its head and sniffed, once, twice, and then slowly, struggling, turned in his direction. It dragged itself toward him, leaving a smear of black in its wake.

Juan stared. It should be dead, it had to be dead, but it was still moving, still seeking him out. It inched closer, driven by unfathomable purpose, and he could only watch.

Then a scratching sound broke the spell.

Juan looked up to see more shapes squeezing in beneath the cafeteria doors. He looked back to the horrible thing crawling toward him. It was just feet away, but he had the knife.

He crouched, getting just close enough to hack at the rat, and brought the knife down. The first swing was a bit off and only managed to sever one of the remaining legs, but the rat simply kept pulling itself forward as best it could, sniffing and snapping its teeth. Juan did better with his next couple of swings, chopping the rat into several pieces that twitched a bit but couldn't really move.

He ran back to the kitchen and to the loading dock, only to stop short. Near the Dumpster, faintly glowing with the emergency lights behind him, were the eyes of several cats, all unmoving. The wind shifted and he was almost overcome with the stench of corrupted flesh. Suddenly the cats lurched toward him, ungracefully moving from side to side. Juan retreated back inside, pulling the steel door shut behind him. He dashed back into the cafeteria, and saw that not only were there several rats, but there were also larger creatures outside, all pressed up against the windows, too dark to see clearly.

*

The stench of the decaying animals hung heavy in the air. He heard them moving everywhere, scratching at the door and the walls, trying to find a way in. Heart hammering madly in his chest and breath coming ragged, Juan looked for something . . . anything . . . that could help him. His eyes paused on a cardboard box. He'd first found the rats in this very room. They'd found a way in before, and that meant it was only a matter of time before the rest of them found a way in. Something "shushed" against the ceiling tiles.

He pressed against the door to the refrigerator and felt the cold metal behind him.

The walk-in! He'd be safe there. The walls, ceiling, floor, and door were all stainless steel. There was no way for them to chew through that. He pulled the lever to open the door, and the cool, clean air puffed out across his face. He flipped the switch to turn on the lights, but nothing happened. There was no emergency light in the fridge. He'd be sitting there in the dark. At least the compressor was off, so it should warm up in there after a bit. Hopefully he wouldn't suffocate.

Juan stepped inside, and as he pulled the door shut behind him he heard the sound of things falling from the ceiling.

He sat in the cold darkness, listening to the soft sounds against the door and trying not to picture what was happening outside. He tried to not make any noise, not even breathe too deeply, in fear that it would attract more of them.

His mind raced wildly. How could this have happened?

One of the rats had clearly eaten the granola before it turned into . . . whatever it had turned into. The granola had been stored with cleansers and was expired. He'd tried to feed the granola to people too. Was he to blame for all of this?

No, that was stupid. Even if the granola was spoiled and contaminated with floor polish, the worst that could happen was that it could kill someone. There was no way it could turn a rat into a monster.

There was a loud crash from outside the fridge. Something was out there, something big.

Then something heavy struck the refrigerator door . . . once, twice, three times.

Not quite knocking, but not pounding either. Much too high up to be a rat and much too loud. Was someone trying to rescue him? Was someone else trying to escape the rats?

Juan held the knife in front of him, not knowing what to expect. There was a click as the latch for the walk-in door was pulled. The door opened and light streamed in silhouetting a man. Relief flared. It was Tony.

But then Juan's heart seized. Tony and his clothes were torn and covered in blood. He looked as grotesque as the rats.

Juan wondered if Tony had eaten any of the granola.

Time War
~ A Crimson Story ~
Stephen D. Sullivan

Award-winning author and artist Stephen D. Sullivan has been working professionally in fantasy storytelling since 1980. He's contributed to projects ranging from Dungeons & Dragons *to* Star Wars *to* Teenage Mutant Ninja Turtles *to* Chill *to* Wabbit Wampage. *His comic* The Twilight Empire *ran for more than 4 years in* Dragon Magazine. *He worked with the Writer's Symposium in its Milwaukee days. In all Steve's work—including more than thirty published books—he strives to both thrill and entertain his audience. He hopes that you will enjoy this new Crimson story—which ties together many diverse pieces from his career—and he'd love to hear what you think of it. Join Steve in his next adventure by signing up for his newsletter and getting other cool free swag at:* www.stephendsullivan.com. — *Adventure guaranteed. (Monsters optional.)*

Our sasquatch battalion storms up the time fortress's left flank, throwing scorpion riders into the abyss along the way. The enemy's ZTZ-99s roll out in defense, so we send our dragonfly squadron on a bombing run, knocking out several of the tanks and pushing the bulk of the enemy's defenders back toward the citadel. Naturally, they call in a retaliatory strike from their starfighters. As is usual with these things, the whole situation rapidly degenerates into a shitstorm of blood and guts and firepower. If war is hell, then Time War is a quadruple-scoop of hell with flaming jalapeños on top.

Magical and technological bolts of energy blaze through a sky filled with stars, planets, galaxies, and some forms of cosmology I don't recognize. The landside battlefield is a broad two-dimensional checkerboard, suspended in thin air, surrounding the fortress. Neither the heavens, the earth, nor anything else around us seems possible—and, of course, without the time meddlers, it wouldn't *be* possible.

My name is Crimson, and today, I'm a grunt. Being semi-immortal, I get swept up in this kind of thing more often than you'd probably believe. Sometimes I even survive. Most who live through a Time War forget it ever happened. *I* remember—thanks to the "gift" from the gods who put me in this situation. That and a talent for killing things is probably why I've been chosen to lead the infiltration squad on the right flank.

While my team is going in on the right, Carnelian Fyre's troops are keeping the enemy busy on the left. Yeah, *that* Lian Fyre, the hero of the Fourth Wizard War—the Fire Mage who can toast you with a glance. I know. I thought she was dead, too. But who knows what portion of space-time the meddlers plucked her out of. We've met before, she and I, either in my past or her future. So, for me, this battle feels like a Warrior Chicks Reunion Tour: Lian and Crimson together again, for the first time. *Scarlet Fire and Red Death* the troops called us—among other, less repeatable things.

My team's job—and the job of our counterparts on the other flanks—is to get inside the fortress, find the woman responsible for this mess, and put both her and the time vortex out of commission. Why? Because you just can't have folks messing around with the timestream, screwing up quadrillions of innocent lives.

Some immortals never learn; they have a pathological need to "fix" the universe, make it over in their own image. So, when this particular galaxy-spanning squabble broke out, the demi-god on our side—Tanalon, Lord of Order—scooped up heroes from all of time and space to prevent his nemesis—Yathmog, Lady of Chaos—from fucking up the cosmos beyond all recognition.

While Lian, the sasquatch, and the rest are keeping things nice and toasty on the left, my squad moves among the troops on the right, looking to bust into the citadel. My infiltration team includes a time traveler known as The Professor and a demon-borne assassin named Pietro "Orm" Ormin. He's the muscle, I'm the finesse, and the Professor is the brains—at least, when I'm not being the brains.

Under covering fire from our dragonfly corps, we make it to the base of the citadel—an architectural monstrosity that looks like it's been cobbled together using cast-offs from all of time and space. I spot a medieval cathedral, a Frank Lloyd Wright building, a Zeppelin, and some kind of gossamer-rigged sailing ship, among other elements, all topped off by a 20th century Russian space rocket, which serves as both an observation tower and a gun emplacement.

My team mingles among the troops—which we hope will conceal us as we break off from the main force and enter the citadel on the sly. Most of our soldiers are samurai turtles, and they're making hay out of Yathmog's Blackwater Mercenaries. (Bitch demi-goddess should have known better than to bring hired help.) Just when it looks like the turtles will wipe out the last of the mercs, Her Wickedness 'ports in the storm troopers. No, I'm not talking about the pansy clones in plastic armor, I mean the real thing.

Of course, there *had* to be Nazis; you can't have a Time War without Nazis. Troopers versus turtles heats up real good, even before the goddamn flying monkeys start swooping over, throwing poo at everyone. The chaos buys my team the time we need to sneak inside the fortress. The Professor uses his cell phone to reprogram the lock on a hidden maintenance hatch, and we're in like Flynn, unnoticed.

None of us expects that will last.

You don't get to be an evil demi-god by leaving a lot of chinks in your defense, but this conflict is so big, some areas are bound to remain vulnerable. The last thing I see as we duck inside are a bunch of chainsaw-wielding rabbits fighting against Neanderthals with Tommy Guns; I have no idea which ones are on our side.

My team and I have a good fix on the location of the time vortex. You need a lot of shielding to protect that sucker, so it's housed in a spherical metal chamber—like a gigantic natural gas storage tank—in the middle of Yathmog's architectural nightmare. We figure that the demi-goddess will be hanging out there, directing the action and making sure things fall the way she wants once the vortex stabilizes. We need to stop her before then, or the Queen Bitch gets to remake the game in her favor, permanently. Other stealthy assault teams will be heading in that direction, too, as well as our main forces. Hopefully, the body of our army will distract Yathmog's internal security and give one of the smaller groups the chance to get through and settle her hash for good.

"Watch yourself!" the Professor warns as Ormin steps toward a doorway that looks like a submarine hatch.

The big man glances back at him but keeps going. I flatten against the wall, pressing the Professor back with me, as Orm crosses the threshold. The fire that bursts from all sides of the portal would cook most people—but I guess there are advantages to having your soul melded with a demon. Orm stands in the conflagration, his armored body seeming to swell in the flames. He sweeps the perimeter of the door with his double-edged sword, shattering the flamethrower jets. His leather-and-plate armor smokes a little, but his hair isn't even mussed when the fire dies away.

"Coming?" he asks in a deep, grim voice.

"You could have been killed," I say.

He turns away. "If only it were that easy."

"It just might be if you keep charging ahead like that!" the Professor responds. "Yathmog knows we're coming now! Didn't you see it was a trap?"

Orm shrugs. "I saw. I just didn't care. Let's get this done."

"Just give me a minute..." The Professor fiddles with his cell phone again, and it emits a high-pitched squeal. The lights go out in the corridor; a moment later, dimmer ones come on. Apparently the Prof can do everything with that gizmo except change diapers. "Okay. Done. I set up an EMP and knocked out all their surveillance and electronics on this side of the vortex."

"Can we go now?" Orm strides down the corridor without waiting for an answer. The Professor and I follow, me hoping his electro-magnetic pulse worked as well as he claims. I don't like working with people I've barely met, but in a time war, one has little choice. I'll just have to trust to luck, Tanalon's good taste in warriors, and my usual skills and equipment. My gear—chainmail, a sword, and a knife in each boot—is not ideal in this kind of temporal clusterfuck, but it's a lot more than the Professor is packing.

The three of us keep moving toward the center, me following my warrior-honed senses, Orm his inner demon, and the Professor checking a readout on his phone. True to the time traveler's word, the surveillance all seems to be knocked out. We don't run into any other traps, either. But that doesn't mean Yathmog hasn't left a few surprises to bar our way.

We turn out of the submarine-style corridor and into an arena-sized chamber filled with machines. Some of them seem to be men mounted atop the bodies of metal spiders; others look like trash cans with black basketballs and lasers stuck on top. Apparently, we've stumbled onto Yathmog's army reserves. That brings all of us, even Orm, to a halt as hundreds of gleaming metal eyes turn and focus on us. Apparently, the EMP didn't affect them.

"Martian Cybos and Robotitons!" the Professor announces. "Back the way we came!"

We turn and run as mini-guns chatter and energy bolts fly. One blast catches Orm in the back, and he grunts in pain—so I know these weapons aren't to be trifled with. It takes a lot to hurt the demon-borne, though the hit doesn't come close to stopping him. There's good chainmail under my maroon tunic, but not good enough to stop this kind of firepower. With angry, metallic cries of "Annihilate!" the mob is after us like hell hounds scenting blood.

"Take the third turn on the right," the Professor calls, lagging slightly behind Orm and me. "That should loop you around toward the vortex."

I glance back at him. "What are *you* going to do?"

"Buy you some time." With that, he presses a button on his cell, and a blast door slides down between us and him, leaving the Professor trapped on the far side with the metal monsters.

I pause, reluctant to leave him, but Orm grabs my arm and yanks me forward. "Make it worth it," he says. "Don't let his sacrifice be in vain."

We start running again, taking the corridor the Professor indicated. The passageways seem impossibly long—the building bigger on the inside than it was on the outside. I guess if you can violate the laws of time, you can bend the laws of space as well.

As we run, Orm keeps glancing back over his shoulder.

"Did the machines get through?" I ask. "Are they coming?"

He shakes his head. "Don't you hear them? Don't you *smell* them?"

Before I can ask *"Hear and smell what?"* he turns, just in time to intercept a hairy body hurtling through the air. His sword flashes and a huge wolf falls to the floor, cut in half. I get my silver-traced blade out in time to put three feet of steel through the eye of a second wolf, trying to pull me down from behind.

"You shouldn't have done that," says a voice even deeper and gruffer than Orm's. "It would have been much easier if you'd died quietly—easier for *you*." A feral hulk of a man steps out of the shadows; behind him, a dozen more wolf eyes gleam.

"Sorry we killed your pets," Orm says, not meaning it.

"Scurry off before we kill you, too, Furball," I add. I'm happy to avoid this fight if possible; it will only slow us.

"You misunderstand," the feral man says. "They're not my pets, they're my *people*." And with that, his body changes, bulking up and sprouting hair, becoming a veritable man-wolf.

In response, Orm changes as well, his body swelling, his face assuming a fiendish countenance—the visage of the demon-borne. "Go, Red Death!" he tells me, his eyes burning with rage. "Complete the mission! I can handle these dogs!"

He charges the man-wolf and its minions. One wolf lunges for me as I turn to leave, but Orm lops off its head before it can pass him. Then, the man-demon and man-wolf crash into each other, the pack swirling and snarling around them. Again, I have to trust my companion's choice and keep moving.

"Happy hunting!" I call to Orm as I run deeper into the fortress.

I sprint down a damp stone corridor, like a passageway out of a medieval dungeon. The tunnel debouches into a broad courtyard open to the stars. On the far side, I see the dome of the vortex chamber.

As I run into the yard, an armored figure steps out to bar my way. He's dressed in black and silver, his armor composed entirely of moving shapes—snakes, scorpions, spiders, centipedes. His face is pale, his eyes violet, and his hair almost silver. With leisurely grace, he dons a horned black helmet.

I know who this is. He's a faerie war-master named Kalil. He's greatly feared on Illion—a world I've lived on occasionally. They say that he's immortal, and that he can kill anything. But he hasn't met *me* yet.

Then I notice his sword; it's not the one he's renowned for carrying. Clearly, Yathmog has bribed him with a present. Its blade is midnight black, traced with ever-changing runes. It's one of the few things I fear in the multiverse—a soul-stealer.

I've lived many lives, but the chances of being reborn are dim if my spirit is trapped within the blade of a sword. I know that even a scratch from this kind of weapon can debilitate, and a solid hit... Well, let's just say that I don't intend to find out if his blade is stronger than my "gift."

He strikes like a cobra, silent and swift, with a powerful, straight-forward thrust, but I'm ready. I parry high and heave to the left. The soul-stealer hisses as it slides against my silvered blade. I let the strength of his counter-parry force my sword to the right—straight at his neck. He wheels away and slashes at my back on the follow-through. But I spin as well, and his blade misses me by inches. We complete our turns and face each other once again.

"Good," his cold voice says, and he laughs under his breath.

"It gets better," I reply.

He lunges. I slap parry and thrust at his outstretched shoulder. The point of my blade traces a gash up the surface of his deltoid. Instantly, his armor repairs itself, the metal creatures weaving their tiny bodies back into a single whole. He slaps his blade back against mine, and my whole body shudders from the impact. He cuts at my exposed flank, but I lean aside, and he only catches my arm with the flat of his blade. The force of the blow still sends me sprawling.

I crash onto my backside and skid across the paving stones, my arm and shoulder numb where the soul-stealer touched me. *And it didn't even break skin!* He's laughing in earnest now as he casually walks toward where I lie sprawled.

"You've some talent, girl," he admits. "Maybe in a few more lifetimes..."

With one swift move, I draw the obsidian dagger from my left boot and throw it into his eye socket. "... Maybe then you'll be able to keep up with *me*!" I say.

Kalil screams with rage but, annoyingly, he doesn't die. Instead, half-blinded, he rushes me. I barely get to my feet in time to parry his arcing swing. Again, the impact from the blow shakes my body to the bones. I fall, roll, spring back to my feet, but he's still on top of me. *Fuck!* Never taunt a faerie war-master!

I parry two quick cuts aimed at my neck and breast, and then kick his left kneecap with all my might. My blow yields a satisfying crunch; the knee buckles, and he stumbles. A defensive swing of his sword keeps me from going in for the kill, so I back away, trying to gain a moment's respite. He pulls my obsidian blade from his eye and hurls it at me.

Luckily, being half-blind, his depth perception is for shit, and he miscalculates the distance; it's only the butt end of the knife that smacks into my left temple. Still, the stone hits with enough force to make me see stars. My knees go loose, and it's only his wounded leg that slows him enough to keep me alive for a few more seconds. I blink, trying to clear my sight, but he's on me, single eye blazing with hate. He bats aside my parry, and my silver-traced blade flies from my hand and scuds across the courtyard.

I know I'm screwed.

Then a hulking shape lunges between us, and double-edged blade clangs against soul-stealer. "Red Death!" Orm shouts, concerned. Though I can barely focus through my concussion-induced haze, I'm very happy to see him. He locks swords with Kalil, and the two of them grapple, like bull oxen, struggling for supremacy.

"When I give you the chance," Orm roars, "take it!"

"Two can die as easily as one!" Kalil hisses.

As if to prove his point, he shoves Orm away and, in a viper-quick move, stabs at my friend's belly. The blade finds a chink in Orm's armor and plunges deep into the demon-borne's gut. I gasp. Kalil laughs, but Orm smiles grimly. He wraps his bulky arms around the faerie war-master and holds him tight, presenting Kalil's back to me.

I draw the flint knife from my other boot, hurl myself at Kalil, and plunge the blade into the back of his neck, severing the spine. Not even a faerie can survive that kind of blow; he slumps to the pavement, dead.

Gasping, Orm pulls himself off Kalil's sword.

"Gods, Orm!" I cry, knowing that, in an instant, he too will fall—his soul sucked from his body. But Pietro Ormin doesn't fall. Instead, for the first time since I've known him, he looks *happy*. His body has changed, too. He's smaller, his armor barely fits him, and his face is no longer angry but rather, serene. He hardly seems to notice the wound in his side, which I can see—thankfully—missed hitting anything vital. His eyes gleam.

"I'm . . . free!"

I realize then what's happened. The soul-stealer ripped the demon from his body, while he—Ormin—remained. It must have taken amazing willpower to force the demon out and not be taken himself. Tears bud in the corners of my eyes.

"Free!"

I re sheathe my weapons and then pick up the soul-stealer. Orm quickly bandages the wound in his side. "Come on," I say to him. "We've got a job to finish."

Just then, the entire fortress shakes as a huge roar shatters the air.

"What in the Seven Hells?" Orm says as the Russian rocket, formerly the tower of this strange citadel, lifts off into the galaxy-filled sky.

"That, unless I miss my guess," says a familiar voice, "is the proprietress seeking greener pastures."

The two of us turn to find the Professor strolling across the courtyard toward us. He glances at his cell phone as we watch the rocket climb into the darkness.

"You mean, one of the other teams got to Yathmog?" I ask. "We've won?"

He checks his cell and shakes his head, holds up a finger for patience, and glances at the retreating missile, then says, "Two . . . one . . ."

KA-WHOOM! The whole rocket goes up in a burst of red fire and black smoke.

As the flaming pieces of the missile fall back toward the

citadel, the Professor smiles. "*Now* we've won. Of course, we've still got a bit of tidying up to do, shutting down the time vortex and such, but, I'd say... Yes. We've definitely won." Then, noticing Orm's transformation, he adds, "What the devil happened to you?"

Orm smiles—a genuine, human smile. "I won, too."

"How did you escape the machines, Professor?" I ask.

"Oh, quite easy, really," he replies. "I set up a feedback loop. Shorted out the whole lot of them. Pretty brilliant, if I do say so myself."

I smile. "And you do."

"Let's finish our mission," Orm says. "I want to get on with the rest of my life. I've been looking forward to it for so long." He sprints toward the submarine-like hatch, leading into the vortex dome, on the far side of the courtyard.

As I follow, I notice that Kalil's body is gone. Goddamn faeries! It'll take him a while to reform, though. At least the warmaster is out of this battle.

"No! Wait!" the Professor cries after Orm—but the warning comes too late.

As Orm opens the hatch, jets of bright orange flame stream out from all directions, engulfing his frail human body. He's dead in an instant, before either he or I can scream.

"Goddammit!"

"I'm sorry," the Professor says, evincing more resignation that sadness.

"What the hell?" I rage. "What was the point of that? We've already won!"

He takes a deep breath. "Winning doesn't mean the fighting is over, Red Death. There's always more work to be done."

"Then deactivate that fucking trap and let's get to it."

He nods, does so, and we step into the dome of the time vortex, avoiding the remains of our friend as we go. Stepping over what's left of the demon-borne tears at my heart.

The room is a sphere of white metal, and we enter through a hatch halfway up the wall. There's a balcony, around the room's circumference, with high-tech instrumentality on all sides, pointing toward the center—which is filled with the time vortex. The vortex itself is almost impossible to describe; it's like a whirlpool sucking in the whole of time and space. I can feel its power tugging at my hair and clothing. When I look at it, I see pieces of the past and the future—some of it my own, most belonging to the rest of the universe. Some is glorious, much terrible.

I look away, fighting the urge to dive in. The maelstrom's power is difficult to resist.

"That's the control panel, unless I miss my guess," the Professor says, pointing to the far side.

To me, it looks like something out of a Flash Gordon serial—buttons, flashing lights, and arcs of electricity with a large triangular viewscreen in the center.

"From there," he says, breathless, "Yathmog could put the universe to right."

My eyes narrow and my gut goes cold.

His eyes sparkle playfully. "Or what *she* saw as right, anyway. Let's see what we can do with it, shall we?"

We circle round the platform, avoiding the vortex's gorgon-stare. We're almost to the machine when space rips open and Tanalon, the Lord of Order, steps through. He looks like a wizard, all flowing robes and white beard. In his left hand, he holds a large silver bag.

"Well done! Well done!" the demi-god says, beaming. "I chose my team well."

"So, Yathmog died in the explosion, did she?" the Professor asks.

"Not quite," Tanalon replies. He reaches into the bag and pulls something out—the scorched and bloody head of his ancient enemy. He tosses Yathmog's head over the balcony railing and into the vortex. The maelstrom quickly pulls her into a billion particles and scatters the remains across all of time and space.

"There," he announces, pleased. "Now it's done."

"And Lian Fyre and the others?" I ask. "They lived?"

"Most of them, yes. And don't you worry. I'll put them all back, right as rain—even the ones who died. I daresay most of them won't even remember the experience."

"Except in dreams—or nightmares," I add.

"What about the losers?" the Professor asks.

Tanalon shrugs. "Who cares? The universe is better off without them."

"And Ormin?" I say.

"I'll put him right as well," the demi-god replies. "It will be just as though he'd never been killed."

"So he'll still be cursed—still demon-borne?"

"Yes. I'm afraid that's the way it must be. He has a part to play, and he must play it—as I'm sure you both know."

The Professor nods sadly. "So we can shut the vortex machine down, then."

"Oh, I think that would be a bit hasty," Tanalon says. "It seems a waste to have come this far and not . . . spruce up a few things, now that we have the chance. In moments, the vortex will be stable. Then I can start setting things right."

I walk past him, examining the machine. "So you *can* fix things?"

"Yes, of course," Tanalon replies. "The things that *need* fixing."

"Just like Yathmog would have done," the Professor notes.

"No. No. Not like that," Tanalon sputters imperiously. "I'll be making things *better*—stopping the spread of Yathmog's cult and the Orlakai—things of that nature."

"Yes, that's *very* different," I mutter.

He turns toward me, but by then I'm already moving. I thrust the soul-stealing blade clear through his chest and out the other side. The demi-god gapes as the weapon drinks in his immortal essence. Tanalon is only an empty, disintegrating husk when I kick him off the blade. His body falls over the railing and into the vortex. I toss the sword in after him, and both disintegrate into the nothingness of never-were and never-will-be—vanishing down a hole, straight to the end of the universe.

The Professor's jaw hangs slack for once, speechless.

"He was just like her," I explain. "Just like Yathmog. One was order, the other chaos, but they were both *wrong*—manipulating people's lives, treating us like playing pieces, every one expendable—just like gods and would-be-gods everywhere."

The Professor cocks his head and cracks his neck. "Well . . ." he says, "I suppose it may have been necessary. After all, nothing good ever comes from meddling with time on that scale."

"You're a bit of a time meddler yourself, Professor."

"In future, I'll keep that in mind," he says. "Assuming you don't want to kill me now."

"I was kind of hoping you could fix things," I say. "Not in the way that *they* intended—just back the way they were before all that . . . meddling. Although, if you could . . ."

The Professor sighs, and in his breath I hear the experience of many years, many lifetimes—and wisdom matching that longevity. "I'm afraid Orm has to stay the way he was when he entered this war."

"Yeah," I say, resigned. "I figured."

"Tanalon was wrong about many things, Red Death, but he was right about that," the Professor continues. "We can put the universe back, but it has to be the way it was—not the way we want it to be. We *can* make things better, of course. We just have to do it one little piece at a time—not by mucking about with the continuum."

"You can do that, though. Right? Put things back the way they were? I was pretty much counting on your being able to fix the universe when I killed Tanalon."

My companion rubs his hands together enthusiastically. "I'm the Professor! I can fix anything! Well... except for plumbing."

And fix it he does, his hands flying across the controls of the vortex machine almost faster than I can watch. On the viewer above the panel, I catch images of others returning to their times: Lian, doomed Ormin, the samurai turtles, and the sasquatch... even the Nazis—may Hitler and his spawn burn in Seven Hells forever.

Then it's done, and the Professor presses the "call" button on his cell phone.

The air shimmers and his time machine appears out of nowhere. It's a surprisingly flimsy looking device—all Victorian knobs and crystals combined with trappings of Orientalist design—not the proud, adventurous ship I was expecting.

"We should get going," he says. "I've set Yathmog's citadel to self destruct. Can't have it falling into the wrong hands—again. It'll wipe out this part of the continuum, too. Fortunately, this whole parsec is uninhabited. Care for a lift, Miss...? You know, Red Death, I don't believe I ever caught your name."

"Crimson," I say. "Just Crimson. And I don't believe I caught yours, either, Professor."

"Herbert," he replies. "But my friends call me George." He gives me a boost into the saddle of his machine. It's a bit cozy, but he's a pleasant enough companion to travel beside. "So, Crimson, where do you want to go?"

I smile as the vortex chamber fades into oblivion around us. "Surprise me."

THE FOURTEENTH VIRTUE
Anton Strout

"The Fourteenth Virtue" was originally published as the lead tale in the DAW anthology The Dimension Next Door. *I actually sold the story in a bar over drinks at Gen Con, where many a bit of business is transacted, no doubt. Kerrie Hughes and John Helfers had met up with me for the first time that year to discuss the state of the publishing business, what with my day job being with Penguin Group USA and all. They mentioned one of the anthologies they were working on concerned alternate worlds and the like. It just so happened that I had a short story on a thumb drive, one set in my Simon Canderous series that concerned a noted historical event from my world. I was all bummed out because it had just been rejected for a different anthology, but I told them about it – the end days of Benjamin Franklin, Necromancer – then slotted my thumb drive into Kerrie's laptop, and by morning I had a sale ... and a bit of a hangover.*

As I mentioned, I am the author of the Simon Canderous urban fantasy series for Ace Books, including Dead To Me, Deader Still, *and* Dead Matter. *I've also appeared in a variety of anthologies – some of which include Simon Canderous tie-in stories – including* Boondocks Fantasy, The Dimension Next Door, A Girl's Guide to Guns & Monsters, Pandora's Closet, Spells of the City, *and* Zombie Raccoons & Killer Bunnies. *Currently I'm hard at work on the next book featuring Simon Canderous, and you can always find me lurking the darkened hallways of www.antonstrout.com.*

"I suppose I don't so much mind being old as I mind being fat, *dead*, and old," said the dried humanoid husk, pausing to catch its breath on the stairs down to the villa's catacombs. If an evil, undead creature had breath to catch, that is.

I leaned against the stairway wall, thankful for the respite myself. Forty-six was far too old for an agent of the Fraternal Order of Goodness to be chasing down the undead, especially if that agent was a research archivist like me.

Evil radiated from the necromancer like a fire's heat in the dead of winter. Yes, I had been hunting the undead and every other manner of curiosity for all my natural adult life, but to catch up to *it* after all those years was on par with discovering the lost city of Atlantis or Shangri-la.

"My name is Thaniel Graydon," I said with a mix of fascination and horror. "And your unnatural life ends here, Necromancer."

My instructor from Opening Threats would have cringed at how pedestrian my declaration must have sounded, but given the dire circumstances I was just happy to have gotten it out at all.

The creature gave me a holier-than-thou look. "I would prefer that you refer to me as Mr. Franklin—or Benjamin, if you must. That title is such an ugly moniker, and perhaps the least of the ones I earned in my lifetime."

The moment FOG had caught wind of the necromancer's existence, they'd sent their foremost expert on it – namely me – out into the field, running me ragged in singular pursuit. The modern marvel of Pierre Andriel's steam-powered vessel had carried me safely (if queasily) out of New York Harbor, and within weeks I'd tracked the creature to this Cologny villa just outside Lake Geneva. My life's study had culminated in this hunt, and I could hardly believe I was finally standing face to face with the creature. I was terrified.

Somewhat rested, I pushed myself off the wall and started

The Fourteenth Virtue

closing in on the foul thing, only for it to raise one of its hands in surrender. We were far underground, with nowhere for it left to run. I held my torch up to get a better look in the clinging darkness.

Despite his years of decay, I could still see hints of the human it had once been, but I had to look extra hard. The long, gray hair that ran in a crescent around the back of its head was snarled and matted with mud. Its garb was at least thirty years out of date, and hung off its pear-shaped torso in tatters that had turned a muted brown with age. The stench of the dead that came off its body was overpowering in the confined staircase, but I did my best to hide my discomfort. Thankfully the burning, pitch-soaked rags from the torch helped mask the stink.

The creature started down the stairs again with defeated resolve, beckoning me to follow. I did so with a healthy dose of reluctance, surprised when he led me past the stone caskets of the catacombs and into a small, furnished chamber that resembled a lonely writer's garret. The creature gestured toward a table in the center of the room, covered with books and scraps of parchment. A chair slid back at its command.

"What sort of trick is this?" I asked, feeling both heady with triumph and a little confused. Did it think I was going to sit down and leave myself defenseless?

The creature shook its head.

"No trick, human," said the walking corpse of Benjamin Franklin. "But if I am to be destroyed, I would first set the record straight whereas it concerns my life. My good friend John Adams once said that I was 'more esteemed and beloved than Newton, Leibniz, or Voltaire.' I would prefer to keep matters that way if it can be helped. Now sit."

The words had power in them. Despite my reluctance and fear, I felt compelled to obey. I found an empty sconce along the wall and slid my torch into it, then did as the creature bade. The creature flicked its wrist. The table's oil lamp blazed to life and pressed back the clinging darkness. The creature reached pulled a blank notebook free from the table-clutter and offered it to me. Despite my unease, I took it without hesitation.

When Benjamin Franklin had been alive, my respect for him had been enormous. My life's pursuit had been to set all manner of his arcane knowledge straight for our archives, and I felt excited at the chance to complete this long labor. If things went well, I would finally be able to transform conjecture into testimonial fact and earn a place of respect among my fellow archivists in the Fraternal Order. I was shaking so much I could barely pull quill from inkwell.

After all my years of study, I hadn't come unprepared. I reached into my satchel and pulled out sheaves of parchment I had "borrowed" from the Order's archives. I flipped through the loose pages. Some had been worn or torn by time and most bore writing by hands much older than mine.

I raised a sheet closer to the oil lamp and read from it, always keeping one wary eye on the creature.

"It says here you were born in 1706 or 1705, depending on how you reckon it by calendar," I said. "You moved it when the colonies switched to the Gregorian."

Franklin chuckled, pulled his glasses from his face, and wiped them with the edge of his tattered coat. He fit them back on his face, dirtier than before, but it was no matter – he had no eyes left in the sockets anyway. I waited for him to settle into the chair opposite me, partly out of courtesy but mostly out of mortal fear. Despite his manners, I reminded myself that I was still in the presence of evil.

"Is something funny?" I asked, then quickly added, "sir?"

"If I'm not mistaken, it's 1818 now, yes?" he asked. "It's hard to tell after so much time . . . that would make me surprisingly lively for a man of one hundred and twelve. I'm in the prime of my senility!"

He continued chuckling to himself. Pretty jovial for the

damned, I thought. I looked back down at my papers, grateful to avoid those dead sockets of his, and reread them. "That's what the record shows, anyway. Of course it also states that you died in 1790."

"Don't you think I know when I died, son?" Some kind of bug scuttled out through Franklin;s nostril and across his cheek, then disappeared into the tangle of his long gray hair. He leaned back in his chair. *"In this world nothing can be said to be certain, except death and taxes.* Well, taxes anyway."

"Sorry," I said. I hadn't been expecting to engage in a dialogue, and felt it was better to act as civilly as I could. The creature was congenial now, but who knew what might set off its evil temper again?

What price had this man paid for so long a stay on God's earth? The creature seated before me was a result of a life pulled far too thin by powers I had barely begun studying, powers that I'd still rather not think about. I tapped my quill against the rim of the well, shedding drops of excess ink, and flipped open the notebook.

"Shall we begin?"

The creature nodded.

"If you would not be forgotten as soon as you are dead and rotten," the rotting corpse said, quoting himself again, *"either write something worth reading or do things worth the writing."*

He held up both of his bony hands. Neither possessed a complete set of fingers. A chill ran down my back and a dark smile crept across his face.

"Since I seem incapable of performing the simple task of setting quill to page, I suppose you will have to do. Before destroying me, of course."

All things considered, he seemed to be taking this rather well.

"Naturally," I said. I lowered the tip of my quill to the blank page and started writing.

"The secret history of our United States is dark material indeed," the extremely elder statesman said. Even given his advanced necrotic state, Benjamin Franklin cut an imposing figure. "And if the greater body of historians and their books are to be believed, not a word of it tells the true tale."

I flipped through a few of the historical pages I had brought with me. "We've done extensive research on mankind's transgressions into the arcane arts, and one common thread has run through the last century: they all seem to feature one of our most senior and well-respected statesmen. You, sir."

I sensed a smile on his decaying face, but it was difficult to tell for sure. Then the creature coughed a laugh, a rattling rising from its chest. The sound of it alone made me want to flee in terror. Maybe another agent of the Fraternal Order of Goodness would have fared better: one who hadn't dedicated his life to the pursuit of this one man, wouldn't be taking this task on with so much foreboding.

Hoping to settle myself, I took a deep breath and let it out slowly.

"You try living more a century and see what polymathic accolades *you* garner," Franklin said.

I stopped writing and looked up.

"Polymathic?" I asked, cocking my head. "Forgive me . . . I'm not familiar with the term."

"From the Greek, I believe," he said, and his voice changed. There was an inherent power when he spoke: I understood why people had listened intently to his every word when he was alive. "Meaning 'having learned much.' I have an encyclopedic knowledge of a variety of subjects. Diplomat, printer, author, activist, scientist, inventor . . ."

He tapped his glasses with his decaying index finger.

"And the study of something a little more . . . sinister?" I asked.

The Fourteenth Virtue

He nodded and leaned back in his chair, crossing his legs and resting his hands on his knees. It was such a dainty gesture for so grotesque a creature, I almost laughed.

"There's a danger in being a polymath," he said. "Adams and Jefferson were quoting me when they said an investment in knowledge always pays the best interest. It *is* true that a little knowledge can go a long way, but an encyclopedic amount? Why, it practically begs questions about the natural philosophy of the world!"

"Meaning the dark arts?"

"For heaven's sake, just say it!" he shouted, slapping his hand down on the table. Bits of flesh flaked off the bone onto my notebook. "*Necromancy.*"

Despite my hatred of the practice, I couldn't contain my excitement. "I knew it. All the other agents in the Order couldn't get beyond your early religious ties . . ."

"But not you." Franklin cocked his head as if studying me. His neck clicked and crackled like dried leather. "I wonder why?"

"*Deism,*" I said. "Everyone says your proclamation of being 'a thorough Deist' was a path that ultimately led to God."

"True," he said, "if you follow Deism through to its logical, reasonable, and very *human* conclusion, Deism does lead to God."

I shook my head, thrilled to be engaged in such a debate with one of our nation's greatest thinkers. It was almost a shame I would have to destroy him.

"Perhaps," I said, "but it just doesn't ring true to me."

I grabbed several pieces of parchment and looked back through his history, searching for an answer.

"You yourself said that 'God shouldn't be found in the supernatural or miracles, but through human reason and things we observe in the natural world,' " I said. "I don't think you believe that, though. You've read too much, studied too much of the world. I propose you don't actually reject the supernatural, but you embrace it."

Franklin's silence was all I needed to know I was right. Despite my fear, I dared to stare into his lifeless eyes. He was truly hideous.

"But why this?" I asked. "Why do this to yourself?"

The creature sighed again. A waft of rot filled the room.

"If you are as learned about me as you seem, young man, I'm sure you're aware of my love for puzzles and codes. Again, another polymath trait. If you understood that love, you could have easily found the reason for my transformation. It's hidden within my Fourteen Virtues."

"Thirteen," I corrected. I might not be the foremost Franklin scholar, but I had learned enough about the man to know he had written his famous Thirteen Virtues – a set of personal ideologies he lived by – when he was only in his twenties.

Franklin raised what remained of an eyebrow. "Does it surprise you that I'm still a virtuous man, despite the black art that keeps me in such a state? *There never was a truly great man that was not at the same time truly virtuous.*"

He produced a well-worn fold of paper from his coat pocket, smoothed it out, and pushed it across the desk. I refused to touch so old a document from so foul a creature, instead using the tip of my quill to hold it open while I read.

The Thirteen Virtues – B. Franklin.
1. *TEMPERANCE. Eat not to dullness; drink not to elevation.*
2. *SILENCE. Speak not but what may benefit others or yourself; avoid trifling conversation.*
3. *ORDER. Let all your things have their places; let each part of your business have its time.*
4. *RESOLUTION. Resolve to perform what you ought; perform without fail what you resolve.*
5. *FRUGALITY. Make no expense but to do good to others or yourself; i.e., waste nothing.*
6. *INDUSTRY. Lose no time; be always employ'd in something*

The Fourteenth Virtue

useful; cut off all unnecessary actions.
7. SINCERITY. *Use no hurtful deceit; think innocently and justly, and, if you speak, speak accordingly.*
8. JUSTICE. *Wrong none by doing injuries, or omitting the benefits that are your duty.*
9. MODERATION. *Avoid extremes; forbear resenting injuries so much as you think they deserve.*
10. CLEANLINESS. *Tolerate no uncleanliness in body, clothes, or habitation.*
11. TRANQUILLITY. *Be not disturbed at trifles, or at accidents common or unavoidable.*
12. CHASTITY. *Rarely use venery but for health or offspring, never to dullness, weakness, or the injury of your own or another's peace or reputation.*
13. HUMILITY. *Imitate Jesus and Socrates.*

"Are you familiar with the term deca-coding?" he asked, once I stopped reading.

"It's a coding system based on a system of tens, isn't it?"

"Correct," he said. His mouth split into a grin, bile and blackness showing instead of teeth. He tapped at the folded paper. "Most of the Virtues listed there are the thoughts of a young idealist. What did I know back then? But once I made my choice to engage in the darkest of necromancy, I really only lived by the Fourteenth Virtue. There may be only thirteen on the page, but my coding points to the only one I truly held any real stock in."

I scanned the page, applying his deca-coding. By starting with a base of ten and beginning to count from the top of his list again, it meant the fourteenth virtue was actually the fourth one on the list.

"Resolution?" I asked.

"Resolution. *Resolve to perform what you ought; perform*

without fail what you resolve. Notice I don't bring up whether good or evil fits into that equation."

"But," I pressed, "a resolution about what?"

"The answer lies before you." He pointed at the piles of paper. "Right there in your histories, the greatest and most defining moment in modern history. *The American Revolution.* Necromancy saved that marvelous homeland of ours. After all, I was – and still am – first and foremost a patriot and a statesman."

I sat there in shock as I let it sink in. "You did this to yourself . . . for our country? But you were one of our greatest leaders! You are *the* elder statesman."

"*Many foxes grow gray but few grow good,*" he said, running a hand along the rotting fringe of his matted hair. "With age, idealism melts away in the face of practicality."

"I'm sorry," I said, shaking my head. "I'm still not following."

It was hard to feel remotely smart talking to Benjamin Franklin, no matter how evil and rotten he might be.

"Remember your history," he said. "The Founding Fathers and I were attempting to declare our independence for the thirteen colonies from the British. Despite what other historians have written, the British *would* have easily overrun this country, even given their distance from England. Action had to be taken to 'secure the Blessings of Liberty to ourselves and our Posterity.' "

"But . . . but giving yourself over to the power of necromancy? It's folly!"

"All wars are follies," he said, raising a finger and waggling it at me. "Very expensive and very mischievous ones. I knew what price I paid when I made my bargain."

"Did they know, too?" I asked, writing as fast as I could. I jabbed the quill back into the well whenever the ink started to run dry.

"They?"

I looked up. "Adams, Jefferson, the Continental Congress . . ."

The creature Franklin shook his head.

"I thought it best they never know. *He that would live in peace and at ease must not speak all he knows or all he sees.* Naturally reports came in from the front concerning the American dead. Generals kept sending in accounts of the dead rising from the battlefield and soldiering on against the British. Most of Congress ignored such reports, dismissing them as fantastical, but I think Jefferson had his suspicions. Always the clever one, Tommy was."

What I was hearing seemed unbelievable. "And you were all right with this . . . *bargain* you made?"

The corpse shrugged. It seemed a gesture beneath a man of his stature, even a decaying one. "All human situations have their inconveniences," he said, "but for the immortal, energy and persistence conquer all things. Think what you will of it, but the power over life and death, limited as I was with it, saved this country. Legions of the living dead founded our freedom. Old boys have their playthings, you know, as well as young ones. The difference is only in the price."

He looked at me with those dead eyes again. I couldn't help but turn away.

"Don't judge my actions," he said, his voice sad. "*Any fool can criticize, condemn and complain, and most fools do.*"

*

Franklin rose from the table while I finished writing my account. I no longer felt the need to keep an eye on him. I was surprised to find that my fear had dissipated after hearing his story. I stood and eyed my torch, sitting in the sconce along the wall.

"You seem rather willing to let me destroy you," I said. "You're turning yourself over for disposal? Just like that?"

Franklin nodded as if he were a parent being patient with a small child. "If you prefer, I *could* swarm you with the contents of these catacombs instead."

With a snarl, he held out his arms. The sound of stone coffin lids sliding free rose behind me, followed by the scratching and clawing of bony fingers fighting to get out. I didn't dare look back. I realized how powerless and insignificant I was in this creature's presence and shook my head in response to his offer.

Franklin dropped his arms. The coffin lids slid shut and once again the room fell silent. A lifetime of studying him hadn't prepared me for this. Several lifetimes wouldn't have been enough.

"I've hunted you my whole life. Why are you willing to die now?" I asked, feeling my own reluctance for the task setting in. "Why ever?"

"Other than the fact that you have me cornered and at a disadvantage?"

His empty sockets looked down at my hands. I was still clutching the quill in one and the notebook in the other. I put the quill back in the well and closed the book before tucking it into my bag.

"This is strictly for my own curiosity, not for our archives," I said. Standing toe to toe with this necromancer, I opted for politeness. It seemed the reasonable thing to do. I'd like to think my brothers back at the Order would have been proud. "If you'll forgive me asking, sir, why do you want any of this on record at all?"

The creature made no move to stop me as I headed for the sconce.

"I first met Mary Shelley in the summer of 1816," he said, letting out another dry, earthy sigh. The humanity of it almost broke my heart.

"The writer?" I said, pausing with my hands on the torch.

Franklin nodded. "Of course, she was only nineteen then, and still Mary Wollstonecraft Godwin. She and Percy hadn't married yet, but that was when she found me."

"Found you?"

Franklin cackled, sounding for once like the evil undead thing that he was.

"My dear boy, it wasn't as if she were looking for me specifically. She simply chanced upon me here in Switzerland that wintry summer."

I stared at him, confused. "Wintry summer?"

He took on the tone my grandfather used when he was recounting his service at Lexington and Concord. As I pulled the torch off the wall, it settled heavy in my grasp. Setting Franklin aflame was going to be harder than I imagined.

"Once I had 'died' for the sake of my country," he said, "I fled the now-United States of America in the hope of obscurity in foreign lands. I found a certain modicum of peace here, high up in the Swiss Alps. All of Lake Geneva had fallen under a volcanic winter that summer, thanks to the untimely eruption of Mount Tambora the previous year." He raised his hands and examined them for a moment, as if he were seeing the skeletal appendages for the first time. "By that point of my transformation, the cold didn't bother me much. Few things did at that point. Anyway, if it hadn't been for that damned book she insisted on publishing, you might never have found me."

"Her damned book?" I repeated, moving back around the table towards him. "You mean *Frankenstein*?"

"You've read it?" he asked, with genuine interest. "It's only been stateside a few months, by my reckoning."

I paused. "Yes ... but what does it have to do with you?"

"Mary was fascinated when she discovered me here – and she had of course heard of my doings in America during my natural life. This *is* the infamous Villa Dondati, after all – the very place she wrote that book. When Polidori, Byron, and Shelley suggested their fateful writing contest in the rooms above these very catacombs, Mary simply couldn't resist recounting my life in her own dark fashion.

"Think about her book for a moment. The evil doctor

attempting to raise the dead? His experiments with electricity to do so? Sound familiar?"

"Surely not..." I started, but he cut me off.

"She even went so far as to name her main character *Franklinstein*, but I objected to so direct a correlation and drew the line."

"I never would have made the connection," I said, "but I see it now."

"You wanted to know why I insisted you write down my account? *Glass, china, and reputations are easily cracked, but never well mended,*" he said. "It takes many good deeds to build a good reputation, and only one bad one to lose it. History will judge me, and I'd rather not have the truth behind *Frankenstein* be the lone record of my dark life. If people ever make that connection, and see the darkness behind this abomination I've become, I want my whole secret history to be revealed. Let the world know that what I did, I did for my country with Resolution... that I *performed without fail what I resolved* for the good of America. A man's net worth to the world is usually determined by what remains after his bad habits are subtracted from his good ones. Let us hope this is true."

He seemed almost at peace as he lowered his head and fell silent. I readied the torch in my hands, knowing my duty, but found myself unwilling to follow through. The heat of the burning pitch washed over me while I hesitated.

Finally, I dropped the torch to the floor. It flickered while it fought to stay alight. "I can't do it," I said.

"You may delay," Franklin answered, reaching over and taking my hands in his. I didn't flinch. "Time will not. I should have no objection to going over the same life from its beginning to the end: requesting only the advantage authors have, of correcting in a second edition the faults of the first. Wish not so much to live long as to live well."

The Fourteenth Virtue

With that, Franklin stepped away from the table covered with his papers. With a wave of his hand, my torch flared to life and leapt from the floor towards him. The crackle of dark magic filled the tiny chamber, and before I could react, the creature burst into purifying flame, a light that nearly blinded me. I raised my arm to shield my eyes as the screams of hell filled the room. I clamped my hands over my ears until the evil slipped from the room, followed by silence.

Flames licked at the beams above me. I gathered what I could of Franklin's papers and stuffed them into my bag. I stayed to watch the flames consume what remained of one of the most revered men in history before racing back out through the villa. I had no idea what I would do upon my return to America, to the Fraternal Order.

Forty-six didn't seem a bad age for retirement.

BLOOD AND LIMESTONE
Richard Lee Byers

Richard Lee Byers is the author of more than thirty fantasy and horror novels, including a number set in the Forgotten Realms *universe. His short fiction can be found in numerous magazines and anthologies. A resident of the Tampa Bay area, the setting for many of his horror stories, he spends much of his free time fencing and playing poker. He's been participating in the Symposium for long enough that he can no longer remember how many years it's been. Visit him online at richardleebyers.com*

"Blood and Limestone" originally appeared in Blood Muse, *an anthology edited by Esther Friesner and Martin H. Greenberg.*

Raoul paced through the chilly expanse of the cathedral, newly completed despite all, drinking in its beauty and grandeur, the darkness little hindrance to his unhuman sight. Slender columns rose past the aisles and triforia to the high, vaulted ceiling. The stained-glass windows, scenes from the Bible and the lives of the saints, along with depictions of all the laborers, stonecutters, mortar makers, plasterers, blacksmiths, and even bakers and farmers who'd helped in one way or another to raise the edifice, shone with the moonlight. Not as they'd shine with the sun behind them, he thought with a pang of sadness, but still, brightly enough to tell their tales to a creature like himself. Alabaster statues of apostles and kings watched him from the shadows, still smelling, like the murals, of fresh paint.

And all the loveliness was gradually destroying him. His head throbbed, twinges stabbed through his joints, and his silent heart ached in his breast. The site had been poisonous to his kind since the bishop—not the current ass but wise old Etienne, dead these sixty years—had blessed the first foundation stone, and every bit of work completed thereafter had made the place deadlier still. It was high time Raoul took himself elsewhere, but he was having difficulty tearing himself away. Because he knew that after tomorrow morning, when the bishop would lead a procession into the cathedral, consecrate the structure, and place the sacred relics in the receptacles prepared for them, the building would become so lethal that he could never return.

At last his discomfort waxed too great to ignore. He turned in a circle, taking a final look, and then, somewhat dizzy, trudged into the south transept, melted his substance into shadow, and tried to slip through the crack between the door and its frame.

Agony, not the dull aches and nausea he'd been experiencing but a sharp, sudden pain, as if someone had thrust a dagger into him, hurled him backward. Solid once more, he sprawled on the floor.

From past experience, he understood what was wrong. Some pious mortal, perhaps employing holy water, or the Host, had sealed the exit against him. Given time, Raoul *might* be able to breach the barrier, but it would be considerably easier to escape via another route if he could find one that hadn't yet received the same treatment. He scrambled to his feet and hurried back into the nave.

A woman's voice spoke. He could tell that she wasn't truly shouting, and yet, to him, the sound seemed excruciatingly loud, jabbing knives of pain into his ears. But despite the apparent volume, he couldn't comprehend the words. She must be reciting a passage from the Scriptures, or a prayer.

Raoul lurched around, to see his tormentor advancing up the center of the nave. He wondered fleetingly how she'd gotten the front door unlocked. She was young, surely no older than seventeen, and painfully thin, with a pinched, prim face that was nonetheless rather pretty, although she seemed to care nothing about her comeliness. She wore a drab, coarse, shapeless gown, and her long blond hair needed combing. A feverish light glowed in her pale gray eyes, and she was clutching a rosary. To his sight, the beads blazed with blue fire, radiating a more potent version of the poison that pervaded the cathedral itself.

Raoul struggled to mask his distress, smile, and bring his supernatural powers of influence to bear. Evidently she'd come here hunting vampires, but that didn't necessarily mean that he couldn't beguile her into believing him mortal. The ploy had worked before. "Good evening," he said.

She sneered at him, then continued her exorcism.

Though his anguished body wanted to recoil from her, he forced himself to move forward instead. It would be impossible to impel himself within arm's reach of the rosary, but perhaps he could make it appear as if he could. "I'm one of the painters," he said. It was difficult to speak in a normal tone. He felt as if he needed to bellow to make himself heard above the din of her voice. "I'm allowed in here, but I don't believe you are, not until tomorrow."

"Liar!" she cried. Probably she'd actually raised her voice, though to him, it seemed to have grown considerably softer. To his disappointment, however, despite the cessation of her litany, the rosary glowed as dazzlingly as before. "I know what you are! Christ showed me your face in a vision! He guided me here to destroy you!"

So much, Raoul thought grimly, *for my hypnotic talents*. Either his current malaise had wiped them away, or a strong will rendered her immune. He wheeled and ran toward the sacristy. There was an exit there.

The girl laughed. "There's no way out, monster! I barred every door!"

When mortals lied, he could hear it in their voices, and she was telling the truth. Then, abruptly, he realized that, unless she could fly, she couldn't possibly have sealed all the potential exits above the ground floor. Perhaps he could leap from the tower!

He pivoted and ran toward the stairs, but his dizziness and weakness slowed him to a hobble. Perceiving his intent, the girl dashed *around* him and blocked his path.

Raoul stumbled to a halt. Panting, she peered at him, and then suddenly lunged forward, brandishing the rosary as if she meant to wrap it around his neck and strangle him.

He made his eyes burn red, his teeth sprout into jagged fangs, and his nails grow into yellow claws. At least he could still manifest his bestial face and weaponry, even if he did feel too sick to injure a gnat. Goggling, the girl lurched to a stop a few feet away.

Raoul shrank his fangs back into puny human teeth. Otherwise, he wouldn't have been able to speak. "Run away," he snarled. "Run or die, and become like me." He hoped that if she did bolt, she'd leave a door open behind her.

The girl set her jaw in resolution. "No," she said. "God sent me to slay you, and I will. To cleanse this sacred place."

If the cathedral awes her, then perhaps, Raoul thought desperately, *I could persuade her to abandon her purpose.* He extinguished the crimson fire in his eyes, and surreptitiously eased his taloned hands behind his back. "I *built* 'this sacred place,'" he told her.

Her mouth twisted. "Liar."

"I wasn't always as I am now," said Raoul. A lance of pain stabbed through his belly. He grunted, and went rigid. "Once upon a time, I was a living human being. My name is Raoul de Cormont, and I was the first master builder here. The one who drew the plans for the cathedral."

"I don't believe you," she said, but he sensed that she did, or at least, was uncertain what to believe. Perhaps she could hear the ring of truth in people's voices herself. "Why should I? Your master is the Father of Lies."

His legs quivered, and he sidled to one of the columns and set his back against it for support. The touch of the sculpted limestone made his skin burn and itch, even through his mantle and jerkin. "I thought I knew everyone living hereabouts," he said, "but I don't recognize you. Who are you?"

She hesitated.

"Are you afraid to tell me?" he asked, arching an eyebrow. "It's a bit late to worry about evading my notice at this point."

She scowled. "I'm not afraid of you! My *faith* will protect me." He reflected glumly that she was all too right about that, at least inside these walls. "My name is Genevieve. People call me Genevieve of Amiens."

He nodded. "I've heard of you." Given to fasting, self-flagellation, and visionary trances from an early age, she'd recently taken up preaching, and sending admonitory letters to bishops, secular lords, and even the Pope. Some people considered her a saint. "And surely such a learned maiden has heard that the undead begin existence as mortals, then change after perishing from another vampire's attentions. So it was with me. A lamia attacked me on the road that runs from the cathedral into town." He smiled wryly. "Well, perhaps 'attacked' is the wrong word. She was lovely, and I thought she was human. When she offered herself to me, I was eager enough to sample her charms. At any rate, she drained me white. I rose from my grave three nights after my friends, the chapter, the quarriers, the masons, the carpenters, and all the others, laid me to rest."

For a moment, he imagined that her expression had softened slightly, as if interest in his tale had taken the edge off her self-righteous loathing. Then she scowled even more ferociously than before, as if now angry with both him and herself. "It doesn't matter who you *were*," she said. "Now you're an abomination." Clutching the rosary, she drew a breath.

Hastily he cried, "How can you kill me when I've done so much good? *Since* I became what I am! How could a just god desire that?"

Genevieve glared at him. "Oh, I've heard about your good

works! The townspeople tell stories about the fiend who kills in the night!"

Raoul was grateful that he'd managed to divert her from a resumption of her exorcism. Evidently, saint or no, she was too enamored of her own rhetorical prowess to resist an invitation to argue. Or perhaps she could tell that his strength was failing. That the power radiating from his own creation would annihilate him soon enough, even if she didn't augment it with her invocation.

"I've never killed anyone intentionally," he said. "And I regret the accidental deaths. But I can no more forego drinking blood than a mortal can survive without water." He wouldn't mention the ecstasy that feeding brought him, even during his first months as a vampire, when he'd struggled to resist it. "And in payment for my predation, I gave the town the cathedral." He glanced around at the arches, the colored glass, the carved wood and stone, and, even now, with his very existence in jeopardy, felt a swell of exaltation. "Don't you think it's a fair trade?"

"I think you share your king Lucifer's pride," Genevieve answered. "For aught I know, you did draw the plans for the church, but you certainly didn't build it. Generations of Christian men did, toiling in the light of God's sun, while you were hiding in your lair."

The bottoms of Raoul's feet began to sting. The power of the cathedral was seeping up from the floor through the soles of his shoes. "I don't disparage the efforts of those good men," he said. "I consider them my friends, for all that none of them remembers ever having met me. But I still say that without me, the cathedral would never have been completed."

He shifted his shoulders in a futile effort to ease the grinding ache in his bones. "After I changed," he continued, "I was tempted to relocate to another town, where no one knew me. My existence would have been easier, and far less lonely, in a place where I could pass for mortal. But I lingered to see the cathedral rise, and it was well that I did. Jehan, the builder the chapter hired to replace me, had a good heart, but didn't deserve his reputation. He lacked any deep understanding of wood and stone, and he didn't know how to talk to the craftsmen. I had to take him in hand."

Genevieve glared at the vampire. "I think you mean that you possessed and enslaved him."

Raoul shrugged. "I taught him the skills a builder needs. He took no harm from it, quite the contrary. Without me, he never could have managed here. And in later years, I kept money coming in, and no great monument can be raised without it."

"So now you're claiming credit for the generosity of all the pious souls who donated to the chapter," Genevieve sneered.

"People are generous when times are good," he replied, "but for the last forty years or so, that hasn't been the case." Though she supposedly preached vehemently against the evils of her age, he wondered if anyone so young, who'd known only the world devastated by the Black Death and the endless war against the English, could appreciate just what a bleak century this was. "How many towns have you heard of that have begun building a new cathedral? Not many, I'll wager. And how many where such an effort has been abandoned for want of cash? When the money hereabouts dried up, *someone* had to prevail upon the rich to open their purses again."

"So you enslaved them too."

"I did only than what was necessary. Over the years, we builders here have had more than our share of accidents and misfortunes. A quarryman crushed. Two wrights fallen from the roof. When lightning struck the tower, people began to whisper that the cathedral was cursed, that their god didn't *want* it finished. Some even advocated razing what already stood! None of the lords and merchants felt inclined to give any more money, nor did many laborers find the courage to work here, until I gave certain influential people a nudge." He sighed. "Even afterwards, things were difficult."

"Perhaps the church truly is cursed," said Genevieve. "Cursed by your presence."

"Look around you," said Raoul, nodding at the vast, imposing space in which they stood, at the organ, intricately wrought screens, richly embroidered cloth hangings, and all the other splendors. "Does it *seem* cursed, or does it seem like a holy place?" He smiled crookedly. "Rest assured, *I* can feel your deity's presence even if you can't."

She grimaced. "I do sense Jesus hovering near," she said grudgingly. "And I've heard tales of saints who compelled devils to build churches and bridges, so perhaps the cathedral isn't tainted. But I'm sure those holy men didn't let the unclean spirits run free when their task was done. They must have driven the demons back to Hell, and that's what Christ has told me to do to you!"

"Are you listening to me?" Raoul demanded, squinting. As his remaining strength faded, her rosary seemed to blaze brighter, until he could barely make our her features beyond the glare. "No priest or magician forced me to shepherd this work to its completion. *I wanted to.* Because I don't like being as I am! I still cherish your god, for all that I can't partake of the sacraments, speak his name, or pray in the usual way. Don't you see, the *cathedral* is my prayer, and my plea for deliverance!" Fleetingly he remembered the sacred imagery he'd sketched for the craftsmen to create from wood, stone, metal, paint, and glass, and the way his hands had ached for hours afterward.

"I don't believe you," said Genevieve. "I hear the gloating in your voice when you speak of this place. You had to see it built out of *pride!* As a monument to your own cleverness!"

Raoul sighed. "That was part of it, too," he admitted. Hot spots of pain began to smolder on his face and hands. He suspected that the malignancy emanating from the stonework and her beads was blistering his skin like sunlight. "This is the grandest thing I ever thought to build, and I yearned to see it live. But that doesn't mean that it wasn't a work of devotion as well. Even mortals rarely have absolutely pristine motives. You preach because you think your god wants you to, but don't you also *enjoy* it? Take pride in your oratory? Don't you relish spinning finely-phrased arguments and exhortations as much as I did raising this magnificent structure?"

Genevieve's gray eyes narrowed.

"I suspect you do," Raoul persisted. "I think that in that respect, at least, we're two of a kind, and so I beg you, as one craftsman to another, spare me. If your god bade you rid the town of me, fine, I'll go far away and never return." He meant it; he had no reason to linger now that his task was done. Only the gargoyle which he'd prompted one of the sculptors to carve in a parody of his own fanged image would remain, crouching on the roof.

She gazed at him for a moment, then gave her head a violent shake. "Your powers are strong," she said. "For a moment, they almost had me sympathizing with you. But my Lord is stronger, and it's time I finished His work." Chanting her deafening, incomprehensible recitation, thrusting out the shining rosary, she marched toward him.

His head pounding in time with her words, he reeled backwards. He hated himself for trying to talk to her. He should have found a way to fight her, or tried to force his way through one of the sealed doors, while he had a little strength left. Now it was too late.

He stumbled past a pillar and into the aisle. As he blundered against one of the pungent, freshly painted murals, a depiction of the martyrdom of St. Stephen, he trod on something which cracked beneath his foot.

Looking downward, he saw that he'd stepped on a clay mortar and pestle. One of the painters must have left them behind. And Raoul realized that there might be a way to strike at his nemesis even if the agonizing radiance of her rosary did keep him beyond arm's reach. He stooped, snatched up the biggest piece of the shattered mortar, and threw it.

He wanted to hit Genevieve between the eyes. Instead, the

shard glanced off her temple, but that was enough to stagger her. Her exorcism faltered, and, its glare dying abruptly, the rosary slipped from her fingers.

Raoul launched himself forward and slammed into her, knocked her down and fell on top of her. Thrashing, she struggled to scramble out from underneath him. At the moment, her merely mortal strength was more than a match for his own.

But he had his claws, and he started ripping at her, shredding her gown and the pasty, dirty, sour-smelling skin beneath. His attacks flung spatters of blood through the air. Despite her frenzied efforts to shield herself, in another moment, he'd rip out her throat.

And then, his fury and desperation notwithstanding, he imagined the possible consequences.

He hoped that if she was no longer alive to hinder him, he could escape via the spire. But if he did, he wouldn't be able to return, nor could he haul her corpse up the stairs with him. He was simply too weak.

And many of the townspeople were still afraid that the church was haunted or accursed. How much more terrified would they be tomorrow, if they entered and found a butchered saint on the floor? Would they still consecrate the cathedral, or might they abandon or even demolish it after all?

As he hesitated, she thrust her arm out and just barely managed to grab her rosary. The beads shone with azure fire as she lashed them against his head.

The worst pain yet blasted through his skull. He collapsed, and she dragged herself from beneath him, already gasping out the words of the exorcism again.

Wracked by convulsions, he tried to crawl after her and claw her, but only succeeded in flopping over onto his back. His body crackled, blackened, and shriveled. The ribbed vault in the section of ceiling above him seemed to rush down like a set of terrible jaws.

ALMOST BROTHERS
Paul Genesse

"Almost Brothers" was the lead story in the anthology, Fellowship Fantastic *from DAW Books in 2008. It's one of the darkest stories Paul Genesse has ever written, and he plans to turn it into a novel someday. When he's not writing short stories—he's sold eleven so far—Paul has found the time to write the first two novels in the successful Iron Dragon series,* The Golden Cord *and* The Dragon Hunters. *An avid participant in the Writer's Symposium at Gen Con since 2005, Paul has become the editor of the free Writer's Symposium Ezine, dedicated to "Helping Writers Write." To sign up for the ezine, or watch a video about the* Iron Dragon *books, visit him online at www.paulgenesse.com.*

The rope sawed into Finn's wrists as he struggled to escape the heavy wooden chair, still stained with the blood and urine from the last child Nagel had captured. The leathery-skinned brute sat on a stool, grinning at the young boy as he sharpened a long rusty razor.

Nagel locked his gray eyes on Finn's wiry twelve-year old frame, then lubricated the crumbling whetstone with blood-tinged spittle. Finn realized that hitting Nagel in the mouth with the rock had not been the right thing to do, but he wasn't going to be captured without a fight.

Finn shifted on the sticky chair, and a splinter poked into the naked flesh on his bum, beaten red and raw by Nagel's calloused hands. The much-too-thin boy glanced at the fireplace. His filthy clothing smoldered there, permeating the shack with a swampy odor mixed with the scent of burning hair.

Despite his hands being securely lashed behind him, Finn arched his back, fighting to escape the fate all the other orphaned refugee children had fallen victim to. Even his best friend Owen had received the "special treatment" at the hands of the Bloody Barber.

Nagel's fierce gaze met Finn's terrified green eyes. "Listen, you rat hunting turd. If you don't stop squirming, the first thing I'll do is shave off that little mushroom cap between your legs."

Knees clenched together, Finn tried in vain to hide his nakedness. He wished he had one of the dried animal skins or furs hanging on the dingy walls to cover himself. If only he could slip his hands free, he could escape out the side window of the trapper's shack. In desperation he thought, *Perhaps the Barber will listen to reason?*

Finn searched for the right words, summoning his beggar's voice. "*Please, sir.* If you let me go I'll—"

"You'll what?!" Nagel furrowed his brow. "Steal more food? Damn Tarnite orphans like you are all the same."

"I swear I didn't eat it! I catch my own food. I swear it on the twelve saints of the Celestrum."

"Eleven saints, stupid boy. You're not in Tarn. Everyone here knows Vivianne is a witch, not a saint." Nagel shook his bald head. "And don't expect me to believe that you be surviving on them skinny rats your ratter dogs kill in the barns."

"We do. The food I . . . found . . . was for—"

Nagel pointed the razor at Finn's crotch.

Trembling uncontrollably, Finn felt blood oozing from where the ropes sliced into his skin. He stopped struggling as pain and cold fear washed over him.

"And don't you go pissing on my chair either. The last one of you orphans to piss themselves was sorry she did."

Finn guessed he was talking about Lynn and saw what remained of her long, blond hair in the corner of the fireplace. The sticky stain on the chair had to be from her.

The Bloody Barber stopped sharpening the folding razor knife and gave Finn a wicked grin, showing all three of his front teeth.

Finn's eyes opened wide as the hulking man lumbered toward him. Finn almost had a hand free when cold iron pressed against his dirt-smudged cheek. Nagel grabbed Finn's unkempt sandy brown hair and stepped behind him.

"No, please!" Finn squeaked. "I swear I won't—"

A rough hand squeezed Finn's throat, choking off his plea. The razor scraped against Finn's scalp, shearing off a swath of hair over his right ear and opening several small stinging cuts.

Finn screamed, "Stop! Please!"

The Bloody Barber's chortling made Finn gnash his teeth. He wished his friends were there to save him, but he was alone. Captured. Helpless. Just like Owen, Lynn, Hazel, and the others had been when Nagel had caught and killed them.

High-pitched barking and loud scratching came from the door of Nagel's shack. Finn knew it was Pip and Fyse. His little black-and-white rat terriers were still free, and at least they hadn't abandoned him.

"Quiet!" Nagel shouted at the door, but the dogs kept scratching and barking. The Barber threw a discarded child's shoe—probably Lynn's—at the door, and the dogs stopped.

A yellow puddle of urine came under the threshold. *Good dogs!*

Nagel stormed toward the expanding puddle. "Stupid mutts!"

Finn pulled at his bonds and excruciating pain swept through him. Skin tore loose from his wrists. *Almost there. Just . . . keep . . . pulling.* The blood made it slippery enough to wrench a hand free. He slid off the chair and nearly fainted as the flesh on his backside separated itself from the splintery wood.

Cursing, Nagel opened the front door and tried to kick the little black-and-white dogs. Both darted away and growled at the huge man brandishing the rusted razor. Pip and Fyse bared their teeth. The dogs weighed less than twenty pounds, but they lunged and snapped at Nagel, determined to save their beloved Finn from a gruesome fate.

The sight of his tiny dogs facing Nagel gave Finn a burst of strength. He slipped his other hand free and darted to the side window and clambered over the sill—remembering too late that he was supposed to grab some clothing. He landed in mud that smelled like it contained Nagel's cast out nightsoil. "Oh, sh—"

Hands grabbed Finn and pulled him up. He expected a cuff on the head but saw Owen's clear blue eyes—and newly shaved scalp—staring at him.

"Owen, you're alive." Hope for the others flashed through Finn's mind as he stared at his lanky boyhood friend, who was already much taller than Finn.

"Come on!" Owen pulled Finn away from the hovel as Nagel came charging around the side of the house. Pip and Fyse were yipping and barking at his heels.

"Get back here!" Nagel shouted.

Owen and Finn sprinted away from Nagel's shack and into the muddy streets of Ryeland. Pip and Fyse caught up as the boys ran past a column of Celestrian soldiers marching south toward the invading Tarnite army. A mounted knight from the Order of Saint Mathias lifted his visor to watch them flee.

The sight of a naked boy running in the street made a few of the villagers shake their heads, but most ignored Finn. A gang of Ryeland's children—all with full heads of hair—laughed and pointed at Finn, making snide comments about the size of his manhood. It took every bit of control for him not to stop and start another fistfight, but his ribs still hurt from the last brawl, and the thought of facing the boys naked gave him pause. And Owen had said Finn was on his own if he started another fight.

After running far from Nagel's shack, the boys stopped behind widow Tillwell's chicken coop to catch their breath. Finn squatted down and covered himself as Pip and Fyse snuffled at his legs before rolling on the ground and showing him their bellies.

"Good girl, Pip. Good boy, Fyse." Their soft brown eyes showed their love for him, and Finn tenderly rubbed his little dogs.

Owen got a whiff of Finn and wrinkled his nose. The brown mess on Finn's knees definitely wasn't mud.

"You've smelled worse." Finn shrugged. "And I should have taken some clothes."

"Nagel gave everyone new clothes once he finished. He was just going to shave off your hair."

"What?" Relief and shame washed over Finn. *They're all still alive.* "How was I supposed to know? I thought—"

"If you hadn't run off you would've known."

"But the locals said he skinned the children he caught alive and—"

"You listened to them?" Owen shook his head in disbelief.

Finn's face turned red as he realized what a fool he'd been by believing the Ryelanders. His shame turned to boiling anger. "I'm not letting anyone shave my head. Especially the Bloody Barber!" Finn stroked the bare spot by his ear and grimaced when he felt the fresh cuts. Finn glanced at the scabs on Owen's freshly shaved head and the little bumps and knots revealed by the absence of his blond hair. "I can't believe you let him do that to you."

"Sir Luther and the Deacons ordered all of us to let him." Owen gestured to the abbey's bell tower dominating the skyline over Ryeland, as if pointing explained everything. "Finn, you've got lice, just like the rest of us did."

"I do not." Finn's scalp started to itch fiercely, but he resisted scratching. Owen was right, but Finn wouldn't yield. "Why do you do everything they say? The Deacons aren't going to let you be a knight."

"Sir Luther's teaching me to ride."

"Only when you're not cleaning steaming piles of shit out of the stables or polishing his shield. We might as well be slaves back home in Tarn."

Owen shook his head. "Sir Luther said he would teach me the lance and sword when I'm fourteen."

"That's two years away! They'll cart us off to the orphanage in

Templemoore, just like they did the others."

"No. The Deacons said they're keeping a few of us here to be in a proper orphanage—like a school—for devout Celestrians like us."

"You mean like you." Finn rolled his eyes.

"They say the Saints have a plan for us. If you'd come to the prayer services you might understand better."

"I've been to plenty back home. I'm not going again. The Saints abandoned us." Finn stared at the dirt, remembering when the Tarnite soldiers dragged away his mother and sister during the attack on their refugee column.

"Here." Owen handed him his tunic, leaving himself with only a pair of rough brown breeches. "It's long enough to cover your—"

"Thanks." Finn put on the itchy wool garment, stitched together by the holy sisters for the refugee children. "I'll give it back later."

"Keep it. Sir Luther gave me an extra one with the coat of arms of Saint Mathias on it. I'll get some breeches for you tonight, but we better not go back to the abbey now. Nagel will catch us for sure."

Finn pulled the tunic down. The rough material chafed against his bum, and he raised an eyebrow at Owen. "Hey, what were you doing outside the Barber's shack?"

Owen grinned. "I figured you'd do something stupid, and we're supposed to watch out for each other. We're almost brothers, you know?"

Finn's stomach growled. "Brother, I don't suppose you have any food?"

The boys laughed and Owen explained, "The holy sisters won't feed us again until sunset. They wanted to get rid of us while they deloused the dormitory, and they won't let you in with that hair on your head."

"I'm not going back anyway."

"You've been hiding out for two days!"

"The farmers feed me and the dogs for killing barn rats."

"You can't stay out there forever."

Finn rolled his eyes.

"Everyone misses you, especially Lynn."

A needle of guilt poked into Finn. "Where'd the gang go?"

"To the river. To find lunch."

"Those carp taste like mud." He thought about stealing some eggs from widow Tillwell's coop, but Owen would probably object.

"The fish taste better than the rats you catch."

Finn sighed. "I know a perfect place to find trout. Nagel will never find us, and it's just a short ways up the Little Iden by the road to Ashkirk."

"But Deacon Nethers said not to go near the road. Bandits and such."

"Who cares? There're lots of trout and big crayfish. Aren't you hungry?"

Owen nodded then chuckled. "Just be careful."

"Why?" Finn's brows narrowed.

"You don't have any breeches on and that thing looks like bait." Owen laughed, and Finn couldn't help but smile—then he punched Owen in the arm. Hard.

Owen ran to get the others, while Finn and the dogs headed for their meeting place at the marshy area outside of town. He snuffled at the swampy air and let the cool mud on the shore soothe his bare feet. His raw backside ached, and just when he was going to sit in the mud Owen and the gang arrived.

The kids, ranging in age from six to ten, almost all held crude fishing poles as they marched behind Owen. Finn hadn't seen any of them since he'd been hiding out and was surprised at how excited he was to see them. Though he barely recognized them with their bald heads and newly sewn baggy clothes. Trailing behind Owen came Lynn, Hazel, Brek, Gael, Lilly, Baird, Watt, Salty, Rhyssa, and little Tupper.

Hazel squinted as she approached. "Finn, what happened to your breeches?"

Finn wanted to say something witty to the ten-year-old girl who had once had long, beautiful raven tresses—often filled with leaves—but the sight of her stark white scalp with nicks all over it made him bite his lip.

"They're still making his clothes." Owen winked at Finn.

"Hey, Finn!" The youngest orphans, Brek and Tupper, both six, ran over to Finn to show him the tiny frogs they had caught. Tupper held up three of the little hoppers, each with a tadpole's tail. "See my frogs?"

"Look!" Brek dug a mass of gray worms and one little frog out of his pocket.

Finn nodded his approval then made eye contact with Lynn. Fuzzy nubs of blond hair shone in the sunlight. Finn remembered seeing strands of her hair in Nagel's fireplace—*Bloody Barber!* Tear marks streaked through the dirt on her face, and Finn decided Nagel would pay for cutting off her beautiful hair. At least she didn't have many nicks on her freckled scalp.

He hugged her close and remembered when he had decided to be Lynn's big brother. It happened the night that her family had disappeared in the flight from the Tarnite soldiers. Plus, Pip and Fyse really liked her. The little dogs ran around her legs yipping. Lynn smiled and Finn took the ten-year-old girl's hand. "Come on, Lynn. Let's catch us some fish."

Finn guided the children toward the Little Iden and the fishing place, a bend in the river where the current slowed and flies swarmed. The kids put their lines into the green water, and Finn wondered how many fish they would catch. Soon, half of the kids took off their barely stained clothes and jumped into the warm water. The kids splashed and dunked each other, screaming with glee as they frolicked in the shallows.

"You're going to scare the fish away!" Owen shouted, his child's voice becoming deeper for a moment.

Finn's nostrils flared. "Nagel will hear us back in Ryeland if they keep this up, and the road to Ashkirk isn't that far either."

The games and shouting continued off and on, and Finn kept an eye out for Nagel. After midday, Pip and Fyse barked at something in the forest, but Nagel didn't appear. Finn guessed it must have been a squirrel, or maybe one of the barn cats that despised him and his dogs.

Late in the afternoon hungry bellies forced the gang of Tarnite children to man their poles in earnest, but still no fish were caught.

"Look what I found!" Lynn's high voice made everyone turn away from the river.

The little girl clutched a big clay honey pot against her body. She could barely lift it and leaned backwards as she waddled forward.

"What's in the pot?" Tupper asked, bounding over to her as Pip and Fyse pranced at her feet, wagging their little tails.

"Honey." Lynn licked her lips and plopped down the pot.

Owen put his hands on his hips. "Where'd you steal it?"

"I didn't steal it!" Lynn's face flashed with indignation. "I found it right over there on the path."

"Some farmer must have forgot it." Finn swished away the flies. "Let's eat it!"

The kids squealed with delight and swarmed around the little girl, dipping their hands into the pot and licking the sticky honey off their fingers. Owen stepped in and made certain the younger ones got their share. Everyone was soon swallowing the sweet, syrupy nectar and joking about sticky fingers.

"How'd we get so lucky?" Hazel asked.

"Who knows?" Finn shrugged, letting Pip and Fyse lick his hands as he yawned. "I need a nap." Finn almost forgot about his tender backside and closed his eyes. Moments later, all of the orphans lay down along the riverbank and fell asleep.

Finn felt himself flying, then he slammed into something hard and wet. River water went up his nose as the ground shifted. He realized he was in the bottom of a leaky boat as two pointy sacks landed on him—then whimpered. Finn could barely open his eyes but realized the sacks were sleeping children; Lynn and possibly Tupper. Owen lay in the boat beside them, apparently asleep, along with others—probably the rest of his friends.

Pip and Fyse barked savagely from somewhere close by, and Finn tried to lift his head when a brown boot caked with river mud stepped beside his head. An older man with a shaggy, gray beard snatched up a crossbow and loosed a quarrel.

A dog's shrill yelp made Finn shudder. "*No!*" Finn's shout came out as a whimper. The barking stopped. Finn tried to sit up, but his body wouldn't move. "*Pip! Fyse!*" Finn could only mumble as the sweet flavor in his mouth turned bitter. Oars splashed into the water, and he fell asleep as lethargy overwhelmed him.

Finn awoke as his body crashed onto a bouncing wooden floor. He heard the clopping of horses' hooves and the squeak of wagon wheels. His hands were tied in front of him and his feet bound tightly together with twine. Owen and the other orphans lay in the wagon, similarly bound.

A vague memory of barking surfaced in his mind. "Pip! Fyse!"

"Shut your mouth, or I'll fill it with sand," a shaggy-bearded man cloaked in shadow warned from the bench in front of the wagon.

Panic filled Finn's entire being as the wagon rumbled down a rocky road that snaked through the gloomy woods.

"You all right?" Owen whispered.

Finn nodded, but he wanted to vomit—or maybe cry. "What happened to . . . the dogs?"

Owen shook his head. The crack of a whip made Finn shrink down.

"They'll never catch us," a man sitting next to Shaggy-beard said, then whipped the horses again.

Shaggy-beard nudged the man with a dirty elbow. "Them Ryelanders wouldn't give the ass end of a skunk for these Tarnite whelps. They're not coming after us."

"Who are they?" Finn scowled at Shaggy-beard and the wagon driver—Whip.

"Slavers."

"How'd they get us?" Finn asked, already knowing as waves of nausea spread from his gut.

"Poisoned honey." Owen shook his head and Finn dry heaved.

Five men on horses charged out from shadowy trees. The wagon jerked to a halt, and the horses snorted with displeasure.

"Celestrian soldiers!" Lynn shouted, sitting up beside Finn.

Shaggy-beard and Whip bellowed with laughter, and Lynn withered.

A man on a tall horse with braided red hair asked, "How many?"

"Twelve." Shaggy-beard glanced back. "Half are girls."

"Good catch." Red-braid peered into the wagon, a hard smile on his ruddy face. "You two wait in the trees. We'll ride ahead and tell the Tarnite soldiers what these will cost them. And don't touch any of them little girls. Sir Maddox is buying, and you know he likes them unspoiled. But you can have one of them boys if you want."

The horseman snickered as Shaggy-beard cast a hungry gaze at the children. Red-braid and the other three rode off, and the terrified kids stared at Finn and Owen. Finn wasted no time in trying to get free. The slavers had bound his hands in front, and he quickly set to work. Owen shielded him from Shaggy-beard and Whip as Finn easily untied his feet, then chewed on the twine around his wrists, wishing his teeth were as sharp as the rats he hunted.

The two slavers waited until the horsemen were long gone,

then stopped to piss beside the wagon. "Doesn't matter to me," Shaggy-beard told Whip. "They both squeal the same when I'm with 'em."

Shaggy-beard growled and shook the wagon, thrusting his hips against it. Lynn and Rhyssa began to cry. Tupper asked for his mother, and Hazel curled into a tight little ball beside Owen.

"What are they going to do to us?" Lynn sniffled as big tears fell from her eyes.

"Don't worry," Owen soothed. "The twelve angels of the Celestrum will watch over us. Say your prayers, and you'll be safe."

Finn bit into his bindings, wanting to say the saints who had supposedly become angels weren't going to lift a precious wing to help them. He knew the Ryelanders—probably the Bloody Barber—had sold them to the slavers. *We're on our own. No one's coming to save us.*

Shaggy-beard stalked toward the back of the wagon. Finn stopped chewing at the frayed twine and held still.

"This one's a boy, isn't it?" Shaggy-beard asked Whip, and seized Lynn's leg, pulling her toward the rear of the wagon.

"She's a girl!" Finn shouted.

Owen sat up. "Leave her alone." His voice sounded like a man's, not a skinny twelve-year old.

Lynn screamed as Shaggy-beard pulled her closer. Owen dove forward and grabbed Lynn. "Please, not her. She's just a little girl. That man said take a boy."

Shaggy-beard's eyes flared at Owen. "You want to take her place, *boy*?"

Finn shredded the twine with his teeth, not caring if they saw him.

Shaggy-beard dragged Lynn out of Owen's grasp and let her fall to the ground.

"No!" Owen shouted, and crawled forward on his elbows.

"Don't worry. You're next, *boy*." Shaggy-beard slapped Owen hard in the face.

Finn tore his hands free and sprang out of the wagon, landing on the grass. Shaggy-beard put a foot on Lynn's neck and pointed a dirty finger at Finn. "Don't you run, or she'll wish she was dead."

Finn found a fist-sized rock. "Shut your mouth!" He hurled the stone as hard as he could. It struck Shaggy-beard in the throat, staggering him.

Owen leaped out of the wagon, his feet and hands still tied. He landed on Shaggy-beard's back and wrapped his bound hands around the man's throat. Owen pulled the twine as hard as he could and Shaggy-beard's face turned red, the veins in his neck bulging.

Whip laughed so hard he fell off the wagon bench.

Finn sprang toward Shaggy-beard, who stumbled backwards as Owen choked him. Finn knelt behind the man's legs, and the slaver tripped over Finn's body and hit the ground, pinning Owen under him. Shaggy-beard pushed Owen's arms away from his throat and rolled off the boy.

Finn kicked Shaggy-beard in the groin and smashed an apple-sized rock into the slaver's skull. He whirled around to see what Whip was doing and spotted the man shuddering and gurgling on the ground as blood leaked out of his slit throat. A huge bald man in fur boots stood over the dying slaver. The man wiped the bloody razor on his deerskin breeches.

"*The Bloody Barber.*" Finn dropped the rock beside Shaggy-beard's body, stifling the urge to run away as fast as he could.

The big man bared his three front teeth and stomped toward Lynn.

"You betrayed your slaver friends?" Finn's mouth hung open, wondering how much they had paid Nagel to help them.

"I'm a hunter, you stupid boy. And the Deacons wanted you tracked down." Nagel pulled Lynn up. She yelped as he sliced the twine binding her limbs.

"They sent you . . . for *us*?" Finn couldn't believe it.

Owen stood, trying to catch his breath. "Thank . . . you . . ."

Nagel cut Owen free and stared at Shaggy-beard. "He's not dead... yet."

Finn noticed the man's chest rose, despite the blood oozing out of his scalp.

Nagel offered the razor to Finn. "Boy, you're going to have to learn to kill men soon enough. Now cut his throat."

Finn reached tentatively for the blade, but Owen snatched it out of Nagel's hand. Owen glared at Finn. "This man should face judgment in Ryeland. In front of the Deacons."

"Maybe so, but we ain't in Ryeland." Nagel's eyes focused on Owen, who turned away and jumped into the wagon where he started cutting the other children loose.

Horses on the road made Nagel duck behind the wagon. "They're coming back."

Owen ushered the children out of the wagon, some of their hands still bound. Nagel lifted the little ones out and Finn herded them toward the woods. Nagel and Owen came behind, and they all rushed into the forest as five horses arrived at the wagon.

Nagel picked up Brek and Tupper and carried them under his arms. Finn held Lynn's hand and guided her through the brush, while Owen held Hazel's. Nagel took the lead and they found the Barber's brown gelding tied near a willow tree. Nagel lifted the five smallest children onto the horse. "Hold on. And no one cry. You boys don't let the others get lost." He pointed at Finn and Owen, who ushered Lynn, Hazel, Watt, Baird, and Rhyssa through the forest.

Nagel led the way through the brush and moonlight flashed off the hilt of a massive sword strapped to Nagel's saddle. Finn recognized the two-handed greatsword and knew it was taller than he or Owen. A stout crossbow also hung from the saddle, and Finn imagined shooting it would be like getting kicked by an angry plow horse.

"Shhh." Nagel raised a big hand and they stopped. Finn heard horses moving ahead of them. A lot of horses. Nagel crept forward, then came back with a foul expression and whispered, "Tarnite cavalry."

Behind them, a horse whinnied and a man cursed loudly. Faint torchlight appeared in the forest, and Finn's heart raced.

"Slavers. Come on." Nagel guided them through the trees, away from the Tarnite column and the slavers. For two hours they tramped through the brush. Finn noticed the five exhausted children atop the horse had fallen asleep. Lynn was nearly asleep on her feet, and eventually Finn had to carry her on his back for a while. She wasn't that heavy at first, but his strength ran out when the forest opened up onto a burned field. Nagel marched them forward without mercy. Lynn kept up with Finn leading her along by the hand.

Lightning flashed, then thunder boomed in the distance. Moments later, rain fell in fat drops. Finn grimaced as Tupper and Brek began to shiver uncontrollably. Tupper nearly fell off the horse as cold, fatigue, and the residual effects of the poison took their toll. Finn poked Nagel in the leg, and the big man turned.

Finn craned his neck to stare upwards. "Listen, you heartless bastard. We've got to stop."

The hulking man scowled at Finn as rivulets of water ran off Nagel's bald pate.

"Finn's right." Owen's voice didn't waver.

Nagel turned and kept marching, but he headed toward a razed homestead in the distance. The house was a pile of scorched timbers, but lightning revealed an intact barn with a patched roof and rotting walls.

Finn entered the empty barn and sniffed a fresh rat pellet. "If Pip and Fyse were with me we'd clean all the rats out of here in one night."

Nagel frowned at Finn. "How long with one dog?"

Finn's heart pounded. "One?"

Nagel sighed. "Your male one is dead."

"Dead? Fyse is . . ." Finn fought back the tears as Lynn hugged him. Brek and Tupper wrapped their arms around Finn and Hazel sobbed. After hugging them back, Finn stomped into one of the empty stalls. All of his friends hovered outside, but Owen held them back.

Finn pounded his fists against the wood. *First father doesn't come back from the war with the Murhatans, then we lose our farm to the baron's taxmen, then mother and sister are taken by soldiers. Now Fyse is killed by slavers? It's not fair! This can't be happening to me!*

Finn slumped to the floor in the darkness. Owen stepped into the stall and sat beside Finn for a long time before saying, "He was a good dog."

Finn's chest shook, but he held in the sobs, taking a shuddering breath. *I'm never going to cry again.* "Now all I've got left is Pip."

Owen punched Finn hard in the arm.

Finn's anger built, but the hurt look in Owen's eyes made him pause. "What?"

"You've still got me." Owen pointed at the other kids. "Us."

Finn fought back the tears, and a frown mixed with hope spread across his face. "I guess we're still almost brothers."

Owen smiled, then Finn punched him in the arm.

The other children came into the stall and surrounded the two boys. They all fell asleep on the moldy hay, sleeping like a litter of puppies.

*

The pounding rain on the roof finally stopped, but water dripped down into murky puddles.

"Riders on the road," Nagel whispered.

Owen and Finn crept out of the stall where the children huddled together in the darkness.

"Too late to run." Nagel barred the doors with a plank. "Boys, close the back way."

Finn and Owen quickly finished their task, returning to find Nagel had loaded his crossbow and unsheathed his greatsword. The big man's eyes were nearly invisible in the darkness, and he kept peering out a crack in the barn doors, watching the riders come ever closer. Finn stared into the night through a knot-hole at six riders bearing torches.

"What do we do?" Owen asked.

"Tell the little ones to be quiet."

Owen held up a pitchfork. "We can help."

Finn raised a stout axe handle.

"Damn Tarnite orphans," Nagel grumbled.

Six horses stopped outside the barn. In the torchlight, Finn saw Shaggy-beard with a bloody cloth around his head. The red-haired man pointed at tracks in the mud. Two men rode to the rear of the barn and Red sent another man—a skinny fellow with a hooded cloak—to the front. Skinny held an axe in one hand as he sloshed through the mud, then peered into the barn.

Nagel plunged his sword through the gap between the doors. The tip pierced the man's gut. Nagel yanked the sword out and Skinny fell into a puddle clutching at his belly.

When Skinny stopped moving, Red and Shaggy-beard circled the barn and spoke with the other two horsemen. They argued, and Finn heard Red say, "We took coin from Sir Maddox. We deliver tonight or he'll have our heads on pikes. He's probably after us already."

Thunder boomed in the distance as two men approached the rear, while three came at the front, all on horseback.

Nagel handed his crossbow to Finn. "Aim, then pull this lever here. Wait until he's close."

Finn nodded, intimidated by the size of the weapon and wondering how to hold it. Nagel sent Finn and Owen scurrying away to hide and pressed himself into a shadowy alcove.

The slavers tossed ropes over the handles of the barn doors and used their horses to tear them open. They dismounted and marched into the barn with torches held high, each carrying a club or axe.

Nagel leaped to attack, his greatsword arcing toward the slavers. Red and the other two men jumped back, recoiling from Nagel's slashing blade. Shaggy-beard came from the rear and checked the stalls, getting closer to where the children huddled together. The kids screamed when he appeared in the doorway.

Finn stood in front of the little ones, squinting in the torchlight. He scowled at the grinning slaver and thought about his dead dog. Shaggy-beard sidestepped out of the way just as Finn pulled the crossbow lever. The bolt *thunked* into the chest of the other slaver as the recoil sent Finn tumbling backwards.

Riding Nagel's horse, Owen burst out of a stall and charged Shaggy-beard with a pitchfork held like a lance. Owen yelled as he attacked, and the slaver dropped his torch to ward off the blow. One of the tines pierced Shaggy-beard's hand as Nagel's horse knocked him down.

Finn screamed and rushed out of the stall with the axe handle held over his head in two hands. All of the children followed him out, makeshift clubs in their hands and feral screams erupting from their lips. They descended on Shaggy-beard and pummeled him mercilessly.

Smoke and flickering orange light made Finn stop hitting the slaver's bloody skull. Flames erupted all around them where the torches had been discarded. The rear of the barn was engulfed in a rapidly spreading fire.

"We've got to get everyone out!" Owen shouted to Finn as Nagel's horse bucked and screamed. Owen jumped onto a pile of hay as the horse sped out the front of the barn, past Nagel and Red.

Finn and Owen herded the children as the flames swept along the floor of the barn and up into the loft. They stopped near the entrance where two slavers lay dead, gruesome gashes across their bodies.

Red and Nagel still faced each other, the slaver staying beyond the reach of Nagel's sword. Red held the blade of a throwing knife in one hand, and an axe in the other.

Nagel could barely stand, a knife handle protruding from each of his thighs, and another in the center of his chest. A cut across the right side of Red's neck appeared to be his only wound.

Finn and the other children reached Nagel as the big man fell hard to his knees, still holding up his sword. Finn and Owen flanked the Bloody Barber, brandishing axe handle and pitchfork. Nagel coughed, and the tip of his sword hit the dirt. Bright red blood leaked out of his chest. Finn reached for the knife.

"Leave it." Nagel shook his head.

Smoke billowed around them and Red backed out of the barn, a content grin on his face as Nagel fell backward. Finn and Owen tried to ease him down, but the big man was too much for them and he fell hard.

Nagel whispered to Finn, "Take my razor. Hide it. Then cut that bastard's throat when he falls asleep."

Finn took the folded razor out of Nagel's hand. "I will."

"When he's dead . . . get the children back to Ryeland," Nagel whispered. "Protect them all. The Deacons want you there. Especially you two boys."

Finn shook his head. "But we're nobody."

Nagel managed a gurgling laugh. "I'm nobody. An orphaned bastard from Tarn who became an unworthy servant of the Deacons. But you'll both be knights in the Order of Saint Mathias. The Deacons told me that."

Finn and Owen exchanged wide-eyed glances. *Knights? Impossible.*

"Now get out of here and let me die in peace." Blood leaked out of Nagel's chest.

"But you'll burn to death!" Finn urgently grabbed onto Nagel. "We'll drag you out."

"No. I'll be dead before the fire comes. Now go."

"We'll pray for you." Owen's lips trembled.

Nagel pressed his greatsword into Owen's hands.

"Go!" Nagel commanded as he coughed and choked on the blood filling his lungs.

Wracked with sorrow for leaving Nagel behind, Finn helped Owen lead the children out of the burning barn.

The slaver waited as horses galloped down the road toward them. Red grinned at the children after staring through the darkness at the incoming armored warriors. "Look! Sir Maddox comes for his slaves. There's nowhere to run." The slaver smirked at the children. "That big man was a fool to steal you from me."

"Shut your bloody mouth!" Finn lunged, but Owen held him back.

"Sir Maddox will cut your tongue out for that." Red turned as the riders emerged from the darkness. "Sir Maddox! I have your slaves."

The leader galloped toward Red and drove a lance through the slaver's chest. Red splashed into a puddle, gasping, "*But . . . I . . .*"

Finn knelt down and put a hand over Red's mouth, then slowly cut his throat.

Shadowy horsemen in full plate armor ringed the children, helms down, faces hidden, lances and swords drawn.

Owen lifted Nagel's sword, his small hands around the massive hilt. The knight who lanced the slaver dismounted, drew his longsword, and faced Owen.

Bloody razor in his hand, Finn stood shoulder to shoulder with his best friend.

"*Yield.*" The knight commanded, his voice muffled by his helm.

Owen's arms trembled, barely able to hold up the heavy sword. "Never," both of the boys said in unison.

The other children stepped forward, some with clubs, others with rocks to throw at the shadow-cloaked knights.

"Go back to Tarn!" Finn shouted.

Laugher erupted from the riders, and many raised their visors. The dismounted knight took off his helm and stared at Finn and Owen, his steely eyes and scarred face revealed in the growing firelight. "Tonight we're headed to Ryeland." The knight's eyes softened. "I'm Sir Gregory of the Order of Saint Mathias. The Deacons sent us to find you. Now I understand why."

The barn fire raged higher, and in the burgeoning light Finn saw emblazoned on their shields a Celestrian angel raising a silver sword. Overpowering relief made Finn's remaining strength fade away.

*

Finn and Owen stared at the burning barn. Celestrian knights stood guard as Owen drove Nagel's sword into the mud, then gathered the children for a silent prayer.

Finn wiped his eyes, telling himself it was the smoke from Nagel's pyre that made them water. As he thought of Nagel's sacrifice, a new path for his life suddenly opened before him. He turned to Owen and looked into his friends clear blue eyes. "Someday, I'm going back to Tarn—as a knight. I'm going to find my mother and sister."

Owen put his hand on Finn's shoulder. "Brother, you're not going back alone."

A lump caught in Finn's throat. He knew they would always be there for each other. No matter what. Until the day they died.

"Let's get you all home." Sir Gregory motioned to his men.

"Not yet." Finn unfolded Nagel's razor and splashed water from a puddle onto his hair. "There's something the Bloody Barber would have wanted."

With slow strokes, Finn shaved his head clean as tears streamed down his face.

The Prince of Artemis V
By Jennifer Brozek

Jennifer Brozek: author, editor, slush reader, and small press publisher. She has been writing RPGs for six years and professionally publishing fiction for five years. In 2010, she has three books and three anthologies scheduled for release. She has been a part of the Gen Con Writer's Symposium since 2006. Oddly enough, she was inspired to write "The Prince of Artemis V" while re-watching The Wizard of Oz. *Often considered a Renaissance woman, Jennifer prefers to be known as a wordslinger and optimist. You can find more about her at her blog: jennifer-brozek.livejournal.com.*

"A princess is a servant to all of her people. She's supposed to care for them and never let them down. Ever," Lanteri said.

Hart nodded at his little sister. "What's the first rule of being a princess?"

"Never, ever abandon your people—for they need you more than you know," she said in a tone so serious that it would have indicated satire if it had not come from an eight-year-old's mouth.

"You're a very good princess."

"I'm trying." She smiled at her older brother. "But sometimes, it's hard."

"I know. As Dad says, 'Nothing good...'"

"'...ever comes easy,'" they both finished together and then grinned.

Lanteri bent over her pixel board and continued to draw her idea of the perfect castle. She drew each line slowly, dragging the pixel pen over the board. Whenever a line was not exactly as she wanted it, she turned the pixel pen over to erase the offending pixels, before going back to her masterpiece. She had been working on this particular picture for weeks.

Hart watched her, envying both her ability to manipulate the pixel board and her imagination. He had never had her artistic talent and had not drawn anything since that night five years ago . . . since Toor was Taken. Though only thirteen, Hart felt old. He felt like his parents must feel after a long day in the fields harvesting the purpuran flower buds. He hoped that Lanteri would never have to feel the way he felt right now. Especially as the double moons of Artemis V readied themselves to rise in their annual double-full arc tonight.

The opening and closing of the front door signaled the arrival of their parents. Neither child moved from their respective places in their shared bedroom. The conversation between their parents, or argument as it seemed to be, echoed through the small Company-provided house.

"They all look at me like she's already been Taken," Hart heard his mother say. He could imagine the distressed flush of his mother's face. "We've got to do something."

"The Company doesn't give a damn what happens to us. As long as the purpuran flowers are harvested and the royal dye is made, they don't care." In his mind's eye, Hart could see his father's drawn face and strength failing in his old man's body.

"We've got to do something. Anything. Stop the purpuran shipments. Get their attention." His mother's voice had softened to the whine of a wounded animal. "I can't go through this again."

"Saneri, the last time we tried something like that the Company almost starved us to death. The only thing that grows on this mud ball is the purpuran flower. The Company doesn't care. The empire doesn't care. The empress herself can't know of this, and even if she did, would she care? No. I don't think so. There are no rescuers. No brave guardsmen. No heroic Hedari. No stranger SLINGing in from another galaxy who'll come roaring to the rescue. We only have us to depend on. That's how it's always been."

"I can't go through this again. I can't lose her."

Hart reached over and closed the bedroom door to shut out their parents' pain and worry, and most of all, their helplessness. He hoped Lanteri had not heard their parents' despair but, as all hopes were dashed on Artemis V, this one was too.

"In my world," Lanteri said without looking up from her pixel drawing of a castle in a beautiful sunny landscape, "there are no Takers, and no one's afraid of losing their children."

*

"I'm going to Nori's," Lanteri called as she headed out the door.

"Wait!" Saneri called.

Hart, sitting at the kitchen table, heard the panic in his mother's voice and hoped Lanteri would not. He also hoped that their mother would not ground Lanteri on what might be her last day alive.

Lanteri stopped, turned, and gave her mother an impatient look. "What?"

"Uh, don't forget your coat."

"I'm just going next door, Mom."

"Don't you sass me. Go get your coat, or you're not going anywhere."

Lanteri sighed and stomped back to the bedroom to get her coat. Hart listened as their mother paced, then fussed with Lanteri's coat. "You be back before dark. You hear me?"

"It's not like it's gonna get all that dark with the double full moon, Mom."

Hart smiled at the defiance in his little sister's voice.

"Lanteri . . ." Their mother's voice had a warning note in it that promised pain and punishment if she were not obeyed.

Another sigh. "Yes, ma'am. Before dark. Can I go now?" Lanteri asked.

There was a pause before their mother's reluctant answer

came, "Yes. Okay. Go."

Hart knew their mother would not make that kind of fuss about him if he wanted to go over to a friend's house today. It made him hurt a little more inside. He waited for his mother to come to the kitchen.

Saneri was wiping at her face when she entered. Seeing her son there surprised her. "Hart? What's wrong?"

"You look at her as if she's already been Taken." His voice was flat and full of anger.

Saneri blinked at her eldest in shock and realization. Shock turned to anger in a tightening of her lips. "You don't know what it's like."

"I lost Toor, too. He was my brother. My twin. He was closer to me than you. You act like . . . like . . . you're the only one who lost him."

The tightened lips turned into a white line while bright splotches of red shone on Saneri's cheeks. "Don't you dare!"

"No, don't you dare!" Hart stood up, his chair falling away from him to clatter on the floor. "We *all* lost him when he was Taken. Now, you act like Lanteri's already gone."

Hart's outrage deflated his mother's anger, and she slumped to the kitchen chair beside her like a spent windsock. She put her face in her hands and silently wept into them, her body shaking with her repressed sobs.

It was Hart's turn to be deflated. He watched his mother break down in front of him for a couple of silent moments before picking up the kitchen chair, setting it right, and sitting across from her. He let the worst of her grief, anguish and rage pass before offering her a kitchen towel as an apology. For several long minutes, the two of them sat there in silence. Him watching her and her wiping at her face, regaining her composure bit by bit.

"Toor," she said, "was special to me. He promised me he'd never be Taken. He promised me . . ."

"He was your favorite." There was no accusation in Hart's

voice; just a simple knowing truth. Saneri looked away but did not deny it. This lack of denial murdered the last bit of his child's heart. He swallowed his own grief and pressed on. "Now, Lanteri's your favorite."

"She's the only girl child of age in this harvest zone. She's special."

"What about Nori?"

"Nori's too old. They haven't Taken anyone over the age of fifteen in at least twenty years."

"Then why aren't you worried about me?" The betraying words were out of Hart's mouth before he knew he was going to ask the question. But now that the words were on the table between them, he could not snatch them back. At least his mother had the decency to look shocked again.

"What? Of course I'm worried about you! What would make you think . . .? Why? Oh, Hart, I love you. Of course I'm worried you'll be Taken." She paused, waiting for him to respond, but he just continued to look at her, stone-faced. "You're different. You're stronger. Solid. Dependable," she tried to explain.

"Not the prize that Toor was and Lanteri is?"

His mother gave him a look. "Now you're just being sullen. Stop it." She wiped at her face again, but this time it was more of a nervous tic.

This casual maternal admonishment made him smile, though he did not really understand why. Perhaps it was that the admonishment was a sign that she really did care about him and what he did.

Saneri took the small smile as a sign of encouragement. "I love you, Hart. You're the one I can depend on. You always have been." She paused, took a breath, and then forged onward. "That's why I need you to protect your sister."

"Because you and Dad can't."

She looked away and nodded, but not before he saw the flinch of pain on her face. "Yes. You're closer to her. She idolizes you.

You ... I ... I think you're her only hope."

Now that the truth was out between them—almost all of it anyway. Hart nodded at her, feeling better. He *was* Lanteri's only hope. He knew it. He had always known it. "Don't worry, Mom. I'll protect her. I promise." The look of gratitude on his mother's face was painful but he smiled at it. "I know what to do."

*

Lanteri and Hart sat in their bedroom not speaking. They both watched the window as the sun set late in the summer's evening. Their silence spoke volumes to each other in sibling-speak. They were both worried. She looked to him for comfort, and he gave it in a sudden slap at the button that closed the blinds and signaled the room's automatic sensors to produce a dim light. Then, he patted the spot next to him on his bed nearest the wall. She came willingly enough, despite wanting to seem adult. There was enough of a child's need for comfort that she took it went it was offered.

They sat like that on his bed, Lanteri pressed to her brother's side and he with his arm wrapped around her shoulders in a protective embrace. When she spoke, her voice was soft. "What was Toor like?"

He did not look down at her. "He was a lot like you. Good with animals. A dreamer. Always forgetting about the time." Hart smiled. "I was always saving him from punishment. Reminding him to do his chores. To come home on time. To remember what Mom and Dad said to do."

"I'm not like that. I remember things."

Hart looked down at her. "You're right. I guess you've got a bit of both me and Toor in you. Part dreamer. Part ... not dreamer."

Lanteri smiled a brave smile at him. "I'm a princess."

"Yes. You are." He returned the smile in kind.

The two of them lapsed into silence again, watching the

minutes tick over on the clock. Hart did not know what she thought of but his mind raced. Finally, he shifted, waking Lanteri from her doze.

"What's going on? Are they here?" There was a hint of panic in Lanteri's voice.

"No, silly. We've just got to get ready."

"Oh," she yawned. "How?"

"Like this." Hart reached up to the shelf above his bed and found a small wad of dingy rope. "You're gonna sleep in your clothes tonight and on my bed with me." He tied one end of the rope around his left ankle and then tied the other end of it around her right ankle. "If they come to Take either of us, this will connect us, and the pulling should wake one of us up. Then, we have to save the other one. Okay?"

"I'm gonna save you?"

He shrugged. "Maybe. I don't know." He kept his head down so she would not see the look on his face. He did not want her to know that he knew what was coming.

Lanteri nodded. "I'll save you." She curled up next to him, facing the wall while he remained on his back.

"Lan?"

"Yeah?"

"What's the first rule of being a princess?"

"Never, ever abandon your people—for they need you more than you know," she said. There was a smile in her sleepy voice.

"Good. And the second?"

Lanteri's body relaxed in the comfort of the familiar game. "A princess is a servant to all of her people. She's supposed to care for them and never let them down. Ever."

"Yep. What's the third rule?"

"A princess must be kind and generous, but firm, because she has to make the hard decisions that others cannot."

"Because 'nothing good ever comes easy,'" he quoted to her.

There was a moment of silence before she spoke again. "Will

you always be my subject?"

"Yes. Always," Hart said. He smiled to himself, allowing his eyes to close and await that which was to come.

*

They came as they had for the last five years. This was the sixth time that Hart would face them, the Takers. They came in light, sound, and beauty. They looked like they could be any one of a dozen humanoid races, but not. They were all beautiful. Shining. Perfect. Too perfect. But, God, they were beautiful. Hart was standing in a field of grass and flowers that could never exist on Artemis V. The sun was shining in that bright, cheerful way that made the Harvesters rush to cover the delicate purpuran flowers that could only survive in the shade.

The air smelled cool, clear, and clean. There was no hint of the musty smell that permeated everything on Artemis V. He knew he was still at home in bed, but at the same time, he was also here, in this impossibly perfect place of beauty and light. There were several of them in the distance, the Takers, watching him. He wanted to go to them but refused to be moved. They had to come to him.

A boy approached. It was the same boy who had approached him every year for the last five years. This boy, with brown hair and blue eyes, grew a year older with each meeting so that he and Hart were always peers. Never one older or younger. "Hart, we're still waiting. Waiting for you."

Hart ached at the sound of his name. "I can't go with you." He saw the boy's smile falter, and it hurt his soul.

"Please. Hart, why not? You deserve a better life. You deserve to play in the sun and the grass. That world is no place for a child."

Hart shook his head. "You aren't real. You can't prove you're real and that what you say isn't a lie."

The boy sighed with weariness of the familiar argument. He

tried something new, "Your brother—"

"Is dead!" Hart interrupted, not willing to listen to anything about Toor. "You killed him five years ago."

The boy shook his head. "No. Far from it. He's here with us and happy. He misses you. He told me to tell you to remember the Day of Purple Hands." For once, the boy did not look happy or sad. He looked confused. "I don't know what that means, and he wouldn't tell me."

Hart felt his stomach lurch. The Day of Purple Hands was the day he and Toor had decided that if they were not allowed to wear the royal purpuran purple color, they would dye their skin with it. It had been Toor's idea; a small act of defiance against the Company and the circumstances that had made their family all but indentured servants to those that employed them. They had gotten in so much trouble. They had been grounded for weeks. But both of them had considered it a victory over the Company. It was something Toor *would* remind him of.

But he could not leave Lanteri.

"It doesn't matter." Hart turned from the boy, though it was hard to turn from that light.

"But, why?" There was a desperate plea in the boy's voice. "Why can't you come with us?"

Hart's answer was a whisper. "Because a prince never abandons his people—for they need him more than he knows."

The boy walked up close behind Hart, putting his hand on Hart's shoulder. "My time is running out. I won't be able to keep coming back. You're my other half. You're the one I was meant to save. If I can't save you, I don't know what I'll do. It might kill me. *Please.*"

The feel of the boy's hand on Hart's shoulder was warm and comforting. It almost unraveled his resolve right then and there. The idea that this boy needed him and needed to save him was almost too much. Then, another sensation distracted Hart from the warmth of the boy's hand. Something was tugging at his ankle.

He looked down and saw the dingy rope from his shelf that he had tied around his ankle pulled tight. It was not a part of this world. It was a part of his home.

Lanteri.

Lanteri was being Taken. From him, from his mother, from his family. Hart shrugged the boy's hand from his shoulder. "My sister needs me." He closed his eyes and groped for his sister. At first, he thought he was too late, and then his hand found his sister curled in a tight ball in the corner of the bed. He grabbed her upper arm and squeezed tight. "Lanteri, stay with us," he whispered to her, praying she could hear him.

Hart opened his eyes upon that field of beauty and light, drinking in the wonder that it was. In his hand, he could feel, but not see, Lanteri's arm. "I can't go with you. My family needs me. And I can't let you take Lanteri." He felt the boy step back from him but did not turn around. He could not turn around to see the sorrow he knew was etched all over the boy's perfect face. It would be too much to bear.

"I'll go now," the boy said. "But I can't wait much longer. We'll meet only one more time, on the next double full moon. You have one last chance to free yourself of that hellish place, and then all hope is lost. Please..."

Hart squinched his eyes shut against the temptation of this place and willed that the boy with his promises of light and joy would just go away. Mercifully, the scent of that place disappeared, and the boy did not speak again.

*

"You bruised my arm," Lanteri said as she looked at the finger shaped marks on her arm in the twilight of the morning. Her voice was subdued, and she refused to look at him.

"I'm sorry," Hart said, apologizing for more than the bruise, as he bent over to untie the rope from around their ankles. As he wadded up the rope again, he could have sworn he smelled that other world on it. He threw it from him towards the shelf and did not bother to see if he hit his mark. He looked down and saw a bruise around his ankle. "You bruised me, too."

Lanteri turned in a sudden motion, threw her arms around him and pressed her face into his chest. Her voice came out in choked sobs. "Why didn't you tell me it'd be like that? Why didn't anyone tell me they'd be so pretty?"

He hugged her to him and petted her hair. "Shhhh," he said as he rocked her. "Shhh, it's okay. You won't remember soon. You won't remember anything about it. It'll be just a dream. No one remembers, really. That's why no one talks about it."

"They were so pretty. It was just like my dream, my picture."

"I know, Lan, I know."

She pulled away from him and looked at his face. "Do they come for you every year? Is it like that every year?"

He smoothed away a tear smug from her cheek and nodded, not wanting to lie to her again. He grimaced at the look of pain on her face.

"How do you not go? Why do you stay?"

Hart closed his eyes and wondered that himself. "I think of you," he said. "I stay because of you. You need me. And so do mom and dad."

"But, what if it's not a lie? What if . . . it's really what they say?"

"You can't think like that. You can't, Lanteri. Think of what it would do to mom and dad if you were Taken. If *we* were Taken. It would kill them." Hart shook his head. "Don't think like that ever." He could hear the lack of conviction in his voice and was certain that she could, too.

She frowned. "I can't remember what she looked like. I can't remember anything but the shining sun."

He turned from her. "Go wash your face and then wake up mom and dad. They'll be glad to know you're still here."

Lanteri got up and walked to the door. She paused, looking back at him. "I want to remember." When he did not answer, she shook her head and left to do as he told her to do.

He shook his own head, murmuring, "No, you don't," under his breath. He did not remember most of the time. It was only in the weeks before the next double full moon that he would remember the field with the flowers and the boy. Last night was the first time the boy had given him proof that Toor was still alive and happy. Last night was the first time the boy had told him how much he needed Hart and that their next meeting would be their last.

For five years, Hart had resisted for the sake of Lanteri, if not for his parents. Now, he knew for certain the Takers wanted both him and his little sister. Next year, they both could be Taken to that place of wonder, to be reunited with Toor, and to live their lives in the sun instead of the shadows and mud. He knew it would kill their parents to lose all of their children to the Takers but, right now, Hart was not certain that knowledge would be enough next time.

STEW
Donald J. Bingle

"Stew" was the first story I wrote on demand. I conceived, researched, wrote, rewrote, and polished it over three days back in 1999 when Jean Rabe tipped me that a Civil War anthology was likely to be a story short. Civil War Fantastic *was published by DAW in 2000 and also made available as an audio book (on cassette tape). Since the turn of the century, I have had another two dozen pieces of short fiction published, along with a couple books (*Forced Conversion *and* GREENSWORD: A Tale of Extreme Global Warming*). Writing eventually replaced competing in role-playing game tournaments as my major non-dayjob, non-sleep, non-TV activity. You can find more about my writing, my role-playing gaming history, my movie and book reviews, and other stuff at www.donaldjbingle.com. I've been a participant in the GenCon Writers Symposium for a half dozen years or so, but who's counting?*

"Pa, I'm goin' to war."

Zeke Daniels looked up with a mild start at his son, but his hands never stopped repairing the worn tack he'd been working for more than an hour.

The boy stood in the doorway of the stable, backlit by the sun sliding behind the hills of their western Kentucky home. The scene was peaceful—the green of the hillsides offset by a luminescent golden glow; the scattered, puffy clouds tinged with a mute rose at their southern and western edges, a tinge that would spread and deepen as the evening progressed toward true night. But the boy was far from peaceful. And it was not just his words of war.

Donald J. Bingle

His brow was furled, his muscles tense, his thin-fingered hands clenched so tight his knuckles were white. Clearly, he expected *words*. His Ma had considered it un-Christian to have an argument with anyone, but even a good, church-going lady could have *words* with someone when they got out of line.

Zeke chose his words carefully, realizing that whatever he said now was more than likely one of the last conversations he would have with his only son—at least for a long, long time. He wanted to keep it civil, unlike the conversations between the politicians of the North and South of these "United" States, which had been uncivil for years and finally led to a God-awful and definitely uncivil war.

"Beau, tain't necessary, you understand, fer you to go. Kentucky here, she's a border state. Allied with nobody and doin' her darndest to just get along best she can. You got no obligation."

Beau had expected a stew, so he had thought about a lot of different responses his Pa might give him. This was not one of them. His carefully practiced lines failed him. Instead, he stammered out, "J-just 'cuz there's a fence at the property line, d-d-don't mean you gots to go and straddle it."

"An' just 'cuz there's a fight in the tavern, don't mean you gots to join it the middle of it, neither," Zeke returned. "Sometimes it's just best to sit in the corner and sip your whiskey, payin' the fight no nevermind. Maybe you're still too young for that wisdom, but it's sho-nuff true."

Beau had anticipated Pa to mention his age—he was barely sixteen, though because of his height and his near-perpetual stubble he looked older. His eyes helped, too, steel gray and always determined looking. "Boys younger 'n me be fightin' already."

"I reckon so, sad to say. But that wasn't my point, son. Tain't your fight. And nobody's gonna come callin' to Beck's Gulch to find recruits. Heck, even the folks over in Hinshaw can hardly find the place back here in the hills. No Army guy's gonna come sweep you up to fill ranks."

Stew

"I'm not volunteerin' 'cause I'm afraid of lookin' like a coward if'n I wait till I'm took." He unconsciously fingered, for reassurance, the pamphlet that was folded up in his right front pants pocket. "It's a matter of justice and honor and duty, that's what it is."

There it was. Honor. Duty. Pride. A man can't argue with that and feel like a man. Zeke still stared at the tack, but he wasn't really seeing it any more. "I reckon it is, son. You've always been real responsible, and for that I've gotta commend you and your Ma, God rest her soul. I guess you're goin' off to war, then. But don't be sneakin' off in the middle of the night. I'll help you pack after I'm done here. An' I'll fix up a big breakfast in the mornin' fore you leave."

Beau visibly relaxed and ran his fingers through his stringy, wheat-colored hair. He felt bad that he had expected worse of his Pa. "Much obliged, Pa. I been teachin' Johnny Horton some of my chores with the horses. He'd be glad to get out of his folks' house, with all them other brothers and sisters an' all, an' stay an' work here, if'n you want. I saved up a bit, too . . ."

"Keep your money, boy. Don't you worry 'bout me or the farm. Sure, the horses will miss you, but they're just animals, boy. We'll all get along."

"Thanks, Pa." Beau didn't know anything else to say, so he turned to leave before he teared up.

The night was mild and the stars shone fiercely as Beau and his Pa finished evening chores and gathered up supplies and equipment for Beau's trip. Pa even offered to let him take one of the horses, but Beau declined. Horses were for officers and cavalrymen. Beau knew he would just be another infantryman. The horse would just be taken away from him, and he wanted his leaving not to hurt the farm's prospects or his Pa's pocket.

They ate in silence in the morning—ham and eggs and grits and brown bread, and some of the fruit preserves Ma had put away before the consumption got her two winters ago. The silence was a good silence, relaxed and comfortable and homey. And all too brief as far as Zeke was concerned.

It was time for Beau to go. The boy shouldered his pack of provisions, and Zeke handed him his cap, which had fallen to the ground. They shook hands.

"One last question, son."

Beau looked at his Pa. He was weary and older than Beau could ever remember him looking. He waited for the question, hoping and praying that Pa would not start a stew now.

Zeke looked at the ground and shuffled a bit, uncomfortably.

"Which side?"

"Huh?"

"Which side you goin' to fight for?"

Beau stared, puzzled. How could he not know? "The United States, Pa. The North. I told you last night, I was fightin' for justice and honor..."

"Everyone thinks they're fightin' for honor, boy. Them Confederate officers are gentlemen, too, fightin' for what they believe in."

"But they keep slaves, Pa. They buy 'em and sell 'em. They whip 'em and work 'em 'til they die. Folks treat horses better'n they do slaves."

Zeke wasn't looking for a fight. He should have known that Beau felt this way—what with his Ma's feelings on the subject and Rev. Throckmorton's sermons. Heck, some of Lincoln's speeches back when he was still in Illinois had been picked up by the Hinshaw paper, with Illinois being so close by and all. Still, he didn't want Beau to be simpleminded about how the world was. "They treat 'em like property, son. *Just like horses*. We break horses, don't we son? Not 'cuz we're mean. We just want to teach 'em the right things to do."

"But it's different, Pa. They're not property. They're people. You know I love the horses just as much as you do, Pa, but they're just big, dumb animals. They ain't got no souls."

Stew

Zeke let it rest, and after a moment Beau turned again to go.

"Just one piece of advice from your Pa, boy."

Beau sighed. Despite his Pa's ambivalence toward slavery, he respected the man, and he owed it to him to listen to his final words of wisdom. "Yes?"

"Fight dirty. It's war, son. Your side only wins if it lives. Fight to win, fight to live, fight to come back to the farm. Heck, fight for justice and honor, too, if'n you want, but fight dirty, 'cause that's how you win."

Zeke turned away and headed straight for the stable to take care of the horses. He did not look back as Beau slowly started off to war.

*

Once enlisted, Beau had little time to think about justice and honor and politics. The outcome of the Great Civil War was in substantial doubt, and there was only time for new recruits to be equipped and drilled and marched—and then marched some more to where they were needed to meet the enemy. Apparently, even the long days of marching weren't bringing up reserves fast enough, for one day the troops met a convoy of half-empty supply wagons waiting to carry them nonstop toward the action. They were loaded onto the wagons with the other supplies—sugar, flour, gunpowder, and shot. But they, the human cargo, were the most urgent supplies needed for the North's war effort.

It was good to stop marching, but the hours of jostling and bumping atop crates of shot and bags of flour were not pleasant, either. Some slept despite the uneven movement, but Beau couldn't. His wagon was in the rear of the convoy and the dust was too thick for comfort for most of the day. As evening approached, the air cleared, and Beau realized it was because they were falling behind the other wagons. Maybe one of their horses was injured or their load was heavier, for eventually the rest of the convoy pulled away out of sight and left them struggling on alone in the twilight. The convoy's supplies were too urgently needed to travel at the speed of the slowest element. The dimming light and clearer air persuaded Beau to try again to doze.

He had barely nodded off when he was awoken by shouts and shots and hoofbeats. A Confederate patrol on horseback was pursuing the wagon. They were probably after the shot and food, but there was no doubt that the Union soldiers would not survive the ambush, even if the driver could be persuaded to stop the team and surrender. A patrol like this, acting alone behind Union lines, would not have the time or patience for prisoners. The Union officer riding shotgun was already slumped over, dead or soon to be, in the seat next to the frantic driver. Eight Rebels were in pursuit from behind; five to the right of the wagon, three to the left.

The Union recruits in the wagon were firing frantically at the group of five and hollerin' for Beau to start up on the three on his side. The defense was not going well, what with the wagon bouncing and the young soldiers panicking. Beau's companions fired quickly, wildly, then cussed as they tried to reload in the midst of the movement and the smoke and commotion of the fight.

Beau grabbed his rifle, flipped up the sight, and tried to steady the barrel atop a sack of flour that had already been tore up by Rebel bullets. His companions were firing repeatedly from the other side of the wagon, but Beau took his time to aim, to get used to the rhythm of the ruts and washboard of the road. He tuned out the shouts from the other side of the wagon, tuned out his fellows yelling his name, telling him to shoot, cussing at him, cussing at the Rebels. He gauged the gait of the pursuers, adjusted his aim, exhaled, and fired . . . straight into the forehead of the big black horse bearing the lead rider of the Rebels.

For a moment, as the smoke swirled around the barrel of his discharged weapon, he thought he saw the horse rear up and leap

Stew

for the sky, but it must have been an illusion. As he reflexively brought down his weapon to commence reloading, he saw the true consequences of his shot. The black horse's head dropped toward the ground, legs still furiously propelling the animal forward for a moment—until suddenly the front legs buckled and the horse plunged into the ground at speed. As dirt and gravel were kicked up, the startled rider was catapulted over his mount. His booted feet cleared the stirrups, but his hand tangled in the reins, and he could not break his own fall into the rutted roadway. He hit headfirst with a sickening, crunching thud.

The horse and rider immediately behind had careened into the dead black horse, tripping badly and falling to the side, still at speed themselves. The rider's leg snapped as his horse began to summersault, and he could not clear his foot from the stirrup. He cried out sharply.

This horse did not fare better, its fall stopped by a protruding boulder along the ditch at the side of the road. The rider continued to scream as he clutched at his grotesquely angled leg.

The third, perhaps wiser, rider had not been so close up on the lead. His horse, a pale gray mare with a mane the color of coal, slowed instinctively as the jumble occurred before it, even before the scene had fully registered on the rider's countenance. But the tangle before it, combined with the screams of the men and the shots from the other side of the road, overwhelmed the mare's training. It reared up, throwing the third rider into a deadfall on the other side of the ditch.

Panicked though they were, Beau's companions peripherally saw the results of his shot. They calmed down and followed his lead and aimed for the horses. The ambush ended quickly after that. The driver halted the wagon, and one of the boys went back to dispatch the wounded. Beau thought the youth seemed too eager to perform the task, but he said nothing.

Then, they all went back to loot the bodies. A muffled snort revealed to Beau that his companion had taken care of the men, but not the wounded horses. He did the duty himself. The pale mare had run off, riderless and unwounded. They did not pursue her.

As they camped for the night, the others talked of the ambush and of Beau's sensible response. "Horse-sense," they called it and laughed at the joke. Beau did not share in their glee but did not decline when they offered to spare him from a shift on watch that night. He bedded down with determination. Not only was he dead tired, but he had just—for the first time in his life—killed a man (more than one, in fact). He worried that he might dream of the Southerners' families or that the foul Rebels' ghosts would haunt him.

Though he did not dream, he did not sleep well either. Nothing as dramatic as a visitation by Rebel spirits, but the whinnies and neighs from the horses at the supply wagon kept waking him. Obviously, he had bunked down too close to where they were tethered—he made a mental note to sleep farther away the next night. His room on the farm faced the stable, and he couldn't remember the noises of the horses during the night bothering him before. Of course, there he had been safe in bed. Here he was on hard, cold ground, with enemies nearby—somewhere.

By the time he awoke, the driver had cooked up something for breakfast that smelled fine. Stew, with plenty of fresh meat. He was on his third bowl before he realized where the meat had come from—the dead horses. No wonder the supply horses seemed skittish.

They caught up with the rest of the convoy and their detachment by mid-morning. Beau's companions recounted the tale of their battle with much bravado, showing off the patches they had cut from the uniforms of the dead rebels and loudly crediting Beau with incredible "horse-sense."

All that day the troops pitched tents, organized supplies, and traded rumors about the coming battle. Beau did his best to help with the chores, but he felt queasy—probably just a delayed reaction to the excitement of the battle.

Early in the evening, one of the patrols that had been sent out that afternoon returned, the men's packs dripping with blood. As a crowd of infantrymen congregated, they excitedly reported their exploits amid the hoots, huzzahs, and hollers of the gathered Union soldiers.

"We gets to this big clearin', see, and we waits for awhile before just steppin' out and wanderin' across there in the open. But we don't see nothin' and don't hear nothin' for about ten minutes. So we start off across. We're close to halfway when this here Rebel cavalry patrol comes chargin' out of the woods along a crickbed, whoopin' and hollerin' with big ole smiles on their faces. Well, one of the guys, Percy here, he just ups an' hollers "Horse-sense, boys, horse-sense!" Tarnation if we don't all take aim at the lead horses and fire off all together like. Next thing you know, there's hooves flyin' and men screamin' and horses rearin' and boltin.' And we'd killed ourselves an entirety of a Rebel patrol, includin' a Lieutenant no less, without takin' a scratch ourselves. Not only that, but we brought dinner!" With that exclamation, the bloody packs were emptied of their contents of fresh horsemeat, and the quartermaster's staff swooped down to fetch the meat up for dinner.

The festivities continued a bit after dark, but Beau was already bunked-out for the night in a pup-tent. There would be a battle coming up soon, everyone knew it, and he still didn't feel that good.

*

He stands in an open bowl of the earth. The ridge about him is dark against a clear blue sky; no tree or structure breaks its journey from horizon to horizon. A soft, cool breeze brushes across his face but is insufficient to stir the grass of the rolling plains. Suddenly, to his left, along the ridge-line, there is a movement. A horse stands silhouetted, black against the blue of the sky. It snorts and shakes its head. There, to the right. More movement. Another silhouette half-circle away from the first along the ridge. Another horse, riderless, without saddle or bridle, like the first.

As he scans back to the first, he sees them coming from behind the ridge. Horses. Dozens. Hundreds. Thousands. They trot up to the ridge-line from behind, then stop, some broadside, some head on to his position. Some whinny, snort, or neigh. A few paw the ground. One or two rear up, then settle down. A large hawk wheels in a lazy circle above his head, then gives a loud scree and dives for him. As it does, the circle of horses begins to tighten. They move down the ridge, picking their way over the steeper, trickier spots but finally achieving good slope and ground. As they do, they move faster. Faster and faster toward the center of the bowl. Toward him.

Now he can still make out individual horses, but as the circle tightens and the pace quickens, the line merges into one huge beast. A closing arc of legs and hooves bearing down, charging, speeding, stampeding toward him. At him. The sound of the hooves on the ground rises from a throaty, irregular clomp, to a deep, constant, and dangerous roar. Like a huge, high waterfall, breaking on the rocks beneath, muffled by the waves of a clear, deep pool. Thundering, breaking like bones covered by fresh, living meat, the sound stampeding through his ears to drown the sound of his heart. Sparks fly off rocks as the hooves slam into the ground. He falls, and a huge crash explodes in his head.

*

Beau awakened in his tent, lightning flickering in the distance, the sound of thunder crashing nearby. Shaking, cold, and wet, he felt his face with his trembling hand. It was wet—the tent must have been leaking. But it was sticky, too. He frantically tore through his pack, looking for the smooth metal mirror Ma gave him one year for his birthday. He waited impatiently for yet another flash of lightening to illuminate his face. When he saw that it was not bloody, his heartbeat began to finally slow to normal. His face was sticky and greasy—apparently the worn spots on the tent were rubbed with bacon fat to attempt to hold out the next rain. He decided that he had been awakened by the storm and frightened by the noise and his knowledge of an impending battle. But his skin was clammy, his breath came in shallow gasps, and the back of his eyelids felt hot against his eyes.

He refused morning stew and tried to prepare with the others for the march to the upcoming battle. But he was shaking and ill. He rushed toward the latrines, but someone left the gate open on the make-shift corral for the supply horses, and a small herd blocked his way. He attempted to dodge past, but his reactions were off from the fever. He bumped against a large pinto, and it skittered and snorted, swinging its head around to snap at him with its yellow teeth. This stirred the other horses, and they began to stomp their hooves on the ground and move in frightened circles about him, herding him with their bodies and angry shoves of their heads. He tried desperately to maintain his path, then merely to maintain control of his own movements, but a hoof stomped down on the side of his foot, and he screamed. He gathered his strength and focused all of his being on just getting away from them, just getting out of this press of flesh . . . of horseflesh . . . alive and whole. But no matter where he turned, he was blocked. Blocked by flesh and hooves and teeth and strength and mass.

Finally, sobbing, he broke. He no longer resisted where he was pushed by the trampling beasts. His fevered body swelled from the bruises and tears as he was brutalized by the herd. Suddenly, they reared up as if one, and he saw a path to open ground. He dove under the flailing hooves, tumbling into an opening in the woods adjacent to camp. And he ran. He ran away . . . away from the horses, away from the camp, away from certain death. At first he heard a few shouts from behind, but soon nothing but the sounds of the woods.

He remembered nothing after that point until he arrived home in Kentucky—sick, malnourished, and delirious. His Pa took him in and nursed him back to physical health, without ever asking him a question; not where, or when, or what happened. And after a bit, he was normal again, but not the same. He worked the farm, but stayed out of the stables. He slept in the storeroom behind the kitchen.

And he never talked about honor or duty or justice. Or pride, which had fled him. He was not proud to have gone to war. He was not proud of what he did. He was not proud to have run. He was not proud to have returned. He was not proud to be alive. And he was not proud when the war was over.

He did not go with his Pa to the parades or the speeches in Hinshaw or elsewhere after the war. He did not read the news accounts of the battles. But somehow, he knew one piece of history about the war: that on the morning after he ran, July 1, 1863, his companions fought in the Battle of Gettysburg, a battle in which fifty thousand men died.

And five thousand horses.

In the Eyes of the Empress's Cat
Bradley P. Beaulieu

Bradley P. Beaulieu is a SpecFic writer who figured he'd better get serious about writing before he found himself on the wrong side of a lifelong career in software. His story, "In the Eyes of the Empress's Cat," was voted a Notable Story of 2006 by the Million Writers Award. Other stories have appeared in "Realms of Fantasy," "Writers of the Future," "OSC's Intergalactic Medicine Show," and several DAW anthologies. He lives in Racine, Wisconsin, where he enjoys cooking spicy dishes and hiding out on the weekends with his family. For more, please visit www.quillings.com.

Al-Ashmar sat cross-legged in the tent of Gadn ak Hulavar and placed his patient, a spotted cat, onto a velvet pillow. Gadn lounged on the far side of the spacious tent, puffing on his hookah and waiting for the diagnosis of the animal, which was grossly thin.

Al-Ashmar held his fingers near the cat's nose. She sniffed his hand and raked her whiskers over his knuckles. When the cat raised her head and stared into his eyes, Al-Ashmar found a brown, triangle-shaped splotch in the right eye, along the left side of the green-and-gold iris. The location of the mark indicated the cat's liver, but it was the strong color that was most disturbing.

"What have you been feeding her?" Al-Ashmar asked as he stroked the cat, inspecting its muscle tone.

Gadn shrugged his massive shoulders. "Nothing. Cats find food."

Al-Ashmar smiled, if only to hide his annoyance. The wealthy always wanted cats of status, but when it came time to care for them, they hadn't any idea worth its weight in sand.

"Not this one," Al-Ashmar said as he picked up the cat. He

stood up, absently rubbing its ears. "Please, go to the bazaar. Buy a large cage and some swallows. Once a day, put her in the cage with one bird. The activity should interest her enough to induce appetite. Do this for a week and her normal eating pattern should return. If it doesn't, send me word."

A bald servant boy rushed into the room and bowed. "Master, if you please, there is a messenger."

"We are done?" Gadn asked Al-Ashmar.

"Yes."

"Then bring the messenger here, Mousaf." Gadn handed Al-Ashmar three coins and embraced him, kissing one cheek, then the other.

The servant boy remained, however. "Begging your mercy, Master, but he asks for Al-Ashmar ak Kulhadn."

Al-Ashmar frowned. "*Who* does, boy?"

"A man, from the palace."

Gadn shoved the boy aside and rushed from the tent. "Why didn't you say so?"

Al-Ashmar was right behind him. Moments later, they reached the edge of the caravan grounds, near pens holding dozens of Gadn's camels and donkeys and goats. A balding man with a reed-thin beard – the current rage in the Empress's courts – and wearing blue, silk finery stood just outside the caravan grounds, on the sandy road leading back toward the city proper. Behind him stood four palace guards.

The first thought through Al-Ashmar's mind was of the beating Gadn's servant would get for referring to Djazir ak Benkada as a mere *messenger*.

The second was what sort of emergency would require the Empress's own spiritual guide and physician to come personally asking for *him*, a simple physic. At the least, it would be to attend to a courtier's cat – he'd been to the palace a handful of times for similar reasons. Since Djazir had come himself, though, he could only assume it was for Bela, the Empress's own cat.

Gadn ak Hulavar, who was the caravan's master, stepped forward to meet Djazir. "Please, Eminence, would you care to join us? A smoke, perhaps?"

He stopped when Djazir held up an open palm, staring at Al-Ashmar.

"You will accompany me," Djazir said.

"Of course, Eminence."

Al-Ashmar left the confused and slightly hurt Gadn and followed the royal guards and physician toward the palace. The walk through the city streets was not long, but neither was the climb easy. Al-Ashmar didn't consider himself old, but he didn't have difficult hikes in him any more – not without gasping for breath, in any case. Djazir, on the other hand, though a good fifteen years older than Al-Ashmar, seemed hardly winded at all.

They walked through the Grand Hallway, with its long pool of water and lily pads, up four sets of stairs to the Empress's personal wing, through a small garden of palm trees and beds of sculpted sand, and finally into the waiting chamber of the Empress herself.

Nearly ten years had passed since he'd had the honor of visiting the Empress's wing, but Al-Ashmar was still surprised to find so many memories in conflict with reality. The room was as opulent as he remembered, but almost completely empty: the only furnishings were the throne itself and a marble table crouched next to it, with three books stacked on top.

Djazir spoke softly. "Understand, ak Kulhadn, you are here to examine the Empress's cat. That is all. You will do your business and you will leave. Is that clear?"

Al-Ashmar bowed his head low. "Of course, Eminence."

"If the Empress decides to speak to you, it will be through her handmaid. But this is taxing upon her. You will formulate brief answers, which will not invite further comment."

"Of course."

Djazir studied Al-Ashmar's eyes. Finally, apparently satisfied, he turned to the guard nearest the rear of the room and nodded. The guard rang a small, brass cymbal. Minutes passed, and Al-Ashmar began to wonder if the cymbal had been heard, but then the door opened, and two huge eunuchs walked in, carrying a covered palanquin between them. The Empress sat inside the conveyance, her form obscured by the green veils that hung down from its roof. The only thing Al-Ashmar could discern was the golden headdress atop her brown hair.

The eunuchs – only their kind were allowed so close to the Empress – set the palanquin down near the throne and, after parting the veils on the far side, lifted the Empress and set her gently on the seat. Then they moved to stand behind her, one on each side.

The Empress was not well. Her eyes drooped, the left one lower than the right. She sat tilted to one side, her head arching back the other way. Her arms were thin, her hands resting ineffectually in her lap. Al-Ashmar barely recognized her – another memory that appeared to have faded to the point of uselessness. Then again, the last time he'd seen her had been years before the malady that had left her in such a state.

Al-Ashmar suddenly realized someone else had entered the room. A woman – young, but no child. She moved with a subtle grace, hips swaying, but looked at no one until she reached the Empress's side. Thus positioned, she turned and regarded Al-Ashmar with impassive, kohl-rimmed eyes. How stunning those green eyes were. How beautiful.

Much of Al-Ashmar's mind wanted to compare her to another beauty in his life – dear Nara, his wife who'd passed years ago – but those memories were still tender, so he left them where they were. Buried.

With no one to perform introductions, Al-Ashmar took one knee before the Empress and her maiden. "I am Al-Ashmar ak Kulhadn, humble physic."

"The Empress knows who you are," the younger woman said.

Movement drew Al-Ashmar's attention away from the Empress. From inside the palanquin leapt a cat: Bela, "the Bright One," the ninth and final companion to the Empress Waharra before she alit for the heavens. Like the animal Al-Ashmar had just treated, Bela was long and lean, but she had the muscle tone of a pet treated well. Her smooth coat was ivory-hued, with onyx spots across her sides and back. Stripes ran down her face, giving her an innocent but regal look. She roamed the room and croaked a *meow* as if she had just woken from a long nap. Wary of Al-Ashmar and Djazir, but she slunk to the foot of the throne, curled up in a ball, and began licking one outstretched leg.

Djazir went to the palanquin and retrieved a crimson pillow dusted with short, white hair. He set it down several paces away from the throne and then placed Bela upon it.

"Please," he said to Al-Ashmar, motioning to Bela, "tell us what you can."

Al-Ashmar hesitated – how rude not to introduce the woman! – but there was nothing for it. He couldn't afford to insult Djazir. As he stepped forward and knelt before the cat, he felt the Empress's eyes watching his every move. Her body may have failed her, but her mind was as sharp as ever.

Al-Ashmar stroked Bela's side and stomach. The cat stretched and purred.

"Her symptoms?" he asked.

He expected Djazir to answer, but it was the Empress's woman who spoke. "Her feces are loose and runny. She eats less than before, though she still eats. She is listless much of the day."

Bela's purr intensified, a rasping sound everyone in the room could hear.

"Anything else? Anything you noticed days ago, even weeks?"

"Her eyes started watering and crusting eight or nine days ago. But that stopped a few days later."

"Has her diet changed?"

"She began eating less, as I said, but Djazir administered cream from cattle of the Empress's reserve herd, laced with fennel."

"She's kept her appetite since then?"

"Yes, but she still seems to eat too little."

Al-Ashmar scratched Bela under the chin. Bela craned her neck and squinted, but when she opened her eyes wide again, Al-Ashmar started. He leaned closer while continuing to scratch, tilting Bela's head from side to side. Bela seemed amused, but on the inside of her iris was a raised, curling mark. It kept the same golden color as the iris, but something was obviously there, just beneath the surface.

Al-Ashmar sat upright again, confused.

The Empress's woman's expression said she'd rather this sullied business be over and done with.

"Do you have a name," Al-Ashmar asked, "or shall I continue to treat you like a talking palm?"

The Empress stirred, making a sound like a cough. Was there a hint of a smile there?

"You may call me Rabiah," the woman said. "Just that."

The height of rudeness! What civilized person withheld her mother's name?

"Where has this cat been, *Rabiah*?" Al-Ashmar asked.

Her eyes narrowed. "What do you mean?"

"I asked where the Empress's cat has been, in the last month."

"In the palace only. She has never left."

"Never?"

"Of course not."

"Enough, ak Kulhadn," Djazir said. "What is it you see?"

"Forgive me. I ask these questions because Bela – long may the sun shine upon her life – has snakeworm."

"What?" Djazir asked. He kneeled beside Al-Ashmar and stared into Bela's eyes.

"Look for the raised area," Al-Ashmar told him. "There."

While Djazir inspected her eyes, Al-Ashmar wondered how this could have happened. Snakeworm was common in his homeland, but that was far to the south, and the worm came from *goats*. There were caravans, of course, like Gadn's, that brought livestock north. It was conceivable that a cat could get it from a transplanted goat, but the worm seemed to have trouble thriving in the north. In nearly twenty years in the capital, he'd seen only three cases, and all of them had been near the caravan landings or the bazaar. How could a cat that never left the palace grounds have contracted the worm?

Al-Ashmar rose. "I can make a tonic and return tomorrow."

"No," Djazir said, standing as well. "You will tell *me* how to make it."

Al-Ashmar dipped his head, breaking eye contact with Djazir. "With due respect, it cannot be taught in so short a time. The balance is tricky, and I wouldn't wish to jeopardize Bela's life over a formula crudely made."

Djazir bristled. "Then you will do it immediately, and return here when it's done."

"Of course, but it will still take nearly a day. The ingredients are rare, and it takes time to find those of proper quality. And then I must boil –"

Al-Ashmar stopped at a disturbing noise from the Empress. The sounds from her throat could hardly be called words, yet Rabiah leaned over and listened attentively, as if she *were* speaking.

Rabiah stood. "Her Highness, Waharra sut Shahmat, wishes for Al-Ashmar to make the tonic. Alone. He will return tomorrow, when it is ready, and every day thereafter, until Bela's recovery is complete."

Djazir bowed to the Empress, as did Al-Ashmar. Again, he thought he saw a faint smile upon her lips and wondered if such a thing were possible. She had enough control still to speak to Rabiah. Could she not show amusement if she so chose?

He supposed so. But the real question was, why? Why him? And why *amusement*?

Al-Ashmar turned to Djazir. "Anyone in close contact with

Bela may have contracted the worm, so it would be wise to examine everyone, and even wiser for everyone to take the same tonic as Bela will receive."

After Djazir nodded his assent, Al-Ashmar inspected the hulking guards, then Djazir. As he held Rabiah's head and gazed into her irises, he smelled the scent of jasmine and felt the warmth of her face against his fingertips. He forced himself to examine her complex, green eyes closely to make sure there were no signs of infection.

He knelt before the Empress next. It took him a moment, for the guards watched him like cobras spying a mongoose. The Empress's eyes were free of the worm, but kept flicking toward the stack of books on the table nearby.

When Al-Ashmar stepped away, he noticed the binding of the top book; it was inlaid with a cursive pattern – one often used in the south, in Al-Ashmar's home. In the center of the leather cover rested a tiger eye stone with a silver, diamond-shaped setting.

Bela, sitting beneath the table, watched him closely. For an instant, it was strange how utterly human she looked.

Al-Ashmar nodded to the Empress. "Our Exalted has fine taste in books."

The Empress spoke to Rabiah. Rabiah said not a word, but after a long moment she went to the stack of books and retrieved the top one. She held it out to Al-Ashmar.

"My lady?" Al-Ashmar said.

"The Blessed One wishes to gift you," Rabiah said.

Al-Ashmar nearly raised his hands to refuse, but considered how grave an insult it would be to reject such an offer. "The Empress is too kind," he said.

Rabiah shoved it against his chest, forcing him to take it.

And now there could be no doubt.

The Empress *was* smiling.

*

Late that night, within his workroom, Al-Ashmar poured three heaping spoonfuls of ground black walnut husk into the boiling pot before him. From behind him came the sounds of his children clearing the remnants of the evening meal. Mia, his second-youngest, sat on a stool, watching as she so often did. She picked up the glass phial of clove juice, removed the stopper, then immediately recoiled from the sharp smell and wrinkled her nose.

Al-Ashmar laughed. "If it's really that bad, stop smelling it."

"It smells so *weird*."

"Well, weird or not, it belongs to the Empress, so leave it alone." Al-Ashmar added minced wormwood root and mixed it with the ground husks. When that was done, he flipped his hourglass over. The sand began spilling into the empty bulb.

Mia leaned over the table and retrieved a thin piece of coal and the papyrus scrap she'd been writing on. "How long after the bark?"

"Four hours, covered. It will boil down, nearly to a paste."

She scratched chicken-prints on the scroll. Al-Ashmar tried to hide his smile; when she caught him, she always got upset. She didn't know how to write more than a few letters, but still she created her own recipes as Al-Ashmar made things she hadn't learned about yet.

"Then what?"

"I told you, the clove juice, then the elixir, then they steep."

"Oh," she said, writing more. "I forgot." She sat up and fixed him with a child's most-serious expression. "Doesn't she have people to heal cats in the palace?"

Al-Ashmar hid another smile. He usually told his seven children about his day over their evening meal, but Mia was the one who listened most often. "She does, Mia, but they rarely see such things."

"Snakeworm?"

"Yes."

"From where you and Memma came from."

"Yes."

"How did it get here?"

Al-Ashmar shrugged. He still hadn't been able to piece together a plausible story. "I don't know."

"Tell me about the woman again. She sounded pretty."

"I told you, pet, she wasn't pretty. She was mean."

Mia shrugged and tugged the Empress's book closer. "She sounded pretty to *me*." She flipped through the pages, pretending to read each one. "What's this?"

"A gift, from the Empress," Al-Ashmar said.

"What does it teach?"

Al-Ashmar smiled. It was a retelling of four fables from his homeland – simple tales of the spirits of the southern lands and how they helped or harmed wayward travelers.

"Nothing," he said. "Now off to bed."

Mia ignored him, as she often did on his first warning. "What's this?"

Al-Ashmar glanced her way, then snatched the book away and stared at the scribbles Mia had been looking at. He hadn't noticed it earlier. He'd had too much to do, and since it had seemed so innocuous, he'd left it until he had more time to sift through its pages. On the last page were the words *save her*, written in an appalling, jittery script. The letters were oversized, as if writing any smaller would have rendered the final text unreadable.

The Empress's hand, surely. But why? Save *who*?

And from what?

Mia dropped from her stool and pushed next to him for a view.

"Enough, Mia," he said. "To bed."

After tucking the children in for the night, Al-Ashmar stayed up, nursing the tonic and thinking. *Save her*. Bela? But that made no sense. He had already been summoned, already been directed to heal the Empress's cat. Why write a note for that?

Then again, there was no logical reason for the cat to have the worm. Coincidence was too unlikely. So it had to have been intentional. But who would dare infect the Empress's cat? Did she fear that the next attempt would be bolder? Was something afoot even now?

Bela, after all, was the Empress's ninth cat, her last. When she died, so would the Empress, and her closest servants with her. That was the way of things. It might explain Djazir's tense mood, and even Rabiah's sullenness. But it didn't explain the smile on the Empress's lips.

Al-Ashmar paged through the tale in which the jagged words had been written. It was a tale of a child that had wandered too far, and would have died alone in the mountains. But then a legendary shepherd found her and brought her to live with him – and his eighty-nine children, others he'd found wandering in the same manner.

Some hours later, Al-Ashmar added the clove juice and a honey-ginger elixir to the tonic and left it to steep. After his mind struggled through a thousand dead-end possibilities, Father Sleep finally found him.

*

The following day, Al-Ashmar was led to the Empress's garden. Wispy clouds marked the blue sky as a pleasant breeze rattled the palm leaves. Bela sat at the foot of the Empress's throne, which had been moved from its cold and empty room. The cat lapped at a bowl of cream, which Al-Ashmar had laced with the tonic.

Odd, he thought. Cats usually detested the remedy, no matter how carefully he hid it. Al-Ashmar's other patients, however, were not so pliant. Nearby, Rabiah took a deep breath and downed the last of her phial. The eunuchs, thank goodness, had swallowed theirs without complaint at a word from the handmaiden.

"Bela will need two more doses today," Al-Ashmar said, "and three more tomorrow."

Djazir stared at his half-empty phial, disgusted.

"Please," Al-Ashmar said. "I know it is distasteful, but you need to drink the entire phial."

"I will do so, physic," Djazir said. "But we will not subject the Empress to such a thing."

Al-Ashmar averted his gaze. "Your Eminence knows best. But if the Empress has the worm, its effects will only worsen with time."

The Empress spoke to Rabiah. Al-Ashmar, listening more closely than the day before, still could not understand a single word.

"Of course, Exalted," Rabiah said. She retrieved the phial meant for the Empress.

Djazir gritted his teeth as Rabiah tilted the phial into the Empress's mouth. The Empress's eyes watered and she gagged, causing some of it to spill onto Rabiah's hands.

"Be careful of her eyes," Al-Ashmar said, stepping forward. "The tonic will sting horribly for quite some time –"

Rabiah waved him away. She took more care how she supported the Empress's head as she dispensed the rest of the tonic. The Empress's coughing slowed the process to a crawl, but eventually the ordeal was over. When it was done, Djazir took Al-Ashmar by the elbow, ready to lead him from the garden and out of the palace.

"I wonder if we might speak," Al-Ashmar said. "Alone, so as not to disturb the Empress."

Djazir seemed doubtful, but he released Al-Ashmar's elbow. "What about?"

"A few questions only, in order to narrow down the source of the worms. If we cannot find it, the infection may recur."

Djazir brought him up a set of stairs to a railed patio on the roof of the palace. Beneath them the city sprawled for miles. The river glistened as it crawled through the city—much like a snakeworm itself—until it reached the glittering sea, several miles away.

Al-Ashmar spoke, asking questions about Bela's activities, the Empress's, even Rabiah's, but it was all a ruse. He'd wanted to get Djazir to agree to a questioning simply so he could ask the same of Rabiah. He had to get her alone, for only in her did he have a chance of unwrapping this riddle.

The subterfuge worked: when he was done, Djazir agreed to send Rabiah up to speak to Al-Ashmar as well. She came and stood a safe distance away from him, gazing out over the city. It took a moment, but Al-Ashmar realized she was staring at the fourteen spires that stood at attention along the shore. Empresses lay buried beneath thirteen of those obelisks, and the fourteenth stood waiting. At first, Al-Ashmar thought she was simply ignoring him, but the anxiety on her face as she stared at the last obelisk made him believe otherwise.

"She won't die from the worm, my lady," he told her. "We've caught it in time."

Rabiah turned to him and nodded, her face blank once more. "I know, physic."

Then realization struck. Rabiah wasn't afraid because of the worm, and never had been. She feared something else, something much more serious. Like riddles within riddles, the answer to this one simple curiosity led to a host of other questions he'd struggled with late into the night.

He hesitated to voice his thoughts – they were of the kind that could get one killed – but he had no true choice. He could no more bury this question than deny any of his children a home to live in.

"How much longer?" he asked.

A muscle twitched along Rabiah's neck. She turned away from him and stared out over the rolling landscape. For a long, long time the only sounds he heard were the call of a lone gull and the pounding of stone hammers in the distance.

"Months, perhaps," she said, "but I fear it will be less."

"You know what she's asking of me, don't you?"

"Yes, physic, but you will do nothing of the sort. I will die *with* her. I will help her on the other shore, as I have helped her here."

This is ludicrous, Al-Ashmar thought. I am jeopardizing my entire family with this conversation. I should leave. I should instruct Djazir in the creation of the tonic, heal Bela, and be done with this foul mess.

But as he stared at Rabiah, he realized how lost she was. She would die the day after the Empress did, would be buried in the Empress's tomb, which waited beneath the fourteenth obelisk along the shore of the Dengkut.

The ways of the Empresses had always seemed strange when he'd been growing up in the southlands, and little had changed his mind when he came to the capital to find his fortune. In fact, the opposite had happened. Each year found him more and more confused.

But that was him. His opinion mattered little. What mattered was why the *Empress* would go against tradition and ask him to save Rabiah from her fate.

The answer, Al-Ashmar realized, could be found by looking no further than his own adopted children. Rabiah had cared for the Empress, most likely day and night, ever since her attacks left her stricken. Rabiah would have become part daughter, part mother. And when the Empress died, Rabiah's bright young life would be forfeit. How could the Empress not try to protect her?

Al-Ashmar regarded Rabiah with new eyes. She had cared for the Empress in life, and she was willing to do so in death, no matter what it might mean for her personally.

"You are noble," he said.

Rabiah turned to him, a confused look on her beautiful face. "You don't believe that."

Al-Ashmar smiled. "I may not understand much, Rabiah of

No Mother, but I know devotion when I see it."

Rabiah stared, saying nothing, but her eyes softened ever so slowly.

"I will need to keep coming here for a week, to ensure Bela's restoration is complete. Perhaps we can stop here and talk. Perhaps play a hand of river."

"I don't play games, physic."

"Then just the talk."

Rabiah held his gaze, then nodded.

*

The next week passed by quickly. Al-Ashmar's oldest son, Fakhir, was forced to take a summons Al-Ashmar would have normally taken himself. Tayyeb, his oldest girl, did what she could for those who brought their cats to his home. And though they hated it, it was up to Hilal and Yusuf to watch over the young ones, Shafiq and Badra and Mia.

The family conversed each night over dinner. Al-Ashmar helped them learn from things they did wrong, but in truth his pride swelled over their performances in jobs he'd thought them incapable of only days ago.

Most of his time, however, was spent creating the tonic for Bela and the Empress, administering it, and teaching the technique to Djazir. Bela continued with her uncanny acceptance of the tonic, as Djazir continued his complaints, but the cure progressed smoothly.

Rabiah held true to her word. She accompanied him to the roof, sometimes for nearly an hour. She was reserved at first, unwilling to speak, so it was Al-Ashmar who told stories of the south, of his travels and his early days in the capital. It was uncomfortable to talk about Nara, but he had to in order to speak of his children.

"You loved her?" Rabiah asked one day.

"My wife? Of course."

"You couldn't have children of your own together?"

Al-Ashmar smiled and jutted his chin toward the city. "She knew what it was like, out there. Why make more when there are so many in need?"

Rabiah regarded him for a long time. "You wanted one, though. Didn't you?"

Al-Ashmar paused, embarrassed. "Am I so shallow?"

"No, but such a thing is hard to hide when you speak of subjects so close to the heart."

He shrugged, though the gesture felt like betraying Nara. "I did, once, but I regret nothing. How would I have found my Mia if I had other mouths to feed? My Fakhir and Tayyeb?"

The silence grew uncomfortable, and Al-Ashmar was sure he'd made a mistake by discussing his children. But how could he not? They were his loves. His life.

"*You* are the noble one," Rabiah said, and left him standing near the railing.

*

Unsure of himself, Al-Ashmar stood before the palace, hugging Mia to his hip.

The eighth day had come: the last time Al-Ashmar would be allowed into the palace. Djazir had mastered the tonic, and had grown increasingly insistent that no one, least of all the Empress, needed to take such a distasteful brew any longer.

Al-Ashmar could hardly argue. The snake-like trails in Bela's eyes were gone, and her feces had returned to its proper consistency. The work was nearly done ... but there was unfinished business still. The Empress's written plea troubled him still.

"Let's *go*," Mia said.

"All right, pet. We will."

They entered the palace. The guards frowned at the unexpected addition of Mia, but Al-Ashmar explained that Rabiah had permitted it. He went to the Empress's garden, where he relieved his aching arms of Mia's weight.

Djazir marched forward to meet them. "What is *this*?"

"Eminence, my sincere apologies," Al-Ashmar said. "With my absence, my business is in a shambles. My other children are old enough to run errands, but I had no one to watch Mia. She will sit here quietly, and bother no one."

"She had best not, physic." Djazir frowned at Mia. "Don't touch a thing, child. Do you hear me?"

Mia hugged Al-Ashmar's waist and nodded.

Al-Ashmar calmed Mia down enough that he could leave her on a bench near the rear of the garden, mostly out of sight of the Empress's three peaked doorways. He went inside the room, where the Empress sat waiting on her throne. The four guards stood at the corners of the room, two more behind the throne, but Rabiah was not to be found. Where was she?

The Empress stared out through the gauzy curtains hanging over the doorways. She studied the garden, perhaps watching Mia play. Then her eyes took in Al-Ashmar.

And a hint of a smile came to her lips.

Al-Ashmar couldn't help but return the smile, but hid it as quickly as it had come.

Bela strutted around from the back of the throne and moved to the bowl of cream Djazir placed there.

"Come, physic," Djazir said.

Al-Ashmar nodded. From inside his vest he retrieved one of the eight phials he'd brought for the final day, but Djazir held up his hand to forestall him.

"I've administered my own tonic," Djazir said. "All that's left is for you to examine Bela."

Al-Ashmar began to worry. He needed to speak to Rabiah one last time. He would never have the chance again, but with the tonic already administered, there was only so far he could extend the examination before Djazir caught on. He did what he could: he kneeled and studied Bela's golden eyes closely even though they were obviously clear of the worm. He checked her muscle tone and reflexes. He examined her teeth.

"Enough," Djazir said, stepping to Al-Ashmar's side. "We both know Bela is fine. The Empress thanks you for your time."

Just then the Empress began to cough: wracking, hoarse spasms that nearly shook her from the throne. The guards moved to hold her, but Djazir waved them away as he rushed to her side. Al-Ashmar waited, hoping Rabiah would step from the rear of the room.

"That will be all, ak Kulhadn," said Djazir.

Al-Ashmar bowed and retreated from the sounds of the Empress's horrible coughing. How painful it sounded. Painful ... but also a touch forced, to Al-Ashmar's ear.

He reached the garden, but could not find his daughter.

"Mia," he called, softly, hoping Djazir wouldn't hear.

She wasn't in the garden, so he moved up the stairs to the rooftop patio. Then he allowed himself to smile. Rabiah crouched next to Mia, and her gaze followed Mia's outstretched finger through the marble balustrade to the city beyond.

"Is that so?" Rabiah asked.

Mia nodded. "And then Peppa brought it to our house. It was big as me – at least, big as I was then, which is *still* pretty big."

Mia saw Al-Ashmar approaching. "I *told* you she was pretty," she said.

Al-Ashmar smiled, his face flushing. He wished he could say the same thing to her, but Nara's memory stayed his tongue. He tousled Mia's dark hair, but shifted his gaze to Rabiah.

"You could help others," he said, "and the Empress will be waiting for you on the other side."

"She'll need me."

"She'll have your predecessor, Rabiah. She'll have the others."

He motioned down toward the sound of the Empress's coughing, which was starting to subside. "She'll be whole once she reaches the far shore."

Her eyes pleaded, as if they *wanted* a reason to come with him. "This is blasphemy."

"Not where we're from," Mia said – as if she, too, were from the south.

Rabiah looked down at Mia, and a sad smile came to her lips. "That's just it, child. It *is*, even where your Peppa's from." When she met Al-Ashmar's eyes again, her expression was resolute. "Please go."

Al-Ashmar hesitated. Words always seemed to flee in the important moments of his life, and this time he knew the reason why. No matter how foolish he considered Rabiah's choice to be, he would never force his beliefs on another. She would have to embrace the Empress's wish herself before she could be saved.

"You would be loved," he told Rabiah, then he picked up Mia and left the palace.

When they were out in the streets, Mia stared at Al-Ashmar. "Is she coming to live with us?"

"No, pet, she's not."

*

Some weeks later, Al-Ashmar woke to the clangor of the great bell atop the Hall of Ancients. A gentle rain pattered against the roof. The bell rang again and again. Al-Ashmar knew, well before the fourteenth peal, that the Empress had died.

When it was over, he sat in silence, feeling as if one of his own family had been lost. No, not one – two. The Empress, even in her state, had smiled upon him in more ways than one. How could he not consider her family? And Rabiah. She'd been so close to walking away from her pointless fate.

A soft knock came from the door. He rushed to open it, and

found Rabiah standing outside, drenched.

"I don't want to die," she said.

Al-Ashmar stepped aside and ushered her into his house. He motioned her to his workroom, where the hearth still had enough embers to stoke some warmth from it. He got a blanket and wrapped it around Rabiah's shoulders.

Fakhir walked in, hair disheveled, a blanket around his shoulders. "Everything all right, Peppa?"

"Fine, son. Go to bed."

Fakhir retired, leaving Al-Ashmar alone with this beauty and the sounds of the pattering rain. He prepared some lime tea, but when he handed it to her she looked distraught, as if coming to him might have been a big mistake.

"There is no shame in living a longer life, Rabiah," he said. "There's so much good you can do. For these children." He paused. "For me."

She looked at him. Her eyes, no longer rimmed with kohl, were just as beautiful in the ruddy light of the hearth. "You?"

Another knock sounded, this one harsher than the last.

Al-Ashmar glanced up, his heart beating fast. "Were you followed?"

Rabiah glanced around, as if specters would emerge from the shadows around them. "I ... I took precautions ...."

Djazir bellowed from outside. "Open up, ak Kulhadn, or we'll break the door in."

Al-Ashmar scrambled to find a proper hiding place, but there was none. He couldn't even spirit Rabiah out the rear door. There was no telling what Djazir would do if he caught them running.

"It will be all right. Stay by my side," he said. As he moved toward the door, four of his children appeared in the doorway of their bedroom. He waved them back. "Fakhir, get them to bed, *now*. Close your door."

Before he could reach the front door, it crashed open. Three guards stormed into the room. Two more stood outside with

Djazir. After the guards had positioned themselves about the room, Djazir strode in as if it were his own home. He looked Al-Ashmar up and down – then Rabiah, who stood nearby.

"Rabiah," he bade, "come."

She stayed still, her gaze darting between Al-Ashmar and Djazir.

"Djazir, please," Al-Ashmar said. "We can discuss this."

Djazir motioned to the nearest guard. Al-Ashmar saw the fist coming out of the corner of his eye, too late to dodge the blow. Then everything was pain and disorientation. He fell, his shoulder and neck striking the low eating table in the center of the room. A piercing pain shot up his neck to the base of his skull.

Before he could recover, the guard closest to Rabiah grabbed the back of her neck and manhandled her toward the exit.

"Stop!" Al-Ashmar cried. "This isn't necessary!"

"Dear physic," Djazir answered, "you have made this *more* than necessary." He knelt next to Al-Ashmar, daring him to rise. "Now I will assume, for the sake of your children, that Rabiah came to you for a bit of advice – to spill her fears of what is to come. It is natural, after all. You of all people should know this. I'll also assume you kindly told her that everything will be fine. Her sacred voyage will be painless, and she should return to the palace, as any good citizen would."

Al-Ashmar opened his mouth to speak.

"But," Djazir continued, not giving him the chance, "if I find differently, or if I see you again before I guide the Empress to the opposite shore, I'll have your head." He stood. "Do we understand one another?"

The door to the children's room was cracked open. Mia's whimpering drifted into the room. Al-Ashmar had no choice. He had to protect them, and though it burned his gut to do so, he nodded.

Djazir smiled, his gaze piercing. "Good. It would be a pity if seven orphans found themselves orphaned all over again."

With that, he left. The door hung open, and Al-Ashmar could only watch as the guards shoved before them, up the street, back toward the palace.

*

The sun had not yet risen. Hours had passed since Djazir took Rabiah, away but still Al-Ashmar could think of nothing to do.

"Peppa?" It was Mia, standing in the doorway to his workroom.

"Go to bed."

"Nobody can sleep, and it's almost morning."

He turned to look. Several of the other children were preparing breakfast in the main room behind her.

"Then eat," he said.

Mia sat on a nearby stool and picked up the Empress's book. "Is she coming back?"

"No, Mia. She's not." Al-Ashmar wanted to cry.

Just then a cat entered through the rear door of the workroom and rubbed against Mia's leg. "Bela!" she cried.

Al-Ashmar looked over in surprise. Indeed, the cat looked just like the Empress's. He picked the animal up and examined her eyes, removing any doubt. It was certainly Bela, but how was that possible? The cat should have died with the Empress.

Bela bit the meat of Al-Ashmar's thumb, and he dropped her in surprise. She walked from the room as if she'd never intended to be there in the first place.

Al-Ashmar followed her out the rear door. She had already slunk beneath the gate of their small yard and out to the alley behind. Al-Ashmar followed and called back to Mia, who was trying to trail him. "Go back, child. I'll return when I can."

Al-Ashmar tracked Bela in the pale light of pre-dawn. She wended her way through the streets, and it gradually became clear that she was leading him toward the palace. She avoided the main western road, however, traveling instead to the rear of the tall, imperial hill. She climbed the rocks, pausing whenever Al-Ashmar fell too far back, then continuing before he could reach her.

The eastern face of the hill was split by a shallow ravine with a trail lined with plants – a gorge carved by waste that flowed from the palace to the river. Bela stopped in this crook. When Al-Ashmar finally caught up, she circled his legs and *meowed*.

Then she vanished into a nearby boulder.

Startled, Al-Ashmar reached out to part a wall of vines that clung to the rock. A low, dark tunnel entrance yawned where the vines had hung. He rushed through, believing that Bela – or, more likely, the soul of the Empress – was leading him up to the palace. He climbed a spiral staircase in utter darkness, as quickly as his burning lungs would allow. Several times the stairs leveled off, leading him a short passage, and beyond it another flight that wound him upward once more. Mostly, it was a grueling uphill climb.

His legs threatened to give out, forcing him to stop, but sunrise was coming, and Al-Ashmar feared that would be when the Empress's retinue would die.

Finally, dim light filtered down from above, and the peal of a bell. Dawn had arrived. Bela *meowed* somewhere ahead. He felt sure he'd climbed thrice the height of the palace, but still he pushed harder. The light intensified, and he came to a wall with a grate embedded in it. The brightness hurt his eyes as he surveyed what he realized was the Empress's garden.

Visible through the three peaked doorways, Djazir paced the length of the throne room. Six of the Empress's personal guard stood nearby, wearing ornate leather armor, with a swords and daggers hanging from their silver belts. Djazir himself wore a white, silk robe embroidered with crimson thread, and a ceremonial dagger hung from a golden belt at his waist. The Empress lay wrapped in folds of white cloth, her face still exposed. Five bolts of white cloth waited on the marble floor to her left.

To her right, on another bolt of cloth, was Rabiah – either unconscious or dead.

Please, Rabiah, thought Al-Ashmar, be alive.

Djazir continued to pace and wring his hands. A young man, wearing clothes similar to, but not so grand as, Djazir's, entered the garden to make a report.

As Djazir and the youth conversed, too quiet and too distant to be heard, Bela slipped out through the grate. Al-Ashmar tried to stop her, but Bela escaped just before his fingers could reach her. She walked up to Djazir as if asking for a bit of cream.

"By the spirits, thank you," Djazir said loudly as he picked Bela up. He turned to the young man. "Prepare the procession immediately. You will find everything ready by the time you return."

The young man bowed and walked back through the garden. Al-Ashmar heard a heavy wooden door close. Moments later, the palace's bell pealed once more.

Breathing hard, Al-Ashmar examined the grate, looking for any sign of a catch. He found something hard and irregular about halfway down on the left side, but had no idea how to release it.

As the Empress's guards lay down upon the white cloths, Djazir used an ornate spoon to ladle a thick, white liquid from a ceramic bowl. He held the spoon to Bela's lips and waited as she lapped at it. Then he set Bela down on a silk pillow upon the Empress's throne and petted her until her movements slowed.

Bela rested her head on her crossed paws and stared directly at Al-Ashmar. Her eyes blinked twice before slowly closing for the last time. Moments later, her lungs ceased to draw breath.

The bell pealed again, long and slow.

Djazir moved to each of the guards in turn and administered a spoonful of the liquid. Each fell slack less than three breaths after imbibing the poison.

Al-Ashmar worked frantically at the catch, thinking, open, damn it! Open!

Djazir ent to stand beside Rabiah's motionless form.

"Stop, Djazir!" Al-Ashmar shouted.

Djazir turned. He stepped toward the grate, squinting. The catch released.

Al-Ashmar stepped out into the light, ready to charge should Djazir make a move toward Rabiah. Instead, Djazir dropped the spoon and pulled his dagger free of its sheath.

"I was willing to let your children live, Al-Ashmar," he said. "But an affront such as this demands both your death and theirs."

Heart beating wildly, Al-Ashmar patted his vest, searching for anything he might use as a weapon. He found only the leftover phials of Bela's tonic. He swallowed hard and pulled one from his vest pocket.

Djazir chuckled. "Are you going to heal me, physic?"

Al-Ashmar unstopped the phial, but Djazir lunged much faster than he anticipated. Al-Ashmar dodged, but still steel bit deep into his shoulder. He flung the phial's contents at Djazir's face. The acidic liquid hit Djazir in the eyes, and he screamed and fell backward.

Al-Ashmar went on top of Djazir, driving his good shoulder into the other man's gut. A deep *whoosh* burst from Djazir's lungs, giving Al-Ashmar time to scramble on top of him. Holding the knife to one side, Al-Ashmar seized Djazir's neck and applied all the leverage he could as the older man writhed beneath him, sputtering and choking, eyes pinched tight. Finally, when the palace bell pealed over the city, Djazir's body lost all tension.

Al-Ashmar gasped, wincing from the pain in his shoulder. He cleaned Djazir as best he could and dragged him into position, upon the remaining bolt of white cloth. Then he rushed to Rabiah's side and tried to wake her. He thought surely she was dead, surely this had all been for naught – but no, she still had a faint heartbeat. She still drew breath, however slowly. He slapped her, but she would not wake.

The bell tolled. He didn't have long before he was discovered.

Al-Ashmar took a bit of the tonic still left in the phial and spread it under and inside Rabiah's nostrils. She jerked, snorting, and her eyes opened. She was slow in focusing, but eventually recognized Al-Ashmar.

"Where am I?" she asked, rubbing her nose.

"Not now. I will explain all later."

Al-Ashmar helped her through the grate, but before he could start down the first stair, she turned him around and wrapped her arms around him.

"Thank you for my life," she said.

He freed himself from her embrace and pulled her toward the stairs. "Thank me when you have your new one."

Al-Ashmar knew they would have to leave for foreign lands, but it couldn't be helped. He hadn't expected this change in fortune, but neither had he expected his wife to die, or to raise seven children on his own. He would take what fate gave him and deal with it as best he could.

With Rabiah.

Yes, with Rabiah it would all be just a little bit easier.

An Animal's Nature
Dylan Birtolo

*"An Animal's Nature" is a story that I wrote as an attempt to try something different than your classical medieval or urban fantasy stories that I have written previously. I wanted to tie in a bit of my knowledge and experience with Native American beliefs and add a bit of a fantastical flair. I currently have a few short stories published and a couple of books available (*The Shadow Chaser *and* The Bringer of War*). I've been coming to Gen Con as part of the Author's Avenue since it's second year. 2010 marks my third year participating on the Writer's Symposium. When I'm not writing, I'm often going out and playing with swords (and axes, bows, lances, etc) and donning real armor (it weighs more than 120 pounds) to perform as an actor combatant. That includes anything from live shows, to film, to even a music video. For more about my writing, fighting, and gaming habits, go to www.dylanbirtolo.com.*

Noah stood in the middle of the dusty path that led through the center of the town. His right hand hung at his side and held a revolver. His thumb idly played with the hammer while his eyes scanned the horizon. He was looking off to the west, where the sun could barely be seen above the distant mountains. A Native American stood a few feet behind Noah with his arms crossed in front of his chest. His eyes were closed and he held his head up at an angle as if in a trance. Along the street, all of the doors and windows were closed and tightly locked.

Something moved out in the distance, drawing Noah's attention. When he focused on it, it disappeared into the darkening air as if nothing was there. He saw more motion, off to his right. But again, when he turned, there was nothing to be seen. He brought his thumb up on top of the revolver's hammer. The clicks echoed through the entire town as it locked into place and presented the next bullet. The next time he caught a glimpse of the motion, Noah brought his gun up and pulled the trigger without focusing on his target. For a few seconds, everything was still as the echo of the gunshot clung to the air.

The growing darkness swirled and collected into the shape of a coyote just outside of the edge of town and off to Noah's left. The creature was sprinting, running past Noah. He swung his gun around, squeezing the trigger as he crossed the coyote with his arc. The bullet bit into the creature's side and there was a brief yip before it disappeared in mist.

Two more of the creatures appeared out of the air in the west and sprinted towards Noah and his companion. One of them tried to run past the two humans, but the second altered his course to charge the cowboy and Native American. It opened its mouth and let loose a howl that made the skin prickle down Noah's spine. He kept his arm steady as he swung it around and fired a shot into the forehead of the creature. It too, disappeared. One final shot felled the third one just before it turned a corner around the nearest stable.

The two men stood at the edge of the town, watching and waiting as the moon rose and offered some limited light. No more creatures came out of the darkness.

Noah turned around and holstered his gun. He nodded, flashed a smile, and stuck out his chest as he spoke to his companion. "We got them wolves before they caused any more trouble. Looks like it's gonna be some more easy cash."

Istaqa opened his eyes and brought his head to a normal position so he could look Noah in the eye. "Those were not wolves; coyotes."

"Whatever, Chief. What difference does it make?"

"They are not the same." He opened his mouth to say more,

but Noah gave a dismissive wave of his hand.

"It don't matter. Just get ready to do your part of the song and dance to chase them away." Noah walked past Istaqa and continued speaking over his shoulder. "Time to get some sleep. Tomorrow we got to see how much the mayor's gonna give up for our expert services."

*

Early the next morning, Noah sat in a comfortable chair in front of the mayor. He leaned back and put his arms up to lace his fingers together behind his head. Istaqa stood behind him, against the wall and to the side of the door. He was straight as a pole and stared at a point just above the mayor's head.

"I hear you've got a ghost problem," Noah said.

The mayor cleared his throat and wiped his face with a handkerchief. "Well, I wouldn't say that exactly, Mister Sands. Just some folk have been reporting seeing some things at night."

"From what I hear, you got shadows turning into wolves and tearing up your cattle; and they aren't leaving no tracks. I heard people shoot at shapes, but hit nothing. And it's more than just what I heard, I saw them last night too. Unlike you folk, I can shoot 'em and kill 'em."

"Yes, well..." The mayor let the sentence trail off into silence. His hand shook as he felt the man's stare measuring him. "That's why you're here, isn't it? You can take care of this kind of thing. I heard you've dealt with—" he paused for a moment and looked at Istaqa, "—their type before. Can we talk in front of him?"

Noah looked back over his shoulder at his companion. Istaqa didn't move. "Old Chief there ain't a problem. He knows which way the way the winds are blowing. We been through most of this pioneer country together. Solved a lot of towns' problems. More of his kind should be like him." Noah uncrossed his fingers and leaned forward on the arm of his chair. "So, tell me what's been going on with your problem."

The mayor took a deep breath before beginning. "The trouble started up when a couple of us ran into a group of them redskins only a few miles away. Claimed we were on their hunting grounds, but the government gave us this land and they aren't supposed to be here. We've been here for months! Ever since then, we've been having these nightmares. And..." his voice grew quiet and he leaned forward to whisper, "we all know those scalpers are unholy types that practice black magic."

At those words, Noah smiled. "I think I can deal with your little problem. You willing to pay?"

The mayor nodded. "Anything to get those redskins to leave us be."

Over the next several minutes, the two men discussed the terms of their agreement. In addition to his fee, Noah insisted on being provided with an extra horse hitched to a cart full of wood. When the mayor pressed about this request, Noah brushed him aside, claiming that it was a complicated but crucial element of the work he was about to perform. The mayor agreed to the terms and paid Noah half of the fee in advance. While the mayor arranged to provide the additional horse and cart of wood, Noah and Istaqa gathered their belongings and prepared their horses.

"Should be an easy job, eh Chief?"

Istaqa said nothing, settling his gear with gentle, deliberate motions. His gaze was unfocused as he moved.

"Relax, Chief. You'll get your cut when we're done. I ain't about to start cheating you now."

Istaqa blinked and turned his head to look at Noah. "Your bullets worked, but the others did not. Why?"

"They probably got all afeared and couldn't hit nothing. It don't matter. After your magic, it'll all be over and you'll get paid."

"I think your bullets were just as useless. Coyote is smart."

Noah tossed the blanket he was holding onto his horse with enough force to make it whinny and pull back against the ties.

"How stupid are you? I shot them and they went gone. This is why you ain't paid to think, Chief. You get paid to work your magic. Leave the thinking to me."

The two of them finished their preparations in silence and then went to retrieve the additional horse from the mayor. Once they retrieved the animal and the wood, they led the three animals out of town. Several people stood in their doorways, watching the two strangers walking through the middle of the main road. Noah stopped them when they were about a mile out.

Noah took a shovel off of his horse and tossed it to Istaqa. Then he sat down and took a long pull from his water bag while the other man measured out paces and marked the dirt with the shovel. Once he had a circle, he began to dig. Noah got the other shovel and helped after a few minutes. The hole was about two feet deep when the sun started to kiss the horizon. A few minutes later, they heard a howl echoing across the plains. It sent shivers down Noah's spine. He stopped digging and whipped his head around to search for the source.

While he was looking around, he bent down, laid his shovel in the dirt, and eased his revolver out of its holster. Another howl surged across the plains, sounding closer, and off to his left. Noah turned, kicking up dirt as he faced that direction. He saw nothing. Just as he was about to turn away, a flicker of motion in his periphery caught his attention. When he looked at it directly, it was gone.

"You see that?" he hissed. He pulled back the hammer of his gun and pointed it out into the darkness. His companion slid forward to stand behind him.

The movement came again, and Noah turned his gun first, firing into the darkness. But when he looked, there was nothing. A growl echoed in his ear, only inches away. He swore he could feel the hot breath of the animal against his cheek. He fired and then turned again, but there was still just empty air. Four more times he turned and fired blindly, trying to hit something that was just beyond his ability to see.

Then he saw it. A coyote ran towards him across the plains with long legs and lips curled back to expose deadly fangs. The beast moved quickly, and his eyes reflected the fading light with a reddish glare. Noah brought his gun around and squeezed the trigger several times, but the hammer fell on spent shells. At a few feet away, the coyote tensed his back legs and lurched through the air.

Scrambling backwards, Noah grabbed Istaqa and thrust him at the wild animal. He rolled away, covering his head and ducking in the hole. The beast dissipated in grey smoke as it hit the Native American. The smoke continued at the same speed, rematerializing into a coyote on the other side of the hole. It continued on its path straight for the town.

Noah picked himself up and wiped the dirt off of him as best as he could. "You are damn lucky, Chief! Did you know that would happen?" he asked with a smile on his face.

Istaqa's face was pale and his eyes were still wide. His chest rose and fell as he panted. He shook his head from side to side. "No."

"I knew it was good to keep you around. Now, let's finish setting up the medicine hut. I want this done tonight. There's more money to be made."

The two of them continued their work, smoothing out the hole they were standing in. When they were satisfied, they crawled out and started a fire with the wood from the cart. While it was burning, Noah removed some large stones from his saddlebags and placed them in the fire, letting them warm. His companion removed the large blankets behind the saddles and unrolled them. They had wooden supports rolled into them at the base. The two men used the blankets and supports to form a covering for the hole, making a half-submerged hut.

While they were waiting for the fire to warm the stones, Istaqa sat down with some red squares of cloth. He placed some sage and tobacco inside each one, tying them shut with the same piece of string so that they formed a chain of beads. He had thirty beads when he was done. During that time, Noah walked the perimeter of their temporary campsite and stared out into the darkness. When the stones were red, Istaqa used a set of metal tongs to pull them out of the fire and carry them into the hut. He removed a pipe from one set of saddle bags and disappeared into the hut with his prayer beads. Noah paced back and forth while he waited for Istaqa to finish.

After what felt like an eternity, Istaqa emerged from the medicine hut carrying the prayer beads. His skin was coated in a sheen that reflected the light of the fire. He stood before the flames and tossed in the chain of beads. As soon as the cloth hit the fire, they burst into flame as if they had been doused in alcohol. The flames gained a light blue tinge and smoke billowed upwards. The smoke tightened and twisted, turning into an identifiable shape. A coyote appeared, solidifying with each passing second as more smoke flowed into the creature. Unlike the beasts that attacked them earlier, this one had bright blue eyes that pierced the darkness. Once the flow of smoke stopped and the fire returned to an ordinary yellow shade, Istaqa gave his command. He spoke in the tongue of his people, so Noah just watched until the animal ran off in the direction of the town.

"That will take care of the problem? Your pet dog will hunt down the other ones?"

"Yes, my spirit guide will find the cursed animals."

Noah grinned and couldn't keep the gleam from his eyes. "It feels good to give them scalpers a taste of their own medicine."

Istaqa offered no response. Instead he moved to start tearing down the medicine hut and store it back on the horses for their return trip.

"Good call, Chief. Let's pony up and get back there. I might just be able to convince the saloon owner to open up the door so I can bend an elbow."

*

The following day, just a few minutes before sunset, the entire population of the town stood in their doorways and at their windows, waiting to see if the beasts would return. Noah and Istaqa stood in the center of town with the mayor. Noah had his chin raised and his chest stuck out as he faced the setting sun. The mayor stood at his side, wringing his hands and glancing at the door to his office every few seconds.

The frontiersmen and women waited as the sun disappeared. More than one door slammed shut as the darkness set in. But, as time crawled on, people crept out of their houses. More and more people came to join the mayor and their saviors in the center of town. A few hours after sunset, all of the townsfolk had emerged and were celebrating their freedom, dancing and cheering around Noah. Despite his part, Istaqa stood at the edge, just outside the throng of people. They were all so engrossed in their revelry that they didn't notice the pack of coyotes creep around the buildings and surround them. The pack was made up of both red and blue eyed beasts and was greater in number than ever before.

One of the townsfolk spun around and found himself face to face with a snarling predator. The man screamed. His scream turned into a gurgle as the coyote clamped down on his throat.

The makeshift celebration changed into a massacre. Guns fired frantically, but the bullets passed through the animals and often hit other townsfolk. A woman broke free of the circle and ran for her home, but a coyote chased her down and grabbed her heel with his teeth. She fell to the ground and scrambled at the dirt to try and get away, but the beast's grip was too strong. Another animal jumped on her back and tore at the flesh over her shoulder.

Noah saw the chaos erupting around him and froze. People reached out to him, pleading, even as they died. He broke out of his paralysis and drew his gun, firing off six shots as quickly as he could. His hands shook as he tried to reload, backing away from a coyote in front of him. He ran into something at knee-level and turned around to see another coyote behind him, tearing at a corpse. It stopped to look up at him and snarl. Noah tried to back away, firing his gun again. Soon he was completely surrounded. He tried to reload, but his hands shook so much that he dropped his gun into the dirt. The coyotes snapped at him when he tried to bend down to pick it up.

He looked around, whipping his head from one side to the other. At the edge of the chaos he saw Istaqa walking forward. The coyotes parted for him, forming a path as he approached Noah. The final circle of beasts stayed tight around Noah, preventing him from escaping. Istaqa stood just on the other side of the circle.

Noah held out a hand and called out, "Help me, Chief!"

Istaqa spoke softly, but it carried over the sound of the carnage. "No."

"What's going on? I thought your magic worked!"

"It worked as it was meant. I tried to tell you, Coyote is the trickster. He watched and learned."

"Chief, you can't . . ."

Istaqa cut him off. "My name is Istaqa. It means coyote-man."

He turned around and Noah screamed as the coyotes lunged forward.

THE SHATTERING
Sabrina Klein

I started worldbuilding when I was twelve, but my imagination started with it much earlier. People and places, both real and fiction, captivated my fascination for as long as I can remember. I have a B.A. in anthropology from the University of Akron, with a specialty focusing on ancient civilizations and a minor in photography. I study anthropology through worldbuilding, but I think telling a story with it is the only real way to see what makes the combination tick. In 2002 I started attending the Writer's Symposium, and learned so very much from the speakers. I then got involved in 2007 thanks to Jean Rabe. This story is a major part of my world, but it's not where the world was born. If I had started at the very beginning, what fun would that be?

Kyrylu closed his dark eyes. The sorcerer's tardiness taxed his patience. The ritual to destroy the plague must be completed by the next moonrise, so time was essential. No one disputed that the current alignment was pivotal to success.

"Where is that swamp skinned charlatan?" He padded to the hexagonal window and looked out, seeing the Weeping Tree's white blooms delicately covered in snow; even in winter it persevered to blossom. Flora here was as persistent as the plague, it just wouldn't die.

Kyrylu turned at a slight sound and watched a stubby gnome enter and bow.

"Master." The gnome looked up, his tattoo of enslavement visible brightly in the light. "Sarosh will be here momentarily. He sends his regrets for the loss of your son." the diminutive creature scurried away, eyes to the floor.

Long minutes later the door opened again.

"Where have you been, Sarosh?" The words came out a sustained snarl.

Sarosh froze, the goblin's shrewd gray eyes betraying a hint of fear.

"You share my eagerness for a cure, Sarosh, and yet you waste time getting here."

"Emperor, the lizardfolk have united under Salya. She opposes you directly, and their shamans show their refusal by leaving. Only a few of their elders remain in this cursed place."

Kyrylu permitted a silence to settle between them. "Kill the lizardfolk elders." He took a few steps toward a furry cat like avian he kept as a pet. "Inform Grandmaster Tehl that this had better succeed." The emperor smiled at the thought of the lizardfolks' painful demise. "Complete the ritual without them."

Sarosh bowed as he backed out of the room, and the heavy doors closed behind him. He wrapped his black cloak around his gaunt frame as he moved in and out of pools of torchlight on his way out of the castle and to his home. The night air was still, but angry whispers were carried from the visitor's quarters. The elven healer in residence was cursed with the moon sickness and fell to its prey on nights of this sort. Sarosh knew the elf was welcome here, however, because the emperor favored his healing skills. The goblin pressed on.

Outside on the winding cobblestones, snow pushed into his boots. Sarosh spat at the white-covered ground. He'd made it clear to the emperor that he preferred the warm beaches of his beloved Soltan Islands, where the moons and stars were easily reflected in tide pools. It was easier to calculate their positions. In the back of his mind calculations flowed with magical theory.

"Does he listen? No," the goblin hissed. "I told Tehl the consequences could be catastrophic if anything is miscalculated."

Lights from the tower formed into windows as he drew near, indicating that most of those in his home were awake and researching the ritual set for the next day.

Fingertips touching the grainy wood of the great door, he coaxed it open with a gesture and took a deep breath of the escaping warm air that was laced with the scents of magical ingredients. He tried to block out the echoing screams of the plague-afflicted—friends from home, allies he worked side by side with, relatives, all staying here as they futilely battled the disease.

Candles dotted tables where books rested one atop another. His sorcerous collaborator, Grandmaster Tehl, sat cross-legged on a pillow against the far wall. The dwarf's skin was the color of cinders, its natural complexion, and tiny gems were encrusted on his hands and forearms in swirling patterns like a second skin.

"What did he say?" Tehl asked, not looking up.

"To kill them," Sarosh replied flatly.

"Mmmm, excellent. So destroy them. Take the young masters Enkae and Dahar with you as reinforcements. Let them prove their worth. I want the lizardfolk dead by dawn."

Sarosh mumbled curses on his way up the spiral stairs where seamless stone work was cut by narrow windows. The lizardfolk were superior warriors, and rumors abounded that Ardiss, the avatar of the Mother Goddess, protected them. Intelligent discussion reached him from a cracked door, and he found Enkae and Dahar together, debating magical theory. Enkae's light elven eyes met his. Hers were accented by the band of tattooed knot work across her parchment white face that faded at her gently pointed ears.

"Continue your discussion later," Sarosh growled. "Tehl wants the emperor's orders carried out before dawn. We have some lizardfolk to slay."

Dahar raised his lip in a sneer. The dark dwarf was Enkae's opposite, his skin as black as ink. Gemstone rings graced each finger, and more jewelry was thick on his right wrist. The dwarf gathered his things quickly, grabbing a staff while Enkae donned her fur cloak.

They followed Sarosh down the stairs.

Calm settled on Sarosh's normally twisting nerves, as the trio walked with purpose through the empty streets. Wet flakes fell heavily now.

"We have the advantage," Sarosh said. "The lizardfolk are creatures of daylight."

The lizardfolk resided outside the city near the iced-over river. Sarosh motioned for them to spread out and surround the hut from which smoke rose. Sarosh watched Enkae creep nearer, slowly raising her hand and spreading her fingers.

"Ardiss is in there," Sarosh whispered. They had discussed Ardiss's immunity to their spells on the way here, and the effects of a death cloud enchantment would be useless. Sarosh had agreed to use an alchemical of goblin origin. There could be dire consequences for attacking him.

Sarosh edged forward with uncommon grace and silence as Dahar and Enkae flanked the door. His specialty was alchemy. Withdrawing a flask from his satchel, he spoke the words to Lightning Rage. The wick ignited and greenish blue liquid glowed brightly. At the same time he loped in toward the doorway, giving the bottle an underhand toss. It hit the hard-packed earth inside. Glass broke and the viscous liquid splattered, igniting. The flames spread with lightning speed, distracting Ardiss, who had been meditating inside.

Two lizardfolk priests rushed out through the fire. Dahar grabbed the first one and cast a spell, the priest instantly falling still. The second priest was struck by a crooked line of blue light emanating from Enkae's palm, dropping him, pale belly blending with the snow.

A third lizardfolk appeared, slitted eyes filled with fury.

"Salya!" Enkae cried.

Salya's outstretched hand glowed gold and white and caused the snow to harden around their feet.

Sarosh saw past her to Ardiss, the glowing avatar. Sarosh moved into the open so the lizardfolk could see him. "Your resistance has caused this, your charge's blood drips from your fingers."

Ardiss stood just beyond the entrance, the flames dying down around him. "Your ignorance and disrespect has brought you to evil, Sarosh." Ardiss's green-blue tattoos glowed brightly amid his mottled scales. He took a step forward, where he could better regard the attackers.

Dahar was able to lean forward just enough. He invoked a spell and stretched, his large hands grazing the flank of the nearest lizardfolk, Salya.

Blue light traced the scales. "Ahhhhhhisssssssss!" Salya screamed as Ardiss yanked her back through the doorway.

"I killed her!" Dahar reported.

Enkae worked to free her feet and at the same time cast another flame spell. Amber flames now engulfed the building, and Sarosh struggled to make Ardiss out.

The trio waited as the crude building burned to its supports.

"It's done," Enkae announced, and hesitated. "But Ardiss's body is not to be found."

Dahar saw a bit of fear in Sarosh's face. "If the emperor or Tehl is angered that Ardiss escaped, tell him nothing else could be done about it. Dawn will bring the ritual, and we will either succeed and stop the plague . . . or the hands of your goddess will come for us."

Sarosh led them back to Tehl. "We may not have to worry about succumbing to the plague," he told the apprentices. "Tehl might kill us for letting the avatar escape."

"But he might not," Enkae said.

"True," Sarosh agreed. "Dark dwarves are as unpredictable as goblins."

Back in the tower Sarosh watched Enkae and Dahar return to their study and their discussion. He climbed the stairs to Tehl's chamber. He heard the scratching of a quill against stiff parchment. Nudging the door open, he stepped inside and let the warmth surround him like a blanket.

Tehl looked up expectantly.

"It is done. Salya and two other priests died. Ardiss was there, but he escaped." The goblin watched the dark dwarf's eyes.

"If Ardiss comes to interfere, he's your problem, then."

"Grandmaster Tehl," Sarosh began. "I have not the sorcery able to best him."

"You will stand between him and the rites masters." Tehl regarded the goblin before adding, "If he doesn't kill you, I will. I think you would rather die at his hands, than mine." Grandmaster Tehl began writing again.

Sarosh shuddered and retired to his own room, where he sat in front of a fire pit, dozing. A knock on the door sometime later roused him.

"Enter."

Dahar appeared. "Dawn is close."

"I'll be a moment."

Sarosh dressed warmly and clasped his amulet of greater sorcery tightly. He was no priest, but his magic—a skittish animal, he called it—came indirectly from the Mother Goddess, and the amulet bore the crest of his clan encompassed by her own. While priests would perform the ritual, sorcerers would be needed to help fuel it.

He and Dahar walked in silence through dawn's light, and all the moons but Cephrine, the Mother's moon, were in eclipse. Cephrine's indigo revealed the disturbed snow of the circular courtyard, making the surface look like water flowing gently over river stones.

The sorcerers and priests were almost done with the preparations.

Minutes later the sun rose above the horizon opposite to Cephrine. Tehl began his spell that would work synchronously with one cast by a high priest. The energy was palpable as light bubbled up through the snow.

Chanting in all four ancient languages mingled like birds singing. Sarosh understood only one tongue.

The prayers of the priests turned rhythmic.

Energy moved and red flame-like pools turned purple, and then blue. Green tangled lines branched together to form another pool, and pale blue swirled the other hues together and expanded outward. Lines ran to a central column that appeared to reach for Cephrine herself.

The effect was at the same time mystifying and terrifying.

Sarosh's skin itched from the magical energy. He was so caught up in the ritual, that he almost didn't see Ardiss, who crouched, tail wrapped around the base of a crenel. The lizardfolk avatar's tattoos shimmered blue-green.

Sarosh motioned to Dahar, and they advanced on the avatar, but Ardiss was faster.

Before Dahar could cast a single spell, a spear appeared in the lizardfolk's hand. Ardiss hurled it with such strength that it went through the dwarf's thick chest, the obsidian tip stretching out his back.

Sarosh rammed his staff against the ground in defense, and a translucent black light jagged across the courtyard, transforming the earth around the avatar into spiking energy. Ardiss screamed in surprise and agony before the light flared brightly and the avatar vanished. Sarosh knew it wasn't he who banished the avatar, and the sky drew his attention.

Overhead, great fissures appeared on Cephrine's surface and ripples of blue fluttered like rain hitting still water. Heartbeats passed and the fissures grew wider, Cephrine burst, and a blaze of light enveloped the land.

The Shattering

The sorcerers sprawled on the courtyard, writhing, as their lives were siphoned by the enchantment.

Sarosh awoke hours later. The sun was setting, and he saw pieces of Cephrine floating in the sky, a pale blue light glowing from each chunk.

"You live, Sarosh, and so do others." Kyrylu was there, looking down on the goblin. The emperor looked different, a broken circle resembling a plate was seared into his pale elven face.

Sarosh's blinked in disbelief. "How?"

"All sicknesses are banished, but life was twisted out of your brethren sorcerers and priests to do it." Kyrylu said. "She appeared to some of us, the Mother Goddess, announcing that we are now forsaken by the primordial gods. She gave us these marks." He pointed to the broken circle. "She's ripped magic from this land, and from us."

"All the gods?" Sarosh asked in disbelief.

"We are forsaken. In my native tongue, the term would be 'Tichryth.'" Kyrylu's voice was heavy with bitterness.

"Now what?" Sarosh stared at the twisted face of Tehl.

"Find new gods and new ways, and then we will conquer the old gods, or find a way to destroy them." Kyrylu reached down and offered his hand.

Sarosh took it. "Goblins are good at surviving. Gods or no gods."

The sun slipped below the horizon. The world was darker than Sarosh had ever seen it. No stars shone down, just Cephrine's pale blue broken shards.

Sarosh recalled Ardiss's words: "Your ignorance and disrespect has brought you to evil." Was this the price of their success?

Staging a Coup
Kelly Swails

When I heard the friend of friend's son was majoring in World Domination at a college in St. Louis, my writer's brain couldn't stop working. What would a school that turned out dictators and anarchists look like? After a month in the back brain and a few days at the laptop, "Staging a Coup" was born. I hope you have as much fun reading it as I did writing it.

I met Jean Rabe in 2005, and she must have seen a diamond in the rough, because she accepted my first story for publication for DAW in 2006. Since then I've published several stories and written several YA novels. My advice to neophyte writers? Persevere. Believe. Write.

There are two things you need to know about me right off. My name is Sally Clark and I'm a horrible liar. Those wouldn't be a problem for most of the world's population, but when you're about to graduate with a degree in World Domination, it's a BFD.

That's Big Fucking Deal for the slow ones in the back of the room.

I mean, really: Sally? No one's scared of someone named Sally. And lying is pretty much the name of the World Domination game. I am so screwed after graduation. How am I going to pay off my loans if I can't blackmail a government somewhere? Maybe if I'm lucky someone will let me be their henchwoman.

So anyway. I wasn't worked up about this until my best friend Marissa Kosinsky dragged me out of my dorm room to check our grades.

"I need the moral support," she said as she grabbed my arm and leaned back, trying to hoist me out of my desk chair.

"Since when?" I said around a mouthful of Twinkie. Marissa

had been one of the top students in the WD program since freshman year. She probably knew her GPA to the third decimal point, so I didn't know why she needed to check her grades anyway.

"Since always," she said.

She gave me her patented *you're not going to let me do this alone, are you?* look. I knew it was no use. She'd gotten the only A in Manipulation Techniques. If I didn't relent now she'd pull out the big guns.

"Fine."

I shoved my hair into a baseball cap, brushed the crumbs off my Machiavelli for Morons T-shirt, and joined her.

Marissa and I met first semester, freshman year, when we were partnered up for a project in our Know Your Nemesis class. We were supposed to pretend our partners were our enemies and devise their "deaths." She killed me the first day – I dropped my guard at a frat party and she drugged my drink, stupid Kappas – and I tried for two weeks to return the favor. I stalked her with no luck. Poison was out because she would expect that. One night I tried getting her in her sleep but she'd rigged her dorm with an elaborate alarm system using fishing wire and wine bottles; I still have a small scar on my hairline from *that* fiasco.

With two days left I managed to sneak behind her in the cafeteria – I had hoped to "strangle" her – but she'd hired a bodyguard to watch her back and he "stabbed" me before I could get within two feet of her. I was twelve hours from failing the project when she jumped in front of me on the front steps of the library.

"Good job," she said.

I blinked. "What?"

"You just pushed me down the stairs." She pointed to the

steep, concrete steps that led from the library doors to the quad. "Nasty fall, too. I'm sure I didn't survive the broken neck I suffered at the bottom."

I had to look at her smiling, innocent face for two long seconds before I got it.

"Yeah, right. I just scragged your ass."

"About time," she said. "I was tired of worrying about it. Glad that's over."

She linked her arm with mine and we've been best friends ever since.

*

We walked across campus to our dean's office, where our grades were posted. I had been avoiding this, and now that Marissa had forced me to go I was glad she was with me. It's possible—hell, probable—that she knew I needed her moral support way more than she needed mine. I can't think of anything more humiliating than checking grades.

The first thing you learn on the first day of the General Topics course freshman year is that every single grade you earn in the program will be posted. Every single one, every single class, all four years. At first I blew that off – I'd been an A student in high school, so how bad could it be? – but that was before I knew how brutal college would be. Grades became one more source of competition in an already competitive field. Every time someone slept through a quiz or botched a paper or failed a midterm, everyone knew about it.

This time, though, it was for all the marbles. Our cumulative grade to this point would determine the time we'd be allotted to take the Comprehensive. Every senior takes the Comp, the one test that covers everything we've ever learned in the program. It's a huge part of our grade, and our scores would pretty much determine what our graduating rank would be, and if you flunked it you couldn't graduate. Marcus Tine had gotten top scores on the Comp four years ago and had recently taken over one of the islands off the coast of Madagascar. He was going places.

Needless to say, one wanted as much time as possible to take the test.

We got there just as Dean Winegarden finished fiddling with the massive wall screen that took up most of the hallway outside his office. He peered over his glasses and made a mental note. "Ladies. You're the first to arrive."

Marissa smiled as he went back to his office.

"Helps if you know when he's posting them," she said once he'd closed his door. "You'd think the dean of the WD school would have better security on his calendar."

"Unless he wants people to hack the system," I said. "Now he knows you knew when he was posting the grades. It's not a big jump to figure out how." That sort of mind game was what I'd come to expect from the program.

"Maybe I'll get extra credit. Or a few more minutes on the Comp."

"One lives in hope," I said.

Marissa gazed at the screen. "Damn. Two points shy of the top."

I pushed her aside. "Who beat you?"

"Cash Powell." She said the name like it was poison.

"Bastard."

"Hello, ladies," someone said from down the hall.

I rolled my eyes. Cash. "Well, if it isn't the man of the hour."

"Marissa," Cash said in that smooth way I hated. He checked the wall. He didn't acknowledge my presence.

I gritted my teeth. Someone of Cash's class rank didn't have to waste his time with someone like me. Just because I understood it didn't mean I liked having it thrown in my face.

"I see that I kicked your ass, Marissa, if you don't mind my saying."

"I wouldn't call two points an ass-kicking," Marissa said.

"Of course you wouldn't." He kept running his finger down the list. My stomach curdled because I knew exactly what was coming. So much for him ignoring me.

"And look who's in last place," he said. "Sally Clark. Can't say I'm too surprised."

"Lay off," Marissa started, but I stopped her with a look. Getting helped only made it worse.

He pointed at the last entry. "Looks like you only get two hours to take the test. Pity."

He lowered himself to smirk at me before walking away.

"Don't listen to him," Marissa said.

I glanced at the list. Yep, I was last all right, by a healthy margin. Marissa and Cash both got four hours, fifteen minutes for their tests. I wanted to cry.

Marissa took one look at my face and entered crisis mode. "It's going to be fine. We'll figure something out."

"What's to figure out?" I said. "Two hours is barely enough time to –"

"Stop it. If there's one thing I know about you, Sally, it's that you're smart as hell."

"All evidence to the contrary." I jerked my head at the screen.

Marissa waved it away. "Whatever. Stop feeling sorry for yourself. Look at it this way – you've got two hours to beat Cash Powell."

She had a point, but how the hell was I going to manage that? I stared at the board, the names and grades blurring together as I tried to formulate a plan. One thing was for certain: I wouldn't be passing my Comp the old-fashioned way.

*

The next few days passed in a haze of coffee-fueled all-nighters and study sessions in the library. My classmates were busy brushing up on Monologues for the Masses and Henchmen Studies. I spent my time tinkering with bots and lurking around the Espionage Applications lab.

Comp Day arrived too soon. Marissa knocked on my door and entered.

"You ready?"

I shrugged and knuckled my eyes. "Sure."

"You sleep at all last night?" She looked perky and awake, and I wanted to hurt her.

"A couple hours," I said. "Enough."

"You're going to do fine."

My stomach rolled as I thought about my preparations. If they failed, I was screwed. "Thanks."

"Let's go."

I gathered my hair into a bun before changing my earrings.

"Those new?" She asked, squinting at my lobes.

"Yeah. You like them?" I tried to appear innocent.

She looked thoughtful. "Where'd you get them?"

"Just this little place in the mall."

She gave me a funny look, but dropped it. I adjusted my pack and tried to relax as we walked across campus to the main lecture hall. It fits three hundred people; with forty WD majors, there was plenty of room to spread us out and discourage cheating.

A small crowd had gathered outside the doors, and the tension was through the roof. If science could figure out a way to harness nervous energy, college campuses at exam time could power whole cities. Maybe if my World Domination career didn't take off, I could go into Research and Development.

Cash was standing front-and-center, but he still managed to notice our arrival.

"Sally. Finishing the exam in two hours is going to be quite a feat. Did Marissa help you study?" he said.

I clenched my jaw. Cash really had a knack for making an insult seem like pleasant conversation. I had to give him that.

"No."

Cash smiled. "Perhaps after graduation I can find a place for you in my team. You know, if the Comps don't work out in your favor."

"That's big of you, Cash," Marissa said.

"Thanks but no thanks," I said as bile rose in my throat. Oh, hell. He and I both knew that if I failed my Comps, working for him would be a gift. Hopefully it wouldn't come to that.

Cash smirked and was about to say something else – intelligent, no doubt – when the doors to the lecture hall opened. The crowd hushed as Dean Winegarden checked his clipboard. He made a show of arranging the strap of a stopwatch around his wrist and cleared his throat. "Cash Powell and Marissa Kosinsky, your time starts now." He clicked the watch.

Marissa whispered "good luck" before walking away. The crowd parted to make a path for Marissa and Cash. Once the doors closed behind them, a low murmur erupted. It was really happening. The test that would determine the rest of our lives had begun. I found a spot against the opposite wall, slid to the floor, and settled in. I had two hours to go over my plan.

By the time Winegarden called my name, my butt had gone numb. I had been alone in the vestibule longer than I care to admit, and the thinking time hadn't been good for me.

"Your bag," he said.

"Oh, right."

I slipped my book-bag off my shoulder and put it with the others along the wall. Bags had never been allowed during tests, to make sure we couldn't bring in cheating materials. I tried to keep my face neutral as I followed the dean into the hall.

My stomach clenched as I looked at everyone bent over their tests. What if this was all a big mistake? I should just take the Comp the right way and see how I fared. I couldn't do worse than last in class, right?

I glanced around: most everyone was at least halfway done.

Cash looked up and smiled blandly just as my eyes passed over him. I gave him my best "oh, were you looking at me?" look. I could swear I heard him chuckle as he tapped his watch and turned back to his test.

That was it. There was no way in hell I could ever work for him. Any hesitation I'd had about what I planned was gone. What was it Professor Markus wrote in *Sun Tzu is a Wuss: The Art of War for the 21st Century*? No risk, no reward. I grabbed the pencil from the desk, ripped the seal on the test booklet, and began.

The first section covered the sciences. I groaned. I had barely scraped a passing grade in my Fun with Nuclear Warheads and Nanotechnology and You classes. Hopefully my theoretical application was better than my memorization skills. I glanced at Winegarden before slowly opening the face of my watch. A cloud of Nanos escaped their confines and hovered over my wrist. These babies only had enough juice for one expedition, so I had to pick right the first time. I bent down to whisper to them.

"Copy Cash Powell, pages one through –" I flipped through my booklet "– fifty-two. Return and report when complete. Go."

The cloud dispersed and flew across the room, invisible to the naked eye.

I grinned as I imagined the bots combing through Cash's test without him having the slightest clue. They returned before I had the chance to pretend to answer the first question. I enclosed them in my watch and pushed a button. Cash's answers scrolled across the face. I copied them as quickly as I could.

The Nanos' energy stores emptied just before I started the last question. Oh, well. Getting one wrong would make this look legitimate, right? I answered as best I could before moving on.

The next section was Psychological/Sociological Applications. I might be lame at hard science, but I got decent grades in all my Psych and Soc classes. I answered everything I knew before twisting my left earring in its hole. This turned on the thought receptor I'd lifted from the lab building.

A jumble of *oh crap I'm so screwed I don't have enough time what does this question even* mean *I can't believe I know this one holy fuck I'm going to ace this thing this test is a load of shit* filled my head.

Too much. I was getting everyone's thoughts around me. I twisted the earring again and homed in on the person closest to me. Brad Stevens was the shy-and-quiet type, and not a genius by any stretch, but he had better grades than me, and beggars can't be choosers. I tried to direct his thoughts to this section of the test but only got *Sally is so hot I can't believe she's sitting right behind me I should really ask her out before we graduate and never see each other again I wonder what she looks like naked* –

I twisted my earring hard, shutting off the flow of words. My face felt so hot, I was probably illuminating the entire auditorium. Well: spy on someone's private thoughts at your own peril. I had no idea Brad felt that way about me.

I stared at my test. Instead of worrying about the questions I hadn't answered, now I wondered what *Brad* looked like naked.

Dean Winegarden broke the silence. "Thirty minutes."

The stress level ratcheted up a notch as everyone shuffled in their seats and checked their watches as though they didn't believe their ears. I pushed Brad from my mind as I tuned my receptor to the next-closest person: Christine Tobin. She gave me the answers I needed.

I flipped to the last section of the test. Essay questions. I'd known going in that there was no way to cheat these without being completely obvious, but I'd hoped to have more than twenty minutes to complete them. Still, they looked like cake. I might be a crappy student and liar, but structured bullshitting? *Totally* my forte. My pencil raced across the page as I answered each question without really answering it. When the dean called time, I had only two questions unanswered.

Not bad.

I closed my test book and left the auditorium with the rest of the class. Marissa caught up with me outside. She slung an arm around my shoulders and gave me a hug.

"How'd you do?"

I shrugged and tried to play it cool. "We'll see."

"I'm sure you did great," she said. To her credit, I almost believed she believed it.

*

The next day Marissa and I joined the throng of students outside Winegarden's office. The results of the Comp and the cumulative grades were always posted at 8:00 a.m. the day following the test. Legend has it that once a few students had camped out to wait for their results, and over the years the tradition had shifted from camping to celebrating. By the time we got there, the remnants of an all-night party littered the hallway. A tame party, sure – no kegs or drugs or anything – but there had been plenty of beer and vodka and snacks.

I wrinkled my nose at the smell. "I'm not going to miss this scene."

"Me neither," Marissa said, but I could tell she sort of would.

Silence fell as Dean Winegarden came down the corridor. The wall panel crackled to life at his touch. Our grades filled the screen, and we scrambled to find our names. Winegarden tried to remain stoic as he fought his way out of the crowd, but I caught him scoffing at our antics. At least someone found this fun.

I hung back at the edge of the crowd until Cash Powell's indignant voice echoed over the din. "No way. No *fucking* way."

He whipped away from the board and scanned faces until his eyes fell on mine.

"*You!*"

I felt my face flush. I must have done better than I'd thought if my grade got this reaction. "What?"

"There's no way you pulled ninety-five on Comp," he said.

I tried to keep a straight face as a murmur ran among my classmates. "What's wrong, Cash? Mad you've been beaten by the biggest dumbass in class? Doesn't bode well for your future, you know."

Marissa looked from me to Cash and back again, her expression somewhere between disbelief and envy. Students parted to let me see my grade. Yep, I'd gotten a ninety-five, which was enough to pull me out of the cellar in the cumulative. I was still going to finish in the bottom third of the class, but I didn't care. I didn't come last, and I didn't fail Comp.

Marissa hugged me. "I knew you could do it," she said. She pulled back and searched my face. I could see the question in her eyes. *How?*

I avoided her gaze as I felt a firm hand fall on my shoulder. My stomach fell at the sound of Winegarden's voice. "Miss Clark? I need to speak with you, please."

"Of course," I said, my mouth dry.

My mind raced as I followed the dean into his office. Clearly he knew something was going on, but what would he do about it? I tried to think through each scenario as he closed the door, cutting us off from the commotion outside. His office was clean and orderly, without any plants or pictures or anything personal on the shelves. It was anonymous enough that it could have been anyone's workplace, which meant it could only be Dean Winegarden's.

He walked behind his desk. "Sit down, Miss Clark."

I sat in one of the cool metal chairs and shivered. It must be a University bylaw to put uncomfortable chairs in offices to keep the students on edge. Or maybe it was just the World Domination teachers using a psych technique on us. Or maybe –

Winegarden peered at the screen in his desk. "I have a copy of your Comprehensive exam here."

"Great, huh?" I asked. I tried for cheerfulness but my voice cracked. See? Terrible liar.

"What's the melting point of plutonium?"

I blinked at the change of subject. What game was he playing? "Six hundred forty degrees Celsius," I said. Everyone knew that.

"I want to show you something." He changed the orientation of the screen so the images faced me. I saw the first section of my test next to Cash Powell's. Shit.

"What's Cash got to do with me?" I asked. I felt a bead of sweat form under my nose, and willed myself not to wipe it. Brushing your nose was the first sign of dishonesty we'd learned in Deception and You. You'd be surprised at how many times that tripped people up. I wanted to sit on my hands to keep from doing it – but that was a sign too.

I tried to relax.

"I think you know, Sally." Winegarden touched the screen and pages whizzed by until he found the one he was looking for. "You and Cash are you only two people in the class that missed question seventy-five. Would you read it and the answer you gave, please?"

My stomach sank as I scanned the screen.

"The melting point of plutonium is ..." We'd both put five-seventy-five Celsius. I fought the urge to swallow, and shrugged. "Must have been nervous or something."

Winegarden sniffed. "Or something." He made a few adjustments. "The next section looks good, except for a few key questions."

Again, there was a copy of my test next to Christine Tobin's.

"What's your point?" I asked. I looked him in the eye.

Winegarden pressed his fingers together. "It is obvious to me that you cheated on this exam, Miss Clark."

He stared at me and I stared back. I waited.

"You do know the rule about cheating," he said.

"Yeah. Don't."

"So I can only assume that you know the consequence of doing so?"

"Expulsion."

"Indeed. Consider yourself expelled, Miss Clark."

My bowels turned to water. Without a diploma of some kind, I was screwed. My student loan balance floated in my head as sweat trickled down my back. Maybe Marissa would give me a job. My mind raced as I watched Winegarden clear his screen. There was only one way to go here. No risk, no reward.

"That's a bunch of crap," I said. "If you don't mind my saying."

Winegarden looked down his nose at me. "Excuse me?"

"You have to admit that a program that grooms dictators and anarchists but doesn't allow cheating is disingenuous at best and inadequate at worst. Our classwork taught us to use *everything* at our disposal to achieve our goals, that *any* means justified the ends. To teach us that, but not allow us to cheat on schoolwork is oxymoronic. How are we supposed to be prepared for the real world?" Winegarden's expressionless face unnerved me but I plowed forward. "Yes, I cheated. I didn't see any other way, sir. I only had two hours, and there was no way to pass without using reinforcements."

He raised his eyebrow. "Reinforcements."

"Yes," I said, and felt a glimmer of hope. "I programmed copy-paste Nanobots –"

"From scratch?"

I shook my head. "No time. I reprogrammed transcription bots," I said. "I turned my watch into a storage and display device. I knew they wouldn't have enough power for the whole test, so I stole a thought receptor from one of the labs and used that on Christine." I pointed to my earrings. "The essay part was all me."

"The most impressive part of the Comprehensive, I assure you."

"If I had it to do over again I'd do the same thing," I said. He didn't respond, so I pushed. "So why'd you give me a ninety-five if you knew I cheated?"

He stared at me a moment, considering. "I wanted to see how you'd react to getting that grade but then getting caught and expelled."

I knew it. Mind games.

"So how'd I do?"

"You saw a hopeless situation, and instead of succumbing, you confronted it. You used skills you'd acquired during your time in the program to work around the roadblocks before you. You displayed ingenuity and quick thinking. Most of all, when confronted, you didn't make excuses or lie. Quite the contrary. You're proud of what you've accomplished." The smallest of smiles graced Winegarden's face. "If that doesn't represent what World Domination is all about, I don't know what does."

I couldn't believe what I was hearing. "So I'm not expelled? I can graduate?"

"If I could give you honors, I would," he said. "Unfortunately, your prior four years of coursework suggest that my peers would frown upon such a move."

I felt lighter and more carefree than I had since coming to college. I wouldn't have to beg anyone for a job. "I don't know how to thank you."

"You can *thank* me by staging a coup."

"Somewhere specific, or is that just a general request?"

"How about a small nation in Southeast Asia?"

I smiled. "I think I can manage that."

Winegarden nodded. "Yes, I think you just might."

I left his office, a stupid grin splashed across my face. I linked arms with Marissa, who was waiting for me, her curiosity only widening my smile. For the first time in my life, I felt on top of the world.

Roadshow
Jean Rabe

I was invited to an anthology about magical toys, and so I relied on a magical memory from my childhood for inspiration . . . a Mr. Magoo car my father gave me one Christmas. I kept it in the box, carefully played with it, and managed to save it for lots and lots of years. The car went missing around the time of a move, and hence the unfortunate plot for "Roadshow" was born. I've been with the Writer's Symposium since the beginning. Heck, I started it . . . at the request of Lou Zocchi. That was lots and lots and lots of years ago. Roadshow first appeared in The Magic Toy Box *in 2006. Read more about me at www.jeanrabe.com.*

The Kingsbury roadster sported tan and tomato-red coats of enamel paint. Thirteen inches long with a rumble seat, the appraiser said it probably dated to the late 1920s or early 1930s, and had original light bulbs, rubber tires, and no visible touchups or rust.

"I found it at an estate sale, in a box with a bald Chatty Cathy, a broken Pops-a-Ball, a dozen naked Action Jacksons, and a bunch of Creeple Peoples tied together with a rotten rubber band. Paid eight bucks for the lot."

"Quite the find!" The appraiser beamed. "I'd say this beauty could go at auction for eight hundred to a thousand dollars."

The toy's owner grinned broadly and gripped the edge of the table for support, and the camera zoomed in for a close-up.

"How about mine? What's mine worth?"

The camera swiveled to the far end of the table, locking in on another toy, this—according to the appraiser—a 1961 Hubley Mr. Magoo Car. It looked like a modified Model T, ten inches long and painted yellow with brown fenders and running boards, a

Roadshow

black cloth top, and plastic gray seats. Mr. Magoo was driving. Made of tin painted bright navy blue, he had a rubber head that turned, and a rubber mud-brown derby hat. The toy was a riot of shiny color.

"I just put new batteries in it." The Mr. Magoo Car rolled forward, wobbly as it was intended, as if the car was drunk. "Watch this." He moved the crank at the bottom of the front grille, then it rolled equally wobbly backward. "So, what's it worth?"

"Fine, fine condition," the appraiser said. He bent near the car and narrowed his eyes. "Where'd you find one like this? Looks like it came right off the toy store shelf!"

"Oh, at some flea market down in Illinois. I think I maybe gave twenty-five bucks for it."

"Liar." This came from Mr. Magoo.

Neither the owner nor the appraiser heard the toy—they didn't speak the language. The other toy cars understood, though.

The Kingsbury roadster flashed its lights to get Mr. Magoo's attention. "So if you didn't come from a flea market, where did you come from?"

"A basement in Burlington. On a high ledge where the damp couldn't get me."

"Burlington?"

"Wisconsin."

"We're in Wisconsin. Milwaukee," the roadster revved. "It's where the Old Things Roadshow is filming for the whole weekend. It's why we're all here. So . . . is Burlington a far drive?"

Mr. Magoo tried to shrug, but the tin shoulders didn't move. "South. It's someplace to the south."

"Why'd he say he got you at a flea market?" The roadster was persistent.

"'Cause he's not going to tell the Old Things Roadshow appraiser that he stole me out of his friend's basement. I belonged to a pleasant woman who rarely played with me. I was a Christmas present from her father when she was a tot, and from the proverbial Day One she treated me like treasure. Kept me for more than forty years before Ol' Five-Fingers Discount there . . . who claimed to be a buddy of hers . . . stuffed me under his coat one day and stuck me in his car while she was out with her dogs. Probably figured she wouldn't miss me, what with all the other stuff piled high in the basement. He knew I was valuable."

The appraiser waived the camera close. "Yes, Mr. Magoo here is quite valuable. I'd say about five hundred dollars. Since you have the original box and since it's in such incredible condition, maybe you could get a little more."

"Gee, I thought it might be worth even more than that, at least as much as that Kingsbury roadster." Disappointment was plain on the owner's face. "But, it's better than nothing."

"Nothing? That's exactly what Ol' Five-Fingers Discount paid for me," Mr. Magoo grumbled. "I was worth more than five hundred dollars to her. To her, I was priceless." If the rubber face could have shed a tear, it would have.

"Sad story," said a 1930 Cortland ice cream truck. Smaller and narrower, it fit in the shadow cast by the Mr. Magoo Car. "See that old man across the aisle there, looking at the Three Stooges bobble-heads? He bought me when he was a kid. Used to race me against his brother's dump trucks."

"Race? Did someone say race?" This came from the replica of a 1961 Chevy Impala sedan.

There were other toy vehicles arrayed on the table at the far end of the convention center. On the other side of Mr. Magoo, a Wyandotte motorcycle made of pressed steel and painted sky blue shimmered under the fluorescent lights. It was appraised at close to one thousand dollars.

"Race? Did someone say race?" The replica of a 1961 Chevy Impala sedan's gear was stuck on the notion. "Va-va-va-varrooooom! A race!"

In the center of the table stalled a glossy pumpkin-orange

boxy-looking car, the smallest of the lot at a mere five inches. Nothing special about it, though the appraiser pronounced it mint and worth at least three hundred.

"I got it for a birthday present," the owner said of the pumpkin car. "Two years ago today, from my wife."

"*Alles Gute zum Geburtstag!*" exclaimed a Schuco-Studio III Mercedes Benz Streamlined W196. Its best wishes were not heard by any of the men standing around the table, but they were heartfelt nonetheless. The angular dark blue toy was a model of the 1954 Formula 1 Mercedes Racer and featured removable wheels and a strong spring-drive. Its greatest feature was its rarity, only two hundred were made. "*Alles Gute zum Geburtstag!*"

"Speak English, you friggin' foreign import," revved the Kingsbury roadster.

"Race?" the Impala cut in. It flashed its turn signal at a miniature 1959 Ford Fairlane Skyliner. "Did someone say race? Va-va-varrrrooooom!"

In return, the Fairlane waved its retractable hardtop. About the length of a G.I. Joe, the appraiser explained that the Fairlane was manufactured by the Cragstan Company in Japan in the early 1960s. Battery operated, it had an attached remote control that steered the wheel. The appraiser noticed a couple of small factory touchup spots on the hood that detracted from its collectability.

"*Kon-nichiwa!*" the Fairlane said to the Impala. "*Kon-nichiwa!*" It repeated the greeting to the Mercedes and the rest of its fellow toys.

"Wonderful," the roadster seized up. "A Jerry and a Jap on our table. Don't you just hate these foreign models? Can't understand a honkin' thing. This is the American version of the Old Things Roadshow, not the one they broadcast over the pond."

"*Kon-nichiwa!*" the Fairlane offered again, with even more enthusiasm.

"Race? Did someone mention a race? Va-va-va-varrrooooooom!"

The roadster turned on its brights. "A race? Yeah, Impala, we could show those foreign models a good what-for."

The cameraman took a wide-angle shot of all the cars on the table, then a moment later the appraiser signaled the toy section finished. The Old Things Roadshow crew moved on to the dolls.

The Impala blinked its headlights seductively at the roadster and wriggled its tailpipe. "Think you can catch me, Kingsbury?"

The roadster let out a little beep. "Been a while since I burned rubber."

"I'm in," the Wyandotte motorcycle said.

"Me too," said an old blue truck, the most valuable of the toy vehicles on display. A Structo Motor Dispatch semi, it haled from the 1920s and stretched nearly two feet long. It came complete with a rear tailgate chain and radiator cap, the decals clean and intact, placing it at worth more than three thousand dollars. "I haven't stretched my suspension in years."

"Race. Race. Race. Race." The Impala had turned the word into a mantra.

"*Das Rennen?*" the Mercedes racer asked.

"Yeah, we race," the Wyandotte motorcycle returned. "What about you, Mr. Magoo? You got new batteries. Want to try them out?"

The tin shoulders tried to shrug. "I suppose it would be all right."

The Impala rolled to the edge of the table.

The roadster honked to get everyone's attention. "We race down this aisle, past the displays for folk art, pottery, and furniture. Got it?" He flicked his lights down an aisle that had been formed by blue drapes stretched on pipes and that was cut at irregular intervals by eight-foot tables skirted with darker blue fabric.

"Got it," Mr. Magoo said. "Then?"

"See that chair . . . the high-backed one painted white? We turn right at it and make for the paintings, paper, and jewelry."

A thin man in a rumpled olive suit with a spotted red tie stood by the chair in question. He gestured to a cameraman and pointed, his words barely heard above the murmur of conversations from people toting boxes filled with their prized old things. "This is an L.& J.G. Stickley chair, circa nineteen seventeen."

"Yeah, that chair'll do," the Impala said.

"*Das Rennen!*" the Mercedes said.

With a throaty "Va-va-va-varrroooooom!" the Impala vaulted off the table and down the aisle.

The Kingsbury roadster followed, honking expletives that the human attendees of the Old Things Roadshow could neither hear nor understand. "I make the rules, Impala. I say when we go."

"Go! The Wyandotte motorcycle cheered. "Go. Go. Go. Go." It rolled forward, dropping off the table and falling on its side. It quickly righted itself and raced after the Impala and the Kingsbury roadster.

The Mercedes hesitated only a moment before flicking a turn signal at the ice cream truck. They sped off the edge simultaneously, tires squealing.

Mr. Magoo tried to put a nervous look on his rubber face as he crept toward the edge and stared down the aisle. The racing toy cars were already yards ahead.

"I have new batteries. I can do this."

"And I'll give you a push!" The Structo Motor Dispatch semi barreled forward, its front bumper slamming into the Mr. Magoo Car and sending it hurtling off the table, inadvertently causing the Mr. Magoo Car to fly over the ice cream truck and hit the aisle running.

The semi lumbered off the edge, its cab angling straight down and smacking against the floor—cement covered by a thin carpet. It had been the most valuable of the toys on the table, but its front bumper snapped off, and the connection broke between the cab and the trailer. A wheel spun away and the tailgate popped open, just as the Japanese Fairlane shouted one more "*Kon-nichiwa!*"

and dove over the side.

The Fairlane had good speed, and should have easily caught the Mr. Magoo Car, but its attached remote-control cable snagged on something. A moment more, and the Fairlane landed on top of the semi, tugging three other toy cars with it.

"I'm not racing," the pumpkin car decided, rolling to the edge and looking down at the tangle of metal and plastic. "It's my owner's birthday, and I think my value just went up a notch."

*

"Va-va-va-varroooom!" The Impala was clearly in the lead, racing down the aisle past the folk art section. It slowed out of curiosity, idling when it spotted a pudgy woman in platform shoes and a flowery print dress.

"My great uncle," she was explaining. "He was in the army and he got around quite a bit. I think he got this here . . ."

"Cheyenne cradleboard," the Old Things Roadshow appraiser supplied.

"Cradle, yeah. I think he got it from a reservation."

The Impala slammed on its breaks, its headlights catching the beaded cradle mounted on buffalo hide. The car was so far ahead it could afford to hear the appraiser's discourse. Besides, the Impala reasoned, if it got too, too far ahead, the other cars might give up and the race would be over before they made it to the white chair.

"See the stylized thunderbirds, and the hawk bells delicately hanging around the opening?"

"C'mon, c'mon," the Impala urged. "Tell her what she wants to hear. C'mon!"

"Well, the cradle is a little out of shape, but I'd place its value at about fifty thousand."

"Dollars?" The woman gasped and patted her chest.

The Impala sped up and caught the woman's swoon in its

rearview mirror, then it zipped around the legs of an old gal in green bib overalls that had been hemmed a little too high.

"I make the rules of this race!" The roadster honked at the Impala, then looked out its side mirrors to spot a line of cars following: the Mercedes Racer, the Wyandotte motorcycle, the Mr. Magoo Car—weaving like it was tipsy, and the Cortland ice cream truck. The roadster flicked its high-beams in surprise—it had thought more cars would participate in the Roadshow race.

"Va-va-va-varrooom!" The Impala squealed.

The roadster cursed and floored it.

*

"My dad left me this, in his will." A man in khaki pants and a purple and white checked shirt ran his hand across the lip of a green vase festooned with ducks and scallops.

"This piece you have here is from a large pottery in Zanesville, Ohio," the Old Things Roadshow appraiser said. "We can see by this mark that it was designed by Weller Rhead, who came to the United States sometime in the early nineteen hundreds. I'd say this vase is worth a little more than two thousand."

"Gosh, I had no idea. In fact, I . . ."

*

The Impala didn't anticipate the surprised pottery owner stepping out into the aisle. The car va-va-va-varrooomed around his ankles, accidentally clipping him. Normally a toy the Impala's size wouldn't have budged the man, but he was already off-balance at the news of the duck-vase's worth. The man wobbled on his feet and stretched out his hands, fell forward into the table and sent his Weller Rhead vase flying. It came down in a hundred or so pieces.

The Impala slowed to sadly survey the damage through its side mirrors, and the Kingsbury roadster took advantage, tires screaming as it passed the competition and rolled over fragments of the duck-vase. The Mercedes Racer, the Wyandotte motorcycle, the Mr. Magoo Car—weaving like it was even tipsier, and the Cortland ice cream truck drew within inches before the Impala bolted forward again.

*

In the distance behind the racers, a distraught man held his hands to the sides of his head. "I'm going to sue, you hear me? This was my only Structo Motor Dispatch semi, from the 1920s. The tailgate chain is broken, the radiator cap is gone. Sure, it had a slight crease on one side of the cab, but now there are creases all over. I'm going to sue!"

"You signed a hold-harmless clause," an appraiser offered.

The distraught man growled.

The pumpkin car made a *tsk-tsking* sound that none of the people heard, and it offered a silent prayer for its brethren broken on the floor.

*

A smallish man in a black suit with a red bowtie, bald on top, but with a gray-black ring of hair around the sides, adjusted his wire-rim glasses with his overly-hairy hands. His rumpled, pale blue shirt added to the professor image. He gestured with a pencil to a massive grandfather clock. He was oblivious to the racing cars headed his way.

"See how long the pendulum is? Longer pendulums keep better time," he explained to a middle-aged couple. "It's also heavy. Weight-driven clocks are simply more accurate. And it has three dials, one for seconds, minutes, and one for hours. That's thought to be more accurate, too."

"What's it worth?" the couple asked practically in unison.

"Well, this dates back more than one hundred and fifty years. German made, I can tell by the signature."

"German made," the Kingsbury roadster hissed. "German made. This is the American version of the Old Things Roadshow, people. AMERICAN."

"What's it worth?" the couple asked again.

"I'd put it in the neighborhood of . . ." The smallish man stared at the aisle and at the line of toy cars racing down it. "Oh my."

"Ah, tell her what it is worth," the Cortland ice cream truck said as it sped by. "Tell her, professor!"

The smallish man scratched his head. "I better call security. Somebody wound up the toys."

"Call security after you tell us what the clock's worth," the couple insisted.

*

The Impala caught up to the roadster when they turned down the aisle by the white chair. The Mr. Magoo Car, with its new batteries, careened drunkenly around the corner, nearly bumping into the Cortland ice cream truck. The Mercedes Racer and the Wyandotte motorcycle fell in behind, fender to fender.

"You're just biding your time, aren't you, Mercedes? You've got more juice than all of them. I can see it in your lines. You're built for speed." The motorcycle popped a wheelie for emphasis.

"*Das Rennen!*"

"Yeah, yeah, I hear you. Shut up and race."

*

The Kingsbury roadster headed toward a string bean of a man with a painting of a wintry scene. Other paintings were displayed on easels behind and between tables. The wintry scene was the largest.

"Va-va-va-varroooom!" the Impala shouted.

The man was standing in the aisle, holding the painting for the camera.

"It's by John Carlson," the appraiser said. "I've done some research on the Internet on the artist. Carlson was a Swede who came to the United States when he was nine years old."

"A Swede!" The roadster cursed. "AMERICAN roadshow, people."

"From Sweden?" The man holding the painting raised his eyebrows, hopeful.

"Carlson was not known for his snow scenes. I'd say this was painted between 1925 and 1935. With a little restoration it could bring thirty thousand or more. I'd insure it for sixty thousand."

The man's fingers and his lips trembled, and the Kingsbury roadster shot between his legs. The man yelped in surprise and dropped the painting. It tottered upright on its frame for a moment, just long enough for the Impala to break through the canvas. Then it fell back, and the Cortland ice cream truck, the Mr. Magoo Car, and the Mercedes Racer trundled over the frame and the ripped snow scene. The Wyandotte motorcycle managed to swerve just in time, slipping around the edge of the painting and avoiding the appraiser's scrambling feet.

Gaining on the Mercedes Racer, the motorcycle popped a wheelie in glee and felt itself being lifted off the floor.

"Mama! Look what I found!" Grubby hands clutched the motorcycle, just careful enough to avoid its spinning wheels. The tot held the motorcycle up to a woman clutching a cardboard box filled with a tea kettle in the shape of a giraffe, a hot pink ceramic bowling pin, an old carved wooden pug dog, and an animated yodeling goat.

"That's nice, Timmy. Put it in my box and you can play with it when we get home. That old toy'll probably last you an hour or two before I have to toss it in the garbage."

"Game over," the Wyandotte motorcycle moaned.

*

The race paralleled a line of people toting their treasures—Kissy dolls in the original boxes, a few Madam Alexandrias with perfect hair, an Operation game with the patient's nose blinking, hand-blown Christmas ornaments, brass doorknockers in the shapes of gargoyles and dragons, Wizard of Oz memorabilia, Civil War sabers, and more. The people chatted about where their antiques came from: grandmother's attic, garage sales, estate auctions, and stores.

"Got this here print of the Founding Fathers out of a Dumpster," one man gushed. "I had it framed and the wife told me to bring it here. Hey, Mary, look at those toy cars."

"*Das Rennen!*" The Mercedes Racer made its move when the course took them down an aisle designated photographs, metalwork and sculpture, and paper. It effortlessly passed the Mr. Magoo Car and the Cortland ice cream truck. The Impala and the Kingsbury roadster were only a few yards ahead of it.

The Mercedes never looked out its rearview mirror. If it had, it would have watched two burly security guards emerge from a gap between "photographs and paintings," leaping over the ruined Carlson winter scene and giving chase. The tallest and fastest was intent on Mr. Magoo. Reaching forward, he tripped over a camera cord and his knee slammed down on top of the Cortland ice cream truck. The little truck let out a final gasp:

"Go get 'em Magoo."

*

"This book is quite extraordinary," the appraiser whistled. He was standing beneath a banner that read "paper," and he was so intent on the book that he didn't notice the racing toy cars and the two security guards chasing them. "It's from the 1500s, from Germany. It has a pigskin cover on a wood board. There are a few worm holes, but I'd place it at twenty-five thousand."

"Germany again," the roadster snarled. "United States, people. This is the United States!"

"Twenty-five thousand dollars. Wow," the book owner said.

"Wow!" the appraiser echoed, catching sight of the racing Impala and Kingsbury roadster. "They belong in the toy section."

Across the aisle from the book appraiser, a stern-looking fellow with trifocals leaned over a table where several metal sculptures gleamed in the bright camera lights. "This cast iron miniature goat cart is circa 1890. See how the goats gallop when it's pulled? There's a hole on the seat where the figure was. As it sits, it's worth about twenty-five hundred, maybe a little more. An easy five thousand if you had the figure."

"Join us?" the roadster called to the goat cart. "We're having a race!"

"To where?" the goats called.

"Uhm..."

"Yeah, just where are we going?" The Impala swept past the roadster.

"*Das Rennen!*" The Mercedes accelerated and drew within inches of the Kingsbury roadster's rear bumper.

The goat cart surged forward, rolling off the edge of the table and landing head-first on the floor. The cart snapped off and a wheel cracked.

"Make that worth three or four hundred now," the appraiser told the goat cart owner.

*

The security guards gained on the racers. There were four guards now, one of them wielding an antique fishing net he'd plucked off a table. All of them were catching up to the sluggish, wobbly Mr. Magoo Car. It tipsily slipped beneath the skirt of a table covered with Egyptian tissue-box holders. King Tut's gold-plated visage wiggled as the security guards thundered past.

The roadster tapped its breaks and avoided colliding with a man appraising an old milk bottle. "Impala, I figure we'll circle 'round the outside, past the paperweights and come back to the toy section. First car to reach the banner wins."

"Wins what?" the Impala posed.

"*Das Rennen!*" the Mercedes keened as it swerved around the roadster and the Impala and took the lead.

"No damn German car is going to beat me!" The Kingsbury roadster howled its rage as it threw everything into the race now. The tread wore on its old rubber tires and its windshield cracked when it hoped over a power cord. "This is the American version of the Old Things Roadshow. AMERICAN. Kapeesh?"

"Va-va-va-varroooom!" The Impala, too, was giving its last measure and managed to nose ahead of the roadster, just as the fishing net came down.

"AMERICAN!" the roadster hollered. "Nooooooo!" Trapped, from inside the net, the Kingsbury roadster read the manufacturer's mark on the curved aluminum frame: *Made in Finland*. "Noooooooooo!"

"Just us now," the Impala hummed to the Mercedes. It was a car-length back, but inching up.

"Va-va-va-varrrrooooom!" the Mercedes cried.

"*Das Rennen!*" the Impala returned.

The cars rounded the corner at the front of the exhibit hall, dodging two men carrying a Victorian roll-top desk. The security guards screeched to a halt to avoid plowing into the antique.

The Mercedes pulled three car-lengths ahead and watched the Impala out of its rearview mirror. It wouldn't do to win by too much. No reason to hurt the American car's feelings . . . the race was the Impala's idea, after all.

Halfway down the aisle they'd just left, the Mr. Magoo Car peeked out from under the table skirting. It rolled forward, no longer hurrying, knowing it was too far out of the race. It reached the front of the exhibit hall, and Mr. Magoo twisted his rubber head to the right, seeing the backsides of a dozen Roadshow security guards and appraisers. At the edge of his vision, between all the legs, he spotted the glow of the Impala's taillights.

Mr. Magoo kept driving straight—right out the convention center doors and onto the sidewalk.

*

Mr. Magoo didn't know that the Mercedes reached the "Toys" banner first. Nor did he know that the Impala scratched its perfect paint job and dented its right front fender on the leg of a century-old coat-rack.

He didn't know that the man who brought him to the Old Things Roadshow was pacing and pulling at his hair, stamping his feet and looking forlornly at the original box.

However, the Mr. Magoo Car knew that Burlington, Wisconsin, was to the south, and that he had brand new batteries that hopefully had enough juice to take him there.

"Va-va-va-varroooom!" Mr. Magoo said.

WALKABOUT PUBLISHING
Great stories by great authors.

Robert E. Vardeman—Michael A. Stackpole—Marc Tassin—James M. Ward
Lorelei Shannon—Dean Leggett—Kathleen Watness—Paul Genesse
Jason Mical—Kelly Swails—Sabrina Klein—Kerrie Hughes—John Helfers
Brandie Tarvin—Donald J. Bingle—Tim Wagonner—Anton Strout
E. Readicker-Henderson—Wes Nicholson—Linda P. Baker—Stephen Saus
J. Robert King—Chris Pierson—Daniel Meyers—Elizabeth A. Vaughan
Richard Lee Byers—Jennifer Brozek—Brad Beaulieu—Dylan Birtolo
Stephen D. Sullivan—Jean Rabe—And More!

Pirates of the Blue Kingdoms • Blue Kingdoms: Buxom Buccaneers
Blue Kingdoms: Shades & Specters
Blue Kingdoms: Zombies, Werewolves, & Unicorns
Luck o' the Irish • Martian Knights & Other Tales
Stories from Desert Bob's Reptile Ranch
This and That and Tales About Cats • Uncanny Encounters: Roswell
Under the Protection of the Cow Demon
And More!

Walkabout Publishing
P.O. Box 151 • Kansasville, WI 53139
www.walkaboutpublishing.com

Official Home of the Blue Kingdoms.

Made in the USA
Charleston, SC
26 May 2010